THE Limits OF Mercy

A NOVEL

JOHN L. MOORE

D1303173

Publishers Since 1798

THOMAS NELSON PUBLISHERS
Nashville • Atlanta • London • Vancouver

Printed in the United States of America

1 2 3 4 5 6 7 - 02 01 00 99 98 97 96

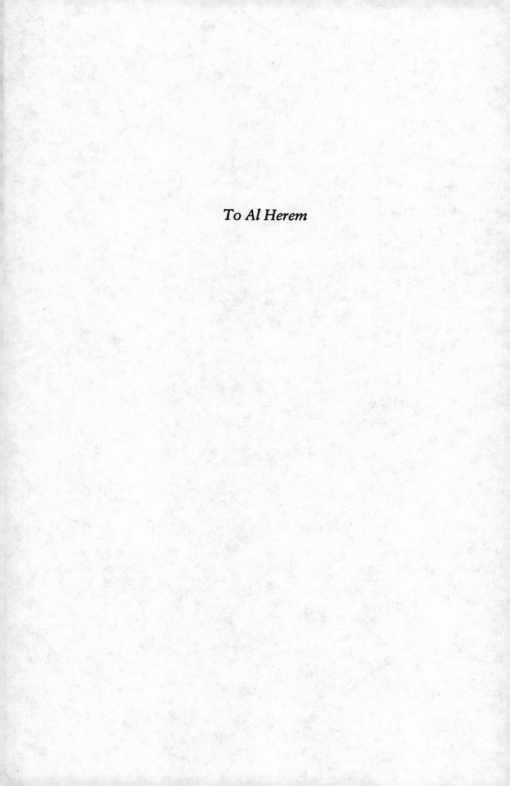

To Al Herem

Acknowledgments

I would like to thank the following for helping make this book possible.

For editorial help, Leslie Peterson, Patricia Moore-Joshi, Jan Dennis, Jennifer Horne, Anna Quinn, Bruce Nygren, and Ken Stephens.

For law enforcement information, Michael Moore, Bob Stabio, Wally Badgett, Don Nees, Chaplain Bill Wholers, Commodore Mann, Tony Harbaugh, and Doug Columbik.

For medical information, Mary Ellen Mehrer, Mal and Beth Winter, Randy Holland, Lew Vadheim, and Mary Margaret Friend.

And a special thanks to my wife, Debra; my son, Jess; my daughter, Andrea; and Loreen Barnaby, Jack Harmon, Doug Nelson, and Terry Sgrignoli for helping do ranch chores so I could find time to write. And to Cathy Bastian for editorial comment and prayer support.

A special thanks to noted western artist and fellow cowboy preacher Chuck DeHaan for another masterful cover.

I

1990 Ezra Riley was a dark figure moving against the November sky, a lone horseman silhouetted on a high, grassy ridge. He sat his horse's gallop easily, as if in a rocking chair. The sky was gray and white, and a breeze from the mouth of the Arctic blew against his face, reddening his already weathered cheeks. Ahead of him the grazing head of a dun horse lifted, and the animal nickered loudly in a laughing call of equine youth that rolled on the wind like fast water over rocks.

The head of a second horse rose, and aged eyes scanned the skyline. Then the ears of both horses, the young dun's and the old paint's, pointed toward the approaching horseman. The dun nickered again, and the mounted horse answered.

Ezra slowed Shiloh to a stiff, fast-paced trot. The sides of his legs felt the sorrel's excitement through saddle leather as they neared Cheyenne and Gusto. Invigorated by the chill in the air, Cheyenne pranced toward them, neck crested, nostrils flaring, front feet pawing playfully, his red mane blowing in the wind. The old paint stood silently and watched.

Ezra dismounted and led Shiloh to the aged horse. He stroked Gusto's dry, brittle coat, and rubbed around eyes still chafed and sore from summer sun and flies. "Howya doing, old man?" Ezra asked. The horse bent his head into Ezra's hand as he rubbed behind the ears. Ezra untangled the mane and scratched beneath the jaw, and Gusto closed his eyes in relaxation while Cheyenne snorted and nosed Shiloh playfully.

Ezra put both arms around Gusto's neck and gave him a strong hug. He smelled dust in the hair and envisioned the summers of years past: the smoke of branding fires, the bitter chlorophyll of cottonwood tree leaves, the white lather of sweat sweeter than fermenting grain, the salty taste of leather reins.

Beneath the black-brimmed cowboy hat, a single tear squeezed from Ezra's eye, ran down a wind-chapped cheek and fell to the needle-and-thread grasses that whipped his denim legs.

"Thank you," Ezra said to the old horse. "Thank you for being my deliverance." He rested his head on Gusto's bony back and stared at the distant badlands. They were growing dark in the overcast of evening, like the hoary backs of hippos covered with coats of clay. Ezra thought of his father, Johnny Riley, who had ridden all of eastern Montana. He thought of Charley Arbuckle and his grandsons, Austin and Cody. He thought of a mean-spirited blue roan named Ribbon Tail. He stared toward a distant coulee where he had nearly frozen to death, his hand gripped in a wolf trap. He thought of his wife Anne and his son Dylan; his uncles, Archie, Rufus, Willis, Joe, Sam, and Solomon; his sisters, Diane and Lacey.

He remembered Jubal Lee Walker and his stylish Thoroughbreds. He and Jubal Lee had raced across this very flat, their eyes dancing with joy, the Thoroughbreds as fluid as water. He thought of Rick Benjamin, Jim Mendenhall; all the men he and Gusto had ridden beside; the partnership of mounted men. In all the turmoil and trials, Gusto had been a constancy, a solace, an anchor in troubled waters.

Ezra looked westward. Below him, in the serpentine twists of Sunday Creek, a single light came on in his house. Anne and Dylan were home from town. The old dog, Blondie, had not barked to announce their arrival. She was nearly blind and stone deaf. She never heard cars driving down the lane to the house.

"Twenty-five years," Ezra said softly to the paint who braced himself on feeble legs once as strong as braided cords of cable. "You saw me through it all for twenty-five years."

He remembered Rick Benjamin's words: "What are you going to do when you have to put Gusto down, sell the ranch?"

He looked into the horse's deep brown eyes. Eyes the size of billiard balls. Dark, clear, wise, and friendly. But tired. Age had stolen their varnish.

"I don't know what my future holds," Ezra told the horse. "I would like you to be there giving your unspoken support, but winter is coming." As if cued, a bitter breeze bit at Ezra's exposed skin. Was it the coming of winter or simply a portent of the future?

Gusto reached out and touched noses with Shiloh.

"Say good-bye, Shiloh," Ezra said. Cheyenne trotted up from the side and touched noses with both horses.

Ezra rubbed the paint one last time behind the ear. "Thank you, again," he said, then he swung quickly up on Shiloh and rode homeward. He did not look back.

II

The following day Ezra left the ranch before dawn for a weeklong elk hunting trip in the mountains of western Montana.

After school let out for the day, Dylan saddled Shiloh, rode into the hills, and caught and haltered Gusto. He led him to a high cedar-topped hill overlooking Sunday Creek. Dylan was intent and serious for a thirteen-year-old. He knew the gravity of his duty as he handed the lead rope to the veterinarian. The man led the horse to a freshly excavated pit. The paint eyed the earthen mound warily. The veterinarian patted the horse twice on the neck, unhooked the halter, and inserted a sterile needle through the sorrel-and-white hide into the corded jugular. The horse tipped quietly into the earth. The veterinarian walked away. Dylan mounted Shiloh. A man on a backhoe drove from around the hill. He lowered the front blade and covered the grave of the redeemer of Ezra Riley's youth.

At that moment, four hundred miles away, Ezra stopped his pickup beside the Blackfoot River. Ahead of him the granite jaws of the eastern front of the Rocky Mountains bit into a kaleidoscoped western sky. He got out of the pickup, stood by the road, and stared to the east. His hat was pulled low on his head, both thumbs were hooked in the loops of his denim jeans, and the trophy buckle on his belt—won by his sister Lacey on Gusto—glowed in the evening's last light. He shuddered once as a cold chill climbed his spine and bit at the back of his neck.

It was finished. Gusto was gone. He felt a part of his soul tear away, take wing, and fly to the air.

One could not put one's trust in horses, he reminded himself. A sudden updraft stirred a dust devil that whirled roadside grit into Ezra's face. If it was a sign, it was an omen of a coming evil, of tests to be faced by a man suddenly dismounted. He was no longer the horseman, the man superior to others. It did not matter that he still owned Shiloh and Cheyenne or that other horses would enter his life. The horse as icon was gone. He was a cowboy afoot, thrown from youth into the realities of middle age. The ground indeed hardened as the body matured.

He heard a distant honking and turned his head upward to a V of geese winging southward. On cue, the leader dropped from the formation and flew by himself until another took his place. The goose then joined the rear. Ezra watched the winged fowl until they were swallowed by the dusky grayness of the evening.

"For everything there is a season," he said to the empty sky.

And what season of his life was he entering?

From the distant mountains came a long, plaintive howl. It rode lightly on the wind, then was gone. Was it a wolf? Ezra wondered.

No, it couldn't be, he thought. He had heard of no reports of wolf sightings in this area. It had to be a hound or sled dog.

As he got in the pickup and closed the door, the howl sounded again. It was louder, as if defining itself, but Ezra did not hear it.

It was a wolf.

III

Three days later he was deep in "doghair," skirting the tree line of granite-topped peaks. He took slow, pointed steps, balancing the weight of his backpack and rifle as his foot settled softly onto the dry mountainside. He moved agonizingly slow through the trashy, high-altitude timber with the pencil-thin, needleless branches. His every sense was electrified as his eyes scanned through the trees, searching for patches of buckskin or black, for irregular shapes, for the twitch of an ear; he sniffed quietly, knowing he might smell the bull elk before he saw him; he strained to hear even the softest snapping of a hoof on a branch or an antler tine against a tree trunk.

His hometown of Yellow Rock seemed as faraway as forever from the edge of the Scapegoat Wilderness. Ezra was alone, miles from anyone. An outfitter friend had trailered him and three horses seven miles the first morning. They rode uphill two more miles, then Ezra dismounted and continued alone. His pack contained the bare essentials: tarp, space blanket, hi-tech lightweight sleeping bag, dried fruit and nuts, camp saw, fishing line, bells, pepper spray, orange flagging, quinine to guard against giardiasis, one pair of wool pants, a wool sweater, extra socks and gloves.

He also carried a pocket-size New Testament. The spiritual failure of his friend Jubal Lee Walker had compelled Ezra to study and pray. He was intrigued by the dynamics of the human heart, and by applying the discipline he had learned from the martial arts, his deep, poetic nature was slowly transforming him into a mechanic of the soul, a lay counselor of inner healing.

He made a fresh camp each night, nestling in among the rocks, his perimeter defined by a square of fishing line hung with tiny bells as a warning in case of a grizzly. His pack was stashed high in a tree five hundred yards away. Grizzlies, federally protected for fifteen years, were a concern. As were mountain lions. But Ezra slept well the first two nights; the exercise and altitude overcame the cold. A canister of red pepper spray and his father's old .30-30 lever-action rifle were kept within reach.

Now he was "in elk." The pungent smell met his nostrils like a heavy cloud of rolling musk. He was close. Very, very close. Ezra froze. Only his eyes moved. He focused all of his attention on looking for the glint of light on antlers, the blink of an eyelid. Silence was a noise of its own. Ezra's heart thumped against his chest; the blood rose in his throat and face. If the elk sensed him first there would be a sudden breaking of tree limbs, a flash of buckskin, the further crashing of timber, and perhaps one quick, fleeting shot aimed between the trees.

In this game silence was everything. Ezra loved it. His senses were heightened. He fought to suppress and control the adrenaline. The only thing more keen than being the hunter, he imagined, was being the hunted. Somewhere the bull lay near, his every fiber an antenna, an amplifier of sight, sound, and smell.

Ezra did not move for several minutes. His heart finally slowed. He took one more careful step. Dusk was settling, and the high, brushy mountain was cloaking itself in darkness. He strained to see, looking through the browns, blacks, and dark greens, looking for the off color.

He saw it. A dark buckskin patch, too soft, too yellowish to be a rock, a segment no larger than a loaf of bread. It was the flank of a large bull not sixty feet below him. He squinted but could see nothing else. His heart rate slowly increased again. The light was going fast. He fought the urge to act rashly. He needed to walk the fine edge between patience and action as his nerves arced with a subtle electricity. He spent months of the year dreaming of this moment. There was no past, no future. His ranch and family problems had been washed away by the immediacy of this second. Of tenths of this second. Concerns for his unpublished book vaporized. He was neither writer nor rancher. He was a predator. He had climbed for days, stretching and conditioning the muscles of his legs and back, forcing himself harder each day, toughening the muscles of his mind and soul while respecting the wild, dangerous world he had invaded. He knew, though he never admitted to Anne, that he could die out here. A chance encounter with a griz, a slip on a rock, a twisted ankle—all could be equally deadly. He enjoyed the risk.

The odor wafted uphill to his nostrils. It was pungent, gamy, and raw. This was the big bull he had been tracking for two days: a monarch that sought the deepest, densest cover, scavenged the worst brush for food, went days without water. Slowly, Ezra brought the carbine up. The caliber was undersized, adding to the challenge. He would need to make a head or neck shot. He took one more hesitant step. He could see ears. They were pinned back and listening. The bull was alert. He could see monstrous antler tines sweeping backward through the brush, curving like long polished tree limbs toward his tail. But all he could see were ears, antlers, and tail. There was nothing to shoot at.

With an intensely solemn trepidation he moved inches uphill, between the many thin trees, their lines like an inverted venetian blind, until he saw one eye. He could guess how the head lay, hoping the 180-grain bullet would crash through the branches like matchsticks, making the kill instantaneous. A wounded bull in the doghair and darkness would be a nightmare to find. He brought the rifle to his shoulder. He slowly cocked the hammer. At this moment he had to be the most efficient killer on the mountain.

Darkness was deepening, and his finger was closing on the trigger when he sensed motion above him at the mountain's crest in the orange glow of sunset. He and the bull were not alone. Ezra's one eye remained on the elk, but the other strayed upward to amber air, to the stark tree line, and he saw a wisp of furtive movement, a ghostly presence. He was filled with a primordial awe. Something moved as gray and vaporous as smoke, yet left a presence as real and burning as fire.

The bull sensed the presence and was instantly afoot, crashing through the timber, his magnificent antlers rattling through the tree limbs like ivory swords, the tips glistening like piano keys. A part of Ezra screamed at himself to whirl and follow the elk's flight, to search for an opening between the trees, to look for bucksin and black flashing across the iron rims of his open sights, but his heart and eyes went back to the skyline where the orange glow was now fading, where something gray and vaporous had come and gone. It had faded like mist. But it had been there.

A wolf.

PART 1

Watchman, what of the night?
Watchman, what of the night?
Isaiah 21:11

CHAPTER ONE

When I was a child my mother used to insist my father take me with him to the cattle sale on Tuesdays. At noon we would have lunch at the Range Riders Bar and Cafe where the surrounding walls were dotted with the black-and-white portraits of grim-faced pioneers. They had been captured stiff and proper, formally dressed in wool suits, silk ties, and John B.Stetson hats. Except one. On the south wall above the door was a photograph of a stocky little man leaning against a rock with a government .45-70 nestled in the crook of an arm and a burdened packhorse standing in the background. I would stare at him while ketchup dripped from my french fries and pooled on the tabletop in big, red blood-like globs. My father would notice my stare and say: "That was old Tom Dilliard, the wolfer. I knew him." He never commented on anyone else. Only the wolfer. But then, I never stared at anyone else. Only the wolfer.

from *Leaving the Land* by Ezra Riley
Stonecreek Press, 1993

1995

Ezra Riley sat on his haunches with the rowels of his plain stainless steel spurs pressing against his buttocks and his back leaning against the cottonwood planks of the corral. Two long soft nylon lead lines trailed from his hand to a young chestnut gelding that stood saddled, bridled, and braced against cooperation.

Ezra talked to the colt softly. "Whoa, Cajun, little fella. Think about the weight on your back. Think about the bit in your mouth. Nothing is going to hurt you, little fella." The colt stared with wide, curious eyes and signaled its own thoughts through the working of its ears. It was the two-year-old's second saddling and first day of being driven with the long reins that trailed from the bridle and through the stirrups. Three trips around the corral to the left, then three more to the right had been his afternoon's instruction.

Sitting on his haunches helped Ezra stretch his aching lower back, and he consciously willed the contracting muscles to relent and allow blood passage to his degenerating lower disk. If he wanted to continue breaking horses, if he was to continue ranching at all, his back would require healing. The ranch had taken the best years of his life and had scarred body and soul with an assortment of pains. He had fought drought, blizzards, poor markets, and conflicts with his sisters and uncle, and now, thirteen years after his mother's passing, he owned little more than he had in the beginning. The Riley ranch was basically two ranches. He and his two sisters owned an undivided interest in the smaller one. Their uncle, Solomon, owned the larger ranch.

Outside the pens a red heeler pup lay with her head on her front paws, her almond eyes glistening with eagerness. She whined softly and wagged her tail each time Ezra spoke kindly to the horse. In an adjoining pen a heavy heifer walked nervously, a balloonlike water bag protruding from beneath her kinked tail. April was calving time. Snow from the last storm had melted and the ground was bare and alternately muddy, frozen, or dry according to its exposure to the warming sun.

A calico-colored cat with six toes and a stub of a tail stepped from the barn's hayloft, stretched, then padded softly down the corral's top railing before seating itself on a railroad tie where it preened while purring to itself.

While the horse, dog, cat, heifer, and cowboy watched one another, Ezra was being watched through Zeiss binoculars from a mud-coated Dodge pickup truck half a mile away. Ezra had paid no attention to the truck. Joggers, aluminum can scavengers, Sunday drivers, and others parked on the highway's edge for various reasons. Especially in the spring.

The watcher was a tall, rawboned man in his early thirties. His straight, brown hair hung over his ears and forehead, and his lean face was covered with a short-cropped beard. His eyes were small and set close together beside a long, slightly hooked nose. His clothes were clean but well worn: flannel shirt, canvas jacket, faded denim jeans, L. L. Bean Maine hunting boots. The truck was plastered with gumbo, obscuring its color and license plates and indicating its use on muddy country roads. A homemade camper shell made of collapsible aluminum framing and canvas sheltered the truck bed.

Although the Riley mailbox was unlettered, Demetrius Pratt knew he was watching the author of the book *Leaving the Land*. There was no blonde dog. He guessed her dead, replaced by the red pup. The paint horse, Gusto, was missing too. He would have been very old, Pratt reasoned, and probably had been put down. That was appropriate. Everything else fit. The bunkhouse near the creek where Riley did his writing, the layout of the corrals, the old white house a mile up the road where the uncle, Solomon, lived. There was no doubt about it, the man sitting in the corral was Ezra Riley.

A thin smile creased Pratt's lips as he watched Ezra rise slowly to his feet. Perhaps it was too easy. Compared to himself, Riley was older, smaller, and stiff with pain. Maybe he was not a worthy challenge for the *soul-talk* of predator to prey, the decisive *conversation of death*. Pratt reached into a coat pocket, pulled out a copy of Ezra's book, and stared at the cover.

Leaving the Land.

Loving the land. Ezra Riley was a lover of the natural.

No, Pratt decided, physical limitations aside, Riley was a challenge. Maybe even a threat. He smiled again as he put the book away. Then again, maybe Ezra Riley could be converted. He could be a scribe in the coming kingdom where Pratt was destined to be chief priest once he found the *thin place*. And the *thin place* was on Riley land, Pratt was convinced of that.

He growled softly like an animal issuing a warning.

On Riley land! No man could own land. The thought was sacrilege. The new kingdom had to be forced into being, ushered to reality with bloodshed if necessary. Wildness must return. Domestication had to die. If he could not be changed, Ezra Riley had to be removed from the land, or the land removed from Ezra Riley.

He put the binoculars away. He dared watch no longer. Three minutes were enough. Besides, he could not trust Diamond long in town. She had her weaknesses. He got in his truck and drove away as quietly as possible.

By the time Ezra had unsaddled the colt, the heifer had calved unassisted. The seventy-pound calf, soaked with amniotic fluid, wheezed and shook its head while the mother stood over it protectively, licking it and glaring fiercely through the corral planks at Beaner, the red heeler.

Ezra waited until the calf rose on wobbly legs to suckle, then walked to the house, the pup dancing joyfully beside him. If he hurried he could make his workout in town with his new friend, Mikal Mora, a fish biologist from Louisiana. Mora would be in town from his camp at Fort Peck Dam to squeeze in some weight lifting between his other errands. Ezra had joined the club as a promise to Anne that he would do stretching exercises for his lower back. Ezra hated stretching. It was incredibly painful and boring. After meeting Mikal he changed his regime to serious lifting instead. Strength training was easier and more fun than pursuing flexibility, and that, he decided, was the curse of middle age: the seduction of building on what was already strong rather than lengthening one's reaches.

Anne Riley was in a hurry.

She rushed from the Yellow Rock Community College where she was a second-year student in a rigorous, accelerated nursing program, to her car. She made a quick stop at the grocery store for bread, milk, and eggs. The night before she had typed a two-thousand-word report on an old portable typewriter—she had stubbornly resisted learning to use Ezra's new computer—and was so exhausted in the morning that she had skipped breakfast. It was her hungry son who noticed they were low on groceries.

Anne was hurrying to get home because she knew Ezra was working the colt alone, and with one little mishap he could lie in the corral for hours before being found. Besides that, it was Tuesday, and Ezra's new friend would be in town. Ezra's workouts with Mikal were a necessary diversion from the routine of feeding, calving, and riding, but he was reluctant to leave the ranch if someone was not there to watch the first-calf heifers.

Anne knew about the need for diversions. She had enrolled in the three-year nursing program not only for a late career and the supplemental income, but to fill her time. Dylan, their only child, would graduate from high school in a month and leave for college in the fall. The thought of him being gone left a huge void in her heart. She wished they had had more children. Even one more.

She nearly ran from the store with her groceries and jumped into her ten-year-old Mercury Sable. She routinely used a dirt road behind the store as a shortcut to get home, and as she drove around the corner of the building she glimpsed a young woman in blue jeans and red sweatshirt leaning against the Dumpster. As Anne watched, the girl took a step, stumbled, and fell. Anne stopped immediately, spilling the bag of groceries across the front seat. The girl seemed small, young, and in desperate need of help. When Anne got to her the girl had risen to her hands and knees.

"Are you hurt?" Anne asked, reaching to help her up.

The girl's head rose. Both eyes were black and swollen, and blood dripped from a puffy lip. She was conscious but dazed.

"Let me help you," Anne insisted, and she placed her hands under the girl's arms and lifted. The girl rose lightly, like clothes on a hanger. "I'll take you to the hospital," Anne said.

"No, no," the girl mumbled, shaking her head. "No hospital." She turned to look behind her as if searching for a vehicle or person. "Gotta find Deemie."

Anne looked angrily, nervously about. There was no one around. Whoever had done this had left her. "Let me take you to the emergency room," she repeated.

"No," the girl demanded, and she tried to pull away, but the effort was too much and she slumped to the ground.

Anne glanced about but there was no one to help her. "I'm taking you to my house," she told the girl. "But if your condition worsens you are going to the hospital."

"No, no. Leave me here," the girl mumbled. "It's not safe," she said, too softly to be heard.

CHAPTER TWO

*The most affable of my father's six bachelor brothers
was obese Uncle Joe. Among the many dilapidated
buildings surrounding my uncles' big white house was
an old schoolhouse. In its narrow, dusty cupboards Uncle Joe found two books by Ernest Thompson Seton and
gave them to me. Soon I was falling asleep with visions
of large-headed, rangy, slack-jawed, red-eyed buffalo
wolves imprinted on the insides of my eyelids. They
roamed my landscape at night. One time I dared tell Uncle Joe that wolves were giving me nightmares. "Ha,"
he laughed. "That's what wolves are for."*

Leaving the Land

P ush it," Ezra demanded. "Push it." He reached down and put his
fingers under the bar. "It's all yours," he said. "Come on, Mikal,
push it."

Mikal Mora's face constricted and reddened. A deep grunt escaped his lips as the Olympic bar, thick on the ends with iron plates, slowly
rose from his chest and toward the bench stand. He was heavily muscled
with biceps like grapefruits and forearms like Popeye the Sailor.

"You got it," Ezra coaxed. "It's all yours."

With a final grimace Mora straightened his arms and the bar collapsed
heavily onto the metal rack.

"Good lift," Ezra said.

Mora stood slowly, sighed, and let satisfaction ripple through the
swelled muscles of his six-foot frame. An audience of high school lifters
turned back to their weights. They had felt young, tough, and strong before
watching Mora and Riley attack the bench press. The older men repeatedly
displayed that muscles could season and strengthen with age.

"Two-seventy," Mora whispered. "Man, I didn't think I had it in me."
He turned his playful dark eyes on Ezra. "Are you going to try it?" he
asked. The challenge was light but direct. Ezra's slight frame carried thirty

fewer pounds than his partner, but his strength lay in his mind. He refused to accept limits.

Ezra shrugged. "Might as well," he said. He dabbed his fingers in a chalk trough, lay on the bench, and reached up and fingered the bar. Mikal moved behind the bar to spot him.

"This will be a personal best if I get it," Ezra said.

Mora smiled. He was impressed that Ezra could stay with him—or a close step behind—when they handled heavy weight. "You'll get it," he said.

"If Anne was here I'd really get it. She thinks I'm doing my back exercises."

Mora laughed, his teeth white against dark skin and hair. "I think she knows better," Mikal said. "She knows you're as stiff as a board, the old warhorse of the weight room."

"Like you're so young," Ezra retorted as he measured his grip on the bar.

"A decade younger than you," Mora said. "What are you now, fifty-three?" he joked.

"Forty-three," Ezra corrected. "*Almost* forty-three."

The teenagers paused to watch. Riley was a phenomenon to them in his faded sweatpants, the streak of gray in his hair, and an obvious dislike for their heavy metal music. They knew him as Dylan's dad, a rancher and writer. Secretly they hoped to be as fit when they were Ezra's age, but being over forty was still incomprehensible to them. Only dinosaurs lived so long.

Ezra closed his eyes, took several deep breaths, and willed his mind to lift more than he had ever attempted.

Mikal was poised above him. "Want a liftoff?" he asked.

"No," Ezra said softly, his eyes still closed. If he couldn't lift the weight off the stand by himself, he knew he wouldn't get it off his chest either.

The bell above the club door tinkled and a tall, brown-haired, bearded man walked in. Mora got a glimpse of him over his shoulder. He saw the stranger enter the office where a young woman worked alone.

"Wait a minute," Mikal whispered to Ezra. He turned and walked cat-like through the weight machines and Stairmasters.

Ezra was deep in a well of concentration and had neither heard nor seen his partner leave. A resolute determination lined his brow. He breathed out three sharp breaths, then hoisted the weight off the stand. He balanced it outright for an instant, his tendons and bones straining, the blood racing to the inflated muscles, then lowered the weight in a controlled drop, catching it as it touched his chest. He strained to start it upward, his back arching slightly, his stomach tightening, and blood pinkening a face lined in grimaces. He willed the weight upward, but it stalled three-quarters of the way up. His elbows began to quiver; his back muscles cramped. He waited for Mikal's encouragement, his deep command to push on. He waited a long instant for the feel of his spotter's fingers lightly assisting the bar, but the assist did not come. Ezra opened his eyes to a bare and ugly ceiling. Mikal was not there, but the immense weight hovered above him like a rock ledge about to topple. From the corner of his eye he saw the high schoolers, noticed their concern, their confusion as to whether to help or not. He could cry for a "spot," but pride stifled the call. A fierce determination rolled up from his belly and chest, exploded from his mind, and demanded more than his muscles, tendons, and bones should have allowed. It willed the bar up slowly, shakily, until his arms locked out and Ezra toppled it backward onto the stand where it dropped forcefully, rattling the entire bench. The high schoolers shook their heads. Dylan's father, the aged wonder.

Ezra rose slowly from the bench, flushed with accomplishment and awash in testosterone, endorphins, and lactic acid. Two hundred and seventy pounds. It felt good. It felt very good. He could no longer run or play basketball, and his karate days were long behind him, but he could push weight. Where was Mikal? He turned to see him hurrying back through the weight stations.

"Whoa, man, what did you do?" Mikal asked.

"I got it up." Ezra smiled.

"No spot?"

"No spot."

"Didn't you hear me tell you to wait?"

"I didn't hear a thing," Ezra said.

"Well, great lift." Mora laughed and slapped Ezra on the back. "For an old guy." The backs, arms, and chests of both men were inflated as if little balloons were bunching under their skin. "Want to go up another five?" Mora teased.

"No way," Ezra said. "No possible way." He walked in a slow circle, breathing deeply, his hands on his hips. "Where did you go?" he asked Mikal.

"I saw a strange guy come in. Linda is in the office alone. I thought I better go check things out."

"Who was he?" Ezra asked in forced breaths, the blood slowly draining from his face. He thought Mikal seemed distracted.

Mora lied effortlessly. "I don't know," he said. "Just some guy looking for health food. Some sort of strange herbal drink." Mora pulled a sweatshirt on over his black tank top. The soft cotton shirt covered the military tattoos on his biceps.

"Are you leaving?" Ezra asked. Their regime was only half finished. "We still have chin-ups and lat work."

"Gotta go. I need to get back to my camp so I can be on the lake bright and early," Mora said. "Besides, you know how I hate chin-ups. But I'll be back in Friday." He rushed off. Ezra watched the bounce of youth in his step, the playful verve in the manhandling of his gym bag. *To be ten years younger,* Ezra thought.

Ezra did one set of chin-ups, knocking out fifteen with little enthusiasm. It seemed rude that Mikal had left so quickly. He did not know his new friend well—they had met in an idle conversation over books; both liked James Lee Burke and Larry McMurtry—but he sometimes suspected that Mikal was too physical, too adventurous to be what he claimed: a married college professor from Louisiana working on a doctorate thesis in warm-water fish biology on the Missouri River. Mora was bright and well read, but he didn't strike Ezra as the egghead type, someone interested in water temperatures and the egg counts of spawning walleye. But Ezra accepted his story. It was the way he had been raised: Take a man at his word until he proved otherwise.

Ezra's enthusiasm left with Mikal. His shoulders burned, and he worried he might have torn a rotator cuff. Weight lifting was an escapist fantasy for a man pushing forty-three, and he knew his body had a date with reality in the morning. He decided to go home.

Early April in eastern Montana is a brown time. Chilly nights prevent the grasses from greening, and the cottonwoods and willows are weeks from budding. The wind blows almost daily, freshening the sky and giving a radiance to sunsets as the low-angle sun bathes the hills in brilliant sheets of orange and yellow slashed by ribbons of stark black shadows.

Dusk fell as Ezra drove home. The Grassy Crown, the highest point on the Riley ranch, held the last rays of the disappearing sun, causing the rounded, sodded ridge to glow above the darkened badlands like a brass doorknob. The valleys were cloaked in a bluish pall that shrouded the mud-covered pickup truck parked on an approach to Ezra's horse pasture. Ezra almost failed to notice it, but when he did he stopped, thinking the driver might be having mechanical trouble. A tall, bearded man emerged from the Dodge. Ezra stepped from his Ford. He wore his black hat pulled low and his trademark black silk handkerchief knotted neatly around his neck. "Having trouble?" he asked. His tone was benevolent but objective. The pickup truck and stranger both radiated a lawlessness that put Ezra on edge. Recent years had seen a wave of misfits move to Montana for the compassion and welfare of the small western communities. Ezra was learning caution.

The man did not answer immediately. Instead, his eyes probed Ezra's shadowed face like two small penlights. His gaze was cold and alien, his stature as imposing as a marble sculpture. Ezra unconsciously took a backward step closer to the coyote rifle in the truck.

The retreating movement startled the man and seemed to make him aware of Ezra as a person rather than an object. "No," he said, as if to be reassuring, "no trouble," but his voice was cool and directed.

Ezra did not intimidate easily—the land on both sides of the highway was Riley land, his turf—but the stranger's arrogance bombarded him in waves. Ezra wanted away from the man's presence. The man smelled of blood though there were no visible stains on his clothing. Yet, he reeked of

death. "Just checking," Ezra said. "Thought you might be broke down."
He opened the door to his truck.

"You live around here?" the stranger blurted.

Ezra froze. He had one leg in his pickup and one hand on the steering
wheel. He could vaguely see the outline of his Ruger rifle. Half a mile away the
lights of his house shone through the bare limbs of the cottonwoods. He dared
not look at them. Ezra lied. "No," he said. "I live up the road aways."

"Oh," Pratt said.

They stared at each other for a moment, neither able to see the eyes of the
other directly, but the air between them scintillated with tension as Pratt tried
to penetrate Ezra's defenses. Ezra finally broke the contact, got into his truck,
closed the door, and pulled onto the highway. When he saw in his mirror that
the man was following with his headlights off, the short hairs on his neck
stood on end, and like a grouse feigning a broken wing, Ezra drove beyond his
own house, over the hill, and past the dim television glow radiating through
his uncle's front door. When the Dodge came over the hill its headlights were
on. Ezra sped up gradually for three more miles then turned right on the Dead
Man Road while telling himself that the diversion was silly, a waste of time
and gasoline, because the man was probably harmless. He crossed the bridge
on Sunday Creek, turned onto a pasture road, killed his lights, and waited. The
headlights of the Dodge illuminated the green highway sign marking the
county road, but the truck continued northward. When its taillights disappeared Ezra let out a deep breath.

He chastised himself for being foolish. He was reacting to a situation,
to the lay of shadows, the mood of the evening, the adrenaline that re
mained after pumping iron.

No he wasn't, he argued. His instincts were often right. The tall,
bearded man was dangerous, and prudence was not a vice. He watched his
rearview mirror all the way home.

In the ranch yard Ezra turned on the corral lights and checked the heifers. The new calf was clean, dry, and resting bright-eyed in a corner of the
corral. Ezra turned the lights off and walked to the house. Anne met him at
the door.

"Sshhh," she whispered, bringing a finger to her lips. "I just put someone to sleep in the guest room."

"You what?" Ezra asked. "It's only seven o'clock." There was no vehicle in the yard so it was someone Anne had brought home. But who,
besides a drunk or a baby, would be asleep so early?

She took him by the hand and led him downstairs to the small bedroom across the hall from Dylan's room. As Anne opened the door, a shaft
of hall light fell on a young Indian woman asleep in the bed, her long black
hair spraying against the white sheet like raven feathers. He also saw the
blue, purple, and red bruises on her face.

"What happened to her?" he whispered.

"I don't really know," Anne said softly, closing the bedroom door as they left the room. "I found her behind County Market. She wouldn't go to the hospital or the sheriff. Her first name is Diamond. That's all I could get out of her."

"How did you get her to sleep?"

"Herbal tea, two aspirin, and two Excedrin PMs."

"Sweet dreams," Ezra said. "Is she all right?"

"She's okay," Anne said. "There's nothing broken."

"Wedding ring?"

"No."

"It was probably a boyfriend," Ezra said, and his mind flashed on the stranger in the truck. He was being silly again, wasn't he?

"Whoever did this," Anne said, "she's really afraid of him."

"Not afraid enough," Ezra countered, "or she would file charges."

They went back upstairs where Anne's homework was spread across the kitchen table. "I have a paper due tomorrow," she explained, "but if you're hungry . . ."

He shook his head. "I had a banana on my way to the club."

"So how was your day?" she asked. "I see a heifer calved."

He wanted to tell her about his bench-pressing and the stranger on the road. One might anger her, the other might scare her. "Just a quiet day," he said. "I worked with Cajun and lifted with Mikal. How about you?"

"The usual, except Pastor Tom called tonight. He wants to know if you can meet with him tomorrow. He will be in his office between ten and twelve."

Ezra nodded and reached into the refrigerator for a Diet Pepsi. "I guess I'll go to the bunkhouse," he said. He knew he needed to give Anne her space. It wasn't easy being an over-forty college student in a competitive program with women and men half her age. "Will Dylan be home soon?"

"He has FCA tonight."

Ezra nodded again. Dylan was a leader in both the Fellowship of Christian Athletes and the church youth group. Ezra grabbed a jacket off a hook, pulled on his hat, and took a flashlight from a cabinet. "I'll be in the bunkhouse. Keep the doors locked until Dylan gets home."

"Lock the doors?"

"Lock the doors," he repeated, nodding toward the basement. He didn't have to say it again. In her concern for the woman and her busyness with schoolwork, Anne had never considered she might have been followed. Maybe the man who beat Diamond was close by.

Anne followed him to the door. "Ezra," she said. "You're not mad at me are you?" Her blue eyes were dimmed by guilt.

"No," he said. "Some people bring home stray dogs and cats. You bring home stray people." He did not tell her that he loved her for it. It was her faith at work, her mercy in action. "Get back to work, nursing student," he said.

His office was cool—accentuating an air of loneliness—so he turned on the small space heater. Because writing was a lonely craft, Ezra had adopted a calico Manx kitten two years ago and named it Hemingway. It was to be his muse, a purring machine of encouragement lying at his feet. But Hemingway disdained people. It paced the office and yowled to be let out. A howling muse. Ezra understood and envied the cat. Sometimes he wanted to pace the room and scream too.

He turned on his new Macintosh and stared at the blank screen. A stack of his published book, *Leaving the Land,* sat on the shelf above him. It had been rejected twenty-one times before Amanda Silverstein, an editor he had met while on horseback near the interstate, moved to a small press in Connecticut. She published *Land,* and though it won two regional awards for western writing, the sales had not even earned back his $5,000 advance. Ezra's first book was an artistic success but a commercial failure. He put his feet up on the desk and stared at the blank computer screen. The posture made his back hurt, so he shifted in the chair. When that didn't help he got up and stretched while looking at objects in the room—two buffalo skulls, a horned cow skull, rows of books, rifles on the wall—then he sat back down and stared again at the screen. His first book had been about his love for the land and its animals. What could he write a second book about: Solomon, his eighty-three-year-old bachelor uncle? No, it would be wiser this time to leave his family out of his book. Relatives did not always enjoy his literary attentions.

Time dragged on. He flipped through books looking for inspiration. He read the openings to *A River Runs Through It, The Prince of Tides, The World According to Garp.* He heard Dylan come home about nine-thirty. The computer screen stayed blank, alternating between a Star Trek screensaver and a wordless illuminated page.

Fifteen minutes later Ezra turned his computer off, left the bunkhouse, and walked through the corral, flashing a light on the heifers, looking for any signs requiring a midnight calving check. He didn't see any.

The stars were brilliant in the night sky—he wished he knew his constellations—and Beaner followed quietly at his heels as he walked to the house. On the steps he stopped and rubbed the pup's head. Ezra appreciated her loyalty. Somewhere in the darkness Hemingway yowled. The cat wanted to be fed but didn't want to be petted. Ezra ignored it. The Manx was a good hunter. Unfortunately it was more fond of birds than mice. He turned on his heels and entered the house. The house was dark, so he quietly pulled off his boots and washed his face in the utility sink. He was turning for the bedroom when he heard a muffled cry from the basement. He tiptoed quietly downstairs to the guest room. Dylan's light flashed on, and his son met him in the hall.

"She's crying in her sleep," Dylan whispered. He was in his underwear and T-shirt, and it always surprised Ezra that Dylan was five eleven and a hundred and seventy pounds. Wasn't it yesterday that he was hoisting him up on Gusto?

"What is she saying?" Ezra asked, his ear against the guest room door. Dylan shrugged. Ezra eased the door open.

The girl had kicked off all the blankets and was curled in a tight ball in the middle of the bed. She clutched the pillow over her head like a shield.

Ezra moved in quietly, picked up the blankets, and covered her.

He heard her voice. Weak, muffled, but almost defiant. "Don't hurt me, Deemie," she said. "Don't hurt me, Deemie."

CHAPTER THREE

The morning dawned cloudy, warm, and humid. A storm from the Pacific had exhausted itself crossing the Rocky Mountains and was passing weakly over eastern Montana. A rim of gray sky was streaked with yellow and orange highlights as the sun tried to burn through the cloud cover.

"I go to class at ten," Anne told Ezra over his usual breakfast of a poached egg on whole wheat toast. "What should we do about Diamond?"

"She's welcome to stay here as long as she wants."

Anne smiled. That was what she was hoping to hear.

"But give her a ride to town if she wants one," Ezra added.

After kissing Anne good-bye he went outside and loaded a half ton of alfalfa and corn pellets in his pickup—fifteen seventy-pound sacks. His left shoulder was sore—he needed to go lighter on the weights—but not nearly as sore as his back. Every morning he awakened feeling as if he was strapped into a girdle of fire.

For the next two hours he drove through the hills feeding cattle coaxed from sagebrush coulees by the blaring truck horn. He enjoyed calving season: the babies on rubbery legs and the maternal confusion of the cows. Spring was a time of rebirth, and he could feel winter's cold fingers slowly leaving his bones, relaxing its grip on his aching back.

Most of the cattle were Solomon's. Ezra's herd numbered short of a hundred head.

With the feeding finished he drove straight to town, casting a critical eye at his ranch yard as he passed it. He saw nothing unusual. Anne had not left for class yet. Ezra was concerned for the Indian girl, and worse, he could not get the bearded stranger out of his mind. He needed to talk to the sheriff.

The lines had deepened on Bill Butler's leathery face and his hair was whiter, but he was still lean and strong, and in spite of two attempts at retiring, still sheriff of Yellow Rock. He smiled when Ezra entered his office. Yellow Rock was a town of familiar cordiality where sons were welcomed in the memory of their fathers. "Mornin', Ezra," Butler said, beckoning to a heavy mahogany chair. "Coffee?"

Ezra shook his head. "I've had my share already." He had tried several times to quit caffeine.

"What brings you to town so early? It's not like you to make social calls."

"Anne brought a young Indian woman home last night," Ezra said. "She's been badly beaten."

"Will she come in?" Butler asked.

"I don't think so."

"Do you know her name or the name of the person who beat her?"

"Sort of. The girl's first name is Diamond," Ezra said. He saw the sheriff's blue eyes flash with recognition. "Does that mean anything?"

Butler was noncommittal. "It might," he said. "Is she about nineteen or twenty?"

"Could be."

"And she didn't say anything about the person who beat her?"

"No, but I heard her talking in her sleep, begging not to be hurt and mentioning what might have been the guy's name."

"Which was?" Butler moved forward in his chair.

"Sounded like *Deemie*."

The sheriff leaned back and rubbed his chin thoughtfully. Even though he was retirement age he had the youthful look of a man who enjoyed capturing bad guys. Law enforcement had not made him cynical. "She's out at your place now?" he asked.

"As far as I know." Ezra was intrigued by the sheriff's undertone of interest. Butler had been a friend of Ezra's father and Ezra knew they shared the same affections: good horses, elk hunts, and coffee brewed stout and served black. Butler got up. "Follow me," he said. "There's someone here I think you should meet." Ezra followed Butler down a hallway lined with small offices, through the jail's kitchen to a door in the back of the building. Ezra guessed it was a conference room.

Butler knocked softly twice, waited, then opened the door and stepped in. A man in a flannel shirt and blue jeans sat alone at a table, a 10mm Smith and Wesson semiautomatic holstered under his muscled left arm. He was studying a pile of papers and photographs. He looked up in surprise when Butler came in with Ezra.

"Mikal," Ezra said.

Mora did not answer. He turned his eyes to the sheriff and gave him an irritated stare.

"You two know each other?" Butler asked, closing the door.

Mora smiled wryly, the surprise slowly fading from his face. "Sort of," he said. There was a mischievous glint in his eyes, the shine of a child caught with the cookies.

"I never really thought you were a fish biologist," Ezra said.

Mora glanced back at Butler. The sheriff took a relaxed seat in an aluminum folding chair. "Ezra has a guest in his house," he explained. "Her name is Diamond."

"Is that right?" Mora said, his voice hinting at both caution and expectation.

Ezra slowly settled in a chair, casually scanning the papers, photographs, and maps as he sat. "So what's going on here?" he asked, directing the question to both of them, knowing one had the ultimate responsibility and authority.

The sheriff took it upon himself to explain, nodding toward Ezra's workout partner. "Mikal Mora—and I don't know if that is his real name or not—is a special agent with the U.S. Fish and Wildlife Service."

"A fed," Ezra said.

Mora nodded. The shared secret drew them closer together, welding a trust that had already been formed in the cooperation of handling heavy weights.

"I have known Ezra and his family for years," Butler explained. "If it is Diamond LaFontaine at his house, he needs to know what he is dealing with."

"I should be out there before she gets away," Mora said.

The sheriff was soft-spoken but adamant. "Give Ezra a few moments," he said.

Mora calculated quietly then pushed a thick brown file folder to the center of the table. It was labeled *Missouri Breaks, 1994–1995*. "You might want to get Miss LaFontaine out of your house and pretend you never met her," he said.

Ezra thought instantly of Anne, hoping she was in class, not alone at the ranch. "What do you mean?" he asked.

Mora began drawing documents from the folder. His eyes were as black as marbles of coal. "You have kicked a hornet's nest, my friend," he said. "I know you didn't do it on purpose, but you did it just the same."

"I am in some sort of trouble?" Ezra asked.

"Trouble?" Mora asked. "Only if you spell it with a capital T."

"The girl is dangerous?"

Mora shook his head. "No, she's a criminal, but she's not dangerous."

"Her boyfriend?" Ezra guessed.

"Her boyfriend," Mora confirmed.

CHAPTER FOUR

Diamond LaFontaine threw back the covers and jumped from the bed. Comfort had awakened her. She stood in the middle of the room, trembling, holding herself, her thin body shaking like a reed. Where was she? Where was Deemie? She sensed she was in a basement bedroom darkened by pulled shades. She felt the eerie sensation of someone nearby and turned to a dim reflection of herself in a full-length mirror. Her bruised face—the colors of eggplant and tomatoes—was not a surprise. A digital clock on a nightstand flashed the time like a pulsating red warning: *9:17.*

All she recalled was a tall, strong woman with a soft touch. What was her name? Anne. Her name was Anne. She heard a noise above her. That would be the woman. Anne.

The blinking clock cast a red line of reflection on the bindings of two books on the nightstand. She curiously picked them up, looking for clues. The books sent terror through her slender body.

The first one was a small black Bible. A part of her wanted to grasp it, hold it to her chest; another part screamed to throw it away. The other book, *Leaving the Land* by Ezra Riley, was equally ominous. Her hands burned in holding them, and she dropped both to the floor, where they landed softly on the crumpled bedcovers.

She had to leave. She found her shoes and sweatshirt. Deemie would be looking for her. Deemie would be very mad. As she entered the hallway she heard footsteps above her moving in a parallel direction.

Diamond hid under the stairwell while Anne came down the steps. When Anne moved toward the bedroom, Diamond slipped up the stairs, her footfall as soft as feathers on stone, and eased quietly out the back door. The last thing she heard was Anne gently calling her name. It was a sweet sound, like a songbird singing to puffy summer clouds. Diamond nearly stopped, but a predatory and carnivorous power pulled her away.

Mikal Mora reached into the folder and brought out an 8 x 10 photograph and handed it across the table. It had obviously been taken secretly. Ezra guessed the blurred lines around the edges to be tree limbs. Framed in the center was a young woman standing over a campfire. "Is that the girl?" Mora asked.

"It looks like her," Ezra said. "But she was asleep when I saw her and her face is badly bruised."

Mora handed him another photo. "How about this individual? Have you ever seen him?"

It was an enlargement of a jail photo marked Missoula County, 1993. The subject was clean-shaven but had longish brown hair, a prominent nose, and the narrow-set eyes of a predator. Ezra's eyes widened by the width of an eyelash, a tiny motion that Mora noticed. "I might have seen this guy last night," Ezra said. "He was parked near our house. I thought he was having car trouble. Who is he?"

"Demetrius Pratt," Mikal said. "He was the guy who came into the club yesterday while we were lifting. I've been hunting him for months, and he comes to me when I'm in my sweatpants with my firearm locked in the truck. I left you to try and find him."

"Pratt," Ezra said. "That name sounds familiar."

"It should," the sheriff said. "Remember Cletus Pratt, Shorty Wilson's friend from Las Vegas?"

Ezra nodded, his eyes glazing with recollection. "Cletus Pratt," he said softly, recalling the buckaroo gangster with the knife in his boot. They had nearly fought each other beneath the shed at the sales barn. "What's the connection?" Ezra asked.

"They were half brothers," Mora explained impatiently. "Cletus is dead, killed in a drug deal that went bad." He rose from his chair. "Discussion time is over," he said. "I need to pick up the girl."

"Do you have an arrest warrant for her?" Ezra asked.

Mora looked down at Ezra. He was a different person from the friend Ezra had gained in the weight room. "She's not wanted for anything," Mora said, "except questioning. And I do plan on questioning her."

"She is a guest in my house, Mikal."

"Pratt is dangerous, Ezra," Mora said.

Ezra noticed that Mikal had balled his fists, causing the tendons in his forearms to rise like coils of wire. He looked at the wall clock. It was a quarter after ten. Anne should be in class. What if she wasn't? What if Pratt *had* returned? "Okay," he said. "Let's go. You can ride with me and fill me in on the way."

"Pratt's game is poaching," Mora explained. His eyes were focused north, toward Ezra's ranch. A Levi jacket concealed his handgun. He glanced quickly at the floorboard of the truck, almost willing Ezra to drive faster. "Big game trophies from Yellowstone Park, Glacier Park, and the Missouri Breaks. Elk, sheep, goats. Anything that brings the big money."

"I get the feeling there is more to this than that," Ezra said.

"I can't tell you any more."

Ezra shot him an impatient sideways glance. "Mikal, the guy's girl-friend is in my house."

Mora gazed at the skyline. He had not told Ezra that this was his first undercover case and he was making the rules as he went. "The guy is loony tunes, Ezra," he said. "He's obsessed with wolves and he hates land-owners. And he's an expert with a recurve bow. He can put an arrow clear through a one-ton Angus bull—he's done it before—then like a wolf he marks his territory. He leaves a *sign*. His sign is a business card with 'Nim-rod' printed on it."

"Nimrod, the mighty hunter," Ezra said. "The legendary king of Baby-lon and the builder of the tower of Babel."

"Whatever," Mora said. "Pratt's spiritual beliefs and the terrorism aren't my concern. My job is to stop the poaching."

Ezra pursed his lips in painful contemplation. "What's he doing in Yel-low Rock?"

"He's camped somewhere in the Missouri Breaks scouting a trophy ram in the C. M. Russell Wildlife Refuge. He either came to town for sup-plies, or he is after a landowner in this area."

"You mean he could be down here as a terrorist? He's here to kill someone's bull or something?"

"Or something," Mikal agreed. "He hates domesticated animals. He's a zealot about wilderness and people and animals living wild and free. So he's anti-technology, too, unless he can use it to his own advantage."

"Do you know who he might be after?" Ezra asked.

Mora shook his head. "I would just as soon not discuss that right now," he said.

Ezra felt a cold dread in his stomach. He glanced at Mora. The agent seemed like a dim shadow, someone whose purpose was important but transitory. "I wonder if it's Shorty Wilson," Ezra said absently. "The tar-get, I mean. Maybe Wilson is the target."

"I have considered that," Mora said. "Wilson is one of the largest landowners in the state."

"And he's my neighbor," Ezra said. He pressed down on the gas pedal, suddenly more concerned for Anne and Dylan, and drove quickly into the ranch yard. Anne's car was gone. The red heeler trotted out to meet him, her tail wagging with its own life. Ezra brushed past her and up the steps to the house with Mora close behind him.

"Anne," he called out. "Anyone home?" There was no response. "The girl slept downstairs," Ezra said. Mora disappeared into the basement.

Ezra went to the kitchen. On the table was a note from his wife: *Ezra, Diamond was gone when I left for class. Will you look for her? I won't be home until five. Love . . .*

Mikal came back upstairs. "Nothing," he said.

Ezra handed him the note. "Where do you suppose she is?" he asked.

Mora crumpled the note in his hand. "She's miles from here by now. Pratt was probably nearby all the time."

Ezra sighed. "Well, I hope I've seen the last of both of them."

Mora's eyes bridged Ezra's with a long ladder of a stare. "You are not out of it, Ezra. You are already a player in this game."

"Why? Because of the girl or because I'm Wilson's neighbor?"

"Neither. I sought you out, Ezra," Mikal confessed. "I made contact with you at the health club for a purpose."

Ezra heard the rattle of heavy weights, the feel of chalk on his fingers, the laughter of two men pressing iron, telling stories, discussing books. "You *sought* me out?" He felt used. His friendship with Mikal seemed tarnished and cheapened.

"I had to," Mora said. "You are my best connection to someone I need to talk to. A prison inmate who spent ten days in the Missoula city jail with Pratt. A guy named Jubal Lee Walker."

Ezra's mouth dropped. He had hardly heard the name in six years. *Jubal Lee*, he thought. *You prodigal phantom, have you returned to haunt me again?* He looked at Mikal. "What do you want from me?" he asked.

"I want you to fly to the state prison with me this weekend. I want you to talk to your old friend Jubal Lee."

Ezra felt the pull of the dark and mysterious. It would be easy to say no, to tell Mikal that he was too busy, he didn't want to get involved, he could not risk putting his family in danger. But his head moved up and down slowly in a nod of affirmation. "I should talk to Anne," he said blankly, but both he and Mora knew he was going. Ezra was now officially involved.

Ezra dropped Mora off a block from the sheriff's office and was almost out of town when he remembered his meeting with Pastor Tom. He was tempted to skip it. It hardly seemed important compared to the new drama he had been thrust into. But conviction and duty turned him around.

He knocked on the door of Tom Jablonski's study. The pastor's voice beckoned him to an office lined with bookshelves, only the shelves were nearly bare—like a forest that had been clear cut—and the pastor was stuffing the books in cardboard boxes and sealing the boxes shut with duct tape.

"Leaving town?" Ezra joked, but there was no humor in his voice. The question was an icebreaker that sounded as distant and mechanical as a rifle shot in a canyon. He was still distracted by thoughts of Demetrius Pratt and Jubal Lee Walker.

Jablonski did not notice Ezra's aloofness. "Yes, I *am* leaving town," he said. "That's why I needed to see you."

Ezra felt forewarned. There was the heaviness of expectation in the air, and he told himself to say no to anything he was asked. He became flippant because it was his quick and reactionary form of self-defense. "Has Betty Lou Barber finally run you out of town?" he asked.

"How ironic that you should bring her up," Jablonski said, adding a box to a small mountain of cartons. "But no, the one-woman lynch mob hasn't run me out of town yet."

Jablonski was unusually lighthearted, Ezra realized. He was normally an idea man, excited by scholastic revelation and systematic programs while maintaining a protective reserve about his personal life. But today he seemed like a child in a roomful of Christmas presents. He finished sealing a box then walked around his desk and sat in his chair where he was suddenly transformed to being businesslike. Missing from the desk were the photographs of his deceased daughters. Ezra guessed they had been packed with the books.

"Darlene and I are going home," Jablonski announced.

Ezra's eyes widened. "Home? To Pennsylvania?"

"To Grove City College. A temporary teaching position, filling in for a sick friend. I don't know which books of mine I might need," he explained. "So I'm taking most of them. We will be gone six weeks. The board has given me the time off. I guess it's time to return and deal with what we left behind."

Pennsylvania, Ezra thought, *where the Jablonskis' only children were killed by a drunk driver nine years before.*

"We have to leave for the Billings airport in an hour. Armon Barber is willing to handle the Sunday night service and the building maintenance. We're canceling the Wednesday night service. I've found another pastor in town to handle funerals, weddings, and hospital visitations should those occasions arise," Jablonski continued. "All I need now is for you to preach on Sunday mornings."

Ezra felt like he was lost in the mountains of sudden decisions with the trail forking in the dark timber. The light was fading and the air was chilling. What direction should he go? Superimposed on the imaginary forest was the face of Pastor Jablonski looking at him hopefully, expectantly. Ezra reminded himself he had heifers calving, cattle to feed, a colt to break. And Demetrius Pratt. He did not need any more obligations.

"You've taught some on Wednesday nights," the pastor said. "Sunday mornings are pretty much the same except you raise your voice and wear a tie. You do own a tie, don't you?"

Ezra shook his head. He didn't. Perhaps that detail would disqualify him.

Jablonski didn't seem surprised. "No problem. Have the church buy you one. We will consider it your yearly clothing allowance. It would be, after all, the only wages you are going to get."

Ezra said nothing. If he did not agree to preach would Pastor Tom cancel his plans for going home? Would he be responsible for keeping a man and his wife from their healing?

"One more thing," Jablonski added. "I will also need you to handle a couple of little counseling responsibilities."

Ezra's eyebrows rose. Christian counseling was an interest of his—his personal faith had been ignited six years before by Jubal Lee, and since then Ezra's personal studies had included in-depth material on inner healing through biblical counseling—but this was too much, too soon. Preaching meant a commitment to Bible study and prayer. Counseling meant a commitment to people, a responsibility to others.

"I know you're not licensed, so you better not get too involved," the pastor said. "Just be a friend, a good listener. Then apply biblical truth for guidance. Don't get too deep. You know I'm not too crazy about most of this Christian psychology stuff."

"But—"

"The first one is tomorrow evening," Jablonski noted, looking through his appointment book. "Lillie Foster. Hmm. The funny thing is she asked specifically if you could talk to her. Do you know her?"

Ezra shook his head. He only knew who she was. She and her husband—was it Brad or Ben?—were new in town. Lillie was in her late twenties and stunningly beautiful. Brad (or Ben?) was small and quiet. They had a little girl. "You say she asked for me?"

"Yes. I guess she's heard about some of the ministering you and Anne have done out at the ranch," the pastor said. "You know I'm not really in favor of that, but I understand there are a few people in the congregation that have trouble with my style. Oh, yes, and speaking of people who have trouble with me, someone else wants to see you this afternoon at four. Can you make it?"

"I don't know," he said. "I'm calving . . ."

"I'll call her," Jablonski interrupted. "She could come out to your place, how would that be?"

The pastor was insisting, Ezra realized. His homeward pull had to be intense. "Okay," Ezra said, and with one word agreed to everything. He would preach on Sundays. He would meet with Lillie Foster. He would take that afternoon's appointment. Whoever *that* was. "Who is it?" he asked.

"Mrs. Barber."

Ezra's face resembled a tombstone. "No, not Betty Lou? Why would she make an appointment with you to see me?"

"She didn't exactly. She was in here an hour ago campaigning to have her husband preach on Sundays. She had a fit when I said you were my choice, and she launched into a tirade about having to see you immediately. Something terribly important. So I said I would arrange it. Otherwise, she would have just barged in on you and Anne. This way you are forewarned."

"Betty Lou . . ." Ezra's voice trailed away like a wounded animal.

Jablonski smiled and his eyes twinkled with a mischievous light. For once he could pawn off, though temporarily, the church's most troublesome member. "Yes, Betty Lou. But don't worry," he said. "When Betty Lou makes an appointment to see someone, she doesn't expect any advice. She comes to complain and give orders. Just listen politely. Maybe you can shovel out a stall while she talks. Shovel fast, though, or she's bound to fill it up again."

"You are going to Pennsylvania for six weeks and leaving me with Betty Lou Barber?" Ezra asked.

"Hey." The pastor smiled, his hands extended as if handing Ezra a package. "What are friends for?"

CHAPTER FIVE

D iamond LaFontaine rested her head against the window of the truck's passenger door. She was in big trouble. Deemie would beat her again as soon as they were in camp. She had it coming. It was all her fault. Her disobedience had thrown them off schedule, causing them to drive back to the Breaks in the daytime. In the daylight they could be seen and remembered.

She had given in to a weakness yesterday. She had purchased the groceries on Deemie's list and was waiting for him behind the store. But she was early, so she went back and bought a soft drink from a vending machine. A Diet Coke. She drank it quickly, but when she returned Deemie was there and he knew the truth. Soft drinks were not allowed because they were not natural. They were evil and had no life force. Deemie had hit her three times before she crawled behind the Dumpster. He was reaching for her when the warehouse door rattled. Deemie jumped in the truck and drove off. Diamond lay unnoticed as two teenage checkout boys shredded cardboard boxes and joked about music and girls. When they left she staggered out. That was when the nice lady came by.

She wished the woman had never stopped, but she did. She took Diamond to her house, washed and treated her face, and gave her strong tea and some aspirin.

When she woke up she knew she had to run away. The lady was too nice. She would try to help. Diamond ran two miles up the creek, then crawled into a culvert under the highway. Every few moments she peeked out and looked for Deemie's truck. She had been lucky. It was the third vehicle to pass.

They drove north on blacktop for almost a hundred miles, then turned on a gravel road, then turned again on a two-track jeep trail.

"So, who took you in?" Pratt demanded. It was the first he had spoken to her in almost two hours.

She shook her head. "I don't know," she said softly. It wasn't really a lie. The tall woman with the sandy-blonde hair had only mentioned her first name: Anne. Diamond was not going to betray her. She hoped the book she had found in the basement meant nothing, just a coincidence.

"I know who it was," Pratt said smugly. His eyebrows rose into his stringy bangs and a thin sneer split his face. "There were only two houses anywhere near where I picked you up. One belonged to an old bachelor in his eighties. I don't think he found you and brought you home."

Diamond felt her insides tighten.

"I found you by accident," Pratt said. "I wasn't even looking for you. I was looking for someone else."

Diamond snuck a peek at him. The long stare of cold light was in his eyes, beaming forward as if seeing something visible only to his infrared vision. He could see light in darkness, and he saw darkness in the light.

"You spent the night in Ezra Riley's house," he said. He coughed a short, guttural laugh. It was the one thing, even more than the beatings, that Diamond really hated. She despised the laugh for its joylessness. It was not even a human sound; it was part animal and part something else that reached out with a cruel and calculated premeditation. She could feel the energy behind the laugh burrowing into her soul.

"Ezra Riley." Pratt chuckled softly. "You better run like the prophet Elijah. You better start hunting your cave."

Diamond hated it when Deemie used biblical terms. She pulled deep into herself. Like a worm inching into the recesses of a rock, she was withdrawing into a narrow tunnel of darkness while pursued by Deemie's menacing laugh, the cold light in his eyes, and the promise of the vicious retribution of his gnarled fists.

CHAPTER SIX

*"Religion?" Uncle Joe laughed, his immense bulk
perched precariously on an overturned five-gallon
bucket. "Ain't no Riley ever been interested in religion."
He cast his line into the bass pond. The red-and-white
bobber plunked on the surface, sending out little ripples
that reached to the edge of the shoreline near his feet.
"Ain't no Riley interested in anything that can't make
money. Religion is just superstition anyway." Later,
when he filleted and fried the bluegills, I saw him throw
a pinch of salt over his shoulder, just in case.*

Leaving the Land

When Ezra got home he walked slowly through his house. Anne had made the bed Diamond had slept in. There was no evidence the girl had ever been there. It was as if nothing had happened; it had all been imagined. He tried to relax, but it was hard to rest knowing Betty Lou was coming for a visit. He wanted to be prepared for her. Instead, he was elbow-deep inside a calving heifer when her Buick pulled into the yard.

The heifer had started wringing her tail and pacing the corral about two-thirty. Ezra gave her an hour while he did other chores. By then it was obvious the heifer needed assistance.

He had hoped for a quick pull. He ran the heifer into the chute, tied her tail up, and eased his right hand inside her vagina. He felt the baby's nose and one front foot, but the other foot was missing. The calf had one leg back. He was pushing forward against the heifer's contractions when Betty Lou arrived for her "counseling" appointment, not just on time, but early. Somewhere on a plane over the Midwest, Ezra guessed Pastor Tom was smiling to himself.

The pup yapped as Betty Lou got out of her car. "I'm over here," Ezra yelled from the corrals.

Mrs. Barber walked directly to the front of the squeeze chute, startling the heifer and causing her to flail wildly between the metal bars. "So, this is the new pastoral counseling office." She sniffed. "Just exactly what are you doing?"

"Mrs. Barber, please," Ezra implored. "Would you step back a little? You're scaring the heifer." Fear had intensified the contractions, making Ezra's right hand seem gripped by a boa constrictor.

Betty Lou moved back defiantly. "Why don't you have a vet do this?" she retorted. The red rinse she used to dye her gray hair left it a dirty pink, and highlighted by the sun, it looked like a wig made of cotton candy.

The woman's dislike of Ezra was common knowledge. She still blamed him for Jubal Lee Walker's sudden departure from Yellow Rock. Betty Lou had been a big fan of Jubal Lee's.

Ezra ignored Betty Lou's remark about a veterinarian. His hands ached from gripping the contracted leg. The heifer had a small pelvis, and the calf was large and slimy with calving fluids. Ezra felt like he was trying to pull Jell-O through a keyhole. "This may take a while," he said breathlessly. "Do you want to come back later?"

"Oh, you won't get rid of me that easily," she said, flinging off a red shawl, startling the heifer again. "I have things to tell you." An old barrel sat beside the chute that Ezra used to place medicine on while doctoring cattle. She dusted it with a handkerchief and seated herself. "I had a dream about you the other night."

"Oh?" Ezra grunted. The calf had a leg distended backward from the shoulder, and the hoof lay under its body. Ezra was now up to his own shoulder inside the heifer, struggling to get a hand under the calf and pull the leg free. Both the heifer and Betty Lou had become a welcome distraction for Ezra. They had taken his mind off Demetrius Pratt.

Betty Lou cleared her throat loudly. "I believe the dream was very important, otherwise I certainly would not come and bother someone as busy as you seem to be." She paused, waiting to see Ezra's astonishment or interest. She saw neither. Ezra now had both hands inside the heifer and was clinging to the hoof of the rebellious foot with his fingernails. His forearms were swelling with fatigue, and sweat rolled from his brow, stinging his eyes.

"Of course, you know I am a seer," Betty Lou continued.

"No, I didn't know that," Ezra said. He had finally succeeded in looping the strap around the ankle. He reached back and dragged the cumbersome calf-puller up to the cow's hindquarters, hooked a cable to the OB strap, and frantically worked the puller's ratchet handle. The cable tightened, and the heifer bellered with surprise and pain as the machine began extracting the calf from her uterus.

"I am trying to tell you an important dream," Betty Lou snapped.

The Manx cat walked with a feline's smug self-importance in front of the headcatch. The heifer bellered and rattled the chute in anger. The cat looked at the cow indifferently.

"Mercy, would you look at that cat," Mrs. Barber said. "It has no tail and six toes."

Ezra continued wrenching the puller's handle. The calf's two front feet, tongue, and nose protruded from the heifer's vagina. "Clear the nostrils," Ezra shouted, forgetting for the moment that Betty Lou wasn't Anne.

"I beg your pardon."

"Mrs. Barber," Ezra implored. "Reach up and poke your fingers in the calf's nostrils. It's sucked in a lot of mucus." The calf's breathing was shallow, raspy, and labored.

"Oh, my word," Betty Lou said indignantly. She daintily reached into the chute and wiped the calf's nose with her handkerchief.

"Thanks."

"Now do you want to know about the dream or not?" she demanded.

"Lay it on me." Ezra grunted and leaned into the puller, using all his might to wrench the calf free. It was now distended as far as its hips.

"It was really more of a vision than a dream," she said.

The calf suddenly burst free in an avalanche of fluid and afterbirth. Ezra fell backward, the cow collapsed in relief, and the ninety-pound baby dropped into Ezra's lap, coating him with odorous afterbirth. The calf flung its head and struck Ezra in the chest.

"Oh my, how dramatic," Betty Lou noted. "I am sure you can work this birthing process into a sermon sometime."

"I may use it Sunday," Ezra said. He struggled to his feet coated with mud, blood, and afterbirth.

"I think you are purposely not wanting to hear my dream."

"Probably," Ezra said softly as he dragged the calf from the alleyway to the headcatch. The heifer stretched her neck down, smelled it, and mooed maternally.

"What is the matter?" she asked. "Do you think I am not worth listening to just because I am a woman?" She was standing with her hands on her hips. Her arms jutted out like pyramids tipped on their sides.

Ezra gave her a wearied look. She was getting on his nerves, and he was afraid he would say something he would enjoy but regret later. "Okay," he sighed. "I'm sorry. Please tell me about your dream."

"You were out in the hills on a horse," she said theatrically. "You rode to a hill, stopped, and got off. Suddenly a coyote rose up out of the ground and began attacking you."

Ezra stopped and stared at Mrs. Barber as he dragged the calf to a dry spot in the corral. This was like the *old* dream. The dream of sixteen years ago when he first returned to the ranch. How could Mrs. Barber know about it? He wondered if he had included it in his book, *Leaving the Land*.

"You fought that coyote off," she continued. "Then a second coyote came down out of the air like an eagle and attacked you. You fought it off as well."

Ezra felt a subtle flow of electricity move through his body. For all her flakiness, he suspected Betty Lou had experienced a legitimate warning for him.

"But then a third coyote—no, this one might have been a wolf, it was much larger than the other two and sort of reddish—came from inside you. It jumped out of your chest then turned and attacked."

"Did I fight it off too?" Ezra asked.

"Oh, I don't know," she said. "That's when I woke up. But I think it ate you. It seems like there was a lot of blood."

Ezra let the calf drop at his feet. "Mrs. Barber," he asked, "have you ever read the book I wrote?"

"Your book?" she exclaimed. "Oh, no, I'm sorry, but I am far too busy for recreational reading."

Ezra moved slowly to the chute to release the fidgeting mother. *Two coyotes and a wolf*, he thought to himself. *One from the ground, one from the air, one from within himself.*

"Well, I have done my duty. I have told you the dream," Betty Lou declared. "I guess I will be going back to the civilized world now."

"Thank you," Ezra said vacantly, but sincerely.

"You're very welcome," she said, walking to her car. "But please don't get the impression that I enjoy dreaming about you, Ezra Riley."

Ezra's eyes followed her car to the highway. Then he watched the heifer lick her baby dry. But his mind was on the dream.

When Anne came home an hour later Ezra had changed clothes and was putting Cajun through his paces in the corral. "Any sign of Diamond?" she called out hopefully.

"No sign," Ezra called back. He tied the colt to a post and walked to the gate. Anne met him with a stack of books in her hands.

"How was your day?" she asked. The question was innocent and routine.

"Interesting," Ezra said. "Diamond's boyfriend is a dangerous poacher, and the law wants me to go to Deer Lodge Saturday because he has some sort of connection to Jubal Lee; besides that, Pastor Tom is going home to Pennsylvania for six weeks and wants me to preach and counsel in his place." He took a breath. "And Betty Lou left here an hour ago after coming out to tell me a dream she had about me."

"Whoa," Anne said. "Back up. Run this by me one at a time."

"Sure. In the house over coffee. By the way, I have another counseling session tomorrow night at the church. I need you to be there."

"I can't," Anne said. "I have a hospital lab. Who is it with?"

"Lillie Foster."

"That pretty young woman who just started coming to church?"
Ezra nodded.

"And Pastor Tom wants you to counsel with her? I thought he was mad about the people who came out here to see us for advice."

"He is, but he wanted to go home, Anne. He packed most of his books and even the photo of his daughters. You'd think he wasn't coming back."

Anne didn't say anything. It took her a few moments to process all the information: Diamond was not only gone but her boyfriend was some sort of criminal; Ezra was going to prison to visit Jubal Lee; Mrs. Barber had had a dream; Ezra was preaching in Pastor Jablonski's place and counseling Lillie Foster. She knew she should be with her husband on Thursday night, but it wasn't possible. Sometimes she hated school.

"No problem if you can't make it," Ezra said. "I can meet with Lillie alone this time, then we can switch the sessions to a night you can come." Ezra was used to making sacrifices to accommodate Anne's college schedule.

Anne stared at Ezra thoughtfully. One time without her would be okay, she decided. She trusted her husband.

He took the books from her as they walked across the yard.

"So tell me about Betty Lou's dream," she said.

He chuckled.

"Was the dream funny?"

"No, the dream was not funny. I was just thinking: We've been married twenty years," he said. "And here I am carrying your books home from school."

Anne smiled and squeezed his arm. But she was suspicious. She was always suspicious when Ezra kidded in the face of difficulty. It was as if he was laughing softly at the devil.

Ezra rushed through chores Thursday hoping to get to church early to pray before his counseling session with Lillie Foster, but nothing went his way. His old Ford broke down in the hills, and he had to cobble together repairs with baling wire and twine. A heifer calved but would not claim her baby, so he milked the heifer by hand and nursed the calf from a bottle. Then, as he was throwing a quick supper together, he got three phone calls. Dylan needed to stay at school to work on the school paper, Anne was staying in town to study before her lab, and Solomon tried coaxing Ezra to his house to watch basketball on television.

Ezra's prayer preparation consisted of a litany of pleas as he drove from the ranch to the church. He entered the pastor's study at ten minutes to seven, still fueled by the adrenaline of his demanding day, so he tried settling himself by looking through Pastor Tom's remaining books. But few of them interested him. There were studies on archaeology, the Greek and Hebrew languages, and Bible commentaries by men Ezra had never heard of. Ezra's interests were psychological and mystical, areas the pastor was wary of.

At precisely seven o'clock he heard the church's front door open, then close. He did not hear any footsteps on the carpeted hallway, but moments later a soft knock sounded on the office door.

"Come in," Ezra said.

Lillie Foster stepped in. Her appearance was demure but casual. She wore an attractive burgundy pantsuit that flattered her slender form. Her hair—how could he describe it, Ezra wondered. Auburn with shadowed depths or a walnut brunette with red highlights?—was parted in the middle and made a glossy curve about her face. Her skin was a Mediterranean olive, flawless, and soft; the eyes were large, wide-spaced and bluish-green; her makeup was perfectly drawn. She was stylish without being flashy.

"Good evening," she said, taking the chair in front of the desk. Her voice was musical, and her motions were casual, fluid, and athletic. Ezra wondered if she was a dancer or a musician. He came to her and offered his hand. "I am Ezra Riley," he said.

She took his hand. "Yes," she said. "I know." Her handshake was gentle but firm, the fingers long and tapered. The hands of an artist. There were layers of light and shadow in her eyes suggesting she was a woman of depth. She looked shyly about the office. "It's just us?" she asked.

The question caught Ezra staring at her beauty, and it startled and embarrassed him. "Yes," he said quickly. "My wife, Anne, has a hospital lab on Thursday nights. She's a nursing student." He retreated around the desk and took a seat in Pastor Tom's chair, not wanting to be too formal but needing to establish a shield between them, a fortress against familiarity, and a declaration of his position and authority. He realized Pastor Tom often did the same thing.

She smiled and moved her hands down her thighs in nervousness. "Well, I guess you want to know why I requested counseling," she said.

"You get right to the point, don't you?" Ezra noted. "We can visit for a while first if you like." He preferred to chat and allow the person's story to unfold in a natural progression of social contact. Preliminary conversation was like two boxers feeling each other out, feinting, jabbing, dancing, getting to know the other's moves.

She shook her head. "No, we can visit later. I am well practiced in being counseled."

He wondered if he had heard an inference in her tone. Was she suggesting she was more experienced at being counseled than he was at being a counselor?

"Let's get to work," she continued. "I don't have time to waste." Her eyes became deep and vulnerable and Ezra had to resist their pull. The books he had read on counseling had stressed the counselor's need to stay in control. "May I call you Lillie?" he asked. "Or would you rather I call you Mrs. Foster?"

"Neither," she said. "I would prefer that you call me Lilith." Her tone was cool, but not cold, and insistent without being demanding, but the demureness had evaporated.

"Lilith. That's an interesting name. Wasn't that the name of a character—"

"Yes," she interrupted. "A character on television. Frasier Crane's wife on *Cheers*."

That's right, Ezra thought. *The cerebral, sultry feminist.*

Lilith waited until she had his full attention again then lowered her voice to a velvety alto. "Can we talk about my problem now?" she asked.

"Certainly." He tried to compare her to others he and Anne had counseled in their home. They had been misfits mostly, church members uncomfortable with Pastor Tom's rigidity. And Ezra knew they had benefited as much from Anne's understanding and compassion as they had from his insight and directives. Lilith seemed distinct from them already, but Ezra did not expect to be surprised by any counselee's confession.

"I have a problem with adultery," she said.

He tried to conceal his speechlessness by waving his hand for her to continue. The sin did not surprise him as much as her frankness.

"I am not involved with anyone right now," she said. "But there are two men pursuing me. For some reason I am never able to hold out for long."

"This is a pattern?" Ezra asked. He wondered if her confession made her less beautiful. To his mild surprise, it didn't. She did not seem wicked or cheap. She simply had a problem, like smoking or overeating.

"It's a pattern," she admitted. "Should I tell you my story?"

"Please."

It came out in a pleasant but prerecorded voice; she had repeated it for counselors so many times. "I grew up in Helena in a very strict, religious home. My mother was overbearing and super-spiritual. She liked organizing prayer groups and Bible coffees. My father was a quiet man who worked for the Bureau of State Lands. I was the oldest of five children. I did all the housework and baby-sitting. There is a term for that—"

She was challenging him, wanting to know if Ezra knew the language. "Parental inversion," Ezra said, describing children forced into parental roles.

"That's right," she agreed. "I was not allowed a childhood. In junior high I wanted jewelry and makeup like the other girls, but it was forbidden. So I shoplifted and kept my things in my school locker. I was very careful not to get caught, and I kept my grades up. My mother expected me to get very good grades."

He felt her challenge again. She was appraising him, wondering if he was really a counselor or simply a cowboy thrown into a substitutionary role. "Performance orientation," Ezra said. "The promise of love and affection as the reward of good works, but it's never delivered." He needed to interrupt her to slow her down and allow him time to digest the information.

"Exactly," she noted approvingly. "My mother always dangled the carrot just out of reach."

"So you began to rebel," Ezra surmised. "You probably had your first sexual contact when you were quite young, and to your surprise you did not go straight to hell. Instead, the naughtiness thrilled you."

"Very good," Lilith said, blessing him with a nod of her head. "I was fifteen when I lost my virginity. At seventeen I became pregnant. My mother kicked me out of the house. I spent my pregnancy in a girls' home and gave the baby up for adoption."

"How did you survive?" Ezra asked. "What did you do for a living?" He looked down at his notepad—he had taken no notes, but looked away because her beauty was mesmerizing. He was pleased so far. Everything was proceeding quickly. Perhaps it helped that she was so experienced at being counseled.

"I waited tables. I got my GED. At nineteen I got married."

"To Brad?" Ezra had forgotten her husband's name and made a guess. He was wrong.

"Ben," she corrected him.

"Sorry."

"No problem. I met him in Spokane. He was very nice, very polite. I decided I needed a sweet, quiet man for a change."

"Like your father?"

She paused. "Yes, like my father."

"Forgive me, but I need to ask about Hillary . . ."

She anticipated the question with an arch of her eyebrows. "Yes," she said. "Hillary is Ben's."

"I didn't mean to be suspicious."

"You would be suspicious if you knew more about me. For example, Ben and I have lived in six different cities. Why do you suppose we move so often?" Her voice was less rehearsed now, more natural.

"Because you become involved with other men. Does Ben know about them?"

"He knew about the first one. The one in Boise. I told him it was rape. It practically was. He hasn't known about the others. I find other reasons for us to move, and he goes along with what I say."

"What reason do you give him for seeking counseling?"

She smiled wryly. "He doesn't ask. I think he assumes I was sexually abused as a child. I wasn't."

The denial of sexual abuse came too quickly, Ezra thought; it was not an area he was ready to plunge into. "And what does Ben do for a living?" he asked, bringing his pen to his lips. He still had not taken any notes.

"He is a salesman for an office supply company," she stated.

His mind wandered when her voice became mechanical, and it quickly flashed from Pratt to Diamond to Lilith's physical attractiveness. He forced himself to pay attention. "So he is on the road often?" Ezra asked.

"Yes," she said, and smiled ironically. "Convenient, isn't it?"

"No, not really." Ezra knew he had to become more forceful. Lillie, no, Lilith, seemed to be enjoying the give and take too much. "So how am I doing?" he challenged.

"I beg your pardon."

"You are very direct, so I will be very direct," Ezra said. "You have been sizing me up. Comparing me to the other pastors and mental health professionals who have counseled you. So how am I doing?" He did not want to know this for his own curiosity, but to reveal and defuse her scrutiny.

She smiled widely. Her teeth were even and white. "You are doing quite well," she said teasingly. "Pretty good for a cowboy."

"Do you want to know my qualifications?"

"You have natural insight. What more do you need?"

"Well." He smiled. "For legal reasons you should know that I am not licensed as a pastor or a psychologist, but I have had some training in biblical counseling."

"You are mostly self-taught," she observed. "So I guess you will be as good as your teacher."

Ezra smiled at her little barb. "Let's get back to Ben. He isn't a challenge for you, is he?"

"Why do you say that?"

"Is he?"

"No. Not at all. He's too nice. All he wants to do is make me happy."

"Some women would consider that to be an ideal situation."

"I am not *some* women."

"So you are not fulfilled by mere attention," he said. "Still, you have this pattern of . . ."

"The word is *adultery,*" she said, her eyes darkening. "And it keeps me in a state of depression. I feel terrible about the things I have done," she said, dropping her gaze to the floor, "but it does no good."

Ezra felt a deep compassion for her pain, but knew he could not dwell there. "Let's deal with the immediate situation," he said. "You say you have two men pursuing you. What are you going to do?"

"I don't know," she said sadly. "Sooner or later one of them will come by while Ben is out of town. I will try to turn him down but I won't succeed. My life will then become a tangled twist of deceits."

"When will Ben be out of town next?"

"Monday." She paused and wet her upper lip with her tongue. "Do you want to know who the two men are?" she asked.

"I don't think that would be professional," Ezra said. But he was curious. He even *wanted* to know, and of course, he wasn't a professional in the strictest sense of the word.

"Sal Santori is one," she blurted.

Ezra paused. Santori was a Yellow Rock businessman. A large, loudmouthed braggart who had inherited two downtown stores and was mismanaging both into bankruptcy.

"He is our landlord," she added. "I can't stand him. He is always dropping by when he thinks Ben isn't home. He hasn't propositioned me yet, but he will soon." She shuddered slightly.

Ezra leaned back in the pastor's chair. He surprised himself with his response. "Tell Sal Santori that you have confided in me, and that if he so much as touches you I promise to break his arm."

Her eyebrows arched again and she almost barked a short laugh. "Did you say 'break his arm'?" she asked. "Isn't this strange behavior for a religious counselor? You are threatening to do bodily violence to someone."

Ezra was bothered by the incongruity, but he pushed past it. She needed help, not sermons. "That's right," he said. "I am promising a little bodily injury to someone."

She smiled. "I like it. I like being protected. If Santori propositions me I will tell him, but aren't you worried about the consequences? What if the word got out? It could embarrass your pastor, couldn't it?"

"It's a risk," Ezra admitted. "But Santori won't talk. He's a phony."

"Okay, I'll do it." She grinned.

"Then consider Santori taken care of." Ezra felt a small surge of satisfaction and knew it was wrong. He wondered if he had crossed from the spiritual to the carnal? Sometimes it was hard to know, the trails were not always well marked.

"The other one—" Lilith began.

"Don't tell me the name," Ezra said, cutting her off. He was afraid of becoming too bold and learning too much.

She pursed her lips. "The other one is more serious. I know his type. He'll push his way into the house someday when Ben is gone. If Hillary is around he will make me put her down for a nap."

Ezra tried not to show his indignation. He hated bullies. He hated the idea of anyone hurting or forcing himself on someone as lovely and refined as Lillie. Stop, he told himself. You are jealous. It makes no difference if Lillie/Lilith is lovely and refined. You must counsel her as you would counsel any woman in trouble. "Call me," he said.

"What?"

"Call me if you know he is coming and I will meet him at your house. If he is already there call me anyway."

"My, are we feeling especially heroic tonight?" she teased.

"No," he said. "We are being practical." But secretly Ezra wondered if he was being too valiant. Perhaps seeing Diamond's bruised face, the threat of Pratt, and the discovery that Mikal was an undercover agent had combined to draw him into a fantasy world of intrigue and chivalry. "Darkness flees at the sight of light," he said.

"Very poetic," she observed. "But if you come to my house won't my neighbors be curious?"

Ezra frowned. He had not thought of that. "We can always tell them that I am a friend of Ben's."

"Hmmm," she said. "I wonder if you will be? Ben could use a friend." She glanced at the clock on Jablonski's shelf. "I need to get home," she said. "Sometimes my daughter takes advantage of my husband and it falls on me to clean up the messes." She rose from the chair.

Ezra came around the desk and opened the office door for her. She stopped there and thanked him. The top of her head came just to his eyes. He could smell the subtle fragrance of perfume. "Same place next week?" she asked.

He nodded. He had planned to change the sessions so Anne could attend, but it had totally slipped his mind, as if forgotten in the maze of an extraordinary week or, perhaps, lured away by a soft beguilement.

She smiled softly as she left the room.

He watched her walk down the hallway, then abruptly looked away when he realized she sensed his gaze. She was a woman with antennas, he warned himself.

CHAPTER SEVEN

"Game wardens!" Uncle Joe laughed and flung his fishing line toward the reservoir like a kid throwing a handful of rocks. "Fact is," he said, "the homesteaders would have et this country plumb clean of game iffen it weren't for game wardens. The law never stopped John though. Your pa killed so many illegal deer and antelope that when he finally killed a legal one he got it mounted. He figured a legal kill was the rarest trophy found in these parts."

Leaving the Land

Ezra met Mikal at dawn on Saturday at the city airport. Mikal was on the runway taking a Cessna 410 through its system checks.

"Where's the pilot?" Ezra called out over the quiet hum of the bird's twin engines.

Mikal smiled. He wore aviator's sunglasses and a leather jacket. "You're looking at him," he said. "Feel lucky?"

"Only if you do."

Mora laughed and slapped Ezra on the shoulder. "I feel lucky. Let's go see your prison buddy."

The takeoff was smooth. As Mikal ascended westward Ezra looked down at the Yellow Rock River reflecting the glow of dawn like a liquid orange and yellow ribbon. He saw geese floating in placid coves where the twisting river bent around brushy islands. "How long have you been flying?" Ezra asked, his eyes entranced by the water.

"Since last week," Mikal joked. Ezra's lips crinkled into a slight smile. "Actually, I got my license when I was nineteen," Mikal explained. "I wanted to be a bush pilot in Alaska, but my wife convinced me it was safer being an undercover wildlife agent."

Ezra saw past his friend's cavalier attitude. "It must be hard being away from your family," he said.

"Let's not talk about it," Mikal said. "You don't want to see a grown game warden cry."

"I don't understand your role in this," Ezra said. "Don't most agents go into deep cover and try to infiltrate a ring?"

"That's right, but in this case Pratt is a loner. There is no ring to infiltrate except a link to a rich South American who is impossible to get close to. Also, your best undercover man is so smart he can act dumb and get away with it. I'm not quite that smart, so they cast me as a fish biologist."

"Do you like undercover work?"

"No, not really," Mikal said, shaking his head. "Most of it is boring. Besides, I'm not a good liar."

"Handicapped by honesty," Ezra noted. Below them light reflected off the wings of geese as the birds took flight above the water. Ezra leaned back in his seat and watched until the earth was too distant and formless to hold his attention. "What did Pratt do to get himself thrown in jail in Missoula?" he asked.

"Your friend Walker will fill you in on that. All I'll say is that Pratt is a very severe critic. You don't want him reviewing your books or movies."

"If being opinionated was a crime," Ezra said, "Montana would be one big prison." He had heard plenty of opinions and criticisms about his own book.

Mora laughed. "Pratt isn't Siskal or Ebert. When it's thumbs-down with him, it's really thumbs-down."

"You haven't told me much, Mikal," Ezra said. "If I or my family is threatened by this guy, I need to know more about him."

Mora shook his head. "I can't tell you any more. I want your own instincts and curiosity to lead you when you talk with Walker. You were a newspaper reporter once. Draw on those old skills. Dig out new information. I don't want you merely confirming information I give you."

"I take it the prison officials are expecting us."

"Let's just say you won't have to break in." He flashed Ezra a closing smile. Officially, the conversation about Demetrius Pratt was over for now.

At the Deer Lodge airport they were met by a county deputy in a brown sedan. There was no exchange of greetings; Mikal simply took a seat in the front and Ezra one in the back. Ezra saw the prison structure looming before them as they drove south of town. It was an imposing, gray fortress encircled by two concentric fences topped with razor-edged wire. The guards in the towers held automatic rifles. The car stopped short of the main gate.

Mikal leaned over the seat. "Unbutton your jacket and shirt," he said.

"Why?" Ezra asked.

Mora held up a small tape recorder and microphone. "You are going in wired," he said.

"You're kidding?"

"No, I'm not. You're going in alone, Ezra. Pratt may have connections inside. It's natural for you to visit Walker; he's an old buddy of yours. But

I can't risk having people wonder who I am." He reached over and taped the recorder to Ezra's chest.

Ezra felt a sudden apprehension. "You could have warned me about this," he said.

"You might not have come."

"You got that right, Mikal. You expect a lot from a weight-lifting partner."

"Think about this, Ezra. Right now Demetrius Pratt could be walking the hills of your ranch, maybe spying on your wife and son." He nodded toward the prison. "Wouldn't you rather have him on the other side of that concertina wire?"

Ezra got out and approached the main gate.

"That's a sixty-minute tape," Mikal said from the car.

At the gate a guard called down and asked him his name and business. Ezra told him. The guard asked if he had any weapons. Ezra said no. Suddenly the large metal gate opened. Ezra stepped through and the gate closed behind him. He had the eerie, doomed feeling of all who visit a prison for the first time: He wondered if they would let him out. A uniformed prison guard met him. "Follow me," he said. Ezra saw inmates in the exercise yard. They wore either blue or tan jumpsuits. Most paid him no attention, but a couple of them stared. Ezra did not want to look at them. At the rear of the compound he saw an isolated concrete compound and a small, ugly trailer house. No one had to tell him what it was. Death row radiated its own identity. The guard took him inside a main building. They passed smiling secretaries who seemed not to realize they worked in a prison. Ezra thought the building grew colder and more sterile as they moved deeper into its stone bowels. They went out a door and entered a separate building marked as the Religious Activities Center. They passed the offices of several chaplains before the guard finally stopped at a large wooden door. "He's inside," he said. "You have an hour. Turn your tape recorder on now." The official turned and walked away.

Ezra opened the door and stepped in. The room was a multipurpose auditorium with a spiritually generic feeling to it. On the back wall hung a cross Ezra guessed had been made in the prison woodshop. In front was a podium, a table for the sacraments, and a candelabra. Off to the side was a small baptismal. He saw a motion in the shadows against a far wall. A small man stepped from the darkness. He appeared to be dusting the pews with a cloth. As he passed beneath a skylight, his hair shone like white frosting. Ezra was about to call out and ask where Jubal Lee Walker was when the man suddenly stopped, turned, and looked his way. Their eyes met. It was Jubal.

Jubal moved forward in brisk steps and they shook hands in the shadowed aisleway. Jubal's hands felt different in Ezra's grip. Firm but knobby. The hair, Ezra noticed on closer inspection, was not white, but laced with gray, and the face had hardened and lined. His eyes lacked the veneer Ezra remembered, but seemed deeper and warmer than those of the charismatic evangelist who had turned the Yellow Rock church upside down. From the grip of the handshake, to the eyes, to the gray in the hair, it was obvious that Jubal had aged in body but had matured in soul.

"They told me to expect company," Jubal said. "I had no idea it would be you." His voice, like his eyes, seemed softer and deeper than the Jubal of the past. They moved to a front pew where the lighting was better. Jubal crossed his legs, leaving his hands to lie in his lap. "I was told to keep the lights dim," he explained. "I assume someone is not supposed to know you are here."

"I am afraid this is a business meeting," Ezra said.

Jubal nodded. He was not expecting a social call. "It's still great to see you, Ezra. What business brings you here?"

"A man named Demetrius Pratt," Ezra said.

Jubal's eyes flared with warning, then softened. "Do me a favor," he said. "Let's forget the affairs of the world for a few minutes. Tell me about Yellow Rock, about Anne and Dylan and Pastor Tom and Darlene."

Ezra agreed. The setting seemed appropriate for stories. He and Jubal had hitchhiked thousands of miles together in their youth and had raced Thoroughbreds side by side. Their present circumstances were simply another crossroads, a place to stop and compare notes. He started closest to his heart. He told Jubal about Anne being in nursing school and Dylan receiving a scholarship to Montana State.

"So, Anne's going to be a nurse," Jubal said. "She will be good at that."

"Yeah," Ezra said. "But it's a tough program. Less than half the women that begin the course finish, and she's by far the oldest student."

"She'll make it," he said, and sighed softly as he thought of his own distant daughters. Ezra saw the pain in Jubal's eyes and thought it better not to inquire. Finally Jubal said, "How's Pastor Tom and Darlene?"

"They're doing fine. They're in Pennsylvania for a while. I'll be filling the pulpit in their absence." That is a strange phrase, Ezra suddenly realized. *Filling the pulpit.* As if you could stand a pulpit on end and enter it like a casket.

Jubal's light laughter barely disturbed the air. "I predicted it, didn't I? I knew there was a preacher in you, Ezra."

Jubal's relaxed sincerity disarmed Ezra, allowing him to feel a deep compassion for his old friend. "What about you, Jubal?" he asked. "How are you getting by?"

Walker smiled. "I love it here," he said sarcastically, the words tailing into a bittersweet laugh. "No, it's terrible, man. The first year was an absolute nightmare. Worse than I could have ever imagined."

"You'll be out soon?"

"Done a trey, a deuce to go. The judge wanted to make an example out of me—the-preacher-turned-coke-dealer—so I got five years without parole."

"You look pretty good," Ezra said.

"Actually, the past year hasn't been so bad. I'm a trustee, so I spend much of my time in here or the library. And I help lead Bible studies with over forty prisoners. There is freedom in my chains."

"I bet you're still playing great music," Ezra said encouragingly.

Jubal winced and shook his head. His hands had remained in his lap and covered by a shadow. He held them up to the light. The fingers were distended, crooked and knobby. They jutted at different angles.

Ezra's mouth opened but he found nothing to say.

"Demetrius Pratt," Jubal explained. "He laughed as he broke each finger. Said he would make sure I never played music again."

Ezra could barely see Jubal's eyes in the shadowed sanctuary. They seemed deep and dark like twin tunnels of regret. "Tell me what happened," he said.

Dylan Riley fiddled with the radio in the pickup as he waited for Uncle Solomon's yearlings to come in for feed. His dad listened to two stations, a conservative Christian station that played what Dylan considered to be funeral music, and National Public Radio. His dad liked NPR because of Garrison Keillor and especially "Writer's Almanac"—*Be well, do good work, keep in touch*—A few moments of culture on the plains.

Dylan liked Christian rock, groups like Petra or The Newsboys, but Christian rock and roll was exiled from the eastern Montana airways. He settled for a Top 40 station but first Madonna's voice came screeching through the cracked pickup speaker, then Michael Jackson's, testing Dylan's moral limits, so he turned the radio off.

He got out of the truck and called to the yearlings. A few of them raised their grazing heads and stared. He petted Beaner, who whipped the air with tail-wagging joy. He honked the horn several times.

The heifers finally came as if of one mind, rolling off the hills like an avalanche of beef. A few kicked awkwardly in the air. Dylan shouldered a seventy-pound sack and streamed out a long green line of pellets. The yearlings fell upon it hungrily.

As he was driving away something caught his eye. It fluttered in the breeze like the wing of a white bird beating against the trunk of a young cottonwood tree. Dylan stopped the truck to investigate. An arrow was stuck in the bark at about the height of a basketball hoop. Attached to the shaft was a single white card.

Strange, Dylan thought. It was an odd time of the year for target shooters. He jumped up, caught a firm limb, and pulled himself into the tree. He could not pull the arrow out, it was embedded in the thick young muscle of tree trunk. So he broke the shaft, removed the card, and jumped lightly to the ground.

The card was the size and thickness of a playing card. There was no name on it. Just a symbol. From his lessons in Sunday school he recognized the Greek symbol *alpha*.

Alpha. Greek for *The Beginning*.

He looked about wondering if there might be another arrow. Perhaps one with the *omega* symbol for "the end." He saw nothing more.

Dylan turned the card over a couple of times, shrugged, and shoved it into his back pocket. *A strange little mystery,* he thought.

He had more cattle to feed, plus, he had to stop in and check on Uncle Solomon before sacking pellets for the next day's feeding. And, if he had time before his afternoon tennis practice, he would work with Cajun. Dylan was good with horses. Like his father, he loved the land and the animals. But having watched his father, Dylan had no desire to sacrifice his sweat and blood to a land that gave so little in return.

He skimmed the radio dial for a listenable tune, finally settling for Garth Brooks on a country-western station, and tapped the steering wheel in time to the music as he drove home. The odd card in the tree was quickly forgotten.

"What happened?" Ezra asked, his eyes on Jubal's crooked fingers.

"Things unraveled, man," Jubal confessed, "and I got desperate for money. I talked Cletus Pratt into fronting me a quarter-kilo of coke. Good stuff, never been stepped on. I sold some of it, snorted the rest, then tried to get away without paying. Cletus had his brother come after me."

"But you and he were in jail together. I heard you were almost friends."

"When I got messed up it happened at night, and I never saw a face. Someone hit me from behind, knocked me down, and went to work on my hands. The only thing I heard above my own screams was a hideous laugh. I was left cold on the street with enough coke in my pockets to get me busted. They knew I'd never roll over on Cletus, so they thought they'd just let me get put away for a while." Jubal turned and stared at his friend with eyes that were dark and hollow like ancient caves lit by primordial fires. "What's this got to do with you?" he asked. "Why are you interested in someone as dark and sinister as Demetrius Pratt?"

"First I have a confession to make," Ezra said, and he unbuttoned his jacket and shirt. "I'm wired."

Jubal's eyes quickened with surprise, then distrust, and finally, amusement. "Have you started a new career in law enforcement?" he whispered. "Guess cowboying doesn't pay enough."

"I'm here because Anne befriended a young woman named Diamond LaFontaine."

Jubal shook his head sadly. His curly hair looked like coils of white wire. "Sometimes Anne is too good for her own good," he said. There was conviction in his voice. He would help Ezra. He would help because Ezra and his family were in danger.

Ezra untaped Mikal's tape recorder and handed it to his friend. "Tell me about Demetrius Pratt," he said.

Jubal spoke clearly and concisely into the small microphone as if he were beginning a sermon. "I can best describe this man with an illustration," he said. "Do you remember the movie *Dances with Wolves*?"

Ezra nodded, then remembered the tape and said "yes."

"What did you think of it?"

"A politically correct attempt at historical revision, but the scenery was beautiful."

"Demetrius Pratt liked it less than that. He was arrested in a Missoula movie theater after he slashed the screen with a knife. He thought the film made the Sioux look like early hippies and the wolf like a friendly German shepherd. To a man who worships what is wild and strong, the movie was blasphemy. Pratt is not a member of the Kevin Costner fan club."

"Tell me about your jail time with him."

"We were cellmates for ten days. I'd already been there twenty days when Pratt got arrested. At first I had no idea he was the one who'd crushed my hands and we sort of hit it off. The guy is really bright. Do you know how we spent our time?"

Ezra shook his head. If he knew he would not have come.

"We studied the Bible," Jubal said. "I mean we seriously studied the Bible. My fingers were bandaged so he turned the pages for me. He already had some understanding, and some misunderstanding, of both the Old and New Testaments, but I was able to take him a little deeper. We read for hours and hours a day. When he wasn't reading the Bible he was doing push-ups and sit-ups, anything he could to stay in shape."

"What was his interest in the Bible?" Ezra was now sincerely and keenly intrigued.

"The weird stuff, man. He was obsessed with the more obscure mysteries in the Old Testament—Baal worship mostly—and the veiled references to incubus and succubus spirits. Anything strange and controversial."

"Why do you think he was so interested in those subjects?"

"Because he's a strange dude, man." Jubal laughed softly. "And because Baal worship was an early nature religion and Pratt worships the natural world. The trees, the rocks, the grasses, the wildlife. He sees himself as a high priest of pantheism, a pagan witch."

In a strange way Ezra was relieved. If Pratt was simply a criminal, he was in a world more familiar to Mikal than Ezra. But if he was a practicing spiritualist, he was on turf Ezra had walked on. "Do you think he's continued on the Baal path?" he asked.

"Oh, man, he's probably gone far beyond it. Most nature religions were rooted in agriculture. They were pagan cries for fertility and rain. That's too tame for Pratt. He hates agriculture."

"Did he mention any of his terrorist activities?"

"He bragged a little, but he seemed to be leaving that part behind. I think he's a stepchild of our own youth, Ezra. Remember our hippie days: the drugs, the Eastern religions, the concern for ecology? He is a product of that taken to its furthest extreme. He can quote the fathers of modern environmentalism, Thoreau, Emerson, Muir, and Leopold, for hours. He's one committed greenie."

"Emerson was a Unitarian minister," Ezra noted, "and Leopold became a convert to Ouspensky's *Organicism.*"

"He stays current, too. Pratt's read Matthew Fox, the defrocked Catholic priest, and a guy named Sydney Singer, who calls himself 'Screaming Wolf.' Singer's book is entitled *A Declaration of War: Killing People to Save Animals and the Environment.* How's that for a rosy title?"

Ezra rose, circled the podium, then leaned against it. He looked down at his old friend sitting in the hardwood pew with his crooked fingers resting in his lap. His hands were cupped and the knobby fingers looked like pretzels in the bowl of his palms. "He had to have been playing with you," he said. "When did you begin catching on to him?"

"Ha. I asked him to pray with me. That bloomin' freaked him out, man. No way did he want to pray with me, and I've learned to be cautious of people who want to study the Bible but don't want to pray." He started to continue then dropped his head and became silent.

"What else?" Ezra asked. "Something else tipped you off that he was a major bad guy, not just a thug who stomped on fingers?"

Jubal shook his head slowly. "It was your book, man," he said. "When *Leaving the Land* came out, I saw the review in *The Missoulian* and bought a copy right away. I loved it. It's pure poetry, man. Anyway, I had it with me in jail and after a week or so I loaned it to Pratt. He read it over and over for two days. Then his last night in the cell he began raging about the evils of technology, Christianity, and Judaism. That's when he began quoting Fox, Singer, and others. He went nuts. He threw your book against the wall a dozen times; kept saying you deserved to die, and then he'd laugh that crazy laugh. That's when I knew who he was. I remembered the laugh. He was released the next morning."

"When he was reading my book did he mention my name?"

"All the time. He thinks you should be killed."

Ezra showed no reaction. He simply filed the information away in his mind. "What else do you know about him, Jubal?" he asked. "Does he have connections? Does he work for anybody?"

Jubal shrugged. "The real radical tree-huggers cut him loose; he was too crazy for them. But he'd just met someone he thought was important. Some rich guy from South America. He was going to be Pratt's gravy train."

"Pratt's now in the major leagues when it comes to poaching trophy game animals. Did this come up in the conversation?"

"Once again, he bragged a little. He said poaching could allow someone to live in the wild and still make big money. Pratt likes nice things, things that last. Good hiking boots are expensive."

"But he's a nature lover. He should hate the type of people who'd pay thousands of dollars for the head of a wild animal."

"He probably does, but he has a greater hatred for owners of private property. In fact, the guy hates the entire human race. He thinks nature must be set free from man."

"And it's up to him?"

"He's the avenging angel, Ezra. He has a warped Messiah complex."

"What is his weakness, Jubal? Is it Diamond?"

Jubal rubbed his chin. "Maybe," he said. "But a man's weakness is usually his greatest passion. With Pratt that would be his own warped spiritism."

Ezra was more interested in Diamond. She was tangible. She had slept in his house. "What do you know about the girl?" he asked.

"Not much. They hadn't been together long then, but he claimed she was descended from a line of tribal shamans and mystics."

"Did Pratt talk about his youth at all? About his brother, Cletus?"

"Not much. Their mother was a prostitute in New Orleans who died of AIDS. Cletus's father had been her pimp, but Demetrius's father had been a professor at Tulane. His childhood was unhappy. He lived for a while with an aunt in some small bayou town and spent all of his time in the swamps hunting, trapping, and fishing."

A child who fled to nature to escape emotional pain, Ezra thought. A child very much like himself.

"He's a poetic sort of guy," Jubal noted. "He writes. He likes symbols and nicknames."

"Nimrod?" Ezra said.

"Yeah. Genesis 10:9. The mighty hunter."

A shaft of light broke the setting as the door in the back opened and the guard stepped into view. He said nothing but by his posture it was clear the conversation was over.

"I guess I have to go now," Ezra said, rising.

The two men stood and faced each other. Jubal seemed younger, less worn, than he had an hour before. He reached out and circled his crooked fingers around Ezra's arm. "One thing before you go," he said. "I want you to forgive me for all the trouble I caused you in Yellow Rock. I nearly had you sent to jail. I could have burned your ranch down, and I almost ruined your church." His eyes were curtains holding back a wall of tears.

"Hey," Ezra said. "Whatever happened back then, it's all under the blood of Jesus. Besides, God used you, Jubal. You were an imperfect vessel, but He used you to get me excited about His power."

Jubal pulled him into a hug. There was an honest ferocity in the embrace, and Ezra yielded to it. For the first time since meeting twenty-three years before, they held each other as brothers.

Finally Ezra tried to break the embrace, but Jubal gripped him harder, and Ezra felt his lips near his ear. "Come back and see me," he said.

"I will," Ezra promised.

"Ezra, one more thing," Jubal whispered. "If it comes down to just you and Demetrius Pratt, forget everything you know about love and compassion."

Ezra leaned back and looked at his friend curiously.

"Show no mercy," Jubal warned, then his arms dropped and he stepped back.

Ezra stood transfixed as he watched Jubal reach down for his dust rag and recede into the shadows. A slim, quiet figure polishing the backs of wooden pews with hands as crooked as hay hooks.

CHAPTER EIGHT

I once asked Uncle Joe why he never went to church. He grunted, threaded a fat angleworm onto a barbed hook, and cast his line into the mossy waters. "This is my church," he said. Then he really surprised me. "Some guy named Thoreau," he stated, "once said 'Wildness is the preservation of the world.' Or something like that. I read the quote in a fishing magazine. I figure he meant we should all fish more." Years later I learned that both Uncle Joe and Thoreau were wrong. It is not in wildness where the preservation of the world lies. It is at the foot of the Cross.

Leaving the Land

The plane's engine hummed quietly as Mikal flew them home. Ezra stared down at the Bible in his lap, following passages he had highlighted in colors of yellow, blue, and green as he studied for the next day's sermon. A yellow marking pen dangled from his lips. The Bible's bonded cover was worn as smooth as latigo leather, and a rainbow of highlights and scribbled margin notes branded the pages. The colors and scribblings were like a map to Ezra. A map of life.

Occasionally he glanced up from his reading and studied the frown on Mikal's face. Mikal was listening to the recording with Jubal through headphones. Ezra smiled at Mikal's befuddlement and returned to the treasury of the Word. He was an Old Testament man. He loved the dramatics of David and Saul, the theatrical power of Isaiah, Elijah, and Ezekiel, the proving of Joseph, and the conquerings of Joshua, Deborah, and Sampson. He was unconcerned about not having a sermon subject for the following morning because each page of the Bible held a message. Ezra merely had to hunt through the words until he found the gems that radiated life. It reminded him of being a child and hunting the gravel bars of Sunday Creek for agates. When his adolescent home life had proven unbearable, Ezra had always been able to escape to the land, to walk the rocky little creeks, staring at mud-crusted gravel until the treasured Montana moss agates showed themselves. Scripture, too, had a way of revealing itself to those who persevered.

"Okay," Mikal said finally, taking the earphones off. "Translate all of this to me in English. What's all this stuff about bale worship?"

"Ba' al," Ezra said. "Baa-awwl. It was one of the world's earliest fertility cults. It had many gods according to tribe and region. They worshiped in groves of trees and also in temples. The temples, usually connected to the goddess Astarte, were really more like whorehouses with prostitutes as priestesses and self-mutilated eunuchs serving as priests or slaves."

"Wonderful. And this incubus, succubus stuff?"

Ezra smiled, foreseeing the challenge to Mikal's pragmatism. "They are spirits that attack people sexually in their sleep."

"What? You gotta be kidding? There aren't such things, and even if there are, why would Pratt care about them?"

"He probably doesn't," Ezra said. "It was just a sideshow on his tour of biblical mysteries. But he is interested in Baal worship because it was in direct conflict with Judaism," Ezra explained. "Throughout the Old Testament the tribes of Israel were judged harshly whenever they compromised and worshiped Baal."

"So? That was thousands of years ago."

"The more things change the more they stay the same. Some of today's environmentalists have beliefs very similar to Baal worship, like spirits dwelling in rocks, trees, grass, and water. They blame the Jewish and Christian religions for the destruction of the natural world. Pratt has probably created his own Baal religion, one based more on wilderness than agriculture."

"I told you he was flaked out," Mora said. "Loony tunes. But he's a poacher," he stressed. "And I'm going to collar him for being a poacher, not for being a nutcase."

Ezra didn't respond. He knew that neither his parochial upbringing nor the police academy had prepared Mikal for the weirdness that was Demetrius Pratt.

Mora was quiet for several moments as he listened to another segment of tape. Finally he asked, "What's this deal between Pratt and your book?"

"It's another religious conflict," Ezra warned him.

Ezra could not see Mikal's eyes behind the dark glasses but knew he was staring at the distant horizon. "Okay," Mikal said. "What is it? I read your book. I didn't see anything to get so upset about."

"You're a lapsed Catholic," Ezra explained, wanting to ease his friend slowly into the bizarre world of spiritualists and nature religions. "To Pratt, I represent cowboying and Christianity, private property and domestication. I am everything he hates. He is a type of warlock or druid. A New Age priest."

There was a subtle tightening to Mora's jaw. "He's still just a poacher to me," he said rigidly.

Ezra returned to his Bible reading.

Mora suddenly dipped the plane to the north. "Have time for a little side trip?" he asked.

"Where are we going?"

"Over the Breaks."

They were there in minutes. Mora followed the Musselshell River to its confluence with the Missouri, then charted eastward above a vista of water and a vast moonscape of seemingly endless badlands. High plateaus stripped by wheat fields and fallow suddenly ended at precipitous mazes of gumbo wilderness. Several million acres of shallow, twisting creeks, deep ravines, caprock, sandrock, clay, cedar, and pine lay below them.

"The habitat of outlaws," Ezra remarked as he stared down at the ill-fitted puzzle pieces of nature. "A hundred years ago it was Big Nose George, Butch Cassidy and the Sundance Kid. Today it's Demetrius Pratt."

"He's just one of many," Mikal said. "Poachers, tax-evaders, militia members, the Montana Freemen, petty thieves. The Missouri Breaks still hides its share of bad guys."

The blue strip of the Missouri widened as they neared Fort Peck Dam, the second largest man-made dam in the world. "And you think he's down there somewhere?" Ezra said.

Mora stared out the window. His sunglassed image reflected back at him. Acres and acres of gumbo wilderness seemed superimposed on his face. "Oh yeah," he said. "He's down there." He said it as if he were linked to Pratt by an umbilical cord of determination—a cop after his man.

Diamond LaFontaine's eyes, as dark and shiny as an otter's, peeked out from the camouflaged tarp that covered the canoe. The plane buzzed by like a big yellow wasp, and she listened to its drone as it continued eastward. When it was out of sight, she crawled from the canoe with the catch from her setline—two catfish and a carp—and ran uphill to where their camp was hidden in a dense cedar cove.

It had been a close call. She had been on the lake in daylight—a severe violation of one of Deemie's rules—hoping to catch fish for his supper if he returned. She didn't know where he was, but she could guess. He had returned to Yellow Rock. She went to their small walltent for spices. Deemie liked lots of red cayenne. As she reached for the pepper, a book toppled from a shelf of cinder block and plank. It landed softly on their sleeping bag, reminding her of the books in Anne Riley's basement. She looked down and was shocked by the coincidence. *Leaving the Land* stared up at her. Deemie had been carrying it with him for weeks. Did he forget it? She picked it up and opened to pages highlighted with colors and covered with Deemie's margin notes. He never allowed her to look at this book. She glanced outside. Maybe he had left the book purposely to bait her, she thought, but she could not resist the temptation. The book was forbidden to her, but she was overcome with curiosity.

Diamond opened it at random: *Thoreau was wrong. It is not in wildness where the preservation of the world lies. It is at the foot of the Cross.*

Her bruised lips parted and her gentle mouth dropped. The book did not fall from her hands but dangled loosely, caught between gravity and control.

It was blasphemy. In the strange netherworld of the half-wild where she and Deemie lived, that statement was blasphemy.

She was saddened by the empathy of sisterhood. Whoever Anne Riley's husband was, to Deemie, he was a dead man. A soulless, domesticated infidel. And Anne Riley was no more than a widow. Or would be soon.

CHAPTER NINE

Sunday morning.

So this is the view from the pulpit, Ezra thought.

When he taught on Wednesday nights it was just him and six or seven others meeting in a small classroom. Sunday mornings produced the added burden of standing before the entire congregation, upraised on the dais for everyone to see, knowing he had to be an example of any message he preached.

He looked out at the people seating themselves in their favorite pews, a curious expectancy etched on their faces. Ezra knew from Wednesday nights that the people liked how he related biblical truth through his earthy, homespun stories. They could relate to him. He was a working man dependent on rainfall and cattle prices for his living, not the gifts and tithes of the church.

Ezra owned but two suitcoats—cold weather and warm weather—and no suitpants. His idea of formal dressing was clean denim jeans, western shirt with a bolo tie, a belt with a silver buckle, and dress boots. Boots were important to him, and he took good care of his. Even his workboots were cleaned and oiled regularly and sometimes worn for dress occasions because of their comfort. To Ezra, comfort was more important than style. More than a few times Anne had insisted his favorite shirts be recycled as oil rags.

Subtle waves of anxiety pulsed through him as he waited to deliver his sermon. He did not hope to please every person. He wanted only to please God with the delicate, deliberate handling of a word spoken from the heart.

Ben and Lilith Foster entered with their little girl—what was the daughter's name? For the moment he could not remember. Lilith walked like a model. She could have balanced a glass of water on her head. Ben followed behind. Somehow he seemed like driftwood in her wake.

Armon Barber assembled the ushers for the morning's offering—a small detail Ezra had forgotten.

Ezra fingered the microphone wire clipped to his jacket. His messages were being taped, not to preserve them for posterity, but as evidence in case someone complained. In case Betty Lou complained.

He closed his eyes and entered a world of prayer and contemplation while Anne led worship on her guitar. The music covered him with a soft mantle of praise. Anne had come to church two hours early to arrange the morning's music and practice with the worship team. He appreciated her devotion.

When he opened his eyes he noticed Lilith was staring at Anne. *She is probably a musician too,* he thought.

Armon came to the microphone to read announcements but was disrupted by his own wife marching to the dais. "The Lord has led me to start a new prayer group," Betty Lou declared. "It is primarily for women," she added with a mocking challenge to her tone. "But you men are welcome to come too."

Fat chance, Ezra thought.

Betty Lou waded into her own mini-sermon on the need for spiritual warfare until Ezra was forced to rise and reclaim the pulpit. She glared at him indignantly, then puffed up her chest like a strutting sage grouse, and stomped back to her seat.

He allowed a moment of quietness to cleanse the room before he began speaking. "Yesterday," he said finally, "I was in the state prison at Deer Lodge, and I bring you greetings from Jubal Lee Walker." Eyebrows raised and eyes brightened with curiosity.

"Jubal Lee Walker is freer in prison," Ezra continued, "than he ever was on the street."

He spoke for half an hour about the liberty of restraints, quoting from the book of Acts about the bondages of Peter and Paul, and concluding with his own parable of two colts born wild in the hills. One submitted to a master's touch and yielded to bit and harness, while the other escaped the corral and enjoyed a few years in the freedom of the wild. But finally, weakened by the blizzards of winter and the droughts of summer, it was pulled down by predators.

"The yoke of our Lord," Ezra surmised, "is gentle and His burden is light, but it is a yoke just the same. It conforms us to His image in civility and service."

It was a short message, and the congregation was unprepared for early dismissal. They were hardened into stoic endurance by Pastor Tom's marathon sermons.

Ezra did not greet people at the door as they left. He stayed at the pulpit reflecting on his message. He was shy about receiving either criticism or praise. When he lifted his gaze from his notes, he looked directly into Lilith's sparkling violet eyes. They were like pools of blue-green water washed by sunlight.

"Excellent sermon," she said softly.

"Thank you," he said. She had a glow about her that made him imagine Mary Magdalene. A contradictory mixture of taintedness and purity.

"No, I came to thank you," she whispered secretly. "Your advice on

Sal Santori worked. I gave him your message yesterday. He won't be bothering me anymore."

"One down, one to go," Ezra said.

Suddenly her husband was protectively beside her. Ezra had not seen him approach. He was a small man with a soft face, wavy blond hair, and a neatly trimmed mustache. "Oh, Ben," Lilith said. "Have you met Ezra?" She took her husband's arm as if to reassure him.

Ezra said hello and they shook hands. Ben Foster's grip was limp. His countenance was pleasant, but Ezra saw a light burning dark and cool in the depths of his eyes. It was like the cloaked light of a child reading comic books under bedcovers by flashlight. Ben Foster was not what he appeared to be. He was a man with secrets.

"Well, I guess we must be going," Lilith said, and she gave Ezra an apologizing smile. She knew he had felt a coolness from her husband.

Ben changed as he backed away from Ezra. A friendlier, less threatened aura surrounded him, and he turned and opened his arms to embrace Hillary as she bounded down the aisle with her Sunday school coloring book in her hand.

Men bother him, Ezra thought. Men his wife paid attention to.

That afternoon he wanted to discuss the Fosters with Anne, but she had a dull headache. "I got it the moment I began to lead worship," she explained, and she retreated to their bedroom for a nap. Dylan talked his father into going outside to shoot hoops.

They played a competitive game of one-on-one with Ezra using experience and shooting touch to try to offset Dylan's youth and size. It almost worked. They were tied at eleven-all in a game to fifteen when Ezra's back stiffened and Dylan scored the next four baskets by blowing past his father for layups. It was twilight when they walked to the house. The western sky was a crimson streak against a cool blue backdrop. Father and son joked as they walked, and Ezra savored the moment, one arm draped over Dylan's shoulders, knowing his son would soon be gone and weeds would grow around the basketball court and the ball would be put away, lost somewhere in the garage behind fencing tools, spare tires, and battery chargers. Ezra's back pained him as he climbed the steps to the house, but he paid it no mind. It was a price worth paying.

Dylan peeled off his sweatshirt and tossed it at the dirty-clothes hamper. He felt in his back pocket and pulled out the white card.

"Look at this," he said, handing it to his dad.

Ezra turned it over. The first letter of the Greek alphabet stared back at him. "Where did you get this?" he asked.

"I found it yesterday when I was feeding the yearlings. It was fastened to an arrow stuck in a tree."

"Show me," Ezra said, his voice undertoned with a quiet but demanding urgency.

Dylan pulled his sweatshirt back on and grabbed a jacket. He led his father to the bend in the creek a half mile from the house.

Dylan found the tree, and with a boost from his father, he climbed through the branches and felt for the wound in the cottonwood's bark. His fingers probed the gash in the tree, but the arrow was gone. "It's not here," he called down.

"You're sure this is the tree?"

"Yeah, I can feel the hole."

A nighthawk swooped in a slow motion glide. In the distance a coyote yapped.

Ezra felt a chill go up his spine.

"Dad," Dylan whispered from the tree. "Do you feel what I feel?"

"What's that?" Ezra asked.

"I feel like we're being watched," Dylan said.

CHAPTER TEN

Uncle Joe sometimes took me arrowhead hunting. Solomon had his own small collection of artifacts, but he never looked for them, he simply picked up the ones he found while herding sheep. "Why don't you hunt arrowheads?" I asked Solomon once. He gave me a hard, long glare, shook his head, mumbled under his breath, and slouched off. "What did he say?" I asked my Uncle Joe. Joe smiled. "He said he's spent his life walking the hills. If an arrowhead wants to be found, it can find him."

Leaving the Land

Demetrius Pratt stood on a high butte in the badlands on the back side of the Riley ranch. By dipping his fingers into three bowls of mud, he painted his freshly shaven face with lines of black, red, and white clay, then removed his shirt—exposing an upper body riddled with scars the size of dimes and quarters—and painted his torso. He put the bowls down and picked up a tied bundle of dried cedar and sage branches.

Pratt set fire to the bundle and held the burnt offering to the spirits of the four winds. He turned slowly to each direction—north, west, south, east—while the pungent smoke drifted skyward as a symbol of his prayers. In a guttural chant he petitioned the spirits of the badlands to aid him in finding the place of power, the *thin place,* where the unseen ones moved easily, coming and going through a portal between earth and heaven. The *thin place* was somewhere on the Riley ranch. He had found traces of its influences in *Leaving the Land.*

He cursed himself for his forgetfulness. That book would be helpful, but he had left it in camp with Diamond. She would find it and read it, and he would have to punish her. He did not like beating Diamond, but discipline was necessary. Besides, he was the new Baal, the new lord of the land, and she was but a possession. He chuckled at the political incorrectness of it. His old friends in Missoula and Los Angeles, even the men, were feminists. They worshiped Gaia, the earth mother. Pratt did not believe in mothers nor in nurturing. He believed in raw, masculine strength. The survival of the strongest and cruelest.

Having finished his ritual, he extinguished the offering and scattered it to the breeze. Then he tied his shirt around his waist, slung his bow and quiver over one shoulder, and broke into a long, ground-covering trot that carried him easily through the hills.

Two hours later he was eight hundred yards from Ezra's home, observing it patiently through binoculars. He saw Ezra come home from a morning of feeding, check the heifers, and walk to the house. The wife and son were both in school. Pratt knew Ezra would eat alone.

"If I were not fasting I would join you," Pratt said softly, imagining himself walking into the house, his face and chest smeared with war paint and a bow and arrow in his hands. It would be a sweet trick, but he was not coyote, the trickster. He was wolf, the scout and hunter. It was not a time for games; it was a time for visions. For three days and nights he had fasted from food and sleep, and the exhaustion was showing. Soon the wolf spirit would take him to the dream world for directions. Until then he would stay at a distance, like an owl, and observe Ezra Riley.

Ezra was washing his dishes when the call came. He recognized Lilith as soon as she said his name. Her voice was light and musical but touched with concern.

"He's coming over in an hour," she said.

Ezra knew who she meant. The other man. Ben had to be out of town. "Do you have a car?" he asked.

"Yes."

"I want you to drive out here," Ezra said, and gave her directions to the ranch.

"Are you sure it's okay?" she asked.

"Of course."

She and Hillary were there in fifteen minutes. Ezra met them in the yard. Lilith's violet eyes were vulnerable and questioning, but her posture was poised and mischievously curious. She wore designer jeans and a short-sleeved white blouse. Beaner trotted up to the child. Hillary drew back for an instant but was coaxed forward when the pup began wagging its tail. Hemingway strutted by, jealous of the pup's attention.

"Mommy, kitty got no tail," the girl said, and clapped her hands excitedly. The Manx ran off.

"What now?" Lilith asked Ezra.

Ezra made sure Hillary was busy with his dog. He never underestimated how much children heard and understood. "You stay here and make yourself at home," he said. "I am going to your house. Do I need a key?"

"The back door is unlocked," she said. "Are you sure this is wise?"

"Do you want to close this chapter of your life?" he asked.

"Yes," she pleaded. Her eyes flashed with a pulsating light that seemed squeezed from the beating of her heart. "I want my nightmare to end," she said.

Ezra parked a block from the Foster home and approached the back door casually but carefully. He did nothing to draw attention to himself. A wallclock read ten minutes before two when he moved from the kitchen to the living room. The house was small and tidy with no visible signs of masculinity. There were no outdoor magazines lying around, no softball trophies or mounted fish on the walls, and the only odor was a lingering fragrance of Lilith's perfume. The framed photographs lining the bookshelves were of Ben and Lilith's wedding and snapshots of Hillary as a baby. To the casual eye they seemed a happy family. The only books he noticed were a physicians reference on prescription drugs and a textbook on the autoimmune system. Ezra wondered if Ben had once tried nursing school.

The knocks—firm but not loud—sounded precisely at two. Ezra took a deep breath and walked briskly to the door thinking the lustful visitor was in for the surprise of his life.

It was Ezra who was the more surprised. The man at the door was Shorty Wilson.

"Ezra Riley," Wilson said. Ezra's neighbor was amused. A childish grin spread across his thick face.

Ezra was not amused. He had imagined Lilith's pursuer as young and handsome, even rakish. Wilson was a slab of mud compared to the flowering beauty of Lilith Foster.

"What are you doing here?" Wilson asked. His pasty complexion was shadowed by the brim of a crisp new baseball cap advertising an Angus ranch, and in spite of his nickname, he was neither small nor particularly short. At five nine he was an inch shorter than Ezra, but from his gray crew cut, through his barrel chest, and to the soles of his lace-up workboots, Wilson was a solid two hundred pounds.

"I'm here because Lilith—Mrs. Foster—told me someone was bothering her," Ezra said.

"Bothering her?" Wilson laughed. "Is that what you call it? Do you think I am over here without a nod, wink, and twinkle from that little spitfire?"

"Are you saying she invited you?"

"You know the kind," he said, and a parade of images—"lounge lizards" in bars, "buckle bunnies" at rodeos, distraught waitresses working the graveyard shift—passed between them like images beamed from a satellite.

"She's not that kind," Ezra said firmly. "And more than that, she's not home. She's out at my place."

"How is it that you are always getting in my way?" Wilson asked. "Seems like you're nothing but a speed bump on the highway of life, Riley."

"Maybe you are the one trespassing, Wilson," Ezra said, but he felt incriminated by his own statement. He had been the one, with Jim Mendenhall's urging and Rick Benjamin's assistance, who had turned a trailer load of yearlings into Wilson's dress store years before on the night of his uncle Sam's wake. In the quiet times before Bible studies, he was often reminded that he had never admitted the crime. It was an unconfessed sin. Ezra softened his tone. "There's no need for us to feud, Shorty," he said. "Actually there's a character in the area you and I both need to be worried about. We should be watching one another's back."

"Who would that be?" Wilson smirked. "Lillie's wimpy little husband, Benny?"

"No. A guy named Pratt."

Wilson's face colored. "He's dead," he said. "He got killed outside Vegas."

"Cletus Pratt is dead," Ezra said. "I'm talking about his half brother, Demetrius."

"I got no dealings with him," Wilson said flatly.

"He might have with you."

"You're blowing smoke, Riley," Wilson said. "Maybe you want to ride herd on this saucy little Lillie heifer all by your lonesome. Then again, maybe you got other woman problems. Problems you don't even know about yet."

"What are you talking about?"

"Have ya heard from your sister Lacey lately?" Ezra felt acid release into his stomach.

"I bet you haven't. I hear tell you and she are hardly on speakin' terms. Maybe she talks more to me than to you. Maybe one of your ranch partners is ready for a family divorce."

"Lacey's in Oklahoma."

"Ever hear of phones, Riley? How about faxes and E-mail? Have you considered there might be an end to Lacey's patience, that she's allowed you to have it your way long enough? You have to give the girl credit, Ezra. She's more shrewd than the rest of you Rileys. She can force your hand or she can let me do it. Either way is fine with me."

The subject of Lilith had vanished like smoke. Wilson was talking about getting the Riley ranch with Lacey's help. "It will take court action to force the sale of the ranch," Ezra said. "Are you saying Lacey is taking me to court?"

"An undivided ranch estate is a messy thing, isn't it? It might be that I could do everyone a favor and clear things up once and for all. There's just you, Lacey, and your older sister, Diane. It only takes one to start the dance, and you can't blame me if I'm whistlin' the tune."

"You've contacted her," Ezra said. "You're putting pressure on Lacey to sell."

"Let's just say that when you're hangin' and twistin' in the wind, I'll be standin' nearby fannin' you with my hat."

"You'd tear this family apart," Ezra said. "The only thing that's ever held us together is the land."

Wilson smiled and pivoted on his worn bootheels. "Land doesn't make for very good glue, Riley," he said. "You might as well call your lawyer." He walked to his "dually" truck with the smug purposefulness of a muscle-bound Angus bull approaching a pen of heifers. "Just remember," he called from the pickup cab, "I can buy you a thousand times and have change left over." He roared away in a cloud of diesel exhaust.

Ezra stepped across the room and leaned against a doorjamb. The bravado of protecting Lilith drained from him like water down a sink. He stumbled through the house, out the back door, and toward his truck like a drunken man. He sat for several minutes staring at the steering wheel. Because the land he co-owned with his sisters was intermingled with his uncle's land, there was no way the ranch could be evenly divided. If Wilson bought Lacey's share, he could convince a judge to rule for a public auction of the smaller ranch. That would force Ezra out of business and give Wilson a toehold into acquiring Solomon's land. And Wilson was ruthless enough to do anything to acquire land.

"I am not going to let it get me down," Ezra said out loud. "I know nothing yet. There are no facts. Wilson could just be bluffing because he's mad about Lilith." He thrust the stick shift into gear and roared away.

As he drove into the ranch yard he saw Lilith leading Shiloh around the corral with Hillary on his back, her little hands knotted with flaxen mane. She flashed him a delighted smile as he stepped out of the truck. "I'm ridin'," she called. "I'm ridin' the horsie."

Lilith reached up and pulled her off. "Hold the horse, sweetheart," she said, handing the little girl the lead rope. "I have to talk to Mr. Riley." She met Ezra outside the corral. "I hope you don't mind us using your horse," she said. "Hillary is crazy about horses."

"No, I don't mind," Ezra said.

"So, how did it go?" she asked, searching the hollow chambers of his eyes for some sign or spark of warmth.

"Do you know who you were messing with?" he asked.

"I wasn't messing with anyone," she said in a sharp whisper. "He was messing with me."

"Okay, okay. I'm sorry," Ezra conceded. "But do you realize who he is?"

Lilith shrugged. "His name's Raymond Wilson. I bumped into him in a store. That's all I know." She glanced into the corral—Shiloh had his head down, receiving Hillary's pats—then back to Ezra. "Why? What happened? This didn't work out right, did it?"

"It worked out okay," Ezra said. "He probably won't bother you anymore."

"Then what's wrong?" she asked, stepping closer and putting a hand lightly on his arm.

"It's a personal thing between me and Wilson. It doesn't have anything to do with you."

"But I've complicated things, haven't I?"

"You didn't start this, remember? You're just a wounded doe leaving a trail of blood. Wolves like Wilson will be following you until your wound is healed."

"But somehow I have made things difficult for you."

Ezra shrugged, folded his arms across his chest and leaned against a corral post. "It has to do with the land," he said. "The ranch is co-owned by me, my two sisters, and an elderly uncle. Shorty Wilson is our neighbor. He surrounds the ranch on three sides."

"And he wants your ranch?"

Ezra nodded. "And he's likely to get it if any one of the four of us wants to sell. He told me today that he has been in contact with one of my sisters. Lacey. She's a horse trainer in Oklahoma."

"And your other sister?"

"Diane. She's a psych instructor at a junior college in Hawaii."

"Family businesses can be so cruel," Lilith said, moving closer, into the aura of Ezra's body warmth and odor. "The problem with land," she continued, "is that it's like a huge video camera. It holds everyone's memories."

"Yeah, I live in a crowd of memories," Ezra said. "It's a wonder I ever get lonely."

She brought a hand to his face. He was surprised how close she was and amazed again at her beauty: her full shining hair, flawless skin, the mixture of blues and greens in her eyes. She hesitated and dropped her gaze for an instant as if weighing her own weaknesses, then stretched up and gave him a light kiss on the cheek. "Thank you for being my protector today," she said.

He held her eyes. She politely took a step back. Ezra reached down and squeezed her hand. "Glad to do it," he said.

"But I have just caused you more trouble."

"All healings have a price. Yours is worth a little trouble."

Hillary stared at them through the corral rails and frowned. She did not like it when another man was that close to her mother. Not even a nice man like Mr. Riley.

She was not the only one watching.

CHAPTER ELEVEN

The bobber twitched. Uncle Joe reeled his line in. The little bluegill was smaller than a child's hand. A biteful. He threaded it on the stringer and hurled his line out again. He fished with three hooks baited with worms. "Fighting and drinking," he said. "It's the Irish blood. An Irishman has to do one or the other but you're a durn fool to do both. Take John—" He meant my father. "He never had to drink to fight. But after he got married he had to fight to get a drink. Fighting and drinking are about the same. In fighting you beat on someone else, with drinking you beat on yourself. There's nothing worse than a dry Irish drunk who's learned to turn the other cheek. He'll self-destruct. An implosion I think they call it."

Leaving the Land

Ezra was imploding. He watched Lilith's car turn onto the highway and start toward town leaving him alone with his demons. As a child, the hills had been his retreat from the ridicule of his uncles and the expectations of his father. They were still there. Shorty Wilson did not own them yet.

The red heeler danced excitedly on her little feet as he saddled Shiloh. "You stay," Ezra commanded Beaner. "It's too long of a ride for you." The pup slunk away to her doghouse and lay with her head resting on her paws. The Manx cat stepped from the hayloft and yowled once as Ezra left the corral. He nudged Shiloh into a brisk trot toward the sun-washed badlands of April.

He was soon swallowed by the wildness of the badlands: the twisting little creeks with pools of coffee-colored water, washouts in the sides of hills like black doughnut holes, buttes layered with the colors of ice cream flavors, gumbo flats as hard and dark as asphalt, and plateaus maned with ivory-colored grasses that waved and rippled in the wind. The hills were always his solace, first as a child hunting rabbits with his single-shot Ithica, now as a man posting in the saddle, his firm body moving up and down in a piston's rhythmic precision.

He tried to quiet his racing mind. If he only had the money to bid against Wilson for Lacey's share. But years of drought had crippled him economically in the eighties, and since Anne had given up her part-time job at the rest home, their finances were shorter than ever. Who was he kidding? No one was going to outbid Wilson for something he really wanted. He thought about calling Diane in Hawaii and asking if she knew anything of Lacey's plans. No. It was better not to get anyone else involved just yet. He wished he had a pastor to discuss his problems with. But he *was* the pastor, at least until Pastor Tom got back, and Pastor Tom didn't see the value of land anyway.

If you are a man of God, he lectured himself, *then act like one. Do not give in to worry, fear, and despair. Pray, then stand your ground in quiet confidence.*

Spiritual battles were the hardest of all. If only his problems could be solved like his father had settled so many of his: with bare knuckles.

He trotted six miles to Krumm Spring where the sweet water gurgled from a rock cove surrounded by an amphitheater of sandstone, cedar, and junipers. Hardy chokecherry trees lined the coulee where the spring overflowed from the wooden stock tank and spilled downhill in a long stream marked by slender green reeds. To the south a high butte was capped by a monument constructed of flat sandstone, a "sheepherder's wife" built to indicate a source of water. It stood like a silent sentinel, a watchman of stone.

Ezra tied Shiloh at the trough and sat against the sun-soaked rocks. There were tracks of bobcat, coyote, deer, and magpies in the sand.

He had made land an idol, suckling from its breast for nurture and spiritual nourishment. Was he any different from the New Agers who worshipped Gaia, the earth goddess? Did he own land, or did the land own him?

The only answer that came easily was the awareness that solitude was now a poor companion for his misery. The hills had harbored him in his youth because he hadn't been responsible. He was but a victim of childhood. But as an adult he had decisions to make, and he could not retreat into a fantasy world. He needed to be around people, and there was only one near, so Ezra decided to watch basketball with his uncle.

His muscular gelding braced himself as Ezra mounted. Getting on Shiloh was like climbing a hill, and once in the saddle there was the sensation of having a mountain of horseflesh beneath you—a solid, reassuring feeling. Shiloh was a horse a man could ride to war on. Ezra adjusted his chaps and recoiled his lariat. He felt naked without a rope coiled on his saddle, the nylon coils brushing against his thigh. The ride home would be cool, so he refitted the nylon scarf around his neck, pulled the brim of his black hat down tight on his head, and buttoned his Levi jacket. From his head to his toes he was a man made of denim, leather, black silk, and felt. His spurs jingled lightly when he rode away. Where two long coulees converged, Ezra reined his horse to the right, toward Solomon's house. From the Grassy Crown he saw the house several miles in the distance. The setting sun made the old white structure stand out like a lighthouse in an ocean of shadowy hills. The house appeared almost comforting, as if no ghosts had ever lived there, no angry voices had ever hurled curses through the rooms, and no child had ever sat trembling, a victim of multiple Irish tempers.

Solomon had waited all day for company. He had phoned Ezra's house three times getting only what he called "the idiot in the box," and he refused to talk to an answering machine. He wanted to remind his nephew of the NBA play-offs, first New York and Indiana, then Phoenix and Houston. Ezra's wind-beaten antenna pulled in only one channel, while Solomon's satellite dish got eighty-six, though some were in Spanish and Japanese.

Several times the old man shuffled on tired feet from the couch to the refrigerator and back, pausing on each pass to stare out the front door and see if Ezra was driving in. By halftime of the Knicks-Pacers game he had about given up. Anne used to come up to watch games, too, and Dylan. Seems he hardly saw either of them anymore. Usually it was just him and Ezra. When Ezra didn't come it was because he was having cow trouble in the hills or he was in church. Solomon wanted to know about the cow troubles. He didn't want to know about church.

It was seven o'clock when Ezra tied Shiloh to a post outside Solomon's house. The horse dropped its head to graze a three-foot circle.

Ezra walked in without knocking, startling Solomon who lay on one of the two old couches that lined the west wall of the room beneath the arrowhead displays. The television set was blaring.

"Who's playing tonight?" Ezra asked loudly as he reached to turn the volume down.

"Knicks and the Pacers," Solomon said, struggling to rise to a sitting position. In defiance of the doctors he had put on more weight, but his face was still remarkably youthful. *Ain't got no wrinkles cuz I ain't been married and ain't got no kids.* His body was not youthful. Arthritis had his joints, and high blood pressure cast spells of weakness and dizziness. Solomon sat up to shotgun his nephew with questions. "What you been doin'? Where ya been ridin'? What horse you ridin'? How does the grass look? How's the calvin' goin'? Any water in the Red Hills reservoir? Seen any hoppers? The cheat grass is takin' the country, ain't it?"

Ezra watched the game and answered the questions one by one. Solomon repeated the same questions every night, and Ezra sometimes answered them in advance. Other times he changed the subject, but once interrupted, Solomon could follow a new trail like a hound on a freshly jumped jackrabbit.

"The Red Hills reservoir got any wat—" Solomon began.

"How many times did you see my dad fight?" Ezra interjected. He had answered the question about the Red Hills reservoir several times this year and there was nothing new to report. The country still needed rain. He wanted to talk about something more exciting than drought.

The old man's face became a stoic mask of thought—How many times had he seen Johnny fight?—then light twinkled in his hazel eyes. "Oh, a dozen, maybe more." He chuckled. "It didn't take much to get John into a scrap."

"Could he box or was he just a brawler?" Ezra asked. He had learned to watch the game and his uncle simultaneously.

"Oh, he could box a little but he mostly brawled. His trick was to put his head down and let the other guy beat on his head and shoulders until he got 'im tired. He did a lotta fightin' out behind the Buffalo Bar in the alley. I woulda seen more of his fights only I mostly stayed in the bar and drank."

"Ever see him get whipped?" Ezra watched John Starks pull up for a jump shot that missed. Ewing got the rebound. He also saw his uncle stare down at the torn linoleum floor.

"Nope," Solomon declared. "Don't think it ever happened. He fought a nigger to a draw once though."

Ezra winced. He had learned to turn a deaf ear to Solomon's profanities, vulgarities, and obscenities. When he took the Lord's name in vain it was merely habit, but the racism was so malevolent and self-righteous.

Solomon was somewhere in a new story. Something about herding sheep on Cow Creek. Ezra kept an eye on the game before jumping back into the conversation like a kid into a water hole. "Nobody fought dirty back then, did they?" he asked. His contact with Shorty Wilson had him thinking about people getting kicked while they were down.

Solomon paused in his verbal tracks. He was talking about sheep, now Ezra was back to fighting again. No matter, he decided. He considered the question, then his swearing laughter rolled around the room like a bag of spilled marbles. "Oh, yeah, some guys gouged eyes and scratched and bit. . . ."

"Did Dad?"

"Johnny? Naw. Didn't have to. And most guys fought clean. The dirty ones were mostly little guys who were afraid of losin' and had no business bein' in the fight in the first place."

Ezra returned to watching the game. Reggie Miller was draining threes from downtown and the Knicks were getting frustrated. Ezra wasn't a Pacers fan, but he rooted for them against the physical, bullying Knicks. Ezra was a fan of the finesse game—basketball as ballet.

"How 'bouch you?" Solomon asked. "Aren't you supposed to be some sorta karate man?"

"Yeah," Ezra said, "a long time ago." His eyes were still on the screen. "But I've never had to use it."

"Ya kick like a girl, huh?" Solomon teased.

"That's right. Elbows and knees too."

"Want some sunflower seeds?" Solomon offered, suddenly going from fight commentator to gracious host.

"No thanks," Ezra said. Sunflower seeds were a trap. Once started on them he would stay and watch both games.

At the end of the third quarter Solomon rose slowly, shuffled to the door, stared out at the descending darkness, then shuffled to the refrigerator. He came back with a handful of store-bought cookies, thrust a couple at Ezra, then backed up to the couch, took aim over his shoulder, and fell backward heavily. Practice had perfected his one-point landing.

"I probably should be getting back," Ezra said, rising from his chair.

"Lotsa game left," Solomon said, a wrinkle of disappointment lining his brow.

"Yeah, but I got things to do before it gets totally dark." He had not mentioned Lacey or Shorty Wilson. Solomon was not a source of understanding or sympathy.

He let Shiloh follow the highway home, and from the crest of the hill Ezra looked back and saw the glare of the television—the only light the house displayed—coming through Solomon's window. It was a cold and sterile light, like a heart that had never known wife or children and was dimming slowly against the relentless attack of time.

Light from one window was all that shone from Ezra's home as well. It came from the basement where Dylan was studying. Anne was still in town. Did she have a hospital lab or was she studying with someone? Ezra could not remember. Shiloh's steps quickened the closer he got to the corrals. Ezra led him into the unsaddling stall beneath the hayloft. This portion of the barn was like a basement: two horse stalls to the west with eight feet of planking, the unsaddling stall and enclosed tack room in the middle, and to the east, a large stall that sometimes served as a carport for his pickup. His father had built the barn just before his death, and Ezra could still remember the old barn in the same location, its tin roof and walls of flat yellow rock packed from Sunday Creek. He used to watch the mice scurry and bull snakes glide through the chinks in the gumbo mortar.

Ezra ran the reins through a large eyelet in a post, opened the door to the tack room, and switched on an electric light. The saddle's back cinch was unfastened first, then he loosed the front cinch and doubled the smooth leather latigo through its keeper. He walked behind Shiloh, one hand on the horse's rump, connected the cinch buckles together, and tied them to his saddle strings. This kept the cinches off the floor, keeping them drier, cleaner, and harder for the mice to get to. He traced his way back around the horse, lifted the saddle and blankets off, and mounted them on pedestals in the tack room. The blankets went on a blanket pile and were turned upward to dry. He rattled a grain bin to warn mice—and later in the season, snakes—then scooped a handful of oats. He let Shiloh nibble from his hand as he led him through the corral to the gate that opened to the creek. The horse lowered his head for Ezra to remove the bridle and bit, then stepped through the gate and stopped with his neck arched and his ears pricked against a moonlit sky. He nickered loudly once to the other horses, then trotted from the corral, splashed across the creek, and galloped up a hill where he stood briefly, waiting for a return call. He heard an answer and loped toward it with his big hooves hitting the prairie sod like iron skillets. Ezra stood and listened. He loved this part of ranching: returning home from a long ride, relieving the horse of its burden, rewarding it with oats, and listening to the hoofbeats as it raced to join its mates. He smiled, looped the reins over one hand, and walked back to the barn, serenaded by the sounds of the rattling bit and the tinkling of his spurs. His only regret was he had no one to share the scene with.

Still, things were not so bad, he decided. He had overreacted in his encounter with Shorty Wilson. Wilson was probably just angry about Lilith. Ezra stepped into the tack room, hung the bridle on a nail, shut off the light, stepped out to darkness, and turned and fastened the door.

Later, he would think back and be amazed at how many thoughts flooded his mind in the instant he was hit.

When the blow struck his right temple, his first thought was *What horse just kicked me?* followed by, *Was it Shiloh? No. Was it another? No. There are no horses in the barn, are there?* Then the conclusion: *This did not feel like a horse's hoof.*

He saw a flash of light, like distant lightning, race between his eyes, followed by a stabbing pain. The left side of his head hit the tack room door. Instinctively, he raised one arm to fend off blows. He was an instant late. The next blow fell like a boulder from a cliff. It caught him behind the head, crumpling him like a feed sack to the dirt floor. He tasted dust and horsehair on his lips, and his nostrils clogged with dirt and manure as he teetered on the edge of unconsciousness. An inner voice yelled at him to rise, another whispered to roll into a fetus position and cry for mercy.

The third blow felt like a kick, something hard and pointed in the notch below his sternum. His breath escaped in a quick, painful burst. The fourth blow landed heavy and hard on his right shoulder. He was falling now into an unseeing, unfeeling world. But could he trust unconsciousness? Could he trust his attacker to relent? He fought for air, sucking in more dust, horsehair, and manure. Then the velvety, enveloping darkness was lit by a golden flash as he remembered the light from Dylan's window and worried for his son. Would the attacker move to the house?

No more blows came. Ezra rose to his hands and knees, coughing dirt and dust, his aching lungs taking in cool draughts of fresh air. He stumbled to his feet and collided with the cold, gritty concrete wall. A throbbing pain arced like an electric snake from his head, flared through his shoulder, and denned in his chest and stomach. He staggered out to a corral lit by starlight and sensed a motion beyond the shadowed iron skeleton of a gate. He froze in a faltering stance, ready to meet his attacker, but it was his dog, Beaner. The pup's whine sounded like a creaky hinge. Ezra broke into a staggering run for the house, with each step his head pulsated like a smashed thumb until he burst through the front door and rushed to the head of the stairs. "Dylan," he yelled. "Dylan."

There was no answer.

"Dylan!" he screamed and started down the steps.

"What?" he heard.

Ezra paused. "Are you okay?" he shouted.

A small wait. "Of course." Dylan's voice flowed through the darkness like sweet water. "Why?"

"You . . . didn't . . . answer." A tidal wave of nausea caused him to collapse against a wall.

"I didn't hear you," Dylan said, his voice nearing. "I had my CD player on. Why? What's the matter?" He appeared below Ezra at the base of the stairs as a fresh, young moon of a face staring up with curiosity.

Ezra's world began to spin. His hand slid on the handrail and he dropped heavily, thumping on his head and shoulders down the steps before Dylan caught him and stopped his fall.

"Dad," Dylan exclaimed, holding his father by his arms and shoulders. "Dad, what's wrong?"

Ezra's head rolled back against his son's chest. "Al-pha," he moaned, then his world was draped in blackness.

Alpha. The beginning. The terror had begun.

CHAPTER TWELVE

*"I remember your pa getting a black eye as big as a
bird's nest and puffier than a mating frog,"* Uncle Joe
said. *"He was tamping post holes with an iron bar and
hit a rock. The bar bounced back and hit 'im in the eye.
Odd part was, your mother was proud of that bruise.
But that was an honest black eye, I guess. He didn't get
it from some fool in the Buffalo Bar or a horse trader beneath the shed at the sales barn. He got it from this
goldarn, unforgivin' country itself. He was a hard man
fightin' the hardpan."*

Leaving the Land

D on't tell your mother," were Ezra's first words as he regained
senses that swirled around him like watercolors. "I don't want
her to worry."

"Dad, what happened?" Dylan asked. "Should I call an
ambulance? And why not tell Mom? She's going to see your bruises."

Ezra had not realized that he was scarred. "I'm okay," he insisted. "It's
just a slight concussion. Shiloh kicked me by accident. Something spooked
him. I think it was Hemingway." He felt guilty, first for lying, second for
tainting his favorite horse's reputation. He wasn't worried about the reputation of the cat. "Help me up," he said.

Ezra climbed the stairs with Dylan's assistance, then walked on his
own power to the bathroom. He switched on the light and stared at himself
in the mirror. A purple bruise, dissected by a thin trickle of blood, covered
the right side of his face. It grew as he stared at it, advancing one pore at a
time. "Not too bad," Ezra said, gingerly patting at the blood with a damp
washcloth.

Dylan watched from the doorway. The bruise did not look serious, but
his father was acting oddly. He wondered about internal damage. "Dad,
are you sure . . ."

"I'll be fine, Dylan. Thanks for the help. You better get back to your schoolwork." He needed his son out of the room so he could make a phone call.

Dylan looked at him quizzically for a moment, then turned and walked away. Ezra waited until he heard music downstairs before pocketing the cordless phone and stepping outside. He dialed Mikal's cellular number. Seven rings finally gave way to a voice clouded in static. "Mikal," Ezra said. "I've had a visitor."

"What happened? Was it Pratt?" Mikal's voice was faint as if fighting through a front of electrical storms.

"Must have been," Ezra said. "I was hit from behind. I didn't see a thing." *Just like Jubal Lee,* he thought.

"Are you hurt?"

"No. Just some ringing in the bell tower." And a lot of static, he thought, wondering if the interference was in the phone or in his head.

"Call the sheriff," Mikal commanded.

Ezra acquiesced. "Okay," he agreed, but he knew his father would never have called the law. His father would have handled the situation himself. "Mikal, do you think he'll come back tonight? Should I worry about Anne? She's not home yet."

"Pratt hits and runs. He won't be back tonight. He's hiding in a hole somewhere."

Ezra sighed with relief.

"Tomorrow we lift," Mikal said. "I will meet you at the club. Don't break any of your routines."

Routine? Ezra thought. *Was anything routine anymore?*

He decided to wait until morning before calling Butler. At the moment he didn't need a hospital and didn't want a sheriff. He just wanted his head to clear and think of a way to keep Anne from being worried.

He was in bed feigning sleep when she came home. Anne tiptoed past their bedroom, put her books on the kitchen table, took her vitamins, and went to the bathroom to change for bed. Anne was easing into middle age gracefully, but the demands of the accelerated nursing program were showing. She had never been a vain or superficial woman—her youthful beauty had been in her naturalness and graceful carriage—but now her sandy-blonde hair was graying, her crow's-feet had deepened, and the classroom had robbed her of muscle tone and a fresh-air glow. She seemed harried at times, as if stretched too far and close to the point of breaking.

Minutes later she eased quietly under the covers. Ezra lay on his right side facing away from her, his bruised cheek pressed against the pillow. He felt her body wind down, the fatigue and restlessness waning, the mind slowing like a phonograph on a turntable that had been unplugged. Soon she was breathing deeply and snoring lightly. It made her mad when he said she snored. One of her hands crossed the sheets on automatic pilot and came to rest against his back. She slept better when touching him, but her touches were less sexual than before. She only had so much energy to give, and school was taking the lion's share.

For a moment Ezra considered waking her in spite of her fatigue, explaining the circumstances, and telling her he needed to make love to his wife, not for sexual satisfaction, but to reestablish the manhood the attack had stolen from him, and to unite her in a common bond against the aggressor. But he didn't. He chose not to bother her.

Sleep resisted him. His head and shoulders throbbed with a dull pain, and his teeth were clenched in anger. Being attacked from behind was a theft of his respect and dignity, and his long-standing hatred of bullies rose up from within him. He wanted Pratt. He wanted to find him, challenge him face-to-face, and return every blow—his and Diamond's—twofold. If Mikal could not find him, Ezra vowed he would.

His righteous wrath was abated by a sudden and disturbing realization: He did not know it had been Pratt. Wilson could have done it or had hired it done. Ezra had ruined his adulterous rendezvous that afternoon.

No, that was silly, he decided. It was Pratt. It had to be Pratt.

Sleep eluded him for several more hours as he schemed of flushing out Pratt. He would ride him down on Shiloh or track him down with his Mini-14. When he wearied of vengeance, his mind strayed to Wilson's threats. Was Shorty in contact with Lacey? Was there a conspiracy between the two? It could happen, he realized.

What a day, he thought. He had been attacked on two fronts. He might have considered the symbolism of Betty Lou's dream had exhaustion not finally forced him to a shallow and restless sleep where he experienced a quick and terrifying dream.

He was in the dark basement of a house with a gun in his hand. The musty odors of oil and coal dust told him he was in Solomon's cellar. He sensed Pratt was nearby. A board creaked above him with the weight of a person's steps. Ezra moved from the basement to Solomon's cluttered kitchen. His shoulders and stomach tightened with apprehension, and he gripped the pistol awkwardly with both hands and stepped into an empty living room bathed in the cold, blue light of a silent television. Solomon was nowhere to be seen, and somehow Ezra realized Anne, too, was gone, not just from the scene, but from his life. So was Dylan. He heard another noise above him. He tiptoed to a door that opened to a long flight of ascending stairs that seemed to stretch to the end of the universe. "Sweetheart," a musical voice called down to him. "Come up to bed." The voice was sultry and soaked with sexual need. It excited and revulsed him simultaneously, but he could not fight its pull. He was sucked upward, embraced in a whirlwind of violent passion.

"Ezra! Ezra, wake up."

He awakened with a dull pain in his head and shoulder.

"Ezra, what happened to your face?"

Anne's voice. The events of the previous night spun through his mind like a ghostly merry-go-round. "I had an accident," he said groggily.

Anne pulled him to a sitting position and examined his face with the critical attentiveness of a nursing student and the concern of a wife. "This looks just like Diamond's bruise," she said. "What happened?"

"It wasn't an accident," Ezra admitted shamefully. "I was attacked in the barn."

"Attacked!" The color drained from her face. "It was him, wasn't it? He came back."

"I told Dylan I was kicked by my horse."

She took him by the hand, helped him from the bed and to the bathroom, where she examined the bruise under better light. "You told Dylan your horse did this?"

"Yeah, I felt guilty about it too. I'm going to apologize to Shiloh this morning," he joked.

"Oh, fine. And how about Dylan? What are you going to tell him now?"

"The truth. I was hit from behind."

She lightly dabbed the bruise with an antiseptic. "Why were you going to lie to us, Ezra?"

"I didn't want either of you to worry. Especially you, Anne. You need to be able to concentrate on your schoolwork."

She gave him a gaze as long and level as a rifle barrel. "Give me some credit," she said. She knew the roots of Ezra's silent protectiveness grew from a bedrock of male pride.

And he knew that she knew. "You *are* hard to lie to," he admitted. "Lying to you is like mugging Mother Teresa."

A sail of white anger crossed her ocean-blue eyes. "I hope Pratt comes back," she said. "I hope he comes back and I hope you shoot him."

"Anne, that's not like you and you know you don't mean it."

"I'm mad, Ezra. He hurt Diamond and now he's hurt you."

"I didn't see a face. We don't know it was Pratt."

"Oh? And who else could it have been?"

"Betty Lou with a sledgehammer," he quipped.

"Funny," she said. "Your gallows humor is delightful." She heard a noise outside and stepped from the bathroom to the kitchen window. A patrol car was approaching the house. "At least you had the good sense to call the sheriff," she said. He couldn't tell her that the good sense wasn't his. He hadn't called Butler yet. It had to have been Mikal.

Ezra quickly dressed, then showed Sheriff Butler the scene of the crime. Butler walked around the corral, into each pen of the barn, and the tack room. He asked Ezra to re-create his actions of the night before. When Ezra was done the sheriff squatted in the stall with his back against the concrete foundation. "And you think it was Pratt," he said.

Ezra squatted against the opposite wall. "I don't know who else it could have been."

"There aren't any tracks," Butler noted.

Ezra wondered if the sheriff was suspicious of his story. "It happened just like I showed you," he said.

"I don't doubt that, but there still aren't any tracks. Now, mind you, it could be done. A person wouldn't leave tracks in that pea gravel in the lane, and he could jump from it onto the corrals and follow the planks down to the barn. Then he could jump onto that big rock you have out there to prop the door back. A long hop and he's in that horse stall. A man could stand in there in the daylight and not be seen. He'd be twice as invisible in the dark."

"But there are no tracks in the stall."

"There's an old gunnysack in there. He stood on that. Your own tracks and your horse's obscured anything else."

"Pratt's a poacher," Ezra noted. "A good one. Agile and patient. He could have done it just like you said."

"Could have," Butler agreed.

They sat quietly for several minutes, neither man in a rush to spill his thoughts, both comfortable with the cowboy way of sitting against their heels. "I'll do what I can," Butler said finally. "What do you plan on doing?"

"Do you think I might do something rash?" Ezra asked. He slid down onto his butt with his knees up and arms dangling across their points.

"I wouldn't blame you if you did."

Ezra didn't smoke but he wished he had a cigarette, or a stem of grass, something to fiddle with. He thought about pulling out his pocketknife and whittling on the closest plank.

"Sheriff," he said, "I lie awake most of the night planning how to get even with Pratt. I suppose I've whipped him ten or twenty times already, but I'm not going to go out hunting him. That's what he expects. I'll leave the manhunting to someone like Mora who gets paid for it."

Butler's eyes were direct and lit with experience. "What if you don't have to hunt him? What if he comes back?"

Ezra had anticipated the question. "There's a martial arts code that says you distribute the punishment according to the situation," he said. "I plan on being prepared for whatever the situation calls for."

"I've learned from bear hunting in the mountains," Butler said, "that sometimes when you are tracking a black bear you better watch out for the grizzly that is tracking you both."

"Meaning what?"

"We don't know it's Pratt. Who else could have done this?" He asked the question as if he were turning over rocks in the Riley family's collective soul.

Ezra wanted to avoid the Wilson issue but he knew he couldn't. He had so much baggage in that area. His strong conscience yearned for a clean slate, to admit his role in turning the heifers into the store, but purity was hard where Wilson was involved. The man did not play by the rules, and Ezra knew his good intentions would never be rewarded. If he exposed himself, Wilson would go for his throat. "You know I do a little preaching," he told the sheriff. "But I'm a pretty sorry example of what I preach when I can't even get along with my own neighbor."

A shade of interest crossed Butler's face. "Having trouble with Shorty again?"

"We had a run-in yesterday afternoon. Shorty's been putting the moves on a young married woman in our church. I called him on it."

Butler shook his head. "Bushwhacking a guy in his barn doesn't seem like Shorty's style. Anyone else?"

"No, I can't think of anyone besides Pratt. He did the same thing to Jubal Lee Walker except he crushed his fingers. I guess he knew I couldn't play music."

"But you write," the sheriff pointed out. "You use your fingers to write."

Ezra paused. He hadn't thought of that. Pratt must not have, either, but he should have. He hated Ezra because of his writing.

"What can you remember about the blows? Odd things stick in a man's mind sometimes. Did the fists seem big? Was he wearing rings?"

"The fists seemed big and hard. No rings. It felt like he had gloves on." The corners of his mouth tightened with thought.

"What is it?" Butler asked.

"The kick to the stomach didn't seem right. It wasn't as heavy as the blow to the head."

Butler waited for more, but Ezra had nothing else to mention, so the sheriff rose slowly, folding out like he was built with hinges. When he stood, his gray hat blended in perfectly with the cement wall. Ezra saw his blue eyes twinkle in the cool shadows of the stall. "You're handling this better than your father would have," Butler said, then he tipped the crown of his hat down for shade and stepped out the door into the stark sunlight of the morning.

Ezra walked into the club that afternoon to the rattle of weights and the laughter of a half-dozen high school kids. Mikal was already doing a warm-up set on the incline bench. He purposely drew attention to Ezra's bruised face. "Hey," he called out, "what plane crashed on your airstrip?"

Ezra felt the curious eyes of the kids as he dusted his hands in the chalk trough. "I got kicked by a horse named Demetrius," he said.

"I'd shoot that horse," Mikal joked.

Their curiosity satisfied, the teenagers resumed their workouts. Mikal and Ezra performed their normal routine of chin-ups, bench press, curls, and leg presses while discussing water conditions at Fort Peck and the latest McMurtry novel. When they were finished, they changed from sweatpants to swimming suits and disappeared into the small sauna at the back of the club. They were alone there.

Mikal was burning to get to business. "So you didn't see him?" he asked. "There's no way you can make a positive ID?"

"Sorry, Mikal. I wish I could, but he was fast, hard, and quiet. Like a ghost with a punch."

"What's your spin on it?" Mikal asked. "Do you think it was a payback for taking in the girl?"

"Had to be, providing it was Pratt."

"Do you have any other enemies?"

"Just relatives," Ezra laughed. "Actually, Butler and I have been down this road. There's nothing there."

"So we're back to Pratt," Mikal said. "You know, the sheriff can get you a permit to carry a concealed firearm."

Ezra grimaced. "I don't know. That's not really my style."

"Change your style. Do you have a handgun?"

"A Ruger .22."

"That's fine for plinking at targets or carrying on a trapline, but it's not likely to stop anybody. I have a backup revolver you can carry. A Smith and Wesson Model 66. It shoots either .38 Specials or .357 Magnums. I'd load it with the Magnums if I were you."

"Thanks," Ezra said. "I'll think about it." The heat was intensifying in the small sauna, but both men were more engaged by the heat of conflict. Ezra mentally reminded himself not to be drawn into a web of excitement. This wasn't a game of playing cops and robbers. He wiped his face with a towel. "There's something I forgot to tell you," he said. "While we were in Deer Lodge, Dylan found an arrow in a tree about a half mile from our house. It had a business card attached to it."

"Nimrod?" Mikal guessed.

"No, it was the Greek symbol for the letter A, alpha."

"He's changed aliases—"

"*Alpha* means 'the beginning,'" Ezra said.

Mora wiped his face. Hundreds of sweat beads dotted the swelled muscles of his arms and chest. "There's another possibility," he said. "In wolf biology the 'alpha' wolf is the dominant pack member. Pratt might be just asserting his dominance, claiming his territory."

Ezra poured a glass of cold water on a rack of electrically heated rocks, causing a cloud of hot steam to rise. "Let's assume it does mean the beginning," he said. "The beginning of what?"

Mikal's pause was the measuring of his next step. "You know about the Buffalo Commons and Big Open proposals?" he asked.

"Sure. Plans by university professors to turn the West into a wildlife refuge for buffalo and wolves."

"Pratt has an unusual and indirect tie to it," Mikal said, breathing into his towel. "He and LaFontaine spent the past winter in Brazil. His sponsor, Antonio de la Rosa, does more than buy trophy heads. He's the head of the International Serengeti Foundation, an organization that plans on securing hunting access worldwide by buying vast amounts of affordable wildlife habitat. Last summer two big ranches in Wyoming were sold. When we untangled the trail of paperwork, it led directly to de la Rosa."

"Buying ranches for hunting rights isn't anything new," Ezra said. "It's been happening around here for years."

"Buying millions of acres is. De la Rosa's group is trying to beat the Buffalo Commons to the punch. They're afraid if the Commons happens, much of the West will be locked up from hunting. They want to get their foot in the door first."

"It all sounds pretty crazy," Ezra said. "It doesn't fit Pratt, does it? He's too much of a loner. He's not an organization man."

"Yeah? Does it sound any crazier than your belief that he's some sort of New Age priest trying to form a warrior cult of nature worshipers?"

Ezra smiled. "They both sound crazy, don't they?"

"Pratt *is* crazy," Mora said. "And I think he's going to stick around here, so I'm moving my base camp from the Breaks down here to Yellow Rock."

"Stick around here? Why?"

"I don't know. It's just a hunch. Besides, the CMR is three million acres by itself, and Fort Peck Lake has over 1,500 miles of shoreline. I might not ever find him in the Missouri Breaks. My chances are better down here."

"But you think he's scouting a trophy ram in the Breaks? What interest could he have in this area?" Ezra pointed to his bruise. "If it's a matter of revenge, I think he's already got it."

"Like I say, it's just a hunch. A gut feeling. I'll use the fish hatchery on the edge of town as my cover."

"We have a bass pond on the ranch," Ezra said.

"Good. I will use it to establish a presence on your ranch." He stepped from the sauna before the heat burned his lungs. Ezra remained on the cedar bench, a long white towel wrapped around his waist, and rivers of sweat running off his face and down his shoulders and arms. A moment later Mora stepped back in. "How can you take this heat?" he asked.

"I'm used to building fence in August. Besides, it's drawing the winter ache out of my back." Ezra wiped his face and breathed into the towel. The heat was making him light-headed. "You know," he said, "when I was a kid my sister Diane actually had a horse named Demetrius. She always gave her horses real unusual names. It was a buckskin gelding. A nice horse. It never kicked anyone."

Mikal looked up, his black hair plastered to his forehead. The shine in his dark eyes said it all, but he put it into words for emphasis. "This horse kicks, Ezra. Borrow my gun and carry it."

Ezra smiled. "It's good guys and bad guys with you, isn't it? White hats and black hats."

"That's right," Mikal said. "I'm a good guy and Pratt is a bad guy."

Ezra shook his head wistfully. He wished it were so simple.

CHAPTER THIRTEEN

*"It's called chivalry," my mother explained to me. "The
real cowboys were chivalrous. They treated women
with respect. They were polite and had good manners,"
she insisted. "I know for a fact that a CBC cowboy once
stopped for a meal at a homestead and left a whole silver dollar under the plate when he left. That was a day's
wages back then." Of course, she knew it for a fact because she had been the woman and my dad, Johnny
Riley, had been the cowboy.*

Leaving the Land

Wednesday it rained. No one predicted it. The clouds simply
rolled in without permission and lingered like Jehovah's
Witnesses on a doorstep. Ezra watched the drizzle through
a window in the bunkhouse. The door was locked and a
loaded rifle was nearby. He did not expect Pratt to return, but his initial
anger had given way to caution and alarm. Pratt was no ordinary foe. He
had an international reputation as a stalker and killer.

A killer of trophy game animals, Ezra reminded himself, not humans.

He wrote a letter to Jubal Lee. He mentioned the attack and asked for
any information that could be helpful. He made several false starts on a
novel knowing they would be fruitless; his mind was too distracted to be
creative. And he roamed the Bible for Sunday morning's message, stopping
to ponder portions of 1 and 2 Kings. He seemed drawn to stories of the evil
queen Jezebel.

Just before lunch he took out a copy of *Leaving the Land* and searched
it for references to his old coyote dream. He found one in the last chapter
of the book. Why hadn't he remembered it was there? It was almost as if he
suffered from partial amnesia.

In the afternoon he went to the Yellow Rock Public Library to research
Baal worship. He found little. Browsing through the shelves he came across
a copy of *Mystic Warriors of the Plains,* a large book on the history and
culture of the Northern Great Plains Indians. He read it cover to cover in

three hours. When he finished he rushed home to check his heifers. Two had calved in his absence.

Thursday the weather was clear. The light rain of the day before had soaked into the dry soil making the ground soft but not impossible for riding. He took Shiloh around the cows. He loved the horse. Through the years the two had forged a partnership from mutual respect. Everything about the animal—his long hip, muscled forearms, thick neck, large eyes — radiated strength and intelligence. Ezra recalled Pratt's hatred of domesticated animals and reconsidered Mikal's offer of the revolver. It would fit neatly in the saddlebag where he normally carried fencing pliers and staples.

On top of the Watkins Flat he stopped and surveyed the several thousand acres of badlands that lay east of the ranch buildings. Pratt could be anywhere. He could be watching at that moment.

He *was* watching. The realization hit Ezra as solidly as any revelation borne from God's Word. He could not see Pratt, but he could sense his presence. Ezra felt violated and the land seemed defiled. Pratt—Nimrod the mighty hunter, Alpha the beginning—was in the badlands seeking something and no handgun or rifle, no matter the caliber or the hands that held it, would deter him unless the shooter was willing to kill.

He rode home gripped by a tormenting ambiguity. There was assurance in knowing—suspecting, he reminded himself—that Pratt was out there. It removed some element of suprise. But he was alarmed by what he didn't know. Pratt was on the land, but what was he looking for?

Thursday evening.

The silence of the empty church was overpowering. Ezra had come early expecting a phone call from Pastor Jablonski that hadn't come. At ten minutes to seven he heard the front door open and assumed Lilith was early for her counseling appointment. It was Betty Lou who strode into the office to Ezra's obvious surprise.

"What are you doing here?" Betty Lou snapped.

"I could ask the same," Ezra retorted. His tone was gentle but the challenge was nonetheless direct.

Betty Lou ignored the joust. "Good grief," she said, her voice lacking any sympathy. "What happened to your face? Have you been playing animal doctor again?"

"Sort of. A horse kicked me," Ezra said. He felt an inner pang. He was lying, but he had to, didn't he?

"Humph, you should leave the animal work to professionals." She began rummaging through the church mail like a dog in a bone pile.

"Can I help you find something?" Ezra asked. "I have a counseling appointment in a few moments."

"Oh, do you? And who would that be with?"

Ezra paused. He wanted to tell her it was none of her business.

"Well?" she intoned.

Ezra did not want to betray a confidence but theirs was a small church where secrets were rarely kept. Besides, Lilith was likely to walk in any moment. "Pastor Jablonski arranged for me to counsel Mrs. Foster," Ezra explained.

Betty Lou's eyebrows disappeared into her pink bangs. "You? Counseling again? I thought Pastor Jablonski resented your counseling? And Lillie Foster of all people. Hmmm, and where is your wife? Do you think it proper to be meeting alone with such an attractive young woman?"

"There is a scheduling conflict," Ezra explained. "Anne has a hospital lab on Thursday nights and Lilith, uh, Mrs. Foster, claims that is the only night she is free."

"Lilith? I thought her name was Lillie. Hmmm. Well, I suppose Lilith suits her better. Lillie sounds a bit cheap, like Lillie Langtry. She was an actress or something, wasn't she? Anyway, I suppose I could sit in on your session."

"I think that would be a breach of confidentiality," Ezra said.

"Confidentiality! Good gracious, Riley, the woman is in my prayer group. I know everything about her there is to know."

Ezra suppressed a smile. The only things Betty Lou knew were her own presumptions.

"But I can't meet with the two of you on Thursday nights," Betty Lou declared. "My bridge club meets in twenty minutes."

"It has to be Thursday nights," Ezra said, trying to conceal his pleasure.

"Well, I just can't make it," she huffed. "No matter. My prayer groups keep me more than busy. We are praying for you, you know. You and that dream I had. Oh, good gracious," she caught herself, "don't assume we are meeting just to pray for you. We pray about a lot of things."

"I'm sure you do," Ezra said. *And the world would be better off if you didn't,* he wanted to add. Betty Lou was ignoring him as she held an unopened envelope up to the light. Ezra was about to stop her when a soft rap sounded at the door.

"That must be Lilith," Ezra said. "If you will excuse me, Betty Lou." He rose and opened the door. Lilith entered shyly dressed in a blue wool sweater and a matching plaid skirt that highlighted the violet in her eyes. She greeted the two of them softly. "I'm not interrupting, am I?" she asked.

"No, no," Ezra said. "Mrs. Barber was just leaving."

Betty Lou glared at Ezra then huffed by, appraising Lilith as she passed. Ezra and Lilith stood quietly until they heard the front door slam.

"You're sure I wasn't interrupting," Lilith said.

"I would have welcomed an earthquake," Ezra said dryly.

"Your face," she exclaimed, seeing his right side as he turned.

"Nice, isn't it?" he joked. "Betty Lou thought it was an improvement. She offered to do the other side. She's the Mary Kay of facial accidents."

"Quit joking," she said. "What happened?"

He hesitated, considering which world he would allow her to enter. "I would like to tell you the truth," he said, "but I must have your complete confidence."

"Of course," she said, and she seated herself in the chair.

"Monday night I was attacked in my barn."

"Attacked? By who?" She seemed personally angry as if it were her turn to protect him.

He seated himself behind the desk. "Ten days ago Anne brought a domestic abuse victim home." He tapped the bruise that had discolored to a moldy green and bluish-black. "This was our reward."

"That's terrible," Lilith said angrily. "I hope he's in jail."

"No, he hasn't been caught."

"Ezra, then he could come back."

"Maybe, but he probably won't. Men who hit women are bullies. Bullies get their revenge then run away."

Her eyes slowly widened and she brought long, tapered fingers to her softly glossed lips. "Are you really telling me the truth?" she asked. "Was it Sal Santori or Mr. Wilson? Did this happen because of me?"

"No, it wasn't because of you. The guy that did this is named Pratt." He said the name softly as if not to be overheard.

"You saw him?"

"No, but it was him. But enough about my misadventures; let's change the subject. Any new problems since Monday?"

"No, thank God, not with men anyway. Mrs. Barber did insist that I attend her prayer group. It's strange, Ezra. I really don't want to go back."

He shifted in the chair and brought a pen to his lips. He knew Betty Lou's gatherings were weird, but he wanted to hear it from Lilith. "Why?" he asked. "What's wrong with her prayer group?"

"I can't put my finger on it exactly. It's just strange. She has to control everything."

"Nothing new there."

"I would have left but I had already arranged for a sitter for Hillary, and besides, she made a big deal about the dream she had about you and the coyotes."

"Two coyotes and a wolf."

"Whatever. She thinks they represent your stubbornness, vanity, and rebellion. She led a prayer that you would recognize your failings as a preacher and step down before God had to forcefully remove you from the pulpit."

"Forcefully remove me?" he asked, a mock concern on his face. He playfully imagined Betty Lou marching to the pulpit, grabbing him in a headlock, pulling him up the aisle, and tossing him out the front door.

"Yes, forcefully removing you. She didn't explain how. I took it to mean an accident or a disciplinary action."

"I was right all along," Ezra deadpanned. "It was Betty Lou who attacked me in the barn."

"I know you are joking," Lilith said, "but just the same, you two must have quite a history. Why does she dislike you so much?"

"Because I stand up to her. Mrs. Barber has problems with male authority."

"It's obvious she doesn't have much respect for men," Lilith agreed. "She reminds me of my mother."

Ezra strummed his fingers on the desk. He was willing for the conversation to lead naturally into a counseling subject. "Does your mother have trouble respecting men?" he asked.

Lilith tilted her head and smiled. The angle accented her cheekbones and fine, straight nose. "I wouldn't call it trouble," she said. "My mother doesn't even make an attempt at respecting men."

"Did she respect your father?" Ezra asked.

Lilith's laugh spilled out quick and hard. It was almost jolting. "You have to be kidding," she said. "No, absolutely not."

Ezra knew he was walking a narrow trail lined on each side with emotional land mines. He was willing to take the risk. "As a child, did she criticize him in front of you?" he asked.

"Daily," she said. There was bitterness in the tone, and she pronounced each syllable with a separate, precise stabbing. Day-lee.

He measured the energy radiating from Lilith as if he were a human Geiger counter. "How did that make you feel?" he asked finally.

Lilith turned her head and stared at an empty bookshelf as if restraining her pain. "It hurt me," she said. "My dad is a nice guy, but my mother was always telling us that he was lazy and had no ambition. It's one of the reasons I detest going home to visit. He seems so small and wounded. More like a child than a man."

"Did you ever wonder why he never stood up to her?"

She turned her gaze back to Ezra. "No, not at all. Betty Lou is a lapdog in comparison to my mother. Everyone weakens around her. Even you would."

"Maybe," he said, not agreeing but not wanting to argue. "Would you like to see your father stand up to her?"

She was intense and adamant. "I would pay to see my father stand up to her," she said. "I would want a front row seat."

Ezra knew he could only go so far in this direction. He needed to turn Lilith toward Scripture. "According to the Bible," he said, "men have a basic need for respect and women primarily need affection. Would you agree with that?"

She crossed her legs. Ezra couldn't help but notice the trimness of her ankles and the definition of her calf muscles. He looked away but not before thinking that she reminded him of an actress on television. Not the "Lilith" on *Cheers*. No. Who then? The girl on *Lois and Clark*, the Superman show. What was her name? Hatcher. Teri Hatcher.

"Do I agree?" she thought out loud. "Well, if you say it's in the Bible . . ."

"But in your heart do you understand a man's need to be respected?"

"A man's need?" she mocked. "I know all about the needs of men. They have been chasing me for the past fifteen years. Except Ben, that is. He never chased me."

"Do you respect *him?*" He asked the question as if rolling her a hand grenade.

Her answer was thoughtful and sincere. "No. I like his gentleness, but I can't honestly say I respect him."

"Does he remind you of your father?"

"Are we going Freudian now? Oedipal?"

"No, just asking," Ezra said innocently.

Her face was cast with a sultry, pouting veneer. "Yes, Ben does remind me a little of my father. Ben would give me anything if I asked for it. Absolutely anything."

"In the affairs you have had," he asked, "do you usually become involved with older men?"

Her glare was sharp and double-edged. "Not *too* old," she said. "What do you think I am, some sort of sicko? I resent your Oedipus complex insinuations."

He held his hands palms up to defuse her. "I am not implying that at all," he said. "I am suggesting there is a type of transference taking place. Your mother disrespects men and some of that has passed on to you. Your attraction to older men might mean the need for a father figure, a male you can respect and trust. And I bet you have heard this before, haven't you?"

"Yes," she said, crossing her legs again and folding her arms across her chest. "I heard it from a counselor in Boise. His idea of a cure was for me to go to bed with him."

"Did you?" He was being purposely bold, risking her anger for the chance of exposing motivations that had escaped his scrutiny. And had probably escaped her own attention as well.

"No," she said purposefully, "and I am hurt that you would ask. Perhaps I'm not the slut you think I am."

"Whoa," Ezra said softly. "I don't think you're a slut, Lilith. You know that. I'm simply digging to get to the root of the problem. We can back off anytime you want."

"Then let's back off," she demanded. "Let me ask you some questions. Did your mother respect men?" She threw the pitch back at him, hard and fast and down the center of his strike zone.

I have to swing at it, Ezra told himself. *I have to play her game.* "My mother had very high standards," he said. "She liked what she called a 'man's man.'"

"And did that include your father?"

"Oh, yes. She wasn't blind to his faults, particularly his temper, but he was anything but a weak man."

"But she was competitive with men, wasn't she? She resented their advantages?"

"Yes." He nodded. Lilith's questions were astute, and he was intrigued with her line of questioning—it revealed a keen and insightful mind.

"And did this competitiveness transfer to your sisters? Have they been competing with you all your life?"

Ezra formed a pyramid with his fingers and rested the index fingers on his lips. "Sadly, they have," he said. "But I understand it. Our mother trained us to compete with one another."

"And what do you think of confident, aggressive women?"

He paused like a soldier taking a hesitant step and hearing the click of an explosive device arming itself beneath his feet. Counseling this woman, he thought, was similar to warfare.

"I'm waiting," she said.

"I have no problem with confidence and assertion in women if they are tempered by a respect for others," he said.

"That's a safe answer," she noted. "And when the confident, aggressive woman does not show respect, does she become a word that begins with a B?"

"Yes, and not just the word you are thinking of. More accurately, she has become a bully."

"A bully? Fascinating. And how is she a bully?"

"Women who use emotions to bombard or manipulate are emotional bullies. They can be abusive because they know the confrontation is not likely to become physical."

"But women are at a physical disadvantage. Your mother knew that—that is why she envied men. Women use their emotions simply to level the playing field. One last question. Am I an emotional bully?"

"I would have to ask Ben," he said.

The response stopped Lilith cold. Her eyes warned him not to proceed in that direction.

"Perhaps we have gone far enough tonight," Ezra suggested. "It seems you did the majority of the counseling anyway. I want you to pray about this respect issue. It may be that the key to your deliverance is learning to respect your own husband. And remember, I am not a professional counselor, Lilith, and frankly, you are quite a handful. I believe there is something within you that subconsciously attracts the wrong type of man. I want to see that wound healed, but, to be honest, I might be in over my head. I wish I had Anne's input. We usually work as a team."

"I thought your wife was going to be here tonight," she said. There was the subtle suggestion of disappointment in her voice.

"Anne can't be here on Thursdays. Is there another night we can meet? Or perhaps a Sunday afternoon?"

"No, not at this time. Maybe later. I was wondering, because you are not really a *professional,* as you say, does that mean we can or cannot be friends?"

He rested his chin in his right hand. "I would imagine that depends on your healing."

"You won't be friends with an adulteress?"

"No, I won't become friends with an adulteress," he stated. "But I don't see you as an adulteress because I don't think you willingly solicit men's interest. I believe you are a victim of adulterers."

"In any case I want very badly to be healed," she said. "I want my husband's trust and I want us to be friends, Ezra."

"Well, we'll see how things go," he said. "Let's take it a step at a time."

"I really do want to know you better," she insisted. "I think the better I know you the better I'll know myself."

"Are we that much alike?" he asked.

"No, we are that much different." Her eyes rested on his as he considered her statement. Then she stood, pressing the wrinkles from her skirt as she rose. "I should get home to Ben," she said. "I need to practice being respectful," she smiled and her eyes twinkled. "Thank you, Ezra. I look forward to seeing you next week." She was out the door and gone before Ezra had a chance to say good-bye. He realized she had had the last word. Being in control was important to her, he noted.

He sat back in the chair and thought about the session for a few moments. She was testing him, and he had to earn her respect by occasionally challenging her, but he had to be careful. He was, after all, an amateur, and she had been handled by professionals. If he pushed her too far the situation could blow up in his face, leaving a bloody mess for Pastor Tom to try and clean up when he returned. Prudence, Ezra reminded himself. *Be prudent.* Caution was not one of his natural strengths.

He sat until he heard her car leave the parking lot, then got up, locked the church, and went to his pickup. He had purposely not walked her to her car. It might not look right if Betty Lou was around, and heaven only knew, Betty Lou could still be around. And what if Lilith kissed his cheek with Betty Lou watching? Ezra shuddered at the consequences. His photo on the front page of the church bulletin, Betty Lou's version of the National Enquirer.

Home was calling him. He urgently wanted to spend a quiet evening alone with his family.

It was dark when he pulled off the highway and onto the ranch lane, but not so dark that he couldn't distinquish the strange vehicle sitting in front of his house. There would be no quiet evening alone with the family.

The vehicle was a mud-coated Dodge pickup. He had seen it before.

It was Demetrius Pratt's.

CHAPTER FOURTEEN

As a child I slept in a house that was never locked. We always had a dog that barked, perhaps even bit. I knew my father was afraid of no one and if he could not whip someone my mother probably could. If she couldn't, we were doomed anyway. I never slept afraid of the enemy from without. I slept afraid of the enemy from within.

Leaving the Land

Ezra killed his truck's headlights and engine, coasted to the edge of the house and pulled his coyote rifle—a Ruger Mini-14, a semi-automatic favorite of survivalists and militia members—out from behind the seat, jacked a .223 hollow point into the chamber and secured the safety. He hoped the pup wouldn't bark. She didn't. Beaner bounded gleefully around the corner of the building, her tail wagging and eyes dancing. Ezra soothed her with a gentle rub of her head. She licked his fingers as he pulled his hand away.

He walked past Pratt's truck casually, the rifle resting on his shoulder. He did not want to overreact. People intent on harm seldom parked boldly in front of their victim's house.

No, that wasn't true, he corrected himself. Psychopaths could be very brazen. He lowered the rifle, eased the back door open and stepped quietly into the dark utility room. His only light was a dim rebound that came down the hallway from the kitchen.

He heard steps coming across the living room carpet. His right index finger rested lightly on the Ruger's safety.

"Ezra," Anne called out softly. "Is that you?" He detected her undertone of fear.

"Yes." His voice was quiet but firm, implying his need for directions or clues. What was going on? Where was Pratt?

Anne appeared silhouetted in the hallway.

"Who's here?" he whispered.

"Diamond," she said.

"Alone?"

"Alone."

He sighed softly and felt a helmet of anxiety loosen from his mind. He leaned his rifle into a corner.

"She took his truck," Anne explained as Ezra followed her to the living room. "I got home just a few minutes ago, and she was sitting on the front steps with Beaner and Hemingway."

The girl sat in the La-Z-Boy in the corner of the room, her body tensed to flee. The room was lit only by a floor lamp near Anne's chair, and Diamond was nearly indistinguishable in the shadows, but he felt her stiffen in his presence.

Anne walked Ezra closer. "I want you to meet my husband," she told the girl.

She would not meet his eyes, but she rose shyly and faintly extended her hand. She was smaller than Ezra had remembered, and her hand seemed like a bird's wing wrapped in flesh, the bones tiny and hollow. Her touch was light and brief, but he felt her pulse, the beating of her heart through the tips of her fingers. She reminded him of a meadowlark chick that had fallen from its nest. Her heart could burst with fear, and she would fold up into a small package of feathers no bigger than a pillow. She receded back into the chair. Ezra took a seat across the room.

"Diamond came to warn us," Anne said.

"Warn us?" Ezra asked. "Warn us about what?"

The girl reached into a pocket inside her jacket and pulled out Pratt's copy of *Leaving the Land*. It dangled from her outstretched hand almost in defiance of gravity until Anne took it and handed it to Ezra. He held it for a moment as if it were a hand grenade then slowly broke it open and let the pages flip. The book was ablaze with markings and scarred with margin notes carved in a fierce black scrawl. Ezra felt as if someone had ripped open and vandalized his soul. He heard Anne take a deep breath, a muffled gasp of fear.

He looked at the girl. She had burrowed into the chair. "What does all this mean?" he asked.

Anne put a hand on his arm. "I don't think she will talk to you," she whispered. "She's afraid of you. Let me do the talking." Ezra leaned back in his chair. Anne leaned toward the girl. "Diamond," she said softly. "Why did you bring us this book?"

The girl mumbled imperceptibly.

"I'm sorry," Anne said. "I didn't hear you."

The words strained through her lips. "Because you were nice," she said.

"Me?"

"Yes."

"Diamond, what do you call, uh, your boyfriend?"

"Deemie."

Ezra broke in. "Is that what he wants you to call him?" he asked.

Her eyes widened and whitened with fear.

"Ezra," Anne reprimanded. "Let me ask. Diamond, does he want you to call him Deemie?"

"No."

"What does he want you to call him?"

"Alpha."

"What do you want to call him now?"

"Deemie."

"Okay. Now, Diamond, why did you bring us the book?"

"Because he hates Ezra Riley," she said quietly.

"Deemie hates Ezra?"

"No. Alpha hates Ezra."

Anne glanced at Ezra then redirected herself to the girl. "Diamond, are we at risk?"

She nodded slowly.

"She's at risk too," Ezra whispered.

Anne ignored him. "Diamond, how are we at risk? What is Dee—, uh, Alpha going to do?"

The girl shook her head sideways.

"Where is he?" Ezra whispered to Anne firmly. "We need to know where he is."

"Diamond, where is Deemie now?"

"Hunting."

"Where is he hunting?"

"In the Breaks."

"Does he know the pickup is gone?" Ezra coaxed Anne. Anne repeated the question.

She shook her head. "Not yet. He will know by morning."

"Does he have another vehicle?" Ezra said. Anne again relayed his question.

"A dirt bike," she said.

"Will he come for you?" Anne asked.

She nodded up and down in a slow, sad, deliberate motion.

"What are we going to do?" Anne murmured to Ezra.

"We have to call the sheriff."

The girl bolted upright, stiff and white with fear. "No law, no law," she said, then collapsed backward trembling.

Anne rushed to her side and held Diamond's hands. "It's okay, it's okay," she soothed. "We won't get the law involved. You have my promise on that."

"Anne . . ."

"Ezra, she's scared to death of the law and of you. You are going to have to let me handle this."

"Fine, and what about Deemie?" Ezra said. "Are you going to handle him too? He is going to come looking for her, and the first place he is going to look is here and guess what, we have his pickup sitting in the front yard."

"I've thought about that," Anne said. "And Diamond and I aren't going to stay here. We're going to the Jablonskis'."

"You're what?"

"We're going to Pastor's house. We have the keys, remember? We will stay there for a while."

"For a while? For how long?"

"I don't know." She turned back to the girl. "Diamond, do you have any relatives anywhere? Is there anyplace you can go?"

"I have a cousin in Kansas."

"Do you know the number?"

"Yes." She pulled a crumpled piece of paper from a front pocket of her blue jeans. "I brought it," she said.

Anne handed the number to Ezra. He punched the number up on their cordless phone. "All I'm getting is a recording," he said. "There's no one home."

"Okay, we're getting out of here. It will take me a minute to throw some clothes together and get all my books."

"But, Anne, what about the pickup?"

"We will leave it in front of the Greyhound station. Maybe he will think Diamond took a bus." She left the girl's side and started for the bedroom.

"If we call Butler he can have someone waiting there for him," Ezra said as she passed.

Anne stopped and drilled him with a hard stare. "I gave my word," she whispered. "No law. Do you want Diamond to get terrified and run away? She has no money and no place to go. We are her only hope."

"Okay," he said, taking her by the arm. "No law until we contact the cousin in Kansas. But we can't leave this open-ended, Anne. I can't put you at risk by having you alone at the Jablonskis' with her."

"Ezra, I've got to do this," she said, pulling away from him. "I'm not afraid of Pratt." She rushed to the bedroom and began throwing clothes into a suitcase.

Ezra turned back and looked at the girl. She had receded deeply into the shadows of the corner and the fabric of the chair, like a cottontail in a clump of brush, pretending no one could see it, pretending it was not there.

Pratt's truck smelled of death. Ezra rolled the windows down, allowing the chilly April air to dispel the odor, real or imagined, that permeated the cab. He drove to Yellow Rock followed by Anne and Diamond in Anne's car, then parked the truck on a side street by the Buffalo Bar. The bus station was across the street. He dangled the keys in his hand. Should he take them or leave them? What would Diamond have done? It didn't make any difference, he was sure Pratt had another set, but what would an abuse victim do in this case? She would compromise, he decided. She might take the truck, but she would leave the keys. He put them back in the ignition.

Ezra sat in the backseat as Anne drove. Diamond was huddled in the front, coiled up no larger than a beach ball. When they got to the house, Anne parked in the driveway, led the girl to the door, unlocked it, and disappeared inside. Ezra surveyed the situation. The lot was too large, the trees too tall and thick, the neighbors too far away. The house would be easy for Pratt to sneak up on. The upstairs windows were accessible from the thick limbs of the towering cottonwood trees.

Anne came back for her clothes and books. "I can't leave her for more than an instant," she said. "She's terrified."

"Anne, this is stupid," Ezra said, following her to the door carrying her books. "This is really, really stupid."

She turned at the door, took the books, and gave him a hard kiss on the lips. "I know it is," she said. "Pray for us."

"Anne, who is going to stay with her while you are at school?"

"I'm skipping school tomorrow. I won't have to worry about classes until Monday."

"Anne—"

"Diamond needs me," she said. "I have to get inside." She closed the door.

Ezra knew a deep tension was pulling at his wife. It involved Dylan about to leave the nest, their unsettled situation on the ranch, and the trials of nursing school. Anne needed to be needed. The Indian girl was fulfilling that need.

Ezra drove past Pratt's truck again on his way home. He had to verify that it was there, that he simply was not having a bad dream. He warred with the idea of breaking his promise, and Anne's word, by calling Mikal's cellular number. But he knew he couldn't do it. Not yet.

The truck was there, as mud-covered and menacing as he remembered. He drove past slowly then stopped for a red light on Main Street. To his left was the Buffalo Bar. He had not been in there for years. He remembered standing next to his dad as a small child, his head six inches shorter than the polished bar, drinking Coke in polished, ice-brimmed glasses while watching beer signs move with a fluid electric light. The Hamm's bear. The Olympia waterfall.

Then he noticed a truck sitting on Main, a one-ton diesel dually, and wondered what brought Shorty Wilson downtown. Wilson was not the bar-crowd type. Two young cowboys crossed the street in front of him, laughing, strutting, overdressed in loud-colored shirts with sunrise patterns. He followed their advance to the bar, saw the door open as they stepped through, and heard a quick rush of music and conversation. The door stalled before closing, allowing a glimpse of a broad-backed man standing at the bar in a crisp, white shirt, and a starched baseball cap on his nearly hairless head. Ezra indulged a fantasy of dragging Wilson from the bar to the alley and pounding on his face as his father would have done.

The man turned sideways, revealing the slender form of a woman standing near him. For a panic-stricken moment Ezra imagined it was Lilith.

A horn startled him. The light had been green for moments. Embarrassed, Ezra thrust the shift into gear and the car lurched forward. He drove home repenting for the murderous intentions of his heart and the suspicious workings of his mind.

Dylan met him at the door. His face was lit with angry concern and he wanted to know where his mother was, where his father had been, and what was going on. Ezra knew Dylan felt he was out of the loop, somehow being ignored and disrespected at a time when his youthful energy lusted for inclusion.

"The Indian girl showed up," Ezra explained. "Your mother is staying with her at the Jablonskis'."

"By themselves?" Dylan said. "You let them stay there alone?"

"Your mother insisted. For some reason the girl is scared to death of me."

"Then I'll go," Dylan said. "I'll go stay with them." He grabbed a jacket and his pickup keys and was started through the door when Ezra grabbed him by an arm. "Dylan," he said, "you can't do this."

The boy whirled around angrily. "Why not? Someone has to," he said, implying he was willing to do what his father wasn't, and he pulled back to break his father's grip.

Ezra only grasped him harder. "Dylan, what's wrong with you? I told you, you can't go."

"What's wrong with *me?*" Dylan snapped. "You're the one getting attacked in the barn then lying about it. And now you're going to let Mom and that girl stay alone in the pastor's house? Why don't you at least call the police?"

"I want to, Dylan, but your mother gave Diamond her word that we wouldn't get the law involved. Not yet."

"Then call your buddy Mikal," Dylan said smugly.

"Mikal?"

"Yeah, he's some sort of cop, isn't he?"

"What makes you think that?"

"Dad, I have friends that lift at the club. They're sure Mikal is some sort of undercover cop, a narc or something."

Ezra smiled and shook his head. "No, he's not a narc. He's an undercover agent with the U.S. Fish and Wildlife Service. He's been after Pratt for months."

"Well, now's his chance."

"Dylan, Diamond has a cousin in Kansas. We want to try to get her out of town before the law gets involved. Come on," he said, tugging gently. "Come back in and let's talk. I don't like this any better than you do. Maybe between us we can come up with a plan."

Dylan shrugged and came back in the house. "My .25-20 is still in my room," he said, as if weaponry somehow qualified him as a warrior.

"Fine," Ezra said. "Keep it there, but keep it unloaded with the bullets nearby."

"Dad, I'm sorry." Dylan said, the hostility draining from his face. "I didn't mean to get smart with you."

"No problem. You're just worried about your mother."

"And I'm mad about you being attacked in the barn," Dylan flared. "That wasn't fair. If this Pratt guy is such a mighty hunter why doesn't he take you on one-on-one in the daylight? I hate bullies."

"Yeah," Ezra said. "I know." He reached into a utility closet, pulled out an eight-ounce canister and handed it to Dylan. "This is the pepper spray I carry when I go elk hunting. It's supposed to stop a bear, so it should stop Pratt. I want you to keep it in your truck."

Dylan rolled the canister in his hand. "Dad, don't you think this 'keeping your word' stuff can get out of hand? I think we should call the cops."

"If you give your word, you have to keep it, Dylan."

"But we're stuck out here, and we don't even have a watchdog. Beaner isn't going to bark if someone comes sneaking up."

"No, but she might lick him to death," Ezra joked.

"Dad," Dylan said seriously, "Mom's right about your sense of humor. This isn't the time for it."

"Yeah, okay, but actually, our best watchdog is probably Hemingway. Pay attention if you hear the cat yowling."

"Dad, Hemingway yowls all the time."

Ezra was exasperated. He had no way to honestly diminish his son's concerns. They were all at risk and had no one but one another. "You have to trust me, Dylan," he asked. "Now let's make sure the doors are locked, then let's hit the sack. We need our rest."

But Ezra did not sleep a wink; he did not even undress for bed. After Dylan's light was off he put on his coat, cap, and gloves, slung the Mini-14 over a shoulder, and went to the corrals to check heifers, praying none would have trouble. He didn't need the distraction of pulling a calf. The heifers stood dully in the pen, chewing their cuds, with their eyes half-closed and their low-wattage minds barely registering consciousness. Ezra turned off his flashlight and squatted against a corral post. Slowly the world of the night unfolded in a subtle display of light and sound. The stars twinkled brightly, and he heard the distant rumble of a coal train as it passed eastward through Yellow Rock on its long, railed passage to Minneapolis. He rested the rifle in his lap with one finger on the trigger guard. Through the night he changed positions several times, moving first to the hayloft—he didn't stay there long because Hemingway began howling, so he left, locking the doors behind him—then the haystack behind the barn, and finally the old boxcar where the feed pellets were stored. When he got cold he walked a perimeter around the house. With the first trace of dawn's light he came back inside and made a big pot of coffee.

At six o'clock the phone rang. He rushed to it. "Anne?" he said.

"No," a husky voice answered. "This isn't Anne."

Ezra paused. The voice sounded familiar but his mind was fatigued and short-circuited by caffeine.

"Ezra, it's Pastor Tom. Are you okay?"

"Pastor? Uh, yeah, yeah," he stammered. "I'm fine."

"I'm sorry I didn't call you last night like I promised—"

Last night, Ezra thought. *Last night at the church.* He had gone early expecting the call. That seemed like such a long time ago. A different time, a different world.

"—some friends took us out for dinner. We stayed out later than I expected. I know it's early there now—it's eight o'clock here—but you ranchers are early risers. So, how is everything at the church? Are you having any problems?"

Problems? "No," Ezra said. "Everything is fine."

"Did the tiles in the ladies' bathroom get fixed?"

Tiles? he thought. *What tiles?* "I don't know."

"Oh? Well, maybe that's something I told Armon about. Speaking of the Barbers, how is Betty Lou doing? Is she rocking the ship?"

Ezra's mind was getting on track. "A little," he said. "She has started a new prayer group."

"Another one?" The pastor sighed. "Oh, well, I hope we don't lose more than three or four members over this one. How about Mrs. Foster? How is your counseling going with her?"

"Fine. Pretty good, actually."

"Anything I should know about?"

"No, not really."

"Marital problems, I suppose."

"Yes, sort of. But everything is going okay."

"So I guess there isn't much new in Yellow Rock?"

"Well," Ezra said. "Actually, there is. Anne brought home a domestic abuse victim the night before you left. I forgot to mention her in your office. The girl ran off but she came back. She and Anne are staying at your house. I hope that's okay."

"My house? Oh. Well, that's fine. There isn't any danger is there?"

Ezra stopped. He did not want Tom or Darlene to worry, but then again, he was using their home. "No," he said. "No real danger."

"Well, I'm sure you have informed the authorities. We'll be praying for Anne and the girl. My, look at the time. My first class starts in ten minutes. Gotta run. See you, Ezra. God Bless."

He put the phone back in its cradle and wondered if he had been deceitful. How much should he have told Pastor Tom? The phone rang like an alarm clock, startling him from his thoughts.

"Hello," he said.

"Ezra." There was a needfulness in Anne's voice that quickened him.

"Anne," he said. His voice was relieved but impassioned.

"I didn't sleep at all last night," Anne said. "How about you?"

"Not a wink. I didn't even try."

"I stayed up with Diamond. I finally got her to sleep about an hour ago."

"Is she okay?"

"Yes. About midnight she began talking. I couldn't believe how much she talked."

Ezra did not have to ask what they talked about, he just waited.

"You need to come by," Anne said. "Maybe about two or three this afternoon. I will let her sleep until noon, but you need to listen to her, Ezra."

"Will she talk to me?"

"No, I don't think so. But she will answer my questions. I'll try and prepare her for you. It's something she will do for me, but don't make eye contact with her, and make sure that I'm always physically between the two of you."

"What's with this girl? Does she think I am the devil or something?"

"Precisely," Anne said. "That is precisely it."

CHAPTER FIFTEEN

My mother, raised on strict Lutheranism, once aban-
doned her faith in favor of the gospel of the National
Enquirer. She believed in Jeanne Dixon, UFOs, and
mysterious mutant children born to out-of-wedlock ce-
lebrities. When she first met my wife, Anne, she took me
aside and whispered she thought Anne was an alien.
A good alien. Perhaps even an angel.

Leaving the Land

Ezra stayed near the ranch house until Dylan left for school, then he loaded the feed sacks and headed for the hills. As he passed Solomon's house he wondered if he should stop and warn him about Pratt. He decided not to. Solomon was a cynic. He didn't believe anything until he saw it with his own eyes. Taking Solomon with him was not an option Ezra was ready for either. With his mind fried from a sleepless night and a pot of stout coffee, he was in no condition for Solomon's endless questions and volatile moodiness.

Ezra called the large herd of cattle together on top of the Watkins Flat, waited until they had gathered hungrily around the truck, then put the old Ford in gear, jumped from the cab, climbed in the box, and began pouring out the twelve sacks of feed in a long, green trail while the old Ford found its own course over sagebrush and badger holes. When the last sack was emptied Ezra vaulted out of the box, jumped in the cab, and slammed on the brakes just as the truck was nosing off the edge of the Flat, the front tires caressing the lip of a forty-foot drop.

It was not the safest way to feed, but it was his only way of doing it alone, and he knew it would get more dangerous the older and less agile he became.

As he was leaving the high plateau he saw one cow nervously leave the feed trail and trot to the north end of the flat. Something didn't seem right so Ezra followed her to a thicket of thick, black sagebrush where the cow circled anxiously while emitting a low, maternal bellow. Ezra stopped the truck and got out. In the midst of the brush he found a package of hair no bigger than a dishtowel. It was the cow's day-old calf. It was slit up the middle and eviscerated as efficiently as a fisherman would clean a trout. Nothing was left of its insides.

It had happened just moments before while the cow had left to feed. Ezra looked around. Not sixty yards away a big, dark coyote sat on his haunches watching him. The moment it felt Ezra's eyes it exploded into a desperate sprint through the brush on a beeline toward the badlands. Ezra jumped for his rifle but by the time the Ruger was shouldered it was too late. The coyote was gone.

He put the rifle down, then picked up the scruffy little carcass and placed it in the back of the truck. The cow watched his every move.

It was Dylan's cow. The calf would have been college money for the fall. The symbolism was not lost on Ezra. A bad coyote was on the prowl.

At noon Ezra sat at the kitchen table sipping a glass of water and half-heartedly listening to Paul Harvey on the radio. He was too tired to eat, or more accurately, too tired to make something to eat. He moved to the couch and was just beginning to doze when he heard a vehicle pull into the yard. He got up hazily, remembering that his rifle was in the house and the front door was locked. He heard three hard raps on the door.

He opened the door to Mikal's smiling face. "Hey, good buddy," Mora said. "You look a little rough. Did you spend the night with your heifers?"

"Yeah," Ezra said, stepping aside to let Mikal into the house. "The whole night."

"Well, I have news for you that will help you sleep. Pratt's truck has been discovered."

Ezra nearly bit his tongue to keep from implicating himself.

"You will never guess where," Mikal said. "Deadwood, South Dakota."

"Deadwood?" Ezra said, genuinely surprised.

"Yeah, I just got a call from Butler on my cellular phone. The truck was found parked illegally in Deadwood. A cop got suspicious and ran a check on the plates."

"How—I mean, why would he be in Deadwood?"

"Costner," Mora said. "That's all I can figure out. Remember, Pratt slashed the screen during *Dances with Wolves*. Costner is building a large development in the Black Hills, in an area that several tribes consider to be sacred. Who knows, Costner might have been the target all along."

"Is Costner there?"

"Oh, I don't know. I doubt it. But if Pratt goes back to his old game of eco-terrorism I'm sure he could have a field day in Deadwood."

"Deadwood is what, four hours from here?" Ezra asked.

"Yeah, about that. I was loaded up to move into Yellow Rock but I'm just going to head on to Deadwood. So, no lifting today, buddy. The way you look I don't think you could have lifted anyway."

"Pratt's in South Dakota," Ezra said, more to himself than Mora.

"That's right," Mora said, reaching for the door. "And in a few hours I will be too."

As Mora drove away Ezra stood on the front step and calculated the numbers in his head. It was one o'clock. If Pratt's truck was found before noon it meant he had left Yellow Rock about six or seven that morning. His camp in the Breaks had to be three hours from Yellow Rock on a dirt bike, maybe four. Pratt must have come back to his camp after midnight, found Diamond gone, and rode the bike to town. Had he been on the ranch? How did he manage to find the truck so fast? And most important, why would he have left it parked illegally in Deadwood?

It made no sense, but nothing made sense to Ezra. The neurons in his mind were spinning in chaotic orbits, crashing into one another and spilling information like a computer having a meltdown. In any case, it must be good news, he decided. He went back into the house and crashed on the couch with his Mini-14 within reach.

At three o'clock he awakened, bathed, shaved, and changed into clean clothes. He now felt reasonably human and prepared for a meeting with Diamond.

Anne opened the door at the Jablonski house. She looked like Ezra had felt a few hours before. "Come in," she said, her brow lined with worry. "The news isn't good," she whispered. "And I'm really sorry."

"Sorry?" he said. "For what?"

Anne's blue eyes were sparked by little lights that marked a path to her depths like a series of night-lights on a staircase. "For making a promise to Diamond," she said. "For not letting you call the authorities."

He stiffened. "Why? Was he here? Was Pratt here? Is Diamond okay?"

"No, nobody's been here and Diamond's fine. We still haven't reached the cousin in Kansas though. She's an evangelist, Ezra. She has an outreach ministry to Native Americans."

"So what's wrong?" asked Ezra. "Why are you so upset?"

"Pratt's crazier than I thought. I spent the morning reading the margin notes in your book. It's all about something called the *thin place* and about the *conversation of death*. And it all revolves around you."

"Me? Why?"

"Because you're everything he hates and everything he loves. I don't know. It doesn't make any sense. None of it makes any sense." She began to cry softly. "I really am afraid."

He held her tightly. "Anne, listen. Pratt's truck was discovered this morning in Deadwood, South Dakota. He isn't anywhere around here anymore."

"Deadwood?" she whispered to the nape of his neck.

"Yes, the authorities think he's targeting Kevin Costner's land development."

He felt her head shake. "I don't know," she whispered. "Deadwood is too close. When you read the notes in the book—" She pulled free and took him by the hand. "You have to come in and listen to Diamond," she said. "But don't do or say anything that might scare her."

She led him to the living room where the girl sat in an overstuffed chair, her legs folded under her. Ezra could not believe the change in Diamond LaFontaine. She had fared the night better than Anne, but he knew it was Anne's work that had accomplished that. His wife's soft touch had penetrated the girl, softening, oiling, massaging her soul, before working its way to the outside, kneading the tension and fear from her body, washing and styling her hair. Diamond was not the half-wild prairie child anymore; rather she was an attractive, feminine young woman. The wariness was still in her eyes, but she was no longer enveloped by a furitive, feral wildness.

Anne took a seat near Diamond, motioned for Ezra to take a chair across the room, and put on her bravest face. "Diamond, I am going to ask you questions about the things we talked about earlier, okay? I need you to speak loud enough for my husband to hear you."

The girl nodded.

"Tell me how you met Deemie," Anne said.

"He came to the reservation when I was fifteen and living with my grandmother," she said in a plain, soft voice. "He wanted to learn the ways of the old people. He performed the old rituals, but my grandmother did not like him. She did not believe in the old ways."

"How long was he there?"

"All summer. Some of the young men laughed at him. They thought he was crazy. But he was a good hunter. He was better with a bow and arrow than anyone."

"Then your grandmother died?"

"Yes. And I had no one. My cousin Melinda was going to come for me. Deemie heard about it and said it would not be wise for me to be with her."

"Because she was a Christian?"

"Yes. He said he would take me away. I did not know what to do. He said he loved me and would care for me, so I went with him." Her voice was growing softer and Ezra had to strain to hear. He also noticed she was referring to Pratt as Deemie, not Alpha or Nimrod.

"Where did you go?" Anne asked.

"We lived in a trailer outside Missoula for a year."

"What did you do for money?"

"Deemie did some sort of work for an environmental group."

"Do you know what kind of work he did?" Anne asked.

"No," she said. "Well, sometimes I did, but not always. I mean, he did certain things. The group backed away from him when he went to jail. They didn't like the publicity."

"You know why he went to jail?"

"He slashed a movie screen."

"Did jail change him?"

"Yes. He hated being locked up. He says he will never go back to a cage."

"Did he talk about his cellmate? Did he mention Jubal Lee Walker?"

"He thought it was funny that he ended up in jail with this Walker guy. I don't know why. He thought Walker was a fool."

"What did he do when he got out of jail?" Anne asked.

"He spent hours reading and writing. He said world history was a battle between the wild, which was good, and the domesticated, which was evil. The main evil was Christianity."

"This was hard for you, wasn't it?" Anne said. "Because of your cousin."

"Yes. Melinda lived with us when I was a child," Diamond said, her voice hinging on breaking. "She told me about Jesus and took me to Sunday school and Bible camps. She left for Bible college when I was twelve. She is all the family I have."

"How did you live after Deemie got out of jail?"

"We tried to live off the land. Deemie hunted and fished, and I gathered wild plants. Sometimes I thought we would starve. He said beef and chicken and store-bought vegetables had no vital force. They caused disease. We moved a lot. Then the wolf woman came."

"The wolf woman?"

"Deemie met her on the Blackfoot River. She was from Los Angeles and must have had a lot of money. She took us to Los Angeles for two weeks."

The Blackfoot. Ezra remembered stopping near the Blackfoot four years before—the day Gusto was put down—and thinking he had heard a wolf howl. Was there a connection?

"What did you do in Los Angeles?" Anne asked.

"We went to a lot of parties. People clustered around Deemie and asked him questions about Indian religion and wolves. Mostly about wolves. They treated us like we were gods. When we came back, he went to Canada and captured wolves. The woman from L.A. paid him a lot of money to transplant wolves into the United States. Then she came to Montana wanting to see a wolf. Deemie had a big male in the mountains in a cage. He was going to turn it loose in the Missouri Breaks."

Ezra periodically snuck looks at the girl. Her body language suggested she was telling the truth, and her story corroborated Mikal's information, but he was amazed at her lack of emotion. She was as stoic as a rock.

"Things went wrong," Diamond said, and she paled and Ezra heard the first tremble in her voice.

Anne reached over and held her hand. "What happened?" Anne asked softly.

"The L.A. woman wanted to pet the wolf. Deemie said that was stupid, but she insisted. They left in her truck. It was many hours before they came back. They drove up to our cabin, and the woman was crying and screaming. Deemie just walked away. The woman was bleeding bad. I drove her to a hospital. One hundred and sixty-seven stitches. It looked like she'd stuck her arm under a lawn mower. That night Deemie hit me for the first time. He said the woman got what she had coming, and I shouldn't have helped her. We moved in the morning."

"Where did you go?" Ezra asked. "Your money source was gone."

"Deemie met a man in Cooke City who said he would pay thousands of dollars for big heads."

"Big game trophies?"

"Yes. Especially big elk heads. Deemie had poached many deer and elk but only for meat. It was hard at first for him to kill trophies for money, but he did it. He killed a big elk in Yellowstone Park for $25,000. That's how it started. Soon he was gone for weeks at a time hunting anything anyone wanted. Bear, javelinas, even gators. We lived in Louisiana for a while because of the gators. Then the man flew us to South America for the winter."

"The man?" Anne asked.

"Yes. Mr. de la Rosa. He had a very large home filled with the bodies of stuffed animals. He and Deemie spent all their time hunting or talking about hunting."

Anne changed the subject. She had one question she needed answered. "Why is Deemie obsessed with Ezra's book?"

Ezra saw Diamond cringe. "He says the book has *bent power,*" she said.

"*Bent power?*"

"Yes. He says Ezra has touched a *thin place* but has corrupted the power with Christianity."

"A *thin place?*" Anne asked. "Is this like a *harmonic convergence?*" Anne had heard the term used in newspaper accounts of New Agers gathering at strategic areas in the West.

"I don't know," Diamond said. "Deemie says it is a place where spirits from the other side and the spirits of the earth come and go, like a doorway."

"And he thinks it's on our ranch?"

"Yes. He says he found clues in the book," Diamond said, then she surprised Anne and Ezra by turning her eyes to him. "He said something else about you," she said. "He said he had to see your eyes when you were in terror. He needed to speak the *conversation of death* with you to see if your soul was wild or free."

Anne had to steel herself to ask the question. "What is the *conversation of death?*"

"I know what it is," Ezra interrupted, his eyes holding Diamond's. "It's the belief that wild prey communicate with predators, giving them spiritual permission to pursue and kill them."

"*Soul-talk.*" Diamond nodded. "That is why domesticated animals can't do it. They have no soul. Man has taken it away." She broke eye contact and dropped her head toward the floor.

Ezra felt Anne's worried gaze. He looked up. *He is stalking you to see if you have a soul,* he felt her eyes say. He knew she would say nothing out loud in Diamond's presence.

Don't worry, his eyes flashed back. *I have a soul. Let the wolf come.*
Her eyes pleaded for caution.

He saw only fear. He shook his head.

Anne quickly broke the contact before Diamond might detect what was passing between them. "I think that's enough," she said. "Thank you, Diamond. How about another massage?"

The girl nodded willingly.

Anne walked Ezra to the door where they stopped and stood hand in hand.

"Are you going to tell her about the truck being found in Deadwood?" he asked.

"Maybe," she said. "I don't know yet."

"I don't like the two of you being here alone. It's not too late to get the law involved."

"What could they do?" Anne asked. "I regret giving my promise to Diamond, but you have told me there are no formal charges against her or Pratt. They are only wanted for questioning. You saw how Diamond was in there. Being questioned by authorities would scare her to death. I need time, Ezra. I need a couple of days to work with her, a couple of days to keep trying to reach her cousin."

"Okay," he said. "But stay near a phone and make sure the doors and windows are always locked."

"Hey," she said. "I'm the safe one. You are the one I am worried about."

He kissed her lightly on the forehead. "Dylan and I can take care of ourselves," he said.

She pulled back, stared deep into his eyes, then kissed him hard on the lips. It was the most passionate kiss he had had in weeks. *Maybe months,* he thought. He wanted to tell her that danger brought out the best in her, but he knew she wouldn't appreciate the compliment.

Her eyes locked on his again. "Ezra," she said. "I don't have a good feeling about any of this. Whatever it is we are up against, it's bigger than we think." She stepped back slowly. Her face was ashen and she seemed to stare through him as she closed the door. He heard the lock click.

CHAPTER SIXTEEN

Saturday morning.

Hemingway took two laps around the inside of the bunkhouse, leaped to the top of the bunkshelf, and yowled at the top of its lungs while novels by Tim O'Brien, Anne Tyler, and Cormac McCarthy spilled to the floor.

"Enough!" Ezra shouted. Catching the cat by the nape of its neck, he tossed it out the door. "Go kill some mice," he ordered.

His writing mood was effectively dispelled, ruined by his howling muse, so Ezra left his bunkhouse for outdoor chores. The ranch seemed empty with Dylan at a tennis tournament in Lewistown and Anne with Diamond at the Jablonskis'. His morning was spent feeding cows and keeping a constant vigil for Pratt—Mikal might be convinced the poacher was in South Dakota, but Ezra wasn't. At noon he fixed himself a scrambled egg sandwich, did dishes, and tried unsuccessfully to study his Bible, but the solitude was slowly eating him alive. He needed to be around people. Anybody. So once again he went to Solomon's to watch basketball.

"Whadya been doin'?" his uncle asked as Ezra walked in the door.

"Fighting coyotes," Ezra said. He still hadn't told his uncle about Pratt or the rumors about Lacey and Shorty Wilson, and these were the coyotes he was referring to.

"Shootin' at 'em or hittin' 'em?" Solomon roared.

"Shooting at them, mostly." Ezra sat in an old wooden rocker near the television set. An NBA play-off game was just beginning, Phoenix and San Antonio.

Solomon was a verbal riot easily incited. In moments he was deep into a story about moonshining during the thirties. He spoke of alcohol like it was a lost love. In 1936 he had wrecked his brother John's new Roadster, ruining the car and nearly killing himself. He quit driving that day. Twenty years later he gave up drinking too.

The details of his current subject were a well-worn path. Ezra had heard the story a dozen times and decided to change the subject. "I see they've turned the wolves loose in Yellowstone," he said. It was like changing dials on the television. One moment Prohibition and moonshiners, the next moment a nature channel.

"Haw," Solomon snorted, and a flood of profanity followed. Somewhere in its muddy stream was the driftwood of an idea, the thought that it was a fool waste of money to bring wolves down from Canada and turn them loose in a national park.

"Did you ever see a wolf?" Ezra asked.

"Once!" Solomon said excitedly. "I was about ten. Me and Archie were herding sheep on Thompson Creek. We saw three of 'em. Charley Arbuckle roped one of 'em. Old Tom Dilliard got its mate. Don't know what happened to the other one." He laughed. "Maybe it's still around. Old like me. No teeth."

"When you were a kid did you hear many stories about wolves?" Ezra's questions were sincere but mechanical. He kept one eye on the game.

"Hundreds. Didn't believe half of 'em." Solomon's eyes sparkled and when he raised his bushy eyebrows they looked like two cocker spaniels rising to stretch. "I know they killed a whole bunch of Arbuckle's mares. Two wolves lay in the brush near a trail to water. Hamstrung each horse as it came by. Twenty-two, I think it was. No. Maybe it was twenty-three." Solomon trekked a long trail about wolves and Charley Arbuckle before retracing his steps to his original moonshining stories. Solomon could not be stopped once he had homed in on a subject. He was a heat-seeking missile of one-sided conversation.

Ezra only stayed for one game. He preferred his uncle's house in the evenings when it seemed warmer and friendlier and the home's sins were obscured by a dim lighting that cast a romantic pallor over the arrowhead displays. Solomon was all business in the daylight, peppering Ezra with questions about grasses, reservoirs, and cows. Same questions. Same answers.

Phoenix lost at the buzzer when Kevin Johnson missed a desperation three-point shot from the corner. Ezra pretended to be disgusted. Solomon's grip of loneliness was more easily escaped if fueled by one of the two passions the old man understood, anger or hunger. Ezra was out the door before Solomon could rise from the couch and coax him to stay.

At home he loaded steel posts, a post-driver, barbed wire, and other fencing tools into his pickup. Beaner watched with melting eyes. "You have to stay home," Ezra told her. "I want you to learn to be a watchdog." The pup shrank toward the ground. "You don't want to be a watchdog, do you?" Ezra said. "You want to be my personal companion." The dog's tail wagged once. "Sorry," Ezra said. "But there's no job opening for personal companions." He drove away wishing he could take her. He wanted a companion, but the dog had to develop a commitment to the ranch buildings, not just to him.

Ezra bounced the truck down pasture roads to the gumbo badlands on the back side of the ranch. He parked on a high ridge, shouldered a brace of posts, and humped downhill to a stretch of fenceline flattened by winter snowdrifts.

Ezra liked fencing. It was mindless and physical and showed results.

He pounded in the steel posts where old cedar posts had rotted and stretched the four wires tighter than banjo strings. Physical labor relaxed him.

He worked west to east, racing long fingers of shadows cast by a lowering sun. He finished in two hours, just as a shadow reached him, took off his gloves, wiped his brow with the back of his hand, and stared at the long climb back to the truck. The taut barbed wires glowed electrically where lit by sunlight, then washed to invisibility in the cloak of shadow.

He climbed the hill with his head down, shouldering the heavy postdriver, and packing an old coffee can of staples, clips, and fencing pliers. He climbed on his toes, his lace-up packers digging for holds in the brittle clay. Halfway up he stopped to rest.

The man's appearance was as sudden and unexpected as the blows Ezra had taken in the barn. He was a silhouette on a sandstone outcropping, a rawboned gargoyle staring down from the walls of a gumbo castle. The outline of a recurve bow and a quiver of arrows encircled him.

Ezra took a deep breath to calm himself. To show surprise was to display weakness. Pratt was between him and the truck, and as he could not outrun an arrow, he decided to take the offensive. "So, you must be Demetrius Pratt," Ezra challenged.

"I am," Pratt said. "But I would prefer that you call me Alpha." His voice was flat and serious.

"Sorry, I can't do that," Ezra said. "You're just Pratt to me." He disliked being literally talked down to and wanted to continue climbing, but the bow and arrows were a halting consideration. "So, what do you want?" he asked. "We need to talk," Pratt said. "Talk away." Ezra scanned his surroundings peripherally. There was a sharp ravine to his left. If he had to run, the ravine might be the avenue.

"I have someone you need to meet," Pratt said. "He has come a long way just to talk to you."

Ezra wished he had packed his rifle down or at least stuck the little .22 Ruger in his belt. His only weapons were a post-pounder and a can of rusty staples. "Someone has come a long way to talk to me?" he said. He remembered Mikal mentioning the Brazilian. "I bet his name is de la Rosa."

"Congratulations," Pratt said. "Someone talks. Either my Diamond or the pest Mikal Mora." Ezra tried to stifle his surprise but Pratt noticed. "You give me too little credit, Riley," Pratt boasted. "I have known about Mora for weeks. He's little more than an inconvenience. I also know that Diamond is with your wife at your preacher's house."

The mention of Anne blew Ezra's self-imposed cool. "You hurt my wife," he warned, "and I'll kill you."

"Relax, Riley. I have no interest in your wife. And no matter what Mora may have told you, I have no interest in your son, your horses, your cattle, your dog, or even your tailless cat for that matter."

"But me?" Ezra asked. "What is your interest in me?"

"That is for a later date. For now I am inviting you to meet de la Rosa. He will be in this area soon."

"And if I refuse?"

Pratt sighed. "Then you cause me to become interested in the afore-mentioned subjects."

"Is that a threat, Pratt?"

"Of course it's a threat, Riley. What do you take me for, some sort of idiot? Don't test my patience. I have been two nights without sleep. How have you been sleeping, Ezra?"

The question made Ezra think about his Thursday night standing guard in the dark. Had Pratt been close by? "What exactly do you want, Pratt?"

"I told you. I want you to meet my friend."

"No. Beyond that. Why are you obsessed with my book and this business about a *conversation of death* and a *thin place?* Why did you attack me in the barn?"

"The answers to the first question will come in due time. As for an attack in the barn, I don't know what you're talking about."

"Leave your bow and arrows and come on down," Ezra challenged. "We can have our little *conversation of death* right now."

Pratt laughed. "You are amusing, Riley. It is not time to end things. It is the beginning. That is why I am Alpha. I am the beginning."

"You know I will have to go to the sheriff."

"No, no, I don't think you will. There are no charges outstanding against me. What are you going to charge me with, trespassing? Look around, we are on BLM ground, Riley. I have as much right to be here as you do. What are you going to tell Sheriff Butler? That there is a crazy man in the hills who believes in *thin places* and the *conversations of death?*"

"You are wanted for questioning, Pratt. They know about your poaching."

"Yes, of course they do. But they have nothing to hold me. I would not even spend one night in jail, Riley. Turning me in would only anger me. Besides, Mora is on a wild-goose chase in South Dakota. Do you think Yellow Rock's old sheriff is going to be able to find me? Do you think any-one can find me if I don't want them to? I am a shape-shifter, Ezra. If any-one gets close I turn into something else."

"So you are coyote, the trickster," Ezra said, remembering his Plains Indian myths.

"No," Pratt said angrily. "I am Alpha, the wolf. I eat coyotes, Riley."

Ezra realized he had accidentally drawn out Pratt's darkest side, and this was not the time or the place to confront the strongest of his many demons. "Okay," he said. "I will make you a deal. If you leave Anne, my son, and Diamond alone, I will meet with your friend, de la Rosa."

"Fine, but one more thing," Pratt said. "You tell no one. No Butler, no Mora, not your wife, no one."

Ezra pondered his choices. He had none. "When do we meet?" he asked.

"Day after tomorrow. The Cattleman's Cafe at two o'clock. Come early and get the booth of your choosing. Remember, Riley, there are no charges against me for anything. Mora has nothing on me. He has never so much as had a good look at my face. If you bring him all deals are off, and I will have my revenge."

Ezra did not even know how to contact Mikal. "Okay," he said. "I give you my word."

"I believe your word, Riley. And you should believe mine. Diamond will return to me. She will not stay with you and your wife."

"I won't discuss Diamond," Ezra said.

"Fine. Then we are through talking." Pratt rose to his feet. "By the way," he added. "I removed the keys from your truck. They're hanging on a fence post. And your little assault rifle is now unloaded."

Ezra was tempted to have the final word. He wanted to rebuke Pratt in the name of Jesus Christ and confront the demons from hell that fueled his wild obsessions, but he knew he had to bide his time. He lowered his head to reach for the post-driver he had dropped at his feet. When he looked up, Pratt was gone. The rock was so suddenly vacant it was hard to believe the man had ever been there at all.

CHAPTER SEVENTEEN

The red and white bobber landed with a soft "ker-plunk" on the water and sent little ripples outward in concentric circles. "You're one of those kids that's gonna spend too much time thinkin' about God and things like that," Uncle Joe told me. "That's all a waste of time. Think about fishin'." He peeled the wrapper off a candy bar and thrust it into his mouth with his meaty hand. "I've never thought about God much," he said. "Thought about ghosts though," he added, and he stared at the water as if he saw something rising from its murky depths.

Leaving the Land

His second Sunday morning in the pulpit, Ezra sat in a front pew and thought about honesty while Armon Barber read the announcements.

Betty Lou came uninvited to the pulpit again and extolled the virtues of her prayer group. Anne led the congregation in worship. No matter the personal trials, Anne always sang with a fullness and purity of heart. She was her most beautiful when praising God, and Ezra wished he could take her home alone for the afternoon.

To the surprise of them all, Diamond agreed to come to church. She sat with Dylan in a back pew and though she was still afraid of Ezra, Dylan did not threaten her at all. The two were even becoming friends.

Ezra saw Lilith out of the corner of his eye. She seemed to be staring at Anne. He noticed that Ben was staring at him. There was an odd intensity in both Lilith and Ben, but Ezra shrugged it off. This was not a time to be analytical or judgmental. It was a time to preach the Word.

He thought again about honesty. He had told no one about meeting Pratt or his meeting the next day with de la Rosa. He had not told Mikal they had Diamond, nor had he told Anne that Mikal was a federal agent. There were so many things he had not told so many people, he was having trouble keeping them straight. He needed a program to keep track of his deceptions, and he was supposed to be a preacher!

The music ended. It was time for the message.

Ezra walked to the pulpit feeling the eyes of the people upon him, especially Anne's, Betty Lou's, and Lilith's. "I do not feel qualified to preach today," he said. "Instead, I would like Anne and the other musicians and singers to continue to lead us in praise and worship, and I invite all of you to come forward toward the altar area. Come forward to pray or to praise or come down to minister or be ministered to." He took a seat in the front pew.

Anne looked as if she had been hit across the forehead with a plank. She walked quietly down to Ezra. "I haven't had time to prepare," she said. "We don't have that many songs ready. What do you want us to do?"

"Just sing," he said. "Sing and praise God, and pray that the Lord will get us out of this one."

Anne rubbed her temples. "I'm getting a headache," she said. "I don't know if I can do this."

"You'll do fine," he encouraged her, but already he could feel Betty Lou's laser-hot vision boring into the back of his own head. He knew she would be on the phone to Pastor Tom before her roast was out of the oven.

Anne walked back to the microphone. "Let us continue to praise and worship," she said. "Please come forward to sing or pray." She led the pianist, bass player, and flutist awkwardly into a chorus. Ezra folded quietly to his knees and dropped his forehead to the floor.

Anne sang one song, then two, then three. Ezra heard the soft rustling sounds of people coming forward and the unpolished voices of laywomen joining in the singing. He knew most of the men were sitting uncomfortably in their pews, glancing at the clock, and wondering if they were going to miss a televised basketball game. After the fourth song he raised his head and looked around. Dylan was at one end of the altar area in prayer. Lilith was at the other. Above her half a dozen women were singing around Anne. Armon Barber was on his knees with his head resting on the front pew. He could not see Betty Lou and did not particularly want to. He was worried for Diamond. She was huddled in the back pew by herself.

Ezra returned to praying. He sensed something unusual occurring. People were responding. Even some of the more stoic men were slowly coming forward. He decided it was time to enter into worship himself so he rose to his feet, and in turning saw Diamond rise from her pew. He was afraid she was going to run. Instead, the girl came cautiously down the aisle and knelt at the altar between Lilith and Dylan.

Ezra breathed a prayer of thanks and closed his eyes.

His eyes opened again at the sound of the shriek. Diamond had jumped to her feet. "No! No!" she shouted and turned and bounded down the aisleway with the grace and energy of a deer. The music stopped, people turned to watch, and Ezra caught Dylan's eye and motioned for him to follow her.

Anne turned toward Ezra. "I must go to her," she said, stepping from the dais. She hurried in Dylan's wake, bumping Betty Lou who was rushing forward to confront Ezra.

"What have you done now, Ezra Riley?" Betty Lou scolded in a harsh whisper. "I'm going back and calling Pastor Jablonski this instant." She turned on her heels and strutted toward the pastor's study.

Though he had been led by the best of intentions, Ezra now felt confused and responsible. The people were looking to him for direction or explanation, but he only wanted to be with his family. While he was considering how to restore order, he felt a tug on his sleeve and turned and looked into Lilith's blue-green eyes. "May I handle this?" she asked.

"Go ahead." Ezra said. He saw a confidence in her that comforted him.

"Everyone, listen," Lilith said. Her voice was a soft command. "Everyone, please, this is a time to pray." She took the microphone and led the congregation in a prayer for mercy and victory for the church, then she broke easily into an a cappella rendition of "Amazing Grace." She was the most competent vocalist Ezra had heard since Jubal Lee. The people stood transfixed, waiting for more. "Ezra," she said, handing the microphone to him, "would you like to close the service?"

"No," he said. "You go ahead." And he left to follow his family.

He did not hear Lilith's prayer, and was only hoping Betty Lou hadn't either, as he left the church. He found Anne, Dylan, and Diamond in an empty lot four blocks from the church. The girl was sobbing in Anne's arms, and Ezra suspected he should keep his distance. "How's it going?" he whispered to Dylan.

"She's okay, I think," Dylan said. "Boy, can she run."

Anne looked at them over the top of Diamond's head. "She says there's an evil in the church," she whispered.

Ezra nodded knowingly. "Of course she thinks it's evil," he whispered back. "Pratt has convinced her that Christianity is evil."

Diamond moaned deeply and her whole body convulsed.

"I think I better get Diamond back to the house," Anne said. "I'll call you guys later."

"Anne," Ezra called after her. "Remember, you have school tomorrow."

"I might not make it," she said. Diamond needed her. Besides, she had such a headache she wasn't sure she could read, let alone study. She walked away with Diamond LaFontaine tucked under her arm like a fledgling under a wing.

"Well," Dylan said, turning his thoughts to matters of importance. "Where are we going to eat? McDonald's or Burger King."

"You pick," Ezra said, as he watched the two women recede into the distance.

They ate at Burger King, and Dylan put away two double-cheeseburgers while Ezra picked at a fish sandwich and sipped his coffee.

"We need to get milk on the way home," Dylan said. "Yesterday morning when I got up to catch the bus for Lewistown, I ate dry cereal. It wasn't that bad, but tomorrow morning I would just as soon have milk."

"Sorry," Ezra said. "I guess groceries haven't been a priority of mine. So how did you do in Lewistown?"

"Won two, lost two," he said and waved at two teenage girls who had just walked in. Unlike many of his peers, it had never bothered Dylan to be seen with a parent. "My serve was awesome," he continued, "but I still don't have a backhand, so I try to run around the ball and hit it with my forehand. That works until I get tired." Dylan took a long sip from his Coke. "Dad," he continued, "do you remember when Jubal Lee took us out to dinner a long time ago, and he said that you'd been trained to kill people in the martial arts?"

Ezra frowned. He wasn't ready for the jump from tennis to deadly self-defense. "Jubal was known to exaggerate, Dylan," he said. "In fact, Jubal's life then was one big exaggeration."

"Yeah, I know, but were you trained to kill?"

"We were trained to distribute the punishment according to the situation."

"But couldn't a situation involve killing?"

"Yes," Ezra admitted, "and we had a couple of techniques that were lethal."

"Cool."

"No," Ezra said. "It wasn't cool."

"Wasn't it?" Dylan smiled mischievously.

"Okay." Ezra grinned. "It seemed kinda cool at the time. But my sensei was very serious, he didn't take life-and-death situations lightly and neither do I. Why do you bring this up?"

"I don't know." Dylan shrugged. "That Pratt guy, I guess."

"He's in South Dakota," Ezra said. "With Mikal on his tail."

"I don't think so," Dylan said. "Diamond's a fox, Dad. Do you think a guy is just going to run off and leave a woman like her?"

"So you think Pratt is still around?"

"Yeah, and you know what else? Diamond was right, there was evil in the church this morning. I felt it when I was up at the altar praying."

"What was it?" Ezra asked.

"I don't know, but it was big-time evil. Big-time."

Ezra brought the Styrofoam coffee cup to his lips and stared out the window, past the throng of junior high kids shouting and laughing, past the elderly couple helping each other over a curb, past everything visible, to the far north where the Riley badlands lay like a convoluted maze of gumbo, sod, and cedar. Pratt *was* out there, somewhere. Even his teenaged son was aware of his presence.

"Dad?" Dylan said.

Ezra turned his attention back to the table. "Yeah, Dylan."

"Are you going to finish that sandwich?"

CHAPTER EIGHTEEN

In the beginning is the land. Silent, unrelenting, and constant. A thin veneer of topsoil over a heart of clay. Short-cropped buffalo grasses circumscribing gumbo mounds like fringe around balding heads; verdant cedar swales, pungent and fertile; rock-capped badlands mystified by aboriginal fears. Then there are the animals. Mule deer, pronghorn antelope, cottontails, bobcats, red-tailed hawks, badgers, and prairie dogs. But first and foremost is the land. It is sovereign. It has its way with men, changing every aspect of our short lives: molding, shaping, and hardening us. For in the end the land is but a tool of a purposeful God, the potter's wheel on which is spun the souls of men. For it is not the earth that is truly the clay, it is the people.

Leaving the Land

A light shower fell all Monday morning, so he cleaned barn stalls and oiled his saddle, applying neat's-foot oil with his fingers, slowly massaging the basket-stamped leather in circular motions as if rubbing a lover's back with suntan lotion. All the time he was thinking about the meeting he had coming up that afternoon with Pratt and de la Rosa. He wished he could tell someone, especially Anne, so there would be no deception between them. And he wished he could tell Mikal. Mikal would be a good man to have covering his back.

Lunch by himself seemed doubly lonesome. He missed lunches with his wife. She made terrific stir-fry with wild rice, steamed vegetables, and cut-up chicken breasts, and they both read the *Billings Gazette* while they ate. Ezra read the sports page first, and Anne read the comics.

Ezra kept glancing at the clock, counting the minutes before meeting with Pratt and his friend, and wondering if he should go armed. He filled the clip of his Ruger .22 with ten hollow-point bullets, then decided taking the pistol was stupid. He didn't have a concealed weapons permit, would probably be outgunned with just a .22, and probably couldn't hit water if he was sitting in a bathtub. Before leaving for town he locked the house, bunkhouse, and the upstairs of the barn.

Ezra took a back booth in the Cattleman's, choosing the side facing the front door so he could watch people enter. It was the same booth he and Jubal Lee had sat in the first time Ezra laid eyes on a Pratt. Cletus Pratt. *Time passes,* he thought, *but while so much changes, so much remains the same.*

People passed by and said hello but were not tempted to join him. Ezra had the radiance of a loner about him, or a person obviously waiting for someone. Waiting with some anxiousness.

He killed time by contemplating the oversize photographs hanging from the walls. They were classics: a band of sheep grazing green hills, a herd of longhorns dotting a meadow, an old-time cattle ranch in a creek bottom, a bronc rider on a dark horse suspended against a blue sky. Yellow Rock was a community famous for its pioneer photographers. Ezra did not know whose work this was, but the hand-tinting was extreme. The grass was too green, the sky too blue, the horses and cattle too dark. That and their size gave the prints a surrealistic quality as if they were dreamscapes that could be entered through prolonged concentration.

The cook bellowed a greeting to Ezra as he emerged from the kitchen. He was also the owner. A greasy white apron hung from his thick shoulders and spread over an expansive belly. He seemed a caricature of a greasy-spoon cook—he lacked only a cigarette dangling from his lips and a heart tattooed on his biceps. Ezra said hello then returned to staring at both the photographs and the front door.

He never saw Pratt come in, he simply materialized in the booth, seated across from Ezra as if he had formed out of the air, a condensing of cigarette smoke, grease, and everyone's fears.

"Where is your friend?" Ezra asked, trying not to show his surprise.

Pratt's cold and level gaze filled the booth, but Ezra sensed Pratt's antennas extended throughout the entire building as if he were seeing or hearing everything in the cafe. Pratt wore a Patagonia jacket and a flannel shirt from Cabela's, and his hair was parted on the left and combed to the side. His eyes burned with a hunter's alertness. Ezra had expected a ruddy, weathered face but Pratt's had the pasty dullness common to mental patients, and though he was groomed for the public, he could not be cleansed from the stench of blood. Ezra sensed there was death in the booth.

"You will meet de la Rosa soon," Pratt said. "First I needed to make sure you were alone."

Ezra watched a policeman enter and take a seat at the counter out of Pratt's range of vision. "I'm alone," Ezra said.

"No wires?" Pratt asked. The way he said it made Ezra think Pratt knew about his trip to Deer Lodge.

"No wires." The policeman was getting a cup of coffee to go.

A young waitress came over with a menu and coffeepot in her hands. Pratt waved her away disdainfully.

"Would you rather have a Diet Coke?" Ezra asked, making a pointed reference to Pratt's beating of Diamond. The policeman was now standing at the till counting change from his pockets.

Pratt gave Ezra an empty stare. He was not easily baited. There was the faint tinkling of the bell above the front door forty feet away. "Has the cop left?" Pratt asked.

Ezra nodded.

"Follow me," Pratt said.

As Ezra trailed behind Pratt, fear tempted him to rise to full height and swell his chest like a badger facing a bear. But he needed to be underestimated, so he slouched, instead, and walked with a slight limp. Pratt led him to a back room reserved for meetings of the local Kiwanis and Rotary clubs. Two people sat alone there at a corner table. One rose as Ezra and Pratt approached. He was a tall, handsome man in an angora sweater and knit slacks. His tanned face was Latin—Or was it Portugese? Ezra didn't know—with dark, wavy hair oiled and brushed back. He reeked of money, charm, and power.

"Ezra Riley," he said, offering his hand. "It is good to meet you." His grip was firm but gentle and he held Ezra's hand for several moments as if massaging it. His dark eyes twinkled with light. Ezra guessed him to be in his mid-forties. "I am Antonio de la Rosa," he said musically. Pratt sat down. The other man did not stand or offer his hand. De la Rosa gestured to him. "This is my pilot, Mr. Sandoval."

They traded stares. Sandoval was obviously more than a pilot. Ezra could feel the eyes sizing him up, checking for weaknesses, motives, and threats. *Mr. Bodyguard,* Ezra thought.

"Sit down, sit down," de la Rosa said, seating himself. "The coffee here is, uh, well, very interesting. I have had coffee this stout only twice before. Once in Alaska hunting brown bear, the other time in the pampas." He filled Ezra's cup from a black plastic pitcher.

"I am a fan of your writing," he continued. *"Leaving the Land* is a beautiful book. Reminiscent of Walt Whitman in many ways. In South America we have many celebrated novelists. We appreciate fine writing." He gestured with his hands as he talked, his three diamond rings glittering in the light like fireflies mounted on manicured fingers.

Ezra felt Sandoval's constant, irritating gaze. He wondered if he was armed. He also sensed Pratt's discomfort and that amused him. Pratt was a social claustrophobic. "So you have read my book," Ezra said. "I imagine you know quite a bit about me."

"Your book tells much," de la Rosa smiled innocently. "But we have filled in the spaces a little." His countenance warmed as easily as the turning of a faucet. "We are here to offer to help you, Ezra Riley. You have a great love for the land and for wildlife. I can respect that. I am confident we can help one another."

He reminded Ezra of a vacuum cleaner salesman. A very rich vacuum cleaner salesman. "Okay," Ezra said. "Give me your pitch."

De la Rosa smiled away the cynicism. "Demetrius has informed us of the intentions of your neighbor, Mr. Wilson. We are aware of Mr. Wilson—"

"*We?*" Ezra interrupted.

"The International Serengeti Foundation," de la Rosa explained. "We monitor wild areas all over the world: wilderness, deserts, jungles, grasslands. We keep a finger on their pulse so to speak. Our objective is to preserve wildlife habitat. We find the practices of gentlemen like Mr. Wilson to be most disturbing." He nodded at Pratt. "Demetrius has informed me that Mr. Wilson is seeking to acquire the Riley ranch. That would be most unfortunate. From what I have been told your land is still rather pristine—numerous species of native grasses and an abundance of wildlife including trophy mule deer and pronghorn antelope. I commend you and your family for your stewardship."

Ezra was unmoved by the compliment. "So you want my ranch too," he said. He and Pratt sat on the same side of a table but several feet apart. It was still too close and Ezra was tempted to get up and walk out. He remembered a cool, dark barn and blows that caused the stars to fall from the sky and into his mind.

De la Rosa leaned back and broke into a broad, white smile, then bent forward, his hands cupped as if praying. "Yes, I want your ranch. It will be a cooperative effort," he explained. "The ISF is interested in not only the Riley ranch, but the holdings of Mr. Wilson as well. We can offer you long-term employment as manager and ownership of your residence including forty, fifty acres around your home and buildings. And you would not only manage the Riley ranch, Ezra, you would have control over Mr. Wilson's as well." He was welcoming Ezra to a land buffet. Eat all you want.

Ezra was not ready to dine. "I didn't know Shorty Wilson's place was for sale."

"It's not. But, Mr. Wilson has ... *difficulties* ... that even he is not yet aware of."

"I know my uncle has no intention of selling."

"I am sure he doesn't. He doesn't need to. Time passes. Your uncle is an old man. When the time comes to settle the estate, we will be there for you. We will protect you from the government and the lawyers."

Ezra glanced at Sandoval, then back at de la Rosa. He did not bother to look at Pratt. He considered bringing the matter of Pratt into the conversation—*And what is your connection with a woman beater and self-styled Baal priest?*—but thought better of it. He was, afterall, outnumbered three to one by men who enjoyed killing. "This is all about hunting, isn't it?" he said.

De la Rosa nodded. "I won't lie to you, Ezra. The ISF is an organization founded by sportsmen. Without habitat there is no game. I know you are knowledgeable of the Buffalo Commons proposal and the Big Open. We believe that some form of prairie restoration is inevitable. The public is for it because the environmentalists have the media in their pocket. In time, much of the Great Plains, from Saskatchewan to New Mexico, will be restored to native grasses and native species."

"Public land or private?" Ezra asked. He knew the question rankled Pratt. He could feel him bristle.

De la Rosa was as smooth as hair conditioner—untangling knots and leaving everything with a shine. "A mixture of both," he said. "I am a capitalist, Ezra. I am hardly opposed to private ownership of land, it's simply that circumstances are likely to be difficult in this area, particularly if one procrastinates. The wave going out takes you to sea; the wave coming in crashes you on the beach."

"Ocean metaphors mean nothing to me," Ezra said. "I'm a cowboy, not a sailor."

"Yes, that is correct. And a good one I am sure."

"There will be elk and bison on this prairie?" Ezra asked.

"The grasslands are their native habitat."

"And wolves?" He slanted the energy of the question toward Pratt.

De la Rosa sighed. "They are inevitable. They will come from Canada and Alaska on their own, and if not, the environmentalists will cry and moan until they have them. We simply do not want the wolves to be the only hunters on the plains."

"You are the human wolves?" Ezra asked.

De la Rosa laughed. His voice was as clear as a school bell on a cool morning. "The ISF wants to be a player. The Buffalo Commons concept has its political dangers. It is not unreasonable to think that the antihunting elements might try to keep the sportsmen out."

"We are not talking about Joe Six-pack who reads *Outdoor Life* are we? This is exclusive. Trophy hunting for the very wealthy."

De la Rosa shrugged. "It is unfortunate, but it is what the world is coming to. Anything rare is valuable and affordable to only those who have the resources."

"You must want a lot of land."

"Our goal is five million acres, hopefully much of it will be contiguous." He said it factually. There was no arrogance or excitement in his voice. It was a figure—a goal—and he was a businessman.

Ezra was not as detached. "Five million acres?" he said, astonished.

"Yes, five million acres. And you can be a part of it, Ezra. In fact, you can be part of the beginning."

Alpha, Ezra thought. *The beginning.* His land was their jumping-off point. "The Riley ranch," he explained, "is less than forty thousand acres."

Pratt broke in. "For who has despised the day of small things," he said. "Zechariah 4:10." There was mockery in his voice, a snarl from the corner of a downturned lip, as he quoted the Bible. Ezra glanced at de la Rosa. He seemed to merely tolerate Pratt, like a general putting up with an annoying but valuable soldier.

"Five million acres," Ezra said again. "There cannot be enough bison in the world to stock such an enterprise."

"It will take years," de la Rosa agreed. "There are only 150,000 bison in America, and most of them are in private herds. In the meantime we will avail ourselves of the best alternatives."

"Which are?"

"Wild horned cattle. Longhorns, Scottish Highlanders, and for the southern states, Brahman. Cattle with heart. *Bos Indicus,* when possible, as opposed to the slow, dim-witted *Bos taurus,* such as Hereford and Angus."

"Wild cattle with horns," Ezra mused. "Cattle with heads that would look good mounted on someone's wall."

De la Rosa nodded. "We *are* hunters," he reminded Ezra.

Ezra could not help but be impressed. The grandeur of the plan was staggering. Millions of acres of restored prairie with wild cattle, elk, bison, and bear.

"I imagine you are an admirer of your state's two greatest artists, C. M. Russell and Will James," the Brazilian said. "Imagine what they would think of such a plan. I can only guess that they would think highly of it indeed."

Ezra thought about it: C. M. Russell painting elk and wolves on the prairie beneath a blazing sunset, Will James sketching a mossy-horned longhorn cow with fire burning in her eyes.

"You have handled some difficult stock in your life, Ezra—*rank,* I believe, is the term you Montana cowboys use. Rank stock. Your uncles once experimented with Highlanders. Imagine crossbreeding them with longhorns and stocking them with bison in pastures of twenty, forty, even fifty thousand acres."

"It could be interesting," Ezra admitted. He imagined making a dead run on Shiloh at a herd of feral cattle: shaggy-haired Highlanders, wild-colored longhorns, their genetically explosive offspring. Horns wider than horse trailers. Ezra could almost feel the swirl of the rope as he built a loop big enough to sail around a seven-foot horn spread.

"I believe your ranch is near the airport," de la Rosa said. "Perhaps if you were to drive me to my jet—just you and I, Demetrius can take Mr. Sandoval—you could show me your beloved hills."

Ezra measured the thought. He was not afraid of being alone with the man. It would be safer than having Pratt and Sandoval along for company. "Okay," he said.

"Excellent," de la Rosa said. "It is important that we get to know each other better." He smiled at Ezra as if together, the two of them could own the world.

CHAPTER NINETEEN

A sleek, silver jet was parked on the runway of the airport. It spoke to Ezra of speed, money, and the future, while he drove a pickup older than his teenaged son. In his rearview mirror he saw Pratt and Sandoval turn toward the jet. For an instant he wondered what de la Rosa's home in Brazil must be like. Then he wondered how the man made his money.

He drove across a high plateau that led to the opening of the wide expanse of the Yellow Rock River's north side, a large canvas of earth tones sprinkled with a hint of green. The short threadleaf sedge, called "nigger's wool" by the locals, was glistening from the morning's shower as were the imported crested wheat grasses and the renegade cheat grass.

The Brazilian was transfixed by the scenery. "*Bromus tectorum,*" he said.

"Pardon me?" Ezra said.

"Downy brome. I believe the local nickname is 'cheat grass.'"

"There's lots of it," Ezra said. It was a tenacious invader plant that was crowding out the native grasses. "But you didn't come all the way from Rio just to see me or look at cheat grass," he added.

"No. I have been at an ISF board meeting in Denver."

"Pratt wasn't at the meeting?"

"No, Demetrius has his social limitations."

They passed Ezra's house, then Solomon's, and turned onto a graveled county road. De la Rosa gestured at a large field of crested wheat grass, last year's stalks standing like straw glued to the prairie floor. "Conservation Reserve Program?" he asked.

Ezra nodded. "CRP. Shorty Wilson's." The disdain in his voice was evident. De la Rosa noted it. "Do not worry about Mr. Wilson," he said. "He shall be taken care of, but I am afraid your friend Mikal Mora will be the cost of my considerations."

Ezra gave de la Rose a glare that said more than words.

"Agent Mora has nothing on Demetrius, Ezra," the Brazilian explained. "Just the same, he has become a hindrance. I do not need your help to remove him, but out of courtesy, I am asking your permission to do so."

"What do you mean, *remove him?*"

"Oh, it's not what you think," de la Rosa said soothingly. "I am an art and antiques dealer, Ezra, not a gangster. But I have friends in your government, including some in the U.S. Fish and Wildlife Service, who are not opposed to the Buffalo Commons idea. Think about it. They need wildlife habitat more than anyone. Demetrius has known about Mora from the beginning. All I need to do is let my FWS friends know that Mora's cover is blown. They will reassign him, probably back to chasing alligator poachers in Louisiana."

"And Wilson? What are you going to do to him?" Ezra asked. Wilson was a contemptible human being, but he *was* Ezra's neighbor.

"Don't worry. It is not what we are going to do, it is what Mr. Wilson has already done to himself."

The gumbo buttes of the Riley ranch rose in front of their windshield like a long row of dark elephants walking trunk to tail. Ezra pulled onto a pasture road that led to a high ridge in the center of the ranch. The Brazilian was beguiling and Ezra felt the need to clear the air. "I want to talk to you about Pratt," he said. "He attacked me in my barn. You and I won't do any business as long as Pratt is involved."

"Demetrius attacked you? Oh, I find that hard to believe."

"Why?" Ezra asked. He noticed two mule deer bedded in the brush in a coulee below them. He glanced at de la Rosa. The Brazilian saw them but made no comment.

"Why do I think it wasn't Demetrius?" de la Rosa laughed and waved one hand in the hair like sweeping a canvas with a brush. "First of all, you are alive. Second, Demetrius has some sense of honor, he would not ambush you."

"He did it once to a friend of mine," Ezra argued. "And he beats women."

"Oh, my, don't be so quick to judge a man for his past," de la Rosa said. "You are a man of the Word, remember? As for striking a woman, it is all a difference in cultures, Ezra. But I am a reasonable man. You let me have Mora, I will give you Wilson, and I will see that Demetrius is sent on a long *scouting* trip. Perhaps Australia."

"Pratt should be behind bars."

"Hmmm, that's asking a little too much. Besides, I still doubt it was he who attacked you. Did you actually see him?"

Ezra shook his head reluctantly.

"No? I didn't think so. Demetrius might 'count coup,' as he calls it, but nothing more, not without staring into your eyes first."

"The *conversation of death?*"

"An interesting concept, isn't it? I don't know if it actually exists or not, but Demetrius thinks so and he is an amazing hunter." A herd of thirty antelope boiled from the sagebrush and fled across a grass covered plain. De la Rosa followed them with the eyes of a German shepherd that lusted to pursue but knew it wasn't allowed. Ezra noted that he seemed more excited by animals that fled than those that lay quietly and watched.

"An amazing hunter?" Ezra said. "More like an amazing poacher."

"Semantics. Mere semantics in our modern world."

"Pratt has been on my ranch looking for a *thin place*. Do you know what that is?"

De la Rosa stared out the window. "No, I can't say that I do. I'm Catholic, Ezra. Demetrius's spiritual obsessions have never interested me. I ignore them."

"You seem to like him." Ezra slowed while a herd of his uncle's cattle crossed the pasture road in front of them. The Brazilian showed no interest in the livestock.

"I am fond of Demetrius," de la Rosa said. "He has been responsible for adding some wonderful specimens to my collection. Now I admit to you, he has his strange side. Does he have an alias currently? He likes to give himself code names."

"I think it is Alpha," Ezra said.

"Alpha. And what does that mean to you?"

"Several things. Christ said He was the Alpha and the Omega, the beginning and the end. Pratt believes he is the beginning of something. Also, he is obsessed with wolves. The dominant male in a pack is called the alpha male."

"That's good," de la Rosa said. "Very good. When I first met Demetrius he called himself Nimrod."

Ezra stopped the truck on the Grassy Crown. They seemed high above everything but the sky itself. Expanses of prairie and badlands, kissed by the morning shower, rolled in every direction, and for every square mile of land there were multiples more of clear sky that loomed above them like a huge concave bowl with bits of cotton suspended beneath its dome. Shadows of high-peaked buttes stretched in long fingers from west to east, while cloud shadows floated softly across an earth that was a quilted work of black, brown, yellow, and green patches. Above it all, the blue ceiling was streaked with slashes of crimson and creamy puffs of white clouds that moved in a floating herd of silent migration.

"Sunset in Montana," de la Rosa sighed. "It is exactly as your Charley Russell painted it. I have an original of his, you know. You must come to Rio and see it sometime." He stepped outside onto the Grassy Crown, an ancient volcanic upthrust carpeted with threadleaf sedge. "Amazing," he said, turning slowly in a circle and drinking in the vastness of the plains and buttes.

In three directions the prairie eventually rolled to land of another color, land either farmed or coated with the straw coloring of CRP. That was the Riley boundary with Shorty Wilson's land. To the north was only the twisted, convoluted clay mazes of the badlands. De la Rosa turned in that direction. "*Mako shika*," he said softly. "You know what it means?"

"It is Sioux," Ezra said, "for 'the no-good land.'"

"Yes. The no-good land. The badlands."

"The badlands have always been my favorite," Ezra said. "They are a place of history and mystery."

"Wildness," de la Rosa said. "The untamable. Now imagine those badlands as home once again to bison, elk, bear, and wolves. And imagine herds of wild cattle with horns the length of fence posts."

"Yes," Ezra said, reliving the dreams of his boyhood. "I can almost see it."

"Excellent," de la Rosa said, his face glowing in the lowering light. It was a healthy face, conditioned by the outdoors, radiant from the luxuries of wealth, and jeweled with twinkling eyes. He opened his arms in a wide gesture as if to embrace and encircle the landscape. "Now imagine it all as yours," he said.

Ezra looked long and hard into the shining eyes. "You mean the ISF's," he said.

De la Rosa laughed. "It can be one and the same," he said.

Ezra looked again. The land seemed to twinkle with a new light as if all his childhood dreams had risen from a gumbo slumber and were bathed in the dawn of hope. "I will prove my good intentions," he heard de la Rosa say. "I am flying from here to a meeting in Calgary. I will take Demetrius with me. You will not have to worry about Mr. Pratt again."

Ezra looked at him suspiciously. "You are a man of your word?" he asked.

"Oh, Ezra," the Brazilian said. His face faded in the decreasing light, and he seemed to fade into the landscape behind him. "I am *definitely* a man of my word." His voice seemed to come from the land itself.

CHAPTER TWENTY

It was his first good night's sleep in a long time. Hard, fast, and heavy. He would have slept longer except Dylan knocked on the bedroom door.

"Dad," he said, "I'm leaving for school."

Ezra rolled over and stared at the clock. It took his mind a few seconds to grasp the details. He was in bed alone. It was Tuesday. He had met with de la Rosa the night before, and it was now 7:28 in the morning.

"You okay, Dad?"

"Yeah, I just overslept," Ezra mumbled. Dylan said good-bye and moments later the boy's pickup left the yard. Ezra remembered he had forgotten to check heifers and roused himself from bed, stumbled to the bathroom, splashed several handfuls of cold water on his face, then dressed, and went to the kitchen.

There was a note on the table from Dylan: *Dad, I checked heifers at 6:15. One calved, and the calf is okay. Hope you had sweet dreams. Dylan.* Ezra sighed with appreciation and made a pot of stout coffee. After his second cup his mind began to clear and his senses sharpened. He called Anne.

"Are you skipping school again today?" he asked her.

"Yes," she said. "I know it's setting me back but Diamond isn't ready to be left alone."

"I think it's time you two moved back out here," Ezra said. "It's safe. Pratt's in Calgary."

"In Canada? I thought you said he was in South Dakota."

"That was a ruse. He's in Calgary."

"How do you know?" she asked suspiciously.

"I have talked with Pratt," Ezra said. "And I've met and talked with Antonio de la Rosa."

"You've what!" she said angrily. "Ezra, you didn't really, did you?"

"Yeah, I did. I met de la Rosa yesterday, and I even gave him a quick tour of the ranch."

"Ezra, I can't believe you did that."

"It's a long story, Anne. I'll tell you about it later. But tell Diamond that de la Rosa took Pratt away. You can come home."

It was a lot for Anne to process. "Give me the day to work on her," she said. "Maybe I can get her to come out tomorrow morning."

"Okay, tomorrow. But, Anne, I'm tired of sleeping alone. Can you leave Diamond there alone for the night?"

"Alone? Oh, I don't think so. She's not going to believe Pratt is in Canada."

"Dylan could stay there."

"Betty Lou would love that, and you know she would find out."

Ezra put the phone down and brought his third cup of coffee to his lips. Pratt was gone. It was time to deal with Shorty Wilson. After doing the morning chores, Ezra visited his lawyer, Jacob Greene, a second-generation Yellow Rock attorney and specialist in land dealings. He was an older man with white hair and a leathery face lined by smoking, drinking, and walking the fairways of the town's golf course.

"Have you heard any rumors about Shorty Wilson making a play for the Riley ranch?" he asked Greene.

"There's been some talk on the street," Greene admitted.

"What kind of talk?"

The attorney lit a cigarette and blew the smoke upward as if dispelling a darker cloud. "The talk on the street," he said, "is that Wilson is about to add to his landholdings."

"My place?"

"That's the rumor."

"He would need the cooperation of one of my sisters, wouldn't he?"

"Yes. Or you. Any three of you could file to have the estate divided. It can't be divided equitably, so the judge would rule for a public auction."

"How about the name Antonio de la Rosa? Have you ever heard of him?"

"No," Greene said and waited for Ezra to tell him more.

"He wants the ranch too," Ezra said. "He approached me yesterday. He's offering to let me keep fifty acres and the house and manage the place for him." He did not mention de la Rosa's larger plans.

"Your two sisters would have to agree to that," Greene said. "And it would involve your uncle too."

"What happens if my uncle dies without a will?"

Greene's eyes became deep and somber. "You are going to have a mess," he said. "One huge mess."

Ezra stared vacantly at the paintings on the wall. The lawyer had an excellent collection of original western art. He wanted to escape into the romance portrayed in the brushwork, colors, and forms.

"There's not much else I can tell you," Greene said. "There's no action until someone puts the ball in play."

"Thanks," Ezra said, rising from the chair. He paused at the door, wondering if he should have Greene try to get information on de la Rosa. But where would the lawyer begin and how much would it cost? He could learn as much from Mikal, he decided, once Mikal returned from South

Dakota. He left the office with a sick feeling in his stomach. Land, lawyers, and family. What an unholy trinity.

He went home and did more groundwork with Cajun, and in a moment of confidence, Ezra climbed into the saddle. The colt stood quietly, waiting with a calm expectation. Ezra let him feel his weight for a few minutes then took a handful of mane in his left hand and swung lightly to the ground. It was a small victory but a valuable one. The first time on a colt had a way of making Ezra young and flexible again.

That evening Ezra knocked out a hundred push-ups before showering—he had to stay in shape to compete with Mikal—then slipped on a pair of Wranglers and a T-shirt. It was exactly two weeks ago that he had come home to find Diamond asleep in the basement. So much had happened in so little time.

He was home alone. Dylan had stayed in town after tennis practice to attend an FCA meeting, so Ezra turned the television to their single channel. Its show was a corny sitcom with an annoying laugh track, so he turned the television off, and picked the latest Anne Tyler novel from his bookshelf. Ezra loved Tyler. Her plots were uncomplicated, but her prose was like vitamins for the soul, and her characters were so believable they followed you to bed long after you laid the book down.

He was in the third chapter when he was startled by a soft rapping on the front door. The porch light illuminated Lilith standing on the steps with a covered casserole dish in her hands. "Hi," she said as he opened the door. "I brought you something." She brushed close to Ezra as she entered. "I didn't know if the girl was staying here or not, but just in case, I thought you could use an extra meal. It's lasagna." She handed Ezra the dish.

"Thanks," he said. "I like lasagna, and Dylan is crazy about it."

"It needs to be cooked at 375 for about an hour."

"Come in," he said. "I'll put this in the fridge." He motioned for her to take a chair at the table.

"Where's Anne?" she asked, seating herself. Her tone seemed childlike in its curiosity.

"Anne and Diamond haven't been staying here," Ezra explained. "We were worried about Pratt. But, as it turns out, Pratt is now in Canada."

"Canada. How convenient. Well, I'm sorry your wife isn't here. You know I haven't really met her. Not formally."

"You haven't?" Ezra was surprised, he had assumed the two knew each other.

"No. We see each other at church, but we've never been introduced."

"I'm sorry," Ezra said, "I thought—"

"That's okay. I'm capable of introducing myself."

In the folds of a short silence Ezra realized the two families had never united. "I don't really know Ben either," he admitted. "When things settle down we'll all have to get together."

"Yes," she said. "We'll have to do that."

"So," Ezra said. "How was your week?"

She smiled and little flashes of light danced in her violet eyes. Her graceful, tapered hands remained folded softly in her lap. "Actually, I'm mad at you. You never told me you were a published writer."

Ezra shrugged. "Just one small book," he said.

"One very good small book," she corrected him. "I was in a gift shop downtown when I saw it. I couldn't believe it was you until I read the first few pages, then I knew. How has it done for you?"

"It hasn't earned back its advance," he said.

"But the clerk told me it had won a couple of national awards."

"Awards can be a guarantee against commercial success."

"Well, I think the book is lovely. I read it in one sitting. Your love for the land and animals radiates from every page, and the writing is very poetic."

"Thank you," Ezra said, embarrassed by the compliments. "Speaking of hidden talents, Lilith. You never told me you sang. I suppose you play instruments too."

"The piano and the guitar."

"The same as Anne."

"Yes. Small world, isn't it?"

"Anyway, thanks for the help Sunday. You got me out of a bind."

"How is the girl?" Lilith asked. "Something at church must have really disturbed her."

"She's fine. Pratt has spent the past five years brainwashing her, making her believe that Christianity is evil. I'm not surprised that she's uncomfortable in church."

"What are you going to do with her?" she teased. "I mean, are you going to adopt her or what?"

"Anne would like to." Ezra smiled. "I don't think Dylan would mind either. We're trying to reach her cousin in Kansas. She'll stay with us until then. She and Anne are moving back here tomorrow."

"She's very pretty," Lilith said. "What is her lineage? Sioux? Blackfoot?"

"Sioux, I think," Ezra said. "She's never really said."

"By her coloring I would say she has some French-Canadian blood."

For a reason he could not explain Ezra became uncomfortable talking about Diamond. He changed the subject. "And you're okay?" he asked again. "No trials or tests this week?"

"No, nothing. My life has been very normal and routine."

"And boring?" Ezra suggested.

She vacillated. "Why? Do you think I bore easily?"

"Yes. You probably do."

"Maybe. But boredom is okay right now. I can live with it. How about you? Your life certainly hasn't been boring."

"I could use a safe, boring week."

Lilith shook her head. "You are more like me than you think, Ezra. Neither of us handles boredom well. That is why you have Anne and I have Ben. They are our anchors."

"You think Anne and Ben are boring?" Ezra asked.

"I didn't say that. They are . . ." She paused, bringing a finger to her lips. "*Grounded,*" she declared. "Very grounded."

Ezra chuckled. "I will tell Anne you said that."

"Don't you dare," she flared. "She will take it wrong. Anne is a lovely woman. I envy her in many ways."

"How is that?" Ezra asked cautiously.

"How she conducts praise and worship. She is so relaxed, so honest. There is not an ounce of performance in the woman."

"I thank you on Anne's behalf. And I'm sure Ben has some very good traits too."

"Ben is Ben," she said. "He's very kind. We have been all through that, haven't we?"

Ezra folded his arms across his chest, knowing it was a defensive posture. "Does he resent me?" he asked.

"Of course," she said, smiling coyly. "But it's nothing you've done. It's what you are. Ben is very insecure in many ways. He thinks he's short, and he doesn't think being an office supplies salesman is very masculine. He would like to be a big, brawny truck driver or a cowboy like you."

"Would he really?"

"No." She laughed. "It's odd that he's a salesman, though, because he isn't at all pushy. But he does quite well. I think people buy from him because they feel sorry for him."

"Do you?"

"Do I what?" Her eyes narrowed as if her mind was squeezing the question.

"Do you feel sorry for him?"

"Is this a counseling session?" she asked. "I thought I was just bringing you dinner."

"Sorry. You don't have to answer that." Ezra knew he too easily became analytical with people. It was as much the poet in him as it was the lay counselor. He naturally sought depth and motivation and shunned superficiality.

"It's okay," she said. "To be honest, you might be right; maybe I do feel sorry for him. But don't all men want sympathy?"

"No. Most men want understanding, not sympathy. And certainly not pity."

"Pity? That's a little condescending, isn't it?" Her eyes narrowed. "You think I'm an enabler, don't you? You think I want him weak so I will appear strong."

"Do you?" Ezra asked. It was his habit to push the limits of a relationship. He was willing to risk his friendship with Lilith if probing dangerous areas helped shed light on the roots of her problems.

Her voice became cool and rich, like good bourbon poured over ice. "I don't appreciate the direction this discussion is taking," she said. "Perhaps I should leave and we can try again when you are less distracted." She shifted in her chair to rise.

"Wait," Ezra said, lifting his hand. "I'm sorry if I offended you. It wasn't intentional. I know you didn't come out here tonight to be counseled. I'm sorry. I slip into my psychological role too easily sometimes."

"Okay," she agreed, resettling herself in the chair. "But turnabout is fair play. Why are you so on edge tonight?"

"Rough week," he said.

"Have you heard from your sister or Shorty Wilson?"

"No."

"Oh." She blushed. "It's Anne, isn't it? I mean, the two of you are separated, you are not sleeping together—"

"I don't think we want to go in that direction," Ezra warned.

"But it has to be hard on the two of you," Lilith protested. "And Anne is in such a demanding nursing program. Taking care of Diamond must be very draining for her."

"It is," Ezra said. "But Dylan is helping with the girl."

"You have a wonderful son," Lilith said. "I'm surprised you and Anne have only the one child. Didn't you want more?"

"Yes, but it never worked out. Finances mostly."

"You wanted a daughter, didn't you?"

"Sure. So did Anne."

"What would your daughter have been like?" she asked.

Ezra smiled. "She would have been tall like her mother but athletic like me. She would have been a tomboy, the kind of girl who was feminine, but happy to be working outside with her dad. Dylan is fortunate— he got both my and Anne's sensitive, creative sides. My daughter would have had some spunk and fire."

"Her daddy's girl, and ornery like you," Lilith joked.

"Spirited," Ezra corrected her teasingly.

"You have described my daughter perfectly," Lilith said. "Hillary is everything you mentioned."

"Well, we know where she gets it," Ezra said.

Lilith laughed. "I have a favor to ask," she said. "For our next counseling session I would like to come back here to the ranch."

"We could all have dinner sometime," Ezra agreed. "Once Diamond is either gone or a little more settled."

"No, what I would really like to do," she said, "is go riding with you. I have this feeling that to really know you I have to see you on horseback."

"Can you ride?" he asked.

"I competed in English for two years. Hunter-jumpers and dressage."

"I should have known."

"Is it a date?" she asked.

"It's a date," he agreed, then quickly regretted the choice of words. *Date.* Her word that he had agreed with.

"Fine. We must do it before the weather gets warm." She stroked her cheek. "The sun, you know. I have this condition." She rose from the chair. "Well, I must get back to Ben and Hillary. Enjoy the lasagna."

He walked her to the door. She paused before leaving and the porch light backlit her hair with a reddish halo. The hallway was narrow and she was pressed close to him.

"You are not a good bachelor," she said. She observed the questioning in his eyes, then brought a hand to Ezra's chest. "Crumbs. You have crumbs on your shirt." Her hand rested there lightly on his chest before she flicked the crumbs off.

He had felt an electricity in her touch.

She smiled, then lowered her eyes. "I better go," she said.

"Yes," he nodded. An arousal coiled within his body that he fought to suppress, forcing it down as if he were compressing a spring. She turned and bounced lightly down the steps. He turned out the light after she started her car.

Ezra fell asleep once Dylan came home. Sleep was like a black ocean, and he sank to its depths. It was a dreamless ocean, no thoughts passed like flashing schools of silvery fish, no colors filtered down, no sounds reverberated.

He was deep, far below the howls of subconscious fears, insulated from the static electricity of his own idling mind. He was like a fetus in a womb, connected to consciousness by the thinnest of umbilical cords.

Suddenly a terrible pleasure descended upon him, sweeping down like a manta ray, spreading and wrapping its wings about him in a fiercely passionate embrace. He tasted its terrible need and zeal, felt himself yielding to its demands and controls.

His flesh erupted with fire, and his breathing became rapid and labored as the terrible pleasure settled heavily upon him.

A sudden alarm rang in Ezra Riley's soul, and he struggled to consciousness, flung the blankets from his bed, and toppled heavily to the floor. He lay there, his body drenched with sweat, his face pressed against the carpet.

"God," he whispered. A prayer, not a blasphemy.

"God, what was *that*?"

PART 2

The watchman said,
"The morning comes,
and also the night."
Isaiah 21:12

CHAPTER TWENTY-ONE

*"Look at this country," Uncle Joe said, his fat arm
sweeping the horizon. "Without rain it looks like asphalt, concrete, and pavement. A man might as well live
in New York City as live here in a dry year. But with
some rain at the right time grass grows everywhere.
This old land changes from being a beggar in dirty
clothes to bein' a pretty woman dressed in her Sunday
best. Dang, a guy can't help but love and hate it at the
same time."*

Leaving the Land

Two weeks later. Early May.

It had become a dream world. Armadas of puffy cumulus clouds patrolled the sky, casting a patchwork of cascading shadows upon verdant land. The hardpan flats were frosted with wild onion flowertops, and the creek banks were freckled with yellow sweet peas. The frequent rainshowers had left a fragrance of fertility and growth wafting on moist breezes. The land seemed to shout with life and applaud its own celebration.

Ezra watched her ride. She was a lone figure against the May sky, her hair rising and falling in rhythm with the powerful gait of the horse. They moved in unity. Certain women had the magic. They more than mastered the animal; they absorbed its very energy with a subtle dominance.

Cajun pricked his ears and watched the display curiously. It was Ezra's fourth ride on the colt. They rested on a high, wide plateau, an epicenter for Lilith and Shiloh as they cirumscribed a perimeter as if defining and possessing both the land and the moment. Their revolutions were the quiet cutting of a glass circle, and Ezra mused that the plateau might break away and become a disk floating in space, reflecting the sunlight like a porcelain saucer.

He watched the sun glisten off her hair. He felt the softness in her hands and the pressure of her legs as she reined his horse in slow figure eights, then slid him on his hocks, his massive hindquarters hinging, absorbing and braking at the edge of the ridge, hundreds of feet above a palette of badlands swirling in a mixture of mauves, beiges, browns, and blues. She executed a perfect rollback and trotted slowly toward Ezra, her slender body rising in a precise and timed bobbing, her face flushed by fresh air, excitement, and power. She rode up to him.

"Shiloh's wonderful," Lilith said. "So powerful, yet so willing."

"He wasn't always so willing," Ezra said. "He gave me a test or two in breaking him."

She patted Shiloh's massive neck and fingered his flaxen mane. "He's a warhorse," she said. "A man's horse." He noticed a tinge of envy and excitement in her tone. She brushed her hair back and sighed, twisting in the saddle to drink in the full circle of scenery. "It's so beautiful," she said. "Thank you for letting me ride."

"You're welcome anytime," he said. "There are plenty of times when I not only like the company but I need the help."

"I would love to help you," Lilith said. "But it will need to be early in the morning or on cloudy days. I have, uh, a condition, that . . . well, I shouldn't get too much sun."

He looked at the Mediterranean tinge to her skin and nodded. She did not seem so fair. She looked like she would tan naturally, beautifully.

"Have you taken Diamond riding yet?" she asked.

"No. She is still very uneasy around me. Anne spends every available minute with her. So does Dylan. But she still looks at me with fear."

"She will learn to love you."

They rode back to the ranch slowly and quietly. It was perfect weather. Ezra wore a black felt hat, denim jacket, and chinks—short chaps he had cut to size from a pair of his father's old batwings. A black nylon scarf was wrapped and knotted around his neck. He let her take the lead as they descended a narrow trail that cut along the lip of a cliff like a razor slash. One hundred feet below them were the rocks and slow streaming of Sunday Creek.

"I better not look down," she joked, and he heard the playful thrill of danger trill through her voice.

He glanced back and caught her looking down.

"I do not know your sisters but I understand them now," she said as the horses splashed through the blue-brown water of the creek.

"What do you mean?" he asked. He stopped to let his horse drink. With the corral in sight neither horse was thirsty but they lowered their heads, nosed the water restlessly, and sipped enough to wash their mouths and bridle bits.

"There are time warps to life," she said. "Times that are so horrible or so magical, or both, that people become trapped in them, like a needle stuck on a phonograph. It must have been similiar to that for your sisters. Imagine their summers! Riding horses under puffy clouds and towering cottonwood trees with the strong, silent presence of a man beside them. I know your father didn't talk to them often. He didn't have to. They read his heart by the set of his jaw, the twinkle of his eyes, the way he set a saddle and held the reins in his hands."

"You are probably right," he said. He let himself look at her and wonder if she were real. She was so beautiful, so contained within the ideal surroundings that she became many facets of young womanhood: sister, daughter, friend. Lover? But he had trouble seeing her as a wife, either his or Ben's. Her independence, he thought.

"It is different between fathers and daughters than it is between fathers and sons," she reflected. "Your sisters probably hated coming home after a day of riding because they had their father all to themselves in the hills. At home they shared him with an envious mother who wanted to be in the hills herself, but was bound by position and duty."

"She extracted her revenge," he said.

"Mothers always do. They have all day to imagine them."

They led their horses into the barn and unsaddled them. She stripped Shiloh of Anne's saddle, placed it on a rack in the tack room, then patted the horse on the neck and kissed him lightly on the nose. The horses were led to the gate and unbridled. They walked far enough to find bare ground, then rolled repeatedly to scratch and dry their backs. Shiloh and Cajun rose, shook a cloud of dust, pointed their ears like gunsights to the south, and galloped down the creek. Ezra thought he could feel the vibrations of their hooves resound through the earth and into his feet.

She watched the horses run. "Wonderful," she said.

They walked back to the barn and hung the bridles on nails in the tack room. As they stepped back into the shadowed saddling stall, she stopped and looked around. "This is where you were attacked?" she asked.

It broke the spell for him, reminding him of another world, a desert planet where dreams did not come true. "Yes," he said.

"I'm sorry," she said. "You didn't want to think about it, did you?"

"That's okay. It happened. It just seems like a long time ago now."

"But no reports on this Pratt guy? No one has seen him?"

"No," Ezra said. He had not told Lilith about his meeting with Pratt and de la Rosa. He had only told Anne. "He has slunk off like a wounded coyote seeking a hole," he said. They stepped from the stall to the corral. He continued walking toward the gate but she stopped.

"You think he's gone for good, don't you?" she said.

He turned and looked at her. He didn't say anything. He simply held her eyes.

Her eyes were sad. "I don't think he's really gone," she said.

The forecast called for more showers that night, but it did not rain. It snowed. The winds began buffeting the house just after dark. Anne stayed in the bedroom and studied. Once she poked her head out and asked: "What's going on outside?"

"Spring storm," Ezra said.

Ezra went to the family room where Dylan was soaking his ankle. He had turned it badly that day on the tennis courts. The divisional tournament was only days away, and it appeared he would not make it. He was disappointed but remained cheerful. "I'm not going to worry about things I can't control," he told his father.

Diamond sat on the floor. She and Dylan were watching *Home Improvement*. Television was strange and wonderful for Diamond. It relaxed her. She seldom talked to Ezra. Sometimes she looked at him and smiled self-consciously, but she never held his eyes for more than an instant.

Ezra went to his corner chair in the living room and sat with a novel in his lap. Lilith's question kept him from reading. *You think he's gone for good, don't you?* Yes, he did. De la Rosa had taken care of Pratt, probably assigning him to caribou poaching in the Yukon.

He thought about how he had heard nothing from Shorty Wilson or his lawyer. It was okay not hearing from them and better yet not to think about them at all. He suddenly wondered if this was what his father had done those quiet evenings when he had sat in this same corner with a horse magazine in front of him. Perhaps he had not thought about horses at all but about other, deeper issues, concerns, or worries.

No, Ezra decided, he had thought about horses.

He put the novel away and picked up his Bible. It was a good evening to prepare for his fourth Sunday in the pulpit. He had played it safe the past Sunday by teaching a simple lesson from the Gospel of John: "For everyone practicing evil hates the light and does not come to the light, lest his deeds should be exposed."

This evening he was drawn to 1 Kings and the story of Jezebel acquiring Naboth's land for her husband, Ahab. Reading about a controlling woman's manipulations to acquire land unsettled him. He put the Bible away and felt drawn to the woman of his heart, his steady Anne, the least manipulative person he had ever known. But he found she had left her books and gone to bed. Maybe she had had another headache, he thought, but her headaches seemed to only occur in church.

Anne was asleep on her side with her back to him when he came to bed. He pressed his body against hers and rested his right hand on her hip. She was blanketed in exhaustion and did not feel his touch. Finally he rolled over onto his other side and they slept back-to-back, their closed eyes facing toward opposite directions.

They awakened to fourteen inches of wet snow. It clung to corral rails and tree limbs, blanketed the pickups and enshrouded the hills.

"This will really make the grass grow," Anne said, staring out the kitchen window.

"Yes," Ezra agreed. He also knew it could cause problems. Cows were still calving and the babies would be chilled, and if the sun shone brightly before the snow melted, the intense reflection would chap the teats and udders of his uncle's Herefords. He rolled his eyes but shouldered his concern privately. There was nothing worse than treating sunburned udders with bag balm. It would have to be done in the hills, roping the sore, engorged cows one at a time, breaking the scabs from the teats and lubricating the udders with lanolin. He should get help, but who? Austin Arbuckle had quit Shorty Wilson and was driving a truck. Ezra's old partner, Rick Benjamin, had never returned from Houston.

He shook his head slowly. Mendenhall. As always, the guardian angel for the Rileys was Jim Mendenhall, the aging cowboy with the liver-flushed, puffy face.

Ezra found Jim later that morning in the Buffalo Bar. He took a stool beside him. Mendenhall was drinking pineapple juice. On the wagon again.

"How's it goin', Ez?" Mendenhall asked.

"Going to be a good year for grass," Ezra said.

"Worlds of grass." Mendenhall's blue eyes sparkled in his puffy face like marbles embedded in flesh-colored pillows.

"Too bad the cattle prices won't be any good."

"You never get everything in this country," Mendenhall philosophized.

Ezra nodded knowingly and sat quietly for a moment. He let his hand run down the polished wooden bartop. It felt oiled by spilled whiskey. He hoped Betty Lou would not see him leaving the Buffalo Bar at ten o'clock in the morning.

"How's ol' Solomon?" Jim asked.

"Ornery as ever."

"I should go see him sometime."

"You should," Ezra encouraged.

"I bet the way the sun's comin' out you're going to have some sunburned Herefords," Jim said.

"That's what I came to see you about."

"When do you wanna start on 'em?"

"We'll give the country time to dry out a little," Ezra said. "Say two, three days."

"Call me," Mendenhall said.

Ezra turned and walked to the door.

"Hey," Mendenhall called after him. "Did you hear about our buddy?"

"Who's that?" Ezra asked.

"Your neighbor, Shorty Wilson."

"Shorty Wilson? What about him?"

Mendenhall raised his juice glass as if offering a toast. "The feds filed papers on him yesterday for CRP fraud and tax evasion."

De la Rosa, Ezra thought. *I will trade you Mr. Wilson for Mikal Mora,* he had said. Ezra's stare went past Jim Mendenhall, past the white-shirted bartender and the two patrons at the end of the bar. It went through the walls of the Buffalo Bar and all the way to Brazil. He thought about Mikal. Where was he? Why hadn't he called?

"What do you look so concerned for?" Mendenhall said. "You should be shoutin' for joy. You look like you've seen a ghost."

"I think I have," Ezra said, and he slid out the door.

The snow was slowly erased. In two days all but the south-slope snow-drifts were gone. The ground absorbed all that it could, then the water began running off in clear little trickles that muddied into bubbling and swollen creeks. Ezra stopped in to check on his uncle.

"Let's go look at the country," Solomon said, his eyes bright with expectancy and demands.

"I don't think we can leave the oil," Ezra said, hoping to convince his uncle to merely take a drive up the highway, let him crane his neck this way and that, say "*Humph!*" a few times, comment on the creek, and come home. Or so he hoped.

"Let's go see what we can see," Solomon said. "I ain't doin' nuthin' here."

Once on the oil Solomon inisted on trying a county road. The road was soft and greasy even though it was graveled with rocks the size of billiard balls.

"Let's look at Cow Creek," Solomon said, his eyes pinned on a distant horizon.

"The ground's too soft," Ezra argued. "We'd never get there."

"Let's try it," his uncle demanded.

They left the gravel and Ezra charged down a pasture road. The wheels dug deep ruts into the ground and flung mud back like flak. The windows became coated with gray globs of gumbo. The pickup strained, the temperature needle leaned past its balance, and the tires slipped trying to grip the greasy slopes. Three miles from the county road Ezra roared over a hill and buried the truck hood-deep in a snowbank. He quickly slammed the transmission into reverse but the truck would not budge.

"We're stuck," he said.

"Guess we shovel," Solomon said.

Guess I shovel, Ezra thought.

He shoveled for an hour, every successive scoop of wet snow increasing in weight. Sweat soaked through his shirt and jacket. It was a beautiful day. The sun was high and warm and the grass was green and nearly noisy in its growing, and Ezra was stuck in a pile of snow and mud eight miles from the house. Every time he tried to get the truck to move the wheels simply spun deeper into snow and mud. Solomon sat in the truck and observed. Once he got out and walked an inspection around the truck, but the gumbo stuck to his shoes like wet cement. He cursed at it, tried to kick it off, then scrape it off, and finally sat back in the truck and let the clay harden around his feet like a plaster cast.

"We're not getting out," Ezra said disgustedly. *Why did I do this? Why do I always give in to Solomon's most unreasonable demands?* "I'm going to have to walk home and get my pickup."

"You goin' by the road or through the hills?" the old man asked.

"Through the hills is faster."

It was closer to the county road, Ezra knew, but if no one came by and gave him a ride it was farther than to the house. Did he feel lucky? Would someone come by? No, probably not. Ezra decided to go by the hills, sticking to the high, graveled ridges.

"You stay with the truck," he told Solomon.

"I ain't goin' nowhere," his uncle grunted.

After a mile Ezra had to stop for a moment to rest. He was exhausted from the shoveling and walking in the mud, and he still had seven miles to go. It would be dark before he got home, and no one would be there. Anne had class. Dylan was taking Diamond to a church youth meeting.

Pace yourself, Ezra instructed himself. Relax and try to enjoy the walk. Escape into your imagination as you did as a child. Pretend you are alone in a world teeming with plants and animals.

His fantasies would not hold. It was not a time for childish dreaming.

It was dusk when he reached the high hills behind Solomon's house. It was another mile to his house, and he was not sure he could make it. His legs were heavy and sore. Solomon's house was locked, but Ezra had a key. Ezra decided to go there and call home. Maybe, by chance, Anne or Dylan would answer. If not, he could walk home on the highway. The paved road would seem like heaven's golden streets compared to the quagmire of creek bottoms that lay before him.

As he neared the old two-storied white house he saw the television's blue light reflecting off a window. Sol had left his television on? *He couldn't have,* Ezra thought. He trudged to the back door and checked the lock. The door was open. Ezra scraped his boots clean and entered the back porch. The noise of the NBA western finals, Houston against San Antonio, was blaring from the living room. Ezra followed the sound through the dark kitchen. Solomon was reclining on his sofa bathed in the television's light. He looked up at Ezra and smiled devilishly. "What took you so long?" he teased.

"How did you get here?" Ezra asked.

Solomon labored to a sitting position. "I got bored sittin' in the truck," he said. "So I walked to the county road. Almost didn't think I'd make it. My feet were playin' out on me. Got a ride in no time, some friend of yours."

"A friend of mine?" Ezra said.

"Yeah, some tall, longhaired guy. Said he was out there lookin' for you. He brought me home. Even came in and took a look at the arrowheads. He seemed to know an awful lot about arrowheads."

"What was his name?" Ezra said. The television screen and its eerie, lifeless light dimmed and left his focus. The room swirled, awash in his fatigue and frustration.

Solomon stared straight ahead as if he hadn't heard the question.

"What was his name?" Ezra asked again.

"Can't remember his first name." Solomon said. "It was long and different. I think Diane once called a horse by something like that."

Demetrius? "What was his last name?"

Solomon spat it out. "Pratt."

CHAPTER TWENTY-TWO

Ezra lay in bed in the dark. Anne came home at ten. He could feel the weariness in her steps. She made ready for bed in the bathroom then came quietly through the darkness and slipped under the covers. One hand reached out to touch him, to know that he was there. It lingered slightly before she began to breathe deeply. Asleep.

Ezra lay awake. In the morning he would tell Anne about Pratt, but for now he would let her rest. There was something more sinister about Pratt's second appearance. His actions seemed so brazen. But Ezra warned himself that he could be overreacting. Perhaps de la Rosa had gotten to Pratt and had convinced him to relinquish his crazy obsessions.

No, the Brazilian had promised to *remove* Pratt. And Pratt was not removed. Something was wrong.

He heard soft footsteps in the hall. Ezra dropped one hand to the floor, his fingers stretching to the .22 pistol he had again placed under the bed. Someone was standing just outside the bedroom door.

"Ezra," a soft voice said.

"Yes, Diamond."

"He's back isn't he?"

Ezra paused. The room was so dark the blackness seemed alive. "Yes," he whispered. "How did you know?"

"I can feel him," she said.

He did not hear her walk away but he knew she was gone. He sensed her move as a breeze, down the hall, down the stairway, down the basement hall, to the guest room, into her bed. He knew she would not sleep well either.

A long time later Ezra succumbed to a deep but troubled sleep. He dreamed someone came to his room and stood at the foot of his bed. He wanted to get up and chase the presence away but he was gripped and unable to move. The presence remained for several minutes. It was tall, dark, and shrouded and it reached out and touched Ezra's foot with an object—a scepter, a wand? Then it was gone, vaporized like smoke.

Anne awakened before six. Sometimes she got up early to pray and read her Bible, and sometimes she went for a short walk outside, but for the past week she was up early to do homework. The days she had missed while caretaking Diamond had jeopardized her entire semester. Ezra did not feel her leave the bed, but he awakened at the sound of her cry.

"Ezra, what's this? *Ezra!* What is this!"

He threw back the covers, sprang from the bed, and stood in the hallway in his underwear, his mind slowly allowing the light and the morning coolness to penetrate his senses. Anne stood rigidly a few feet from the kitchen table. She looked at him. Her right arm stretched out and pointed at the table. "What is this?" she repeated.

In the crack where the table leaves joined was a single tail feather from a golden eagle.

"Pratt," Ezra said, and he approached the table slowly.

"How did he get in?" Anne asked. "I locked the door when I came home. Weren't the other doors locked?" Then another thought suddenly pushed the thought about doors aside. She looked at Ezra and her mouth dropped. "Diamond," she said. Ezra pulled on a pair of Levis and followed Anne downstairs. Dylan's and Diamond's doors were both closed. The hallway was dimly lit by a single night-light near the bathroom. Anne approached Diamond's door. As she reached for the knob her bare feet touched something on the floor. She jumped back.

"What is it?" Ezra asked.

"There's something on the floor." Anne flipped on the hallway light.

Two tail feathers from a magpie lay crossed at their stems. They fanned out in a glistening black and white semicircle.

"He was down here too," Anne said. "He was down here."

"Is she still here?" Ezra asked and pushed the door open. Diamond lay in the bed clinging to sleep as tightly as she held her pillow. Ezra slowly closed the door.

"What does he want?" Anne whispered. "And how did he get in?"

They went upstairs and tested the front door and the back. Both were locked. "The other door," Anne said. They went to the living room and tried the seldom-used door that opened to their southside deck. It, too, was locked.

"He must have come in this door," Ezra said. "He simply locked it when he left."

"Ezra, what does this mean? What's with the feathers?"

"He counted coup," Ezra said. "Indians were awarded feathers for simply touching an enemy."

"You don't think he—"

"Yes, he touched me. I remember feeling something now, a presence at the foot of the bed."

Anne's mouth dropped and she stared at the floor. She shivered. "Oh, Ezra," she said. "I feel so violated. He was in this house. He was in our bedroom. I had hoped he was gone. I wanted your talk with the Brazilian to clear things up. What do the other feathers mean, the ones at Diamond's door?"

"I don't know," Ezra said. "A sign of ownership, I think. A message that he will be coming back for her or that he has the power to make her come to him."

"Ezra, we left the feathers down there. She will see them."

Footsteps sounded in the hall and they both stiffened. Dylan stepped into the kitchen, his face foggy with sleep, hair ruffled. He held the two magpie feathers in his hand. "What are these?" he said.

"Give them to me," Ezra said. "Pratt was in the house last night. We can't let Diamond know." Ezra walked to the coal-and-wood stove in the utility room, crumpled up a newspaper, put the paper in the firebox, and laid the feathers on top of it. He scratched a kitchen match against the stove and dropped it in. A blue and red flame erupted from the paper and began melting the feathers like plastic. The smoke was black and thin. Anne and Dylan stood nearby watching. Neither of them heard Diamond approach.

"He was here last night, wasn't he?" she asked from the hallway.

They turned to her dark, questioning eyes. Her body trembled like a colt twitching flies.

"Yes," Ezra said. "He was."

"I must leave," she said. "Maybe I should go back to him."

Anne encircled the girl in her arms. "No," she said. "You can't do that. You must stay with us until we reach your cousin."

"What if my cousin is gone for good?"

"She's not," Anne said. "And even if she were I would not let you go back to that man. You would stay with us."

Ezra spoke to Dylan quietly. "Do you still have those CDs of Jubal's?" he asked. The boy nodded. Ezra stepped up to the women. "Diamond," he said softly. "I want you to listen to some music this morning. I want you to listen to it carefully, and I want you to realize the man who made the music will never play again because of Demetrius Pratt."

She looked up, her dark eyes peering over Anne's shoulder as bright and curious as an otter's.

"I'm not going to school today," Anne said. "I'm staying home with Diamond."

"I can stay home too," Dylan said. He was a high school senior. Missing a day or two of school wouldn't matter.

"Okay," Ezra said. "Both of you stay with Diamond."

"What are you going to do?" Anne asked.

He looked past Anne to the Indian girl. "I'm going to the sheriff," he explained. "I will not have my home, my family, or my friends threatened. I'm sorry, Diamond. But Demetrius Pratt must be taken care of."

Sheriff Butler ushered Ezra into his private office and offered coffee, which Ezra accepted. "What's going on?" Butler asked.

"Pratt was in our house last night. He left a feather on the kitchen table and two more feathers downstairs by Diamond's bedroom door."

"Diamond's?" The sheriff's eyes were quietly demanding.

"Yeah," Ezra said. "We've had the girl with us for almost two weeks. Anne gave the girl her word that we wouldn't turn her in."

Butler nodded. He understood principles. He went to the next base. "Do you have the feathers?" he asked.

"No," Ezra confessed. "I burned them."

Butler gave him a simple look that made Ezra wish he had not reacted so quickly. The feathers were evidence.

"He is on the ranch," Ezra insisted. "Yesterday my uncle and I got stuck in the hills. I walked eight miles home. In the meantime Pratt came by and gave my uncle a ride."

"He's toying with you," Butler said. "We have a word for what he did last night. We call it a 'hot prowl.' The criminals who do hot prowls are often the most dangerous. What do you think he's after? The girl?"

Ezra nodded toward the entry. "May I close the door?"

"Sure."

Ezra leaned over and pushed the door shut. "The girl isn't it, Sheriff. She's a possession of his, not an obsession. If he loses her he will get another one. Pratt is a spiritualist. Pragmatic Mikal has a hard time believing this, but Pratt is obsessed with our ranch because he believes it has a sort of supernatural power center. He calls it a *thin place*."

Butler leaned back in his wooden chair, scratched his head, then hooked his long fingers in his gun belt. "I learn new things in law enforcement all the time," he said. "But I haven't heard this one before."

"Sheriff, I've been a lay counselor in our church for several years. I have seen much of the same stuff you've seen. Domestic abuse. Sex abuse. Alcoholism. Even rumors about satanic ritul abuse. Pratt is a new type of criminal, and his motivation is definitely spiritual."

Butler smiled wryly. "So what would you have me do, deputize a posse of priests and exorcists?"

Ezra returned the smile. "No, not unless they can shoot straight. Actually I don't know what to do. I just want you to understand the man's motivations."

Butler considered the situation. "You can file harassment and trespassing charges against Pratt," he said. "But we really don't have any proof. The girl is your key. If she would talk about the poaching, I'm sure Mora could hit your place hard. Planes, dogs, helicopters. One way or another he would flush Pratt out."

"Have you heard from Mikal?"

"Not a word, but that's not unusual. He's undercover and doesn't report to this office. The day you came in to report on the girl was only the second time I had met him. The odd thing is, I got a call from a USFWS officer yesterday. He was looking for Mikal."

Ezra shifted in his chair as he thought of de la Rosa. Maybe the threat against Mikal wasn't merely political. Should he tell Butler? Maybe he could back into the subject. "Have you heard the news on Shorty Wilson?" he asked.

Butler smiled. "Yeah, seems like Shorty himself is in a bind."

Ezra leaned forward. "Two weeks ago I met with Pratt's moneyman. I didn't think it could hurt, and I thought I might learn something. The guy is a Brazilian named de la Rosa. He told me he would have Shorty taken care of, but he needed Mora in exchange."

"How was he going to do this?"

"He must have political ties. He's blown the whistle somehow on Wilson with the feds. In turn, he's going to have Mora called off the Pratt case."

"Maybe he already has been, then. Perhaps Mora's on his way back to Louisiana."

"No. Mikal would call me. He would let me know if he was being reassigned. Besides, why would you get a call asking about him? They either got to him, or he is still in South Dakota following a trail of false clues."

Butler shrugged. "I don't have any pull with the U.S. Fish and Wildlife Service," he said. "And I have no idea how to contact Mora. If he is out of the picture then we have to deal with Pratt by ourselves. It's time to anyway. Do you think you can get the girl to talk?"

"Maybe," Ezra said. "I will have a better idea by tonight. Until then I am going to take Mikal's advice. I need to do some paperwork."

"Paperwork?"

"I want a license to carry a concealed handgun."

Ezra watched himself in a wall of mirrors.

He stood in a karate horse stance on the hardwood floor of the health club's aerobics room, his fists cocked in the hollow notch of his hips. Each fist gripped a five-pound dumbbell. He loosed a punch at a time with a harsh expulsion of breath, bringing the fist up, rotating at the forearm, and imaging a strike at one of ten vital areas of his opponent. The fist then pulled back to a cocked position like the hammer of a revolver. He did this repetitively, making his forearms and shoulders ache, while critically assessing his reflection for form and power.

Pretty pathetic, he realized. He looked like a cleaning woman washing windows. If he and Pratt went hand-to-hand Ezra would need more than his physical skills.

He laid the dumbbells down and went into a T-stance, his left arm up in a horizontal block, his right hand fisted on his hip. He rotated the block vertically while stepping into a front snap kick.

The kicks were worse than the punches. His hamstrings were as short and tight as paper clips and the power generated by his leg would have dribbled a football twenty yards. The wall of mirrors condemned him. He was trim and muscular but his body could no longer perform the way his mind so vividly remembered.

Where had the years gone?

Push-ups. He could always do push-ups.

He dropped to the floor and knocked out forty push-ups on his fists.

He barely felt the hard wooden floor. In his younger days he had trained on concrete. He then attempted twenty push-ups on his fingertips but collapsed on the fourteenth. He lay there quietly as if the smoothly polished floor were a pillow.

"Meditating or sleeping?" the voice asked from behind him.

Ezra raised his head toward the mirror. Mikal Mora's smile reflected white in the glass. "Actually I was praying for an angel," Ezra said. "And look what the Lord brought me."

"With wings," Mora said.

Ezra rolled over and slowly brought his knees to his chest to stretch his aching lower back. "Where have you been, Mikal? I was beginning to get worried."

The agent dropped his gym bag and collapsed to a squat. "Goose chase in Deadwood," he said. "Pratt's truck was near a bike trail that led to a little cabin where a couple of Indians were selling illegal artifacts to tourists. I had to wrap them up. The paperwork was endless. Then I spent a week around Costner's Dunbar development, but no sign of the bad guy."

"It sounds like a vacation in the Black Hills at taxpayers' expense," Ezra joked. "Meanwhile, I've talked with your bad guy, met with de la Rosa, and even gave him a tour of the ranch."

Mora's jaw dropped. He let loose a stream of vulgarities that rivaled Solomon's best.

"Not only that," Ezra continued, "but Pratt tepee-creeped my house last night. Left an eagle feather on my kitchen table and a couple of magpie tail feathers downstairs by Diamond's room."

"Diamond's room?"

"Yeah. Diamond LaFontaine is living with us. She arrived the night before you left for South Dakota."

"And you didn't tell me?" Mikal's eyebrows formed a V that pointed straight at Ezra.

"Couldn't," Ezra said. "I gave her my word." He said it with finality, a warning to Mikal not to question his decision.

"She's at your house now?" he said hopefully.

"Yes, but she's not ready to talk yet. Give me a little time, Mikal. The girl is adjusting to the real world slowly."

The agent took a moment to let the facts settle. "It seems I have a lot of catching up to do," he said.

"Mikal, are you still officially on the Pratt case?" Ezra asked.

Mora's black eyes slitted and hardened. "No," he said. "I've been pulled. I'm on comp time. How did you know?"

Ezra had much to tell but the tension in the room was building. He knew he needed to break it. "I'll explain as we get a lift in," he said. "You look pretty soft and puny. Vacations with Costner aren't good for you, Mikal."

"Dancing with wolves isn't what it used to be," Mikal retorted.

"Well, welcome back to the Riley resort," Ezra said. "Today we lift weights and compare notes. Tomorrow we ride horses."

CHAPTER TWENTY-THREE

There was little art in my family. My father's side was a
desert of culture. No one sang or played an instrument,
and no one drew or painted. The closest anyone came to
approaching art was my uncle Willis who taught me
how to build a loop, hold and twirl it correctly, throw,
jerk my slack, and dally. A thirty-foot nylon lariat was
his brush, and a corral filled with cattle was his canvas.
To be a roper was to be cultured. The only other artistic
exemption in the Riley clan might have been my father.
Some said he was a craftsman with his fists. A Picasso of
pugilism.

Leaving the Land

The morning dawned cool and fresh with orange clouds rising like shadow-coated eyelids in the eastern sky. Mikal and Ezra were saddling horses when Jim Mendenhall's one-ton dually Ford and twenty-four-foot horse trailer rattled into the yard.

Dylan's saddle was on Cajun, and Mikal was slowly tightening the cinch.

"He's just a colt," Ezra warned him. "But he's gentle. The ground is soft, and he'll wear out, so you'll need to rest him often."

"You're putting me on an unbroke horse?" Mikal asked.

"Have to," Ezra said. "I'll need Cheyenne and Shiloh today. Me and Jim will be doctoring cows in the upper pasture. Pratt might be watching us. If you find us and stay about a mile away, you might flush him."

Mora took something from his pocket and put it in Ezra's saddlebag.

"What's that?" Ezra asked.

"My Model 66."

"I won't need a gun, Mikal."

"Then you won't have to use it."

Ezra didn't argue. He led the colt to the creek and held the bridle by the cheekpiece as Mora mounted.

"You're sure he doesn't buck?" Mora asked.

"Tame as a kitten. He just doesn't know much yet. Be patient with him."

Mora nodded, plow-reined the colt to the north and started away at a walk. Ezra returned to his own horses. He had told Anne that Mikal was riding to the bass pond to take water temperatures. He wasn't sure she believed him. He wouldn't tell Mendenhall anything unless he happened to see the rider. Just a government guy borrowing a horse, he would say. That would suffice. Government guys did strange things.

Ezra jumped Shiloh and Cheyenne into the trailer then crawled into the cab with Jim. "Mornin'," Jim said stoically. His blue eyes were puffy but clear.

"Mornin'," Ezra confirmed, and the rig rattled off in search of sore-uddered Herefords.

They unloaded their four horses nine miles from the house, near the bass pond off the Dead Man Road. Two horses were left haltered and tied to the trailer. The horses they were riding were cinched tight, breast collars were pulled snug, and extra lariats were tied to the back saddle strings. Ezra also carried a pair of saddlebags. In the left pocket was a jar of udder balm, a bottle of long-acting penicillin, three disposable syringes with needles, and a pair of pocket binoculars. In the right bag was a soft cotton footrope, two sandwiches and apples, and Mikal's Model 66 Smith and Wesson loaded with .38s.

Covering country on soft ground was hard on horseflesh, not to mention the chasing, roping, and holding of full-grown cows. Ezra chose to start his day with Shiloh's strength and experience. At some point the two cowboys would return and switch to fresh horses.

Mendenhall rode a big black. He sat in the saddle upright but casual, like an aging monarch on a leather throne. The air was crisp and moist, and the horses started with energy as the sky lightened to show lines of geese flying north. Mendenhall looked up at the distant honking. "Guess it's spring," he said.

They eased down the sagebrush draws, looking through little bunches of cattle for mamas kicking their ravished calves off from swollen udders. It wasn't long before they found their first one. Jim thundered after her, twirling a loop big enough to hold Connecticut. The cow soon slowed to an awkward lope, and he dabbed the rope on her, dallied, and turned off to his left, throwing extra weight into that stirrup to help brace for the impact. The cow hit the lariat's end like a harpooned whale and turned bawling to face the rope until the loop choked the squawling out of her. Ezra trotted up behind her and swirled a heel loop that stood upright in front of her hind legs. Mendenhall spurred his black horse forward, dragging the cow into the loop. Ezra jerked his slack and pulled back on Shiloh. The sorrel backed until the cow was stretched out like a clothesline. Ezra was tied on hard and fast, his rope knotted at the saddle horn and lined through a neck rope to keep Shiloh pointed forward. He dismounted, took the udder balm from the saddlebag, and approached the cow from her back side, away from her feet in case she slipped from the loop and began kicking.

All four of the teats were raw and scabbed. He broke the scabs off the ends and massaged each teat with the lanolin balm. The lanolin was thick and greasy on his hands. The doctoring took only a minute, then Jim rode a step forward giving Ezra the slack to pull the headcatch off. As the cow floundered, Ezra led Shiloh up and the cow kicked the heel loop free, struggled to her feet, looked at both men fiercely, then headed for the gumbos on a stiff-legged trot, her calf bouncing hungrily behind her.

One down, Ezra thought, *probably another thirty or forty to go.*

If Solomon had been there he probably would have insisted they doctor every cow they saw. But Solomon wasn't there. He was back in the big white house grumbling about the work Ezra and Jim were doing. Ezra and Jim only doctored the worst cases. The others, they knew, would heal on their own, or in some cases, the calf was big enough to fight the cow for the milk. It was the cows with the really swollen bags and the young, weak calves that needed their attention, and there were enough of those.

An hour later they had doctored seven head, and their horses were frosted with white lather. Ezra was too busy to look for Mikal, and knew he couldn't be anywhere near yet anyway. It would be a long, slow ride from the ranch on a colt. Nor did he think about Pratt. He had his hands full.

The snowstorm had scattered the livestock in twenty-five sections of prairie and badlands, and the two cowboys had to hunt cattle like they were elk. They didn't talk much except to comment on a particular cow or calf or laugh at a missed loop. But mostly it was business. The work was strenuous and talking just wasted air.

About noon they were ready to double back for fresh horses when they crossed near the Krumm Spring.

Mendenhall looked down at the water tank sitting like a small boat in a harbor of chokecherries and sandstone. "Better give 'em a drink," he said, and they reined toward the spring. The horses lowered their necks and gulped thirstily.

"Want a sandwich and an apple?" Ezra asked.

"Might as well," Jim said. "Didn't have no breakfast."

They tied their horses, and Ezra took the lunch from the saddlebag and walked to the sandstone rocks. The yellow stone, dried and baked in the sun, made for comfortable sitting. The two ate quietly, each scanning the skyline of his own private thoughts. Jim looked at the distant hills trying to spot cows. He lifted his sandwich and extended his index finger to a high cedar-fringed butte overlooking the spring. "Thought there was a sheepherder's wife on that hill," he said.

Ezra looked at it. "There was," he said.

"I wonder what happened to it."

Ezra knew. Pratt. "Someone probably tore it down," he said.

Mendenhall shook his head, dumbfounded. "Wonder why anyone

would do that? Climb all the way up that hill and tear down a pile of stones. Lotta work."

Ezra knew why. The rocks were a symbol of domestication. A pioneering sheepherder working for a dollar a day had built the monument as a sign of water while his band bedded and watered near the spring. The rocks had stood for a long time since then, enduring maybe eighty, ninety, or more years of rain, snow, heat, and blizzards, until one madman on a mission toppled them.

Jim took another bite of his sandwich. "It took a lot of work," he said again, "to climb that hill and scatter those rocks. It doesn't make sense that someone would do that."

"The man who did it doesn't make sense," Ezra said. He rose and went to where his horse was tied by the spring.

"Where you goin'?" Jim asked.

"For a walk," Ezra said. He went to his saddlebag, pulled the revolver out, and stuck it in his belt behind his back. "I'll be right back," he said, and he started climbing the butte.

Mendenhall shrugged. That Ezra Riley, long as he had known him, had been a different sort. Jim pulled a can of Copenhagen from his left shirt pocket, dipped a pinch, and stuffed it under his lower lip. He reclined against the sandstone. The rocks were warm under his legs. He watched Ezra climb the steep hill. It was the best show around.

One thing Ezra could still do was climb hills. Even wearing slick-soled cowboy boots he was agile as he climbed on his toes, his body bent forward like a sprinter's. He slipped twice but didn't fall. Just watching him made Jim tired, and he slowly succumbed to the solar-heated arms of gumbo and stone.

Thirty feet from the top Ezra stopped to catch his breath. The air was cool and clear and filled his lungs like the springwater had filled the bellies of the horses. He was surrounded by a tapestry of badlands like a small figure woven into a Persian rug.

A sense of déjà vu nearly knocked him backward. He had been to Krumm Spring hundreds of times, but he remembered being on this exact spot only once before. And that was in a dream.

The feel of the cool breeze against his neck brought the dream back in vivid detail. It was a bitterly cold night in the winter of 1979, and he had just returned to the ranch after leaving it as a teenager. He, Anne, and their baby were living in a trailer house a mile down the creek from his mother.

In the dream he had ridden on horseback to a high ridge and dismounted. Two other riders were nearby. He guessed they were Jim Mendenhall and Rick Benjamin. The grass was green, and red cattle grazed nearby. He noticed a coyote in the breaks below him. To his surprise the predator was loping slowly toward him. Ezra thought his scent would turn the coyote, but he kept coming closer. Then he realized the coyote saw him. It was coming to him on purpose. As it neared, he was stricken with fear. A thin, weak voice was crying from the belly of the beast. His father's voice: *Release me, release me.*

The coyote came close enough to stare Ezra in the face. *I have your father,* the animal seemed to say, *and soon I will have you too.*

The dream seemed like a demonic welcoming from a curse lying fallow in the land. It had been so real he had awakened on a subzero morning wet with perspiration.

The land had appeared so lush and beautiful.

The grass was greening now and far to the south, against Shorty Wilson's fenceline, he saw a small herd of red cattle trailing to a reservoir.

Down at the spring Jim was asleep on the rocks. Somewhere to the south, Mikal—who resembled Rick Benjamin in coloring and build—was riding Cajun.

Two riders.

This was the reality of the dream. Demetrius Pratt was the coyote. Ezra felt for the pistol against the small of his back. It was still there.

He climbed to the summit, eye level with prairie stretching northward in a long blanket of grass. At his feet were the ruins of the sheepherder's wife. Most of the flat sandstones had been thrown off the southern slope of the butte. On the rock base Ezra saw some small moss-colored spots. Blood. He followed the trail to the southwest, picking out a drop every four or five feet until he looked into a small grassy hollow and saw the sad, fearful eyes staring up at him. He stopped, startled. Then reached back for the gun.

The gunshot popped Jim Mendenhall from the lap of a curled catnap. A single crack magnified by the clear air echoed in the gumbo amphitheater. He awoke confused and amused, not knowing why Ezra was packing a gun or what he could be firing at. The ears of the horses pointed at the high butte.

Jim gathered himself to his feet and walked on his high, underslung bootheels to the spring. He swung into his saddle and took Ezra's horse by the reins.

He found Ezra at the top of the ridge standing above a big, grassy hollow. A red cow was lying dead in the swale. Jim sized it up in an instant. The snowstorm had blown the cow to the ridge and into the washout where she had lain down to calve. The calf had been big and maybe backward. Either way, it hung up and the cow spraddled herself—tore up her hip muscles—in trying to push it from the birth canal. The calf died half-in, half-out. The cow had been unable to rise. When the coyotes came she thrashed in fear while they ate the calf first, pulling it from her as they fought, then dragged it across the rocks and off the ridge. Later they returned to work on the cow, tearing at the thick red meat of her hindquarters. They would have eaten her alive if the riders hadn't arrived. Ezra stood with the pistol dangling from his right hand. He had put one bullet behind her right ear, killing her instantly.

Jim couldn't figure out how Ezra knew the cow was up there. Why else would he have climbed the hill with a pistol?

Ezra met Jim's eyes and saw the questions. He said nothing. He walked over and took Shiloh's reins. He holstered Mikal's Smith and Wesson and put it back in the saddlebag. He swung up on Shiloh's back. As he gripped the reins, Jim saw that he had a small white card in his hands. Ezra handed it to him.

"Whatzis?" Jim asked. It was just a white card about the size and thickness of a playing card with a horseshoe-shaped object on it. Nothing else.

"That's the Greek alpha symbol," Ezra said. "*Alpha* means 'the beginning.' I found it on what was left of the herder's monument."

Jim chuckled. "What's this all about?"

Ezra's gaze was serious. "Jim, I must ask you not to tell anyone about those rocks down there. There's an oddball loose in these hills. He tore the sheepherder's wife down."

Jim pointed to the distant skyline. "Is that him?" he asked curiously. Danger was never a serious consideration to Mendenhall. If he couldn't outride it or outdrink it, then it was inevitable that it overtake him.

Ezra saw the lone figure topping the far ridge. It was skylined for an instant—a man on a horse—then dropped out of sight. "No," Ezra said. "That's not him. That's a lawman who's hunting him."

Mendenhall smiled wryly and reset his dirty felt hat. "Okay," he said. Okay. Nothing more. Whatever Ezra said was fine with him, and now it was time to go back to work. They pointed their tired mounts in the direction of fresh horses.

CHAPTER TWENTY-FOUR

J ust before dark Ezra and Jim happened to meet Mikal near the bass pond. Cajun was spent. Ezra told Mikal they would haul him and the colt home. He introduced Jim. The two only nodded; they didn't say hello and they didn't shake hands. Mikal was still unofficially undercover, and Jim wasn't eager to know who he was or what he was doing. It wasn't his business anyway. When things were resolved—whatever those things might be—it would make good barroom conversation in the Buffalo, until then he wanted to stay blissfully ignorant.

The trip home was in tired silence. "Again tomorrow?" Jim asked after the three Riley horses were unloaded.

"Yeah, we better ride through them again," Ezra said.

"Same time?"

"Same time."

Mendenhall's rig bounced away, the red taillights doing a happy jig down Ezra's washboarded gravel lane.

"So did you see anything at all?" Ezra asked as they led the horses to the barn.

"One set of footprints," Mikal said, his voice thin with weariness. He walked stiffly like a cartoon character clipped from the Sunday paper. "He has big feet. Size twelve or better. I casted them."

"Where were the prints?"

"About half a mile south of where you shot the cow. What was wrong with her anyway? She was half eaten-up."

"She spraddled calvin'. The coyotes ate the calf then began working on her. My guess is Pratt watched it happen. He tore down that sheepherder's wife and left another Alpha card."

"With all the snow and mud this country's had the past few days his tracks should have been everywhere, but they weren't. He's like a ghost. Either that or he has wings."

Thoughts of ghosts and winged things brought an idea to Ezra. "I need to talk to Jubal Lee again," he said. "Can you arrange it?"

Mikal looked at him curiously, then shrugged. "With luck I can have him call you tonight."

Ezra had unsaddled his two horses before Mikal was done with Cajun.

They led the horses to the gate by the bunkhouse and turned them into their pasture. Shiloh and Cheyenne trotted down the trail, but Cajun followed in a slow walk.

"That colt is really tired," Mikal said.

"Yeah, I guess we better rest him tomorrow. You're a pretty fat boy for him to pack around all day," Ezra joked.

"Fat? It's all muscle."

Ezra let the joking drop. "So what's your plan for tomorrow?" he asked.

"I guess I walk—burn off some of this fat you think I'm carrying. I'll park at your bass pond."

"You should be home with your wife," Ezra said.

"Yeah," Mikal agreed. "But I'm here."

They walked to Mikal's truck and leaned on the hood. The stars were bright in the night sky. Beaner was nosing Ezra's boots and tail-whipping Ezra's legs with excitement.

Mikal glanced toward the house. Ezra knew he was thinking Diamond was in there, and he still wanted to talk to her. Ezra realized Mikal had never met Anne and Dylan, but this didn't seem like the right time for introductions. Mikal looked back to the north at a velvet outline of distant hills. "He's back there somewhere right now," he said.

"Maybe. Or he could have a motel in town. The fact is, Pratt could be hiding anywhere," Ezra said. "I think what we have to do is find what he's looking for before he does."

"You mean this *thin place* stuff?"

"Exactly."

"Holy crow, Ezra, you're going to turn me into a witch-hunter."

Ezra smiled a good-bye. "Get some sleep, Mikal. You're going to be stiff as new wire in the morning. And don't worry, you keep hunting the man, I'll do the witch-hunting." He walked slowly toward the house.

"How are you going to find this *thin place*?" Mora called after him.

Ezra laughed. "God's going to show me," he said. "Put that in your file, Agent Mora."

Anne and Dylan were both home for a change, and Diamond was alone in her downstairs bedroom. She had been upstairs before Ezra came home.

"Did you or Mikal see anything?" Dylan asked as he met his father in the hallway.

"Mikal found a set of footprints," Ezra said. "And I found another calling card."

"Mikal?" Anne said from the kitchen where she was making Ezra a supper of corn bread and taco soup. "I thought he was just checking the bass pond."

Ezra had neglected to tell Anne that Mikal was not a fish biologist. He gave Dylan a nod of permission. He would let his son spill the beans.

"Mikal is an undercover federal agent," Dylan explained. "He works for the U.S. Fish and Wildlife Service."

"Only he's not really under cover," Ezra said. "Pratt's known who he is longer than I have."

"So have half the kids in town," Dylan bragged.

"Well, I haven't," Anne said. "It would be nice if someone would let me know what's going on around here."

"Sorry," Ezra said. "Little details slip by when we're all having so much fun. So what's new here?"

"Diamond spent the day listening to Jubal's music," Dylan said.

"Good," Ezra said, seating himself at the table. "Mikal is arranging for Jubal to call me. Dylan, when he calls I want you to bring Diamond upstairs."

"Ezra," Anne warned, "what are you going to do?"

"Trust me," Ezra said.

The call came after Ezra had showered and eaten. "Jubal?" Ezra asked. "How are you doing?"

"Fine. What's going on?" His voice was expectant.

"Pratt is still a problem and I need some help. Can you do some research for me?"

"The library here is limited," Jubal said. "But I will do what I can."

"Pratt is on the ranch looking for what he calls a *thin place*. Some sort of harmonic convergence site. Today I found where he tore down a sheepherder's rock monument. That got me to thinking there could be a rock formation on the ranch that I don't know about. Something the Indians made."

"You could have a medicine wheel," Jubal said.

"How about some sort of altar?"

"I don't think the Plains Indians built altars. They were nomadic. You might have a natural formation—an upthrust or stratification of some sort—that was considered a holy site."

"You know Pratt, Jubal. Help me find out what he is looking for."

"I'll try, Ezra. It just so happens we have experts on just about everything in here. A prison is sort of like a university."

Dylan brought Diamond into the room. She stood behind Dylan using him as a shield.

"Jubal," Ezra said, "there is someone here I want you to talk to. Just let the Lord use you and say anything that comes to mind." He cupped his hand over the phone's mouthpiece and motioned for Diamond. "This is Jubal Lee Walker," he told the girl. "I want you to tell him who you are. Tell him you listened to his music today."

Anne stood by like a pillar of concern. Dylan coaxed Diamond forward. She took the phone. "Hello," she said timidly.

"Hello," Jubal said. "Who's this?"

"Diamond LaFontaine."

"It's nice to talk to you, Diamond," Jubal said.

"I listened to your CDs today," she said.

"Good. I hope you enjoyed them."

"You can't play music anymore?" she asked with concern.

"No, not too well."

She became sad and serious. "I'm sorry," she said.

"Don't be," Jubal said. "I have given it as a sacrifice to God."

"You make sacrifices?" she asked, thinking of Deemie cutting small strips of flesh from his body.

"Only ones of the heart," Jubal said. "They are the only ones that matter."

"Deemie makes sacrifices," she said, her mind trailing away to the netherworld of chanting and the smoke of cedar and sage.

"Diamond," Jubal said firmly, "listen to me. You can trust Ezra and Anne. Whatever they ask you to do, do it. They will not hurt you. Do you understand?"

She turned slowly and stared at Ezra. Her face was a mask of confusion as confidence and fear battled for control.

"Diamond." Everyone heard Jubal's voice through the receiver. "Do me a favor. Ask Ezra to pray for you."

She stiffened, shivered, and her face paled. She looked up at Anne. A tear from each eye was running down Anne's face. Diamond looked at Dylan, then at Ezra. His eyes were soft and nonthreatening. "Okay," she said to the phone.

"God bless you." Jubal's good-bye sealed the room.

Diamond put the phone carefully into its cradle. She took a deep breath, squared her small shoulders and turned to face Ezra. "Please pray for me," she said.

Ezra smiled and nodded. He motioned Anne and Dylan to draw near, and the four were forming a circle for prayer when the phone rang again. Ezra reluctantly answered it.

"Ezra, my good friend," the voice said.

"De la Rosa?"

"Yes, it is I, Antonio de la Rosa. I am above you, flying at about twenty thousand feet. I've called to warn you, my friend. Demetrius and I had an argument in Calgary. I told him to go to Wyoming, to some holdings I have there, and wait for me. But he isn't there. I am afraid he is back in Yellow Rock."

"I know he is," Ezra said. "And he has bad intentions."

"Oh? I am so sorry. I did my best, but you were right about him. I am afraid he has crossed the line."

"You're not telling me anything I don't know."

"Do you still have the girl?" de la Rosa asked. "She has a cousin who is a missionary. I can help you locate her. If you want my help, that is."

Ezra desperately wanted to locate Diamond's cousin, but he wasn't sure he wanted de la Rosa involved. "I think we can find her," he said.

"Very well. I just want to make sure that the young lady is . . . taken care of." His voice trailed off into an abyss of implications.

"She will be," Ezra answered sternly.

"Well, I must go," de la Rosa said. "I am sorry about Demetrius, Ezra. I failed you there. I will make it up to you."

A chill seemed to have entered the room, and Anne felt it the strongest. "Who was that?" she said. She saw the concern on her husband's face as he put the phone down.

Ezra stared through the living room picture window toward a night sky pinpricked with stars. "That was a warning from on high," he said. A warning from the Brazilian that Diamond Lafontaine had better not talk to the authorities.

There is someone in the house.

Ezra awakened at two in the morning thinking someone was in the house. For several minutes he lay quietly, straining to hear, but all that came to his ears was Anne's slow, measured breathing. He reached under the bed, his fingers walking the carpet like a large spider, feeling for his Ruger .22 pistol. They touched something, and he slowly pulled it out, but it was only one of Anne's shoes. His fingers continued walking until he felt the hard, gritty surface of the pistol's grip. His clothes lay beside the bed. He cradled them and the pistol in his arms and tiptoed from the room.

He stood silently in the hallway. He could hear nothing. The furnace came on, and warm air hissed from a vent near his feet. He pulled on his clothes, stuck the .22 in his pants, and grabbed a flashlight. He did not turn the flashlight on as he walked through the house, unlocked the front door, and stepped out into a cool and very dark May night.

He walked to the corrals by instinct. He heard Beaner leave her doghouse and trot across the yard to follow him. "Stay," he commanded her as he opened the corral gate. Somewhere up the creek an owl hooted.

He stepped into the pen and only then did he turn the flashlight on for one quick sweep of the corral. There were two heifers left to calve and both were lying comfortably. He turned the flashlight off. The owl hooted again. A coyote yapped.

As his bare hand touched the cool iron of the corral gate the thought struck him it was not an owl or a coyote that was calling from the dark. The owl hoot sounded again. Ezra turned, walked back through the pens, and followed a fenceline behind his bunkhouse up the creek toward a high cliff. Every few paces he stopped to let his eyes adjust to the surroundings and to listen for the owl. He stopped finally in a grove of cottonwood trees beneath the cliff. The owl hooted from a maze of black, leafless branches.

"Pratt," Ezra said quietly.

"I'm here," a voice said from the darkness.

"What do you want, Pratt? Why did you call me out here?"

"I called to see if you could hear."

The imposing sheer wall of the cliff created an echoing effect that kept Ezra from pinpointing the location of the voice. Pratt seemed to surround him. "I'm tired of playing games, Pratt."

"So am I, Ezra Riley. Did you have a nice ride today?"

"I killed the cow, Pratt. You wanted her to die slowly, didn't you? You wanted the coyotes to eat her alive. You called them to her."

"My little friends feasted well, and it doesn't matter if a cow dies slowly. They have no soul. Neither do horses. Only that which is wild and natural has a soul. Do you have a soul, Ezra Riley?"

Ezra still couldn't determine his exact location. "You attacked me in the barn, Pratt," he said. "You snuck into my house. Why don't you just step out into the open, and we will finish this?"

The voice came from above him. It was a snarl. "I did not attack you in your barn, and I have not been in your house."

The adamancy in the voice froze Ezra for a moment. He slowly reached back and pulled the pistol from the small of his back.

"You treat me with dishonor, Riley," Pratt continued. The voice now came from the west. "Put the peashooter away. Guns are disrespectful. I've never hunted with a gun, Riley. They are the crude weapons of beer-drinking white trash."

"But you hide in the shadows and darkness," Ezra said. "And you co-operate with the Brazilian who lives only to hunt. What is your interest in de la Rosa owning the ranch, Pratt?"

His laugh moved through the tree limbs as if it was made of feathers and wings. "I am your dark side, Ezra Riley. I am the lover of the land, the lord of the land that you could have been. Let Antonio put together his millions of acres of hunting preserve. When the chaos comes it will all be a wild and uninhabited land. Uninhabited by domesticated, soulless mankind, that is."

"Chaos?" Ezra said.

"Yes," Pratt said zealously, almost as if chanting. "A cleansing chaos is coming upon the land. You could have been a part of it, Ezra Riley, if you hadn't bent your power in the wrong direction."

"Forget about your apocalypse. I have found your *thin place,* Pratt," Ezra bluffed. There was only silence from the trees. He didn't take the bait. "You are a better hunter than I," Ezra continued. "I admit that all the advantages are yours if the battle is physical. You are very likely the world's greatest poacher," he flattered. "You are strong, silent, and ruthless." He waited.

"Go on," Pratt said softly from the north. "What is your point?"

"You are desperate, Pratt. De la Rosa cut you loose, didn't he?"

"Antonio is a fool like you, Riley, except he has money."

Ezra moved slowly to the sound of the voice. He held the .22 below his waist gripped in both hands.

"When an animal is in a corner it must fight or die," Pratt said. "I have you in a corner, Riley."

"I am willing to fight you, Pratt."

"No, no, not yet. Timing is important, Riley. Everything depends on timing." The voice came from the south. Pratt was between Ezra and the house. "You fight to defend your home and loved ones. That is honorable. I can respect that."

"You forced the issue. You came into my house."

"No!" he hissed. "Why do you lie? I have never been in your house, Riley."

"Okay. Have it your way."

"I have told you, I am not interested in your wife or son. I am not even interested in Diamond at this time. Protect them; it is the honorable thing to do. I do not attack women or children. I do not ambush people in their barns."

"Jubal Lee Walker," Ezra said. "What about Jubal Lee?" *And what about Diamond?* he was also thinking.

"Walker was a long time ago." The voice now seemed to be above him again. "That was a favor to my brother, nothing more."

Lies, Ezra thought. The man was possessed by demons and demons were incapable of telling the truth. "So if you are not after my wife, my son, or Diamond, what corner do you have me in?"

"Land," Pratt said. "I am the lord of the land. De la Rosa will not help you. Shorty Wilson knows you are the source of his troubles. Your uncle and your sisters do not matter. I shall own the land, Ezra Riley. I shall own the land because I am the lord of the *thin place*. I am Alpha. I am the high priest of the new kingdom."

He's delusional, Ezra realized. And there was no way to reason with a crazy man. "I am going back to the house," he said. "If you are a man of honor, tell me what the conditions of our battle are."

"Battle? There will be no battle, Ezra Riley. I shall simply come for you. You are to be a sacrifice. I will hear in your eyes *the conversation of death*. You will bow to me. You will give me permission."

"Permission for what?"

"Permission to kill you," he said.

He heard a twig snap and wheeled in that direction, the gun raised. "I leave you with a Scripture," the voice said from behind him. "*'Watchman, what of the night? Watchman, what of the night?' The watchman said, 'The morning comes, and also the night.'*"

Ezra turned slowly around. There was only blackness surrounding him. "The night comes," he heard Pratt say, and then Ezra knew Pratt was gone. There was no sound of his leaving, just an effortless absence as if he had taken wing.

CHAPTER TWENTY-FIVE

When Ezra got back to the house, Anne was sitting at the kitchen table waiting for him. "Where have you been?" she asked.

He kept his coat on so she would not see the pistol. "Pratt was here," he said. "I talked to him down by the cliff."

"Oh, God," she said. "What does he want, Ezra?"

"I don't know." He lied; he wasn't going to tell her that Pratt had promised to kill him. "He's delusional."

"What are we going to do?" There was a soft emphasis on the word *we*.

"You, Dylan, and Diamond are moving back into the Jablonski house," Ezra said. "Mikal can move in with me."

"No," Ann insisted. "I don't want to be away from you."

"You will be safe in town. Pratt is not after Diamond. Not yet."

"I'm not worried about us. I'm worried about *you*."

"Mikal will be with me."

"Why can't someone just go arrest him?" Anne asked in frustration. "Let Mikal talk to Diamond. Then he can go get Pratt."

"Anne, it's not that simple. Pratt has thousands of acres to hide in. Besides, I told you about de la Rosa's phone call. It was a thinly veiled threat. He doesn't want Diamond to talk."

Anne shivered and held herself. "Ezra, I don't like this. I don't like any of this."

"Neither do I," he said. He moved behind her chair and put his hands on her shoulders. "This is reality, Anne. It's not a bad dream that we will suddenly awake from. You have to try and concentrate on school and taking care of Dylan and Diamond. Mikal and I will get Pratt. I guarantee you, we will get him."

"But I don't want you going after him. Leave it to Mikal and the sheriff."

"Anne, no one knows the ranch better than I do."

Anne looked down at the table. For the first time ever she seriously hated the ranch. She hated the land.

Just before dawn Mikal pulled into the yard. Ezra had already saddled two horses and was in his bunkhouse waiting. He stepped out and waved Mikal in.

"Nice office," Mikal said, scanning a room decorated with buffalo and cow skulls, and deer antlers. "So this is where an award-winning writer works."

"This is where I sit and stare at the computer screen," Ezra said. "Once in a rare moon something gets written."

"I've got news," Mikal said.

"I do, too," Ezra said. "Is your news good or bad?"

"It's not too good. My SAIC got me on the cellular last night. He was beaucoup displeased that I was still in this area. He ordered me back to Louisiana ASAP."

Ezra nodded. Even when he had told Anne that Mikal would be staying with him, backing him, looking for Pratt, he had doubted it would really happen. "It's okay, Mikal," Ezra said. He did not even bother to mention that Diamond had talked. It was unimportant now. "When do you leave?"

"I'm going to drag my feet, but I better be out of Yellow Rock by Sunday morning." The two of them stared at each other as if measuring time and space by some invisible ruler of possibilities. "So what's your news?" Mikal asked.

"Two things," Ezra said. "I was contacted last night both by the devil and his chief demon. De la Rosa called, claimed he was overhead in his jet flying home. He's cut Pratt loose. So Pratt's answerable to no one now. De la Rosa also intimated that Diamond better not talk. No matter where she goes he can reach her."

Mikal pursed his lips and silently cursed his luck.

Ezra took a deep breath for strength. He had been up since two. "When I checked heifers this morning, a noise pulled me to the trees up the creek. Pratt was there, talking to me from the darkness as if he were omnipresent."

"What did he want?"

"He talked a lot of craziness, said he wasn't interested in the girl. He also swears he never hit me in the barn or did the hot prowl in my house."

"He's lying." Mikal's assertion was short and hard, like a punch to the ribs.

Ezra could see a growing hatred in his friend's eyes. Mikal was beginning to take the case more and more personally. "Of course he's lying," Ezra said. "But he may not know it. He thinks he's a man of honor and I have shown him disrespect."

"Do you think he's found his *thin place?*" Mikal's voice was mocking when he mentioned Pratt's quest.

"I don't know, but I get the feeling he's close. Why? Are you starting to believe in the spiritual dimensions of this case?"

Mikal snorted. "Hey, I'll believe in telepathic frogs from Mars if it helps us collar this guy. How about Walker? Is he going to be able to help?"

"He'll try. If anyone can dig something up, Jubal Lee can."

"If there's time," Mikal said. "But there may not be time. The girl has to talk, Ezra. If she talks maybe my SAIC will change his mind."

"I can't allow it, Mikal. Anne, Dylan, and Diamond are moving back into my pastor's house today. I was hoping you could come stay here."

"Sure. For two nights. That's all I have."

They heard the metal-clanging rattle of Mendenhall's truck and trailer. "Jim and I are going to doctor a few more cows," Ezra said. "If you want, you can take a horse and ride back to the spring. If Pratt's out there that's where I think he'll be."

They stepped outside. Mendenhall's truck was still running, the bright beams of the headlights stabbing the corrals with light. "Ssshhhezzraaa," Jim mumbled, stepping from the cab. "You ready to r-r-ride?"

"Great," Ezra whispered. "Jim fell off the wagon."

The big man stumbled around the front of the truck then leaned on the hood, blocking one headlight. "Ize ready to ride," he chuckled.

Ezra walked to the truck. "Jim," he said, "you're in no shape to ride, let alone rope."

"I can r-r-r-ride," he giggled. "And I can r-r-r-rope." The endearing trait about Mendenhall was that he was a likable drunk. His pink face was lit up, his eyes sparkled, and he puckered with giggles as if he were sucking pickles.

Ezra lapsed into a counseling mode. He wanted his friend healthy and walking a straight line. "Who put you up to this, Jim?" he asked. "You've been on the wagon too long to dive off by yourself."

Mendenhall chuckled and pointed to the truck cab. The passenger door burst open, and a man fell out onto the ground. He cursed, brushed himself off, and stood up. "Ezra Riley, you sum—"

Ezra's mouth dropped. Seeing Shorty Wilson drunk in his yard stole any thoughts he might have corraled.

Ezra's neighbor stepped forward spewing a stream of vulgarities like verbal vomit. He punched a blunt finger into Ezra's chest. "I don't know how you did it, but you got the feds on me somehow, didn'tchya?"

Mendenhall cupped a hand over his mouth to contain his chuckles. His round, pink face jiggled like a beardless Santa Claus in a Christmas commercial.

Ezra stepped back. "You're drunk, Wilson," he said.

"Drunk, I ain't drunk." He pushed Ezra with an open hand. "You got it in for me, don'tcha? First it was the yearlin's in the store—I know you done that, Jim even said so—then the fire in the CRP, then foulin' me up with Lillie Foster, and now callin' in the feds claimin' fraud. . . ."

Mikal moved forward to restrain Wilson. Ezra motioned him to step back.

"I know you done it," Wilson accused. "A man even told me how you done it. You used some South American. Some Argentine or somethin'," he blubbered.

"Who have you been talking to?" Ezra demanded. He was more concerned about catching Pratt than he was worried about Wilson. "A tall guy with a beard?"

"Makes no difference," Wilson said, and he pushed Ezra with both hands.

Ezra went backward a step and caught his balance. "Back off, Shorty," Ezra warned. "This is my place. I won't let you push me around on my place."

Wilson took another step but the heeler pup rushed in from the shadows, grabbed his pantleg, and pulled. Wilson fell forward. Ezra spun out of the way and let him drop face first into the gravel.

Mendenhall doubled over the pickup hood, laughing uncontrollably.

Wilson staggered to his feet. "I'll kill that dog," he said, and he whirled and kicked. His lace-up farmer's boot caught Beaner in the ribs, lifted the dog off the ground, and tossed the pup ten feet into the side of Mendenhall's trailer.

Ezra's scream was not of fear or anger, it was the *kia* cry of the martial artist erupting beneath years of inactivity. Ezra took one step forward, blocked a roundhouse punch from Wilson with a left rising block, and thrust the heel of his right palm through Wilson's nose. There was a sickening popping sound followed by a geyser of blood.

Wilson collapsed to his knees. "My nose," he moaned, bringing both hands to his face. "You broke my nose."

Mendenhall laughed so hard he slid off the hood, tipped over backward, and hit the ground like a coffin full of sand. He lay there bathed in his own headlights.

Ezra's heart was pounding and adrenaline raced through his body. He balanced lightly in a T-stance, his right leg cocked to kick if Wilson got to his feet.

Wilson didn't try to rise. He simply sat in the gravel, his hands to his face and blood streaming through the fingers as if he were a punctured container of tomato juice. "My nose, my nose," he said over and over.

Mendenhall began groaning painfully from the ground. Mikal bent over him. "Where does it hurt, Jim?" he asked.

"Ma jaw," Jim said. His voice was weak and his breathing labored. "And get that cow offa my chest."

Mora looked up. "Heart attack," he said. "He's having a heart attack."

Ezra rushed past Wilson. "Are you sure?"

Mendenhall's face was turning a silvery pale in the glow of the headlights. "Jim," Mora said. "Do you feel pains running down your arm?" The big man nodded. "Come on," Mikal said, getting one arm beneath Jim's thick shoulders. "Help me get him up. We have to get him to town." Ezra got under the other shoulder and they hoisted Jim to his feet. "To my truck," Mora said. They toppled him into the front seat. "Call the hospital," Mikal told Ezra. "Tell them I'm coming in."

Wilson had staggered to the truck, his face and shirt covered with blood. "Whadabout me?" he said. "I gotta go to the hospital too." Mora grabbed him by a belt loop and the top of his shirt collar, threw him in, and slammed the door. He raced around and got in the driver's seat. "Go call!" he yelled at Ezra, then he roared toward the highway.

Ezra glanced at his dog. The pup rolled over and looked up at its master. "You okay?" Ezra asked. The dog whined and got to its feet. "You're okay," Ezra said, and he ran to the house.

Anne met him at the door; she was ready to leave for school. Dylan had already left for an early tennis practice. "What's going on out there?" she asked.

"Jim had a heart attack," Ezra explained. "Mikal's taking him to town."

"You should have called me," Anne said, following her husband to the phone. Ezra punched 911 and told the police to meet Mora at the Yellow Rock Bridge.

"Is he going to be okay?" Anne asked as Ezra hung up the phone.

"Yeah, I think so. He just overdid it on the laughing."

"Laughing?"

"Yeah," Ezra said sarcastically. "Jim's been drinking and it was an unusually entertaining morning."

"What are you going to do now?" Anne asked. "Do you want me to stay home and help you ride? I want to help." Her insistence was sincere, but halfhearted.

Diamond came upstairs and Ezra lowered his voice so she couldn't hear him. "You can't rope," he told Anne. "Besides, what about Diamond? You are her security blanket."

"Okay," she said, reaching for her coat and books. "I have hospital lab later this morning. I'll check on Jim and give you a call."

He gave Anne a quick kiss. Diamond said good-bye with her eyes. As they drove away he realized Jim's pickup was still running with its headlights on and his two horses standing saddled in the trailer. That seemed like a good omen. The truck was Jim's alter ego. If it was still running, so was Jim.

Ezra unsaddled and penned Jim's horses and tossed them some hay from the loft. He was surprised his right hand wasn't sore, but he knew that was from striking with the palm instead of the knuckles, and amazed that his long-dormant training had returned so fast and furiously. Only a sliver of guilt irritated him for having broken Wilson's nose. He whistled for his dog. "He shouldn't have kicked you," he said as he crouched and rubbed Beaner's head. The red heeler whined and cuddled into him for more attention. "But that doesn't mean you can go with me today. You can't rope either," he told the dog.

He hooked his pickup to his old four-horse Hale trailer—if Mikal returned he would take him along to doctor cows—tied Cheyenne and Shiloh to its railing, and went to the house to phone the hospital. No one could tell him anything. Looking out the window he saw a car driving down the lane. He was surprised to see that it was Lilith. He went outside to meet her.

"Good morning," she said. "How are you? I was worried about you all night. I've tried calling but no one answers."

"I had quite a night," Ezra said. "And an even more bizarre morning. I broke Shorty Wilson's nose, and my hired man had a heart attack." He walked past her and toward the corrals.

"You're kidding," she gasped, following him. "No wonder the Lord kept waking me up all night to pray for you. He kept telling me to pray the Psalm 91."

"The psalm of protection against evil spirits," Ezra said. He had read it a dozen times in the past three weeks. "Well, I feel as if there has been a legion of them loosed against me."

"*You shall not be afraid of the terror by night, nor of the arrow that flies by day,*" Lilith quoted.

"Well, that's fitting when it comes to Pratt, isn't it?" Ezra said. He untied the horses and opened the trailer door. Shiloh loaded obediently, but the dun balked and Ezra had to slap him on the butt. "I appreciate your prayers, Lilith," Ezra said as he slammed the trailer door shut and latched it.

"Where are you going?" she asked. "You seem to be in quite a hurry."

"I have cows to finish doctoring," he said. "And all of my help is presently at the hospital." Beaner waited nearby. Ezra's stern glance told her she wasn't coming, and she slunk quietly away.

"You're going alone?" she asked. "Don't you need help? I can help you."

He gave her a doubting look. "I don't suppose you can handle a rope?" he said.

"No," she argued. "But I can hold your horse or something."

"What about Ben and Hillary? We'd be out there for a while."

"Ben's on a road trip and took Hillary with him. She's going to stay with my parents for a few days. I'm all alone and my boots are in the car."

"Okay," he agreed. "Pull your boots on. I could use the help." He had mixed feelings about taking her. Pratt was out there somewhere, and besides that, he had already turned down his wife's offer to help. But Anne was busy and Lilith wasn't. And as far as roping was concerned, even if Mikal had returned, he couldn't rope either. It wasn't a skill someone learned in a day.

They unloaded the horses on the lower end of Dead Man Creek in an area Ezra and Jim had not covered the day before.

"I have to be honest," Ezra told Lilith. "It may not be safe for you out here. If you want to go back, let me know."

"I'm not afraid of Pratt," she said. "I'm really not. And he probably won't do anything with a witness around, so you are safer with me than without me."

"Okay," he said, and he tightened his cinch and swung into the saddle.

"What are we going to be doing?" she asked as she mounted Cheyenne.

"Doctoring sore-teated cows. I'll double-hock the cows and pull them down. Then you dismount, break any scabs, and rub the teats with the udder balm."

"I can do that," she said confidently.

They rode through several small bunches before finding an old Hereford with an udder the size of a laundry bag. Ezra trotted Shiloh toward her until an opening in the thick brush allowed him to cast his loop and pick up both hind legs. He dallied, slid Shiloh to a stop, and collapsed the cow onto her side.

"Dismount and drop your reins," Ezra instructed. "The lanolin is in your right saddlebag." She swung to the ground, found the medication, then looked up to him for further directions. "Approach the cow from the back side," he told her. "Stay clear of the rope and her hind legs. Reach over her back, break the scabs, and coat her teats."

Lilith approached the cow slowly. "Whoa there, girl," she said softly. "This isn't going to hurt. This will make you feel better." She leaned over its hindquarters and treated the cow as she had been told.

"Okay," Ezra said. "Get back on your horse." When Lilith was remounted, Ezra nudged Shiloh forward and the cow kicked the slackened rope off, rose awkwardly to her feet, and stared at them angrily.

"She doesn't appreciate what I did," Lilith joked.

"The rewards of ministry," Ezra said.

They hunted cattle for another three hours, doctoring only the worst cases. Lilith became quick and efficient at her chore, and Ezra roped better than he had in years. It became a beautiful day in spite of its beginnings, Ezra's moodiness faded, and everything went so smoothly he almost felt enchanted.

"We're a pretty good team," Lilith said after doctoring her tenth cow.

"It's working out better than I thought it would," Ezra admitted.

"I bring you luck," she said.

She was disappointed when Ezra told her they were done. "That's all?" she said. "It was just getting to be fun."

"All good things come to an end," Ezra said dryly, pointing Shiloh back toward the trailer.

They loaded the horses and headed for home. "That was refreshing," Lilith said. "And my hands feel wonderful. No dishpan hands for a week, that's for sure."

"And it was a partly cloudy day too," Ezra noted. "So you didn't get too much sun."

"It was perfect," she said. "And I do want to ride again before the weather gets too hot. If there was one place on the ranch you would show me where would it be?"

He wanted to say Krumm Spring, but knew he couldn't, not with Pratt still at large. He had already shown her the high Watkins Flat. "The cedar hills where Gusto is buried," he said.

"Gusto?" she asked.

"Yeah, the best horse I've ever owned. A horse that made me think living was worthwhile."

"Great," she perked. "Sounds like there is quite a story behind this horse. Let's visit the grave before Hillary comes back so I don't have to worry about a sitter. How about Monday?"

"I don't know," Ezra vacillated. "It's subject to circumstances. If Pratt isn't caught by Monday I don't want you around."

"I told you I am not afraid of Pratt." She laughed lightly with a hint of mockery in her lilt.

They were several miles down the oil and close to Solomon's house when Ezra saw a foreign object in his uncle's pasture. It was about half as tall and twice as wide as a fence post. "What's that?" he said, braking slowly to a stop.

"What do you see?" Lilith asked.

He reached for his binoculars. "There's something odd out there." He focused the glasses. "It's Solomon," he said. "It's my uncle just sitting out there." As they watched, the old man got slowly and awkwardly to his feet and began walking toward the pickup. After several minutes he made it to the highway and shuffled to Ezra's door. He had been out enjoying the springtime, but he had enjoyed it all that he could.

"What were you doing out there?" Ezra asked.

"Went for a walk," Solomon said. "My feet played out on me. Had to rest." He glanced at Lilith. He didn't recognize her. That made him nervous, but he wanted a ride home.

"Well, get in," Ezra said. "We'll give you a ride."

Solomon moved slowly around the front of the truck with one hand on the hood for balance, opened the door, and struggled into the seat. Lilith moved over, almost into Ezra's lap.

"Uncle Solomon," Ezra said, "this is Lilith Foster. She helped me doctor cows today."

"Oh?" Solomon grunted. He did not look at her or acknowledge her extended hand.

Ezra caught Lilith's eye and winked. Ezra expected Solomon to ask why Lilith was helping instead of Jim, but Solomon didn't ask. He just stared straight ahead, forming a shell harder than the dashboard and grittier than the highway.

"Jim had a heart attack this morning," Ezra announced loudly, certain this would crack his uncle out of his withdrawal.

"I know," Solomon spat.

"You know?" Ezra asked, surprised. "Did Anne call you?"

"No! Your friend came by. He told me."

"My friend?"

"The tall beardie," Solomon roared. "The one who likes arrowheads so much."

"Pratt?" Ezra said with alarm, and he felt Lilith tense beside him. "Pratt was in your house this morning?"

"Yup," Solomon declared. It was a simple fact, nothing he planned on elaborating on. "How's Jim? Dead yet?"

"I don't know," Ezra said. He had almost forgotten about Mendenhall.

Solomon grunted. "Well, you better find out," he said. He cared, but he didn't want to show it.

Ezra let out a deep sigh as he made a slow and careful turn into his uncle's yard. He could not let his uncle be unwarned concerning Pratt. "Sol," he said. "I've been meaning to tell you to watch out for that Pratt guy. He's dangerous."

"Dangerous?" Solomon guffawed. "He don't seem so dangerous. What is he, a murderer or sumpin'?"

"Well, no, not yet. He's a poacher—"

"Poacher! Haw! All the Rileys been poachers. Johnny killed more illegal deer than legal ones. Fact is, most everyone was a poacher at one time. Poachin' ain't nuthin'. Besides, what's he poachin' now? Ain't no time of the year to be killin' nuthin'. The deer don't even have no antlers."

Ezra winced. He felt a wave of empathy from Lilith. He knew he couldn't tell his uncle about *thin places* and *conversations of death*. Sol wouldn't believe a word of it. And he had not mentioned those details to Lilith either. He had let her assume Pratt was after him because of Diamond.

"So what's he done?" Sol asked again, his face aimed forward like a hood ornament.

"He's crazy," Ezra said, hoping his uncle would respect craziness. "He is dangerously nuts. There are several law enforcement agencies looking for him."

"Then why don't they just come get him? He wouldn't be hard to get."

"No, he's hard to get," Ezra argued. "Sol, what kind of vehicle was he driving this morning?"

"Vehicle? I didn't see one."

Ezra pulled up to his uncle's front door. The old man struggled with the handle to get out.

"It was nice to meet you," Lilith offered.

"Humph," he grunted, and pushed his way from the cab. He walked away without saying anything more to either of them.

"He's uncomfortable around strange women," Ezra explained as he pulled away from the house. "Especially when he has to sit right next to them."

"Am I so strange?" she teased.

"Well, at least you finally found a man who didn't hit on you."

"Hit on me?" she laughed. "He wouldn't even look at me." She moved over a little since Solomon was gone, but not very far—she was still close to Ezra. "How old is he?" she asked.

"Eighty-three," Ezra said. "And destined to outlive me."

"And Pratt comes to see him? I wonder what he wants?"

"He does it to annoy me, to let me know he can do anything he wants anytime he wants, like sneaking into my house at night."

"That must be terrible." She shuddered. "It gives me the creeps to think that someone comes into your house and walks around while you're sleeping."

"It's called a hot prowl," Ezra said. "Some people get their kicks out of it."

"He's a coward," she said. "And I'm still not afraid of him. He's just a bully."

Ezra pulled up in front of his corrals. "Don't underestimate him," he said. "Make sure your doors and windows are locked tonight and keep a light on. Pratt could strike at you to get back at me."

They unsaddled the horses and released them down the creek. Jim's horses, still confined, whinnied from the corral. Ezra walked Lilith to her car. "Thanks for the help," he said.

Her face was flushed by the fresh air, and her eyes were the color of a lavender sky at twilight. Her teeth glistened when she smiled. "It was my pleasure," she said. "I can't wait until Monday." She leaned up and kissed him lightly on the cheek; he did not see it coming or expect it. Before he could say anything, she was in her car, smiling, and waving good-bye.

The lingering touch of her lips made him uncomfortable. He washed his face in cold water from the hydrant at the horse trough, but her touch still burned softly.

CHAPTER TWENTY-SIX

As a youngster I had few neighbors or close friends. My childhood centered around work—4 A.M. saddlings and fourteen-hour days in the saddle. The life was romantic in retrospect, but to the child the summers were an imprisonment of labor, harsh expectations, and sudden danger. Town schools revealed me as a social misfit trained for emotional conflict, not cooperation. I was a Spartan child. I had been trained for war.

Leaving the Land

It was dark when Mikal returned from the hills. He walked into the house carrying his sleeping bag and an overnight kit. He looked exhausted, and tiredness was as much emotional as physical; his day had obviously produced nothing. "After I left the hospital I took a back route to Krumm Spring," he explained to Ezra. "I don't think he's back there. In fact, I'm sure he's not back there," he declared. "What's new here? Have you heard anything about Jim?"

"Anne left a message," Ezra said. "It was a minor attack. They'll cut him loose in a few days."

"Well, I guess it's not too bad of a day if the hired help doesn't die."

"You look starved," Ezra said. "Just drop your stuff, and we'll go to town to get something to eat." Ezra was equally tired and wasn't up to cooking.

They got a booth in the back of the Cattleman's Cafe. It was after seven so the cafe was quiet. Mikal had chicken-fried steak with mashed potatoes and salad. Ezra had a piece of apple pie. In times of stress he had his mother's nervous stomach. Food did not digest; it lay as a lump that rusted into heartburn.

"So?" Ezra asked. "What do you think Pratt is up to? He stopped in to see my uncle this morning, and according to Shorty Wilson he was in the Buffalo Bar last night."

"He could be staying right here in town," Mikal said. "He has to be close, and he must have a vehicle."

When they had finished eating they walked down the street to the Buffalo Bar. It was just beginning to hum with activity. Ezra greeted the bartender by name.

"Evening," the man said. "How's Jim doing?"

Ezra told him Jim was fine. The barroom did not seem right without Mendenhall in it. It was like a Catholic church without any statues. Ezra asked the bartender if he had worked the night before and if Shorty Wilson had been in.

"I was here," the barkeep said. "And so was Shorty." He smiled at Mikal as if sharing a private joke, but Mikal didn't smile back. "I heard you broke Wilson's nose," he whispered to Ezra.

"I heard that too," Ezra said, not wanting to get into details. "Who was Wilson drinking with?" he asked quietly while glancing around. He did not want to be heard making inquiries about Shorty Wilson, especially not after the events of that morning.

"Shorty's not too popular right now. Can't say there was a line waiting to buy him a drink."

"How about a stranger?" Mikal broke in. "Tall, bearded guy about thirty-one years old? Did you see Shorty with him?"

"Might have seen him," the bartender said. "A strange sort of duck who wasn't drinking at all. He didn't stay long, and I don't think Shorty was that glad to see him."

"Why?" Mikal asked. "What gave you that idea?"

The bartender did not like the cool light he saw in the eyes of Ezra's companion. "What's this all about?" he asked. "I have customers to wait on. I know you, Ezra, but I don't know this guy. Does he have a badge or what?"

Ezra remembered the legal problems Wilson was in. It was natural people would be suspicious of a stranger with questions. "Do you want to see his badge?" Ezra asked.

"No, but I have to get back to work."

"Listen," Ezra said. "Call me if the bearded guy comes back in."

"You guys want a drink?" the bartender asked.

Ezra shook his head.

The barkeep moved away to wait on paying customers.

Ezra and Mikal walked back to the truck.

"Pratt's playing games," Ezra said as he drove home. "He's trying to force me into this *conversation of death* thing."

"And then what?" Mikal challenged. "He kills you and you become the cowboy-preacher martyr?"

"No, that's too obvious," Ezra said. "I think he wants me to kill him."

It was an angle Mora had not considered. "You think he wants to be the martyr?" he asked.

"What else does he have? He needed de la Rosa but couldn't submit to him. Now he's lost in his own fantasy. He must make the fantasy come true or destroy himself in the process. He wants a righteous death. The Old West—me, as a cowboy—kills the New West—Pratt as the ultimate environmentalist. It's performance art on a macabre level."

"Is that why you won't take my pistol?" Mikal asked. "You are afraid he's setting you up to use it?"

Ezra did not want to talk too much about death. It caused something black and ugly to stir within him. "That's part of the reason," he said dryly. "But mostly it's your terrible choice in weapons, Mikal. I mean, a Smith and Wesson? Get real, man. I don't want to be caught dead holding anything but a Ruger."

Mora smiled. He recognized the gallows humor. "You keep insisting on a Ruger and you will be caught dead," he said.

"But dead with style," Ezra retorted. He knew both brands were excellent weapons and didn't have the expertise to argue one over the other. He was only baiting Mora to keep a lightness on the edge of their tension.

They shared a relaxed smile, as if Pratt was just another burden, a heavy weight on an iron bar and each of them was spotting the other. The smile carried them off the highway, down the lane, and to the steps of the house. It faded when they saw the note taped to the door.

Evening, boys. Did we have fun in town?
P.S. Ezra, I never went in the house. I don't do those things.
Alpha

Ezra could not think of anything witty to say. Mikal folded the note neatly and put it in his pocket. A brooding anger clouded his eyes. He had nothing to say either.

Mikal would not sleep downstairs. He slept on the floor next to the woodstove in his sleeping bag. He awakened early, pulled on his pants and shirt, ran a hand across his dark stubble of beard, decided against shaving, and walked to the kitchen where Ezra was making coffee. "So what's for breakfast?" he asked.

"Dry cereal," Ezra said. "Because I keep forgetting to buy milk." He dug two big scoops of ground coffee from a container. "I'm also out of eggs and bread. The coffee is good though. Anne grinds her own beans."

"Just coffee for me," Mora said, and he settled into a kitchen chair and rubbed his face with his hands.

"You look a little rough," Ezra said. "Were you up checking heifers for me?"

"I had a terrible night," Mora groaned. "Nightmares all night long."

Ezra's interest was piqued. "Oh?" he asked. "What kind?"

"The kind a man has when he's been away from his wife too long," Mora said bluntly. His tone hid an undershadowing of sheepishness.

"But they were especially vivid?" Ezra suggested. "As if it really happened?"

"Exactly," Mikal admitted. He was uncomfortable talking about the encounter but was intrigued by its power. "I've never had a dream that seemed so real. It was eerie."

"And a little scary?" Ezra asked.

"Yeah, I guess you could say that," Mikal confessed. "Sexual dreams aren't all that unusual for me, being away from home for as long as I am, but this one was pretty intense."

"What if I told you you were attacked by a spirit?" Ezra asked.

Mora frowned. "I'd tell you you were nuts," he said. "Pratt's getting to you, Riley."

Ezra shrugged. He knew his friend's understanding of the matter simply suggested medieval castles and shrouded priests performing exorcisms. "Yeah, you're right," he relented. "Pratt is definitely getting to me."

Mora stared down at the floor. The mentioning of Pratt had pushed him past his nightmares and into the conflict of the morning. He had to go home, and as badly as he missed his wife and daughters, he did not want to leave a job unfinished and a friend in danger.

Ezra poured a large cup of black coffee and took it to him at the table. "So what's on the agenda today?" Ezra asked.

"I'm going to go to town," Mikal said. "Check the hotels, motels, recent apartment rentals. I'll visit with Sheriff Butler. What are you going to do?"

"The usual grunt work. Feed cows."

"Do you want me to leave my Smith?"

Ezra decided not to make any more jokes about Mikal's gun. Mora was obviously not in a good mood. "No, I don't think so," he said. "I have my Mini-14, a .22 pistol, and an old .30-30 carbine."

"The Mini is a good weapon," Mora said. "But you can't pack it on your person, and if Pratt charges you wearing a down vest and a Carhartt jacket, that .22 isn't likely to do anything but make him mad."

"Five smooth stones," Ezra said. "That's all David took with him when he faced Goliath."

"Stones," Mikal emphasized. "Not pebbles." He dropped the subject. He wasn't going to argue Bible stories with a preacher. "I'm going to town," he said—his stomach was pulling him to the Cattleman's—"I'll meet you back here at noon."

Ezra drank coffee, poured grain out for the horses, filled the food dishes for Beaner and Hemingway, then came back in and called the Jablonskis'. He was surprised, but pleased, when Diamond answered the phone. It showed the girl was adjusting to civilized life. "Diamond, how are you?" he asked.

"I'm fine," she said politely. "How are you?"

He could still detect apprehension in her voice. Her continued fear of him was discouraging. He asked if Anne was available.

"She's still asleep," Diamond said.

That was good, Ezra thought. Anne needed her rest. "How about Dylan?"

"He left early this morning for a tennis match in Billings."

He wanted to keep her talking. He wanted her to know that he was not only human, but a good person. "He's playing?" he asked. "Is his ankle better?"

"Yes," she said matter-of-factly. "We prayed for it last night."

"That's great," Ezra said. He could feel her courage slipping. "Well, tell Anne I called and that I'll call back later."

She hung up without saying good-bye.

Well, I guess she isn't healed yet, Ezra thought.

He reminded himself it was Saturday and he had a sermon to preach in twenty-four hours. He grabbed his Bible from his nightstand. He would study while waiting for the cows to come in. The phone rang when he reached the door.

"Ezra," Lilith said. "You kept me awake most of the night."

"I did?"

"I'm just teasing you," she chided. "Actually, I have been real concerned. Are you okay?"

"Yeah, just a little hungry—" He let the remark drop before he could stop it. Lilith didn't know he and Mikal were baching.

"Hungry?" she said. "Did your family move back into the Jablonski house?"

"Yes," he admitted. "I didn't feel it was safe for them here." *And it's not safe for you out here either*, he wanted to tell her. He was afraid she would insist on helping him.

She surprised him. "I have to go," she said. "I just wanted to know you were okay."

At noon Ezra was burning hamburgers under the broiler when Mikal came in. "What did you find out?" Ezra asked.

"Not a thing," Mikal said. He'd brought back a package of hamburger buns and a quart of milk. "There is no one matching Pratt's description in any of the motels. Same on the new rentals. Butler had a man check on all the public camping areas. *Nada*."

"So what's your guess? Pratt's camped in the hills?"

"That's right. Unless he's living here with you."

"He could be," Ezra said. "The laundry hasn't been done in a while. He might be sleeping in the hamper."

Mora sniffed the air. "Do you have a burn permit for your cooking?" he asked.

"I was going to barbeque outside but the propane bottle is empty," Ezra explained as he put the platter of burgers, buns, and condiments on the table. "I hope you don't mind," he said, "but I always say grace before eating."

"Mind?" Mikal said, looking at Ezra's cooking. "Today I insist."

Jokes aside, they ate hungrily. When they were finished, Ezra wiped the table while Mikal did the dishes. When he was done, Mikal went to the living room and pulled a small box out from under his leather aviator's jacket. "Here," he said, handing the box to Ezra. "Now you can stop complaining."

Ezra gave him a quizzical look then opened the box. Inside was a stainless steel small-framed revolver.

"A Ruger," Mikal said. "So no more excuses."

Ezra held it in his hands. It was small and compact with a rubber grip. "Mikal, where did you get this?" he asked.

"Traded in my 66. That's an SP101, .357 Magnum. It only has a five-shot cylinder, make sure you remember that. It's not a Smith, but it's a good weapon and very concealable."

Ezra felt humbled by the gift. The last time a friend had given him a present was when Rick Benjamin gave him a silver inlaid bit. "Mikal, this is very nice. But your Model 66 was your personal weapon. You shouldn't have done this."

Mikal tried to shrug off the sacrifice. "Wheel-guns don't interest me anymore," he said. "Everybody shoots semiautos. Besides, I can't stay, so I thought I better leave something with you."

The revolver's finish glowed softly. Ezra dry-fired the weapon at the floor. He was touched by Mikal's generosity, but the idea of packing a concealed weapon still challenged his ideals. "Mikal," he said. "I can't promise you I will pack this."

"I'm not asking you to," Mikal said. "But I do want to put you through a training session this afternoon."

Ezra realized he had only been given one other gun in his life. On his twelfth birthday his father had brought home a single-shot Ithica .22 rifle. When Dylan turned twelve, Ezra had passed it on to him. The old .30-30 did not count as a present. He had inherited it. There was not the physical transference of one hand passing the weapon to another, and in spite of Mikal's excuses, Ezra knew Mora had sacrificed a friend in trading off the Model 66. Guns were to Mikal what horses were to Ezra.

That afternoon Mikal tacked up a man-shaped target on a dead tree in the creek. "I'm going to start you from fifteen feet using what's called the Weaver Stance," Mikal explained. He stood at a forty-five-degree angle from the target, raised the Ruger in both hands, and dry-fired three times. *Click. Click. Click.* "Your front sight should be sharp and clear and the target slightly out of focus."

Mikal had Ezra dry-fire several times then handed him five bullets. "Try to maintain your sight picture all through the trigger squeeze," he said. "It's like the follow-through when shooting a basketball."

Ezra squeezed off five rounds. They were all low and to the left. Only one winged the man-shaped outline. "Am I doing anything right?" he asked.

"Not really." Mikal took the revolver, explained the basics again, then ripped off a staccato burst, putting all five holes in a three-inch group in the silhouette's chest. He tacked up a new target and handed the Ruger back to Ezra.

Ezra fired four more groups of five and paid careful attention to Mikal's coaching between each cylinder. He slowly relaxed and was just beginning to enjoy himself when a voice sounded from behind him. It was as soft as falling cotton but as piercing as a hawk's scream. "What are you doing?" it asked.

Ezra turned to see Anne standing on the creek bank. He cringed like a boy caught with dirty magazines. "Hi, sweetheart," he said. "Mikal's showing me some self-defense techniques."

She only glanced at Mikal even though she was yet to meet him. Her eyes were on the revolver in Ezra's hand. "Whose gun is it?" she asked.

"Well, it's mine. Mi—"

"Ezra. We need to talk. Alone." She turned and walked to the house. The afternoon cooled from her tone.

Ezra handed the Ruger to Mikal. "Excuse me for a minute," he said.

The house smelled of smoke. "What have you been burning in here?" Anne asked.

"That was lunch. The smoke was from the burning hair," Ezra joked. "We branded the cow before we ate her."

Anne shook her head and inspected the sink. "At least you are doing the dishes."

"Mikal did the dishes," Ezra said. The criticism in her voice and eyes was uncommon. "Anne, what's wrong?" Ezra asked. "What's wrong?" she said with some dramatic mockery. "I'm living in a strange house away from my husband who is being stalked by a madman, and I find you shooting at a human-shaped target with a handgun you say is yours."

"Whoa." Ezra held up a hand. "The revolver is a gift from Mikal. He's leaving tomorrow."

"So it's a gift. Does that make it any less a handgun? And he's leaving? So you are going to be out here alone? No way," she said. "I'm moving back."

"No, you are not," he said adamantly. "Not until Pratt is caught."

"And who is going to catch him if Mikal is leaving? You? Ezra, you are caught up in Mikal's world. It might be real for him, but it's not real for you. You are not a law enforcement officer. You are going to play around with this game and get yourself killed." Her eyes began to moisten with tears.

"No, I'm not," he said. He wanted to soothe her, but he resented the accusation. She made him sound like a boy playing with toys.

"Yes, you are. It's your death wish coming back," she said. "I can feel it covering you like a coat." Vivid in Anne's memory was a suicide attempt years before that miraculously resulted in Ezra's spiritual conversion.

"This is because it's a handgun, right? Rifles have never bothered you."

"Ezra, you know how I feel about handguns. They are designed to kill people."

"Anne, it's a gift from Mikal. He sold his first weapon to get it for me."

"Please give it back," she pleaded.

He moved a tentative step closer to her. "Anne, I may not ever see him again after tonight. He gave me a piece of himself with his best intentions. I can't give it back."

"So you're telling me you are going to stay here alone with a handgun and face Pratt. You have watched too many westerns, Ezra."

She was right, Ezra thought—not about watching westerns but in what he was telling her. He was staying alone to face Pratt.

"I'm moving back," she said.

"No, you're not," he countered.

She was exasperated. "Ezra, I don't want to lose you," she said. "I feel like something is trying to take you away from me."

"You're not going to lose me," he said.

Her blue eyes were piercing. "Do you mean that? Are you sure you don't have a death wish?"

"Believe me, I do not have a death wish."

"Is Mikal showing you how to use that gun correctly?"

"Yes, he is." He reached over, took her by the hand, and pulled her to him. "Anne, you have a lot of pressure on you right now. You're worried about me and Dylan and Diamond and trying to take finals at school. Hang in there, sweetheart. This will all be over soon."

"Are you sure?" She could smell the faint scent of soap on his skin. It seemed like years since she had swooned in that odor.

"I'm sure," he said. "Are you still having headaches?"

"No. They just seem to come when I'm leading worship at church. I came out because I need more clothes," she said. "And I brought you some milk and butter. I don't suppose you ever remember to get groceries."

He smiled, but he didn't answer. He was afraid it would reflect on his competence. Would she believe that someone who could not remember milk and butter could be trusted with a handgun?

Probably not.

That evening Ezra visited Jim Mendenhall in the hospital. Jim was sitting up in bed, kidding the nurses, and complaining about hospital food. He returned Ezra's greeting with a false gruffness as if Ezra was intruding on his fun.

"Are you going to live?" Ezra asked. "Or are you going to giggle your way to another heart attack?"

"Might do that," Jim chuckled. "If'n I knowed I was gonna be waited on hand and foot, I mighta got a room here earlier."

"Don't get too comfortable. I understand they're cutting you loose in a few days."

"Heck, I'm leavin' here tomorrow whether they like it or not. Doctor says he wants me to lose weight and quit chewin'."

"Are you going to listen to him?"

"Nope." He laughed as the two nurses gave him a dirty look and left the room. Then his face became serious. "How are my horses?" he asked.

"They're doing fine. I turned them out with mine today."

"I'll pay ya for your trouble."

"No trouble," Ezra said. "No payment expected."

"You really did break Shorty Wilson's nose?" Mendenhall grinned, still trying to remember the hilarity of the morning before. "He suin' ya yet?"

"Not that I know of. By the way, the night you were drinking with Shorty do you remember seeing a tall bearded guy?"

"Might have," he said. "But everything's still a little fuzzy."

"Well, I'll leave you to your recovery," Ezra said and started for the door.

"Hey, Ezra," Jim called after him. "Sorry about yesterday morning."

The sudden sincerity in Jim's voice was startling and stopped Ezra like a command. "Sorry for what?" Ezra said.

"For havin' a heart attack," Jim said. "I wasn't much help to ya lyin' on the ground dyin'."

Ezra smiled and nodded. Only Jim Mendenhall would be unrepentant about drinking but apologetic for having nearly died.

"Don't do it again," Ezra warned him. "Or Solomon will dock your wages."

That evening Ezra and Mikal sat at the kitchen table and discussed the situation as calmly as a card game. Mikal was angry and frustrated about having to leave, and Ezra was concerned about facing Pratt alone, but neither showed their emotions. Mikal insisted that Pratt would be undone by his own craziness. The Baal worship, the *thin place,* and the *conversation of death* were all evidence to Mikal of someone about to self-destruct.

When the conversation became too serious, they joked about weight lifting and teased one another about their individual weaknesses.

Then Mikal announced he was quitting undercover work and going back to a uniform. "I've been thinking about what you said," he told Ezra. "It's true that I am very black-and-white, good guys and bad guys. An agent can't have that mind-set and be good under cover. You have to be part outlaw or at least have some sympathy for the outlaw."

"You're probably right," Ezra said. "The high school kids had you pegged for some sort of lawman."

"I'm not much good at it, but you would make a good undercover agent, Ezra."

"Oh?" Ezra said. "Am I part outlaw?"

"Aren't you?" Mikal asked.

Ezra didn't ask him to elaborate and a long silence followed as if each was waiting for the other to deal another card.

"I'm going to quit being a lay counselor in my church," Ezra said finally. "For the opposite reason that you are giving up undercover work. I'm not black-and-white enough. Too much empathy."

"I thought mercy and compassion were Christian virtues," Mikal said.

"They are," Ezra said. "Within the proper limits."

Another silence followed as if their conversation was timed by cycles. When the mood in the room became uncomfortable both strained to find a new topic. Ezra finally broke the pause. "You know, I have to ask this," he said. "Is Mikal Mora your real name?"

"No," the agent replied. "My real name is Mark Anderson. Pretty boring name, huh?"

"How did you pick Mikal Mora?"

"Michael, spelled the regular way, is my middle name. Jim Mora is the coach of the New Orleans Saints, and I'm a Saints fan."

"So what do you want me to call you now?"

"I'm Mikal," he said. "Until Pratt is taken care of. After that you can call me anything you want."

They sat silently again. The only sound in the room was the quiet hum of a wall clock. They both knew that Pratt was somewhere in the surrounding darkness, but it accomplished nothing to talk about him. In his own, lapsed-Catholic way, Mikal had tried to tell Ezra that he had faith. Faith that things would turn out okay.

Ezra was too close to the fire to see its light. He only felt the heat. He finally expressed the last thought on his mind. "Mikal, if anything happens to me, no guilt, okay? Just consider me a poor student."

Mikal nodded.

They were like warriors separating from one another before battle and sealing their friendship in that very detachment.

"Well," Mikal said finally. "Know any card games?"

"Not many," Ezra said. Duty told him he should be in his room preparing Sunday's sermon. Friendship told him to stay with Mikal.

Mikal pulled a deck of cards from his pocket. "What ones do you know?" he asked.

"My father taught me Casino and Pitch, but I've forgotten them."

"You don't know any others?"

Ezra smiled. "Solitaire," he said. He was grinning at the realization that the only card game he knew was based on singleness. As a writer he appreciated the symbolism. Beginning the next day, he would definitely be alone.

CHAPTER TWENTY-SEVEN

My father insisted our family stop attending church over an argument about putting a church sign on ranch property. Nothing was ever said about religion in our home again. The only reference to God was in profanity, and my father and uncles were masters at profane speech. Their language was so blasphemous I often wondered why God never struck them dead with lightning. Then one day He did. Willis, Archie, and Rufus were killed when lightning hit a fenceline they were repairing—a fenceline torn down by a stampede I had caused. I never again wondered why God didn't strike the profane dead. I was afraid He would and I would get the blame.

Leaving the Land

He knew he was in trouble when Betty Lou entered the church carrying a yellow legal pad. She even took a pew several rows closer to the front, followed complacently by her husband, Armon, as if he existed only to sharpen her pencils.

Worship went poorly. Anne was distracted. Her heart wasn't in her singing; she kept rubbing her temples as if her head ached, and she and the pianist were not synchronized. Ezra couldn't tell if she was angry with him, exhausted from her studies, or both.

Dylan had talked Diamond back to church, and they again sat in the back—the better to be farther from him, Ezra thought, and less far for Diamond to run. Then he chided himself for being cynical.

Lilith, Ben, and Hillary had moved to the front pew. He knew she was there to be supportive. After the incident two weeks ago with Diamond, Lilith walked in a new authority. One granted to her by Ezra's trusting her with the microphone.

He felt Anne watching him, and he knew her thoughts. She was worried and confused and wondered if she knew this man who was about to stand and preach. It didn't help that she was sleeping in town and he at the ranch. She was worried, too, because Mora was gone.

Ezra had put Mikal on the plane that morning. They had loaded his bags in the dusky grayness of a clouded dawn and shook hands with the promise to call the other. The sun broke through, painting the sky aqua, amber, and silver when the plane took to the air. In moments it was high and westward, looking no bigger than a single Canadian goose.

He was stirred from his thoughts by the silence of the congregation staring at him. The songs, the announcements, and the offering were over, and it was time for the sermon. He walked to the pulpit like a guiltless man approaching the gallows. It was time to lay down his life, in a proverbial sense.

"You know," he said, leaning against the dais. "The safest thing I could do is teach a little moral lesson from the Scriptures. I can't do that today. Today I have to talk from my heart." Lilith gave him a look of keen anticipation. Betty Lou's face was stitched in a smug self-righteousness. Anne looked concerned.

"I don't know everything there is to know about evil, but we do live in an evil age and no amount of right-living can ensure that evil will not cross our threshhold. Jesus said that in this world we would have tribulation. We spend much of our time avoiding, ignoring, and denying that very tribulation." He noticed that Betty Lou could scribble as fast as he could talk.

"I want to talk to you about a hero of mine," he continued. "His name was Guy V. Henry, and he won the Congressional Medal of Honor in the Civil War at Old Cold Harbor. Later on he was a cavalry officer assigned to this general area.

"Shortly before the Battle of the Little Big Horn, Colonel Henry and his men were attacked by the Sioux and Cheyenne led by the famous chief, Crazy Horse. While rescuing, rallying, and steadying his troops Colonel Henry was struck by a rifle bullet that went under his left eye, through the upper part of his mouth, under his nose, and exited below his right eye." Several women grimaced, but the few men in the church, including Ben Foster, came awake and paid closer attention. Betty Lou gave him a disgusted look and pointed at her notes.

"Though badly wounded, Colonel Henry led one more charge before losing consciousness and falling from his horse. Friendly Shoshone scouts fended off the enemy until Henry could be removed to the rear. There he mumbled to the attending surgeon: 'Fix me up so I can go back.'

"He was not to go back that day. While the battle raged through the hot afternoon, Colonel Henry lay on the sod, his only shelter the shadow of his horse. During a lull in the fighting, an officer accompanied by a war correspondent from the *Chicago Times* checked on him.

"Henry saw the concern on his fellow officer's face. 'It's all right, Jack,' he gurgled through bleeding lips. 'It's what we are here for.' He then tried to convince the war correspondent to quit civilian life and enlist in the army.

"Colonel Henry lived to become a general and the military governor of Puerto Rico. He was also known as a kindly, wise, Christian man who regularly taught Sunday school.

"My point is this," Ezra said. "In our battle with this present age of darkness and its wicked leaders, there are many of us—most of us—that are wounded in one way or another. But what is our attitude? Do we want to leave the battle, nurse our wounds, and moan in self-pity, or are we like Colonel Henry, eager to get patched up so we can get back in the fight? And like the good colonel, even while wounded are we still trying to win others for Christ? Are we encouraging civilians to become members of His army?"

He coiled the microphone wire as if it were a lariat and stepped away from the dias. "I know this message might anger some of you," he said. "And I know Pastor Tom will listen to it on tape and maybe I will get called on the carpet. But the truth is, I think most of us Christians are just big crybabies. We hide in our church world as if it were a fort and never dare to take our faith outside the church walls. And once the enemy shoots an arrow or two at us, we rush madly back to safety to wail in pain and beg for healing. The funny part is, even after we are healed we complain about the scars. Don't we realize that scars are battle emblems and proof of our healings?

"I don't know," he said, shaking his head. "Maybe I am off base, but I think the church in America is largely filled with whiners, and we are good examples. *I* am a good example. I think we need to repent of our defensiveness, self-indulgence, and self-pitying, and throw away our long lists of excuses and simply get back in the fight."

He did not say anything more. He simply stepped off the stage and took a seat in the front pew while the congregation sat nervously for several minutes. When they realized he was done many got up to leave. A few came to the altar to pray.

Lilith touched his arm as she passed on her way to the altar. "Excellent," she whispered. Ben followed closely behind her. He gave Ezra a vague, searching look that showed both confusion and respect. On any other morning the look might have bothered Ezra, but on this day it meant nothing to him. He watched as they knelt together to pray and earnestly hoped the best for them, for their marriage and future. He wanted Lilith healed and Ben strengthened.

Across the platform Anne stared at him through pondering eyes. Her look was honest but blank as if she had something to say but no words with which to package her thoughts. Then she looked away.

He twisted his neck to see if Diamond was still in her pew. She was and he felt relieved.

The relief didn't last long. He felt someone sit beside him and knew who it was without looking.

"You have done it this time, Ezra Riley," Betty Lou said. "Do you think people come to church to hear gory stories from Indian battles? Do you realize you never mentioned the Bible once?"

"You are right, Betty Lou," he said. "I never used the Bible once."

"This has just gone too far, too far," she said. "You know I will have to call Pastor Jablonski about this."

"I would be disappointed in you if you didn't."

"Well, you certainly seem unfazed."

"Do what you have to do, Betty Lou."

"Hmmm, I heard you were seen walking out of the Buffalo Bar Friday night. Would you like to explain just exactly what you were doing in a bar?"

Ezra rose to his feet, collected his Bible, and looked down at her. "I was in there trying to forget about you," he said sweetly. Her eyebrows almost disappeared into her scalp. She rose and stormed away, huffing like a locomotive. Armon came by, wrapped in his usual blissful ignorance, and shook Ezra's hand. "I enjoyed that story," he said, then he left to follow his wife.

Ezra sighed and looked back to Anne. She was focused on playing the piano—soft mood music for the people still praying, of which there were only two: Ben and Lilith. Ezra got up and walked out. He thought about greeting his son and Diamond but was afraid to. He wasn't ready for another panic attack from the girl.

Anne watched him leave. She saw the weariness in his step and the weight on his shoulders, and she wondered again if the man she had known and loved for over twenty years was irreversibly changing in front of her eyes.

Lilith looked up from praying and watched him leave. Ben kept his eyes closed.

No one tried to stop Ezra. They just let him go.

That evening he sat on the front steps with a cordless phone beside him and Beaner at his feet. Hemingway occasionally marched past to yowl, accept a brief rub, then proceed on her territorial duties of being the superior beast that she was.

He expected the phone to ring. He was sure Anne would call him, but she hadn't.

He thought maybe Dylan would. He had tried calling the Jablonskis' earlier but the line was busy.

He hoped Mikal might just to let him know he had arrived safely. But Mikal was in the arms of his wife and children. His was a different world now.

A call from Jubal Lee would be most welcome, but he didn't expect one. Not yet.

Pastor Tom would call, he knew that. If not that night, then soon. Maybe in the morning.

The sky was an ashen blue with crimson stabbings of long, angular clouds backlit by the setting sun. Barn swallows were busily mudding nests under the eaves of the barn. He wanted to shoot them, but Mikal had told him he couldn't. They were federally protected. So were the magpies, he discovered.

Heck of a world, he thought. Pests were given so much sanctuary.

He looked to the hills. Pratt was out there somewhere, maybe only yards away. "Where are you sleeping at night?" Ezra said softly, directing the question at the vastness of the surrounding prairie. Beaner cocked an ear and looked at him, sure he was talking to her. "It's been cool lately," Ezra continued. "If you have a tent we would have seen it by now. Are you simply denning up in a hole like a coyote? I'm not saying you're not tough enough," he said, "but doesn't it grow old? How do you brush your teeth? Where do you bathe? Do you bathe at all? You must, don't you, Pratt? If you didn't I would smell you coming." He waited as if expecting his adversary to answer.

The phone rang.

"Ezra," the voice said. "How are you doing?"

This time he recognized his pastor. "I'm okay, Pastor Tom."

"Are you? I mean, seriously, Ezra, are you okay?"

"Yeah," Ezra sighed. "I'm okay. Just going through a tough time, that's all."

"I heard church was a little, uh, different, this morning."

Ezra rubbed his temples as if massaging away a headache of his own. "Yes, it was," he admitted. "I'm sorry if I'm not meeting your expectations. I hope I'm not ruining your sabbatical."

"Oh, don't worry about it," the pastor said. "Darlene and I are having a wonderful time. We are very grateful to you for taking such a responsibility with no warning whatsoever."

"I'm probably screwing things up."

"That remains to be seen. It sounds like you gave a hard word this morning. The church probably needed it. Anyway, it is better coming from you than from me."

"True. They can't fire me," Ezra joked. "Or cut my wages."

"That's not what I meant," Tom said. "I mean you are one of them, one of the people. That is all but impossible for a pastor no matter how hard he tries. It's just something about the nature of the job, I guess."

"Well, it's a hard job and I'm glad it's not mine." He was watching the sunset fade. The last stabbing rays lit the orange in the barn swallows' tailfeathers, making the birds look like tiny fighter planes with flaming engines.

"Ezra," Tom's voice became pastoral. "When I asked if you were okay, I wasn't thinking about the morning service. I understand your life may be at risk. Is this true?"

"It's possible. I really don't know."

"But you have moved Anne and Dylan and the Indian girl back out of your house again?"

"Yes, I'm afraid we are using the Jablonski Hotel."

"That's fine, don't worry about that. But who's there to help keep an eye on you?"

"No one. Just me, my pup, and my cat. The pup doesn't bark, and my cat doesn't like me very much."

"I'll come right home if you want me to," Pastor Tom said. "I will stay out at the ranch with you."

Pastor Jablonski, the old offensive lineman, Ezra thought. *Ready to get dirty in the trenches.* "No," Ezra said. "I appreciate it, but I really want you and Darlene to stay. I just wish you had somebody else to preach."

"Ezra, I heard you were packing a handgun."

"Well, not exactly packing it. But I was given one."

"Look, if your life is in danger, pack it. Get a little shoulder holster, something that's comfortable. Get a concealed weapons permit. Don't get hung up on spiritual appearances. You are not being more godly by facing evil unarmed."

Ezra smiled with relief. His pastor was blessing Mikal's gift. "Thanks," he said. "I needed to hear that. I'm sorry this is disrupting your time back home. I know you don't enjoy getting calls from Betty Lou."

"Betty Lou?" Tom said. "Oh, Betty Lou didn't call me this time."

"She didn't? Then who did?"

"Anne," the pastor said. "It was Anne who called me."

The emptiness of the house was overwhelming when Ezra awakened Monday morning. Everyone was noticeable by their absence. Anne's books were not stacked on the table, Dylan's tennis bag was not an obstacle in the hallway, Diamond's faded jacket did not hang from a nail, and Mikal's heavy steps could not be heard coming down the hall. Ezra made a full pot of coffee knowing he had no one to share it with.

He did not call Anne. He was a little angry that she had called Pastor Tom without talking to him first. He felt like a schoolboy who had been tattled on. He knew it was silly—it was his male pride taking control—but he could not bring himself to dial the Jablonskis' number though he did want to talk to Dylan. The tennis divisionals were coming up, and Ezra wanted to wish him luck. But he didn't call. It was Monday and Dylan had an early staff meeting for the school paper. If he called the Jablonskis' he would only reach Diamond. What would he say to her? *Good morning, Diamond. Are you still scared to death of me? Do you think I am evil incarnate? Are you secretly working for your boyfriend, Pratt?*

The solitude he knew when writing in the bunkhouse had now expanded and taken the entire ranch as if he had pulled within the pages of one of his own stories. Even Solomon was not an alternative. What would Ezra discuss with his uncle? *What's new? Well, I have had a federal agent staying with me. He's been hunting the poacher I told you about, a guy who has promised to kill me, but first he has to find this* thin place *he's looking for. You wouldn't know where it is, would you? But the agent is gone. He gave me a handgun before he left, and I'm packing it in my pocket. A .357 Magnum. Oh, and Anne and Dylan are living in town with the Indian girl. The Indian girl? Gee, I guess you don't even know about her, do you?*

It was a good thing he was a writer, Ezra decided, because he could create all the imaginary conversations he needed.

The phone rang. He hoped it was Anne. Or Mikal or Jubal or Dylan.

It was Sheriff Butler's office telling him his concealed weapons permit was ready. Ezra said he would be right in to get it. He needed to buy a holster anyway. The Ruger fit well in the deep, slanted pockets of his Carhartt vest but he couldn't wear the vest all the time, could he? Well, he could, he thought to himself. After all, who was around to care? He could wear it to bed with the .357 in one pocket and the .22 in the other.

"Stop talking to yourself," Ezra said angrily. He shook his head. "Too much coffee. Way too much coffee."

The last heifer finally calved. Ezra didn't pay it much attention. It was always a relief to have the last one done, but it didn't seem very exciting compared to his circumstances. Hemingway yowled at him as he threw the heifer hay from the loft. Darn cat thought it owned the barn. He wanted to take his pistol out and use the Manx for target practice.

On the way to town he noticed a bunch of Shorty Wilson's cows grazing the wheatgrass and dryland alfalfa Ezra was hoping to save for hay. He cussed Wilson—"I should have broken more than his nose," he declared— then descended into a shallow pit of remorse. He was not a great preacher, but he was still a Christian and Wilson was his neighbor. *Love your neighbor as thyself.*

He had hoped Butler would be in, but he wasn't. His concealed carry permit was handed to him by a young deputy who didn't look old enough to shave.

"Has the sheriff been flying lately?" Ezra asked.

"Flying? Why would he be flying?" the deputy asked. He thought he had authority simply because he had a badge and a gun.

"With the ADC," Ezra explained. "He said he would fly over my ranch a little."

"ADC? The sheriff isn't the government hunter. He doesn't fly for Animal Damage Control." The deputy's tone was sarcastic and condescending.

Ezra tried his best to be reasonable. "No, I know that," he said. "But he said he would fly to look for someone who is hiding on my ranch."

"Hiding on your ranch?" The deputy laughed. "Who are you, anyway?"

Ezra just shrugged and walked away. It was not going to be a day for getting help. As he was turning to leave the courthouse, he saw three people enter through a different door and walk down a hallway away from him. One was Shorty Wilson; his nose was still bandaged. Ezra guessed the other two were high-priced lawyers from Billings.

Ezra thought about stopping Wilson and apologizing for breaking his nose.

"The heck with it," he said to the marble floor and wainscoted walls. "Forgive me, Lord, but I'm just not sorry I did it." A clerk in a nearby office looked at him suspiciously. Ezra gave her a roguish smile, tipped his hat, and left the building. It was Monday and he knew he had something to do, but other than putting Wilson's cows out of his hay meadows, he couldn't remember what it was.

CHAPTER TWENTY-EIGHT

Uncle Joe watched as I tried my new fly rod. He didn't think much of fly-fishing. "You can spank that water all you want," he said, "but you can't make it give you fish." I shrugged it off. My uncles teased me about anything I truly valued, like writing, basketball, and especially my treasured paint horse, Gusto. Only the ridicule about the horse really hurt. "You just gotta be different, don'tchya?" Uncle Joe said. "Just like that paint horse of yours. Tryin' to show the rest of us up." He threaded worms on his three hooks and whirled the configuration of sinkers, hooks, and bobber toward the water where they splashed in a tangled mess. "No one in this country rides paints," he said, speaking to himself. He was a huge man in bib coveralls, sunglasses, and a brightly colored Hawaiian hat sitting on an overturned five-gallon bucket. "Paint horses draw too much attention," he said. "I favor discretion myself."

Leaving the Land

Beaner didn't bark when the car pulled up, but Hemingway gave a distinctive yowl—a disembodied wail that reminded Ezra of how Jubal Lee had described Pratt's laugh. Ezra was in the barn saddling Shiloh, and the cat's screech nearly jolted him out of his chaps.

When he looked out he saw Lilith in the yard rubbing the Manx behind one ear. The cat's back was arched and its stub of a tail pointed straight up. After being appropriately anointed, the cat strutted off. Lilith stood, stretched, and looked around for Ezra. She wore a white blouse, short black jacket, and denim pants tucked into the tops of English riding boots. "Ezra!" she called out.

"In the barn," he answered. He had forgotten all about their date to visit Gusto's grave.

She walked to the corral carrying her English saddle and leggings. "Good morning," she said cheerfully. "Is it okay if I ride English today?"

"Listen, Lilith," he said. "I don't know if this is a good idea. Pratt hasn't been caught, and I'm out here alone."

"You're not alone," she said. "I'm here." She walked past him and into the corral. "Do you want me to ride Cheyenne or the colt?" she asked.

"You better ride Cheyenne," he said. He knew there was no denying her wishes, short of physically forcing her into her car.

She bridled the dun and led him to the saddling stall. "It's a beautiful day," she called out while brushing him. "It is going to be warm but not too sunny—I'm going to take a chance and not wear a hat, but I have tons of sunscreen on. And," she continued, after taking a deep breath, "the birds are singing and the cottonwoods are even beginning to bud."

"Yeah, beautiful day," Ezra said.

"You don't sound very cheery," she scolded.

He felt the distance between him and his wife, the loss of an ally in Mikal, and was tortured by the thought that yesterday's sermon had been an abysmal failure. "I've had better days," he said.

"Oh, quit feeling sorry for yourself," she teased. "Remember your sermon yesterday, which was wonderful, by the way. You are a wounded warrior, Ezra. Let's get back on the horse and get back into the fight just like ol' what's-his-name."

"Colonel Henry," he said. He certainly did not feel as full of spunk and heroism as the late colonel.

"Right." She led Cheyenne from the stall. Ezra had never seen an English saddle on one of his horses before. The stout dun looked as if it were wearing a leather napkin on its back. "No jokes about the saddle," she warned him.

They led their horses through a gate to the creek. Ezra pulled the brim of his hat down, hitched up his pants, and reached for the saddle horn to mount.

"Ah, Ezra," Lilith said. "I need a leg up."

"A what?" He turned to look at her, his one foot already in a stirrup.

"A leg up. It's customary when you ride Eng-leesh," she said, drawing out the noun with a false snobbery.

He led his horse over to her. Her eyes were especially bright and her complexion was soft and glowing, causing her face to seem especially warm and inviting. For an instant he was tempted to kiss her. Her lips were full, pouting, and painted. He pulled back, he had not kissed another woman since marrying Anne. "What do I do?" he asked.

"Cup your hands," she said. She put her right boot into the cradle his hands formed. "Now boost me up."

He lifted her lightly and easily into the saddle.

"See," she said. "Nothing to it."

He nodded and put his spurred boot back into his stirrup. "Leg up?" he asked.

"No way." She laughed. "You're a big boy."

They rode slowly down the creek. Ezra whistled for Beaner. The pup came running, overjoyed with the invitation.

"You're letting the dog come?" Lilith asked.

"If he can heel Shorty Wilson, he's old enough to start heeling cows," Ezra said.

They rode in silence through sagebrush and cottonwoods. Ezra dismounted to open a wire gate. They rode through.

"You seem distracted," Lilith said.

"It is distracting to know we are probably being watched." He glanced at the surrounding hills knowing Pratt would not allow himself to be seen. He was too cagey for that.

"You think he is watching us now?" She looked around too.

"You can bet on it." He had the same feeling when hunting bull elk in timber. The air was electric with conflicting awarenesses as if with each step, he was pushing through Pratt's radar. That web of psychic vibrations seemed to cover the entire ranch like a net, and he often felt strangled by its clutches.

The tension built in Ezra as they approached Shorty Wilson's cows. He wanted to inflict punishment upon them, make them feel enough pain to deter them from ever straying again. The cattle were smart and devious like their owner. They knew they were in the wrong pasture and began to gather themselves as they saw the horseman coming.

Ezra approached them at a gallop, his lariat in his hand. He used twenty feet of uncoiled rope like a bullwhip—snapping the cattle with the rawhide honda on the rope's end. "Ssss'get'em out," he yelled at Beaner. "Sss'get'em out." Instinct rose in the heeler, and she laid her ears back and attacked the fleeing cows with a vengeance. "Ssss'get'em out, sss'get'em out," Ezra encouraged. The pup grew bolder with success like a twenty-five-pound piranha attacking a school of thousand-pound fish. The cows ran purposely to where they had rubbed the fence down and leaped the wires in desperate, ingracious bounds. Beaner pursued them through the fence for twenty yards, then stopped and looked eagerly back to her master for further instructions.

"Come," Ezra said, slapping his leather thigh. He stepped off his horse and crouched. The pup ran deliriously into his arms, washing his neck with sandpaper licks and wagging her tail ferociously. "Good girl," Ezra said, patting her. "Good girl."

Lilith had been but a spectator, a horse and rider in tow to Ezra's anger and the dog's joyful delirium, but she had enjoyed the chase. She brought Cheyenne alongside Shiloh. It was almost a look of jealousy that came across her as she watched the pup lavish its affections on its master. "That was fun," she said, as if to no one in particular.

"Harassing Wilson's cows," Ezra noted, "is one of my few joys in life." He hunted in the grass for the loosened staples and pounded the fence back up with his fencing pliers.

"Will they stay out?" Lilith asked.

"No," Ezra said. "It's a constant battle. One I have been fighting for years. It will only be over when Wilson is no longer around."

"Any hope for that?" she asked.

"Some," he said, and he remounted and followed the fenceline across a sodded flat, through the creek, and up a rising staircase of cedar hills. Shiloh's thick shoulders and massive hindquarters labored mechanically and his breathing deepened like bellows on a forge. When they reached the top, the horses stopped immediately and sucked air in voluminous breaths. Both branches of Sunday Creek and all of their little tributaries were spread out before them, the grassy meadows and prairie spread like a giant green tablecloth, the distant hills rising like closed fists placed upon an open, outstretched palm.

"It's beautiful," Lilith sighed appreciatively.

"Yes, it is," Ezra said. He dismounted and led Shiloh to the tip of the hill. Lilith dismounted with a bounce and followed.

"He's buried here, beneath us," Ezra said, crouched on the lip of the hill. The needle grass, yucca, and cactus had reclaimed the sod. There was no scar of a grave.

"No monument?" Lilith asked.

"No, you couldn't put on a monument what that horse meant to me. Besides, this way it is not a grave. It is simply where he returned to the soil, where he reentered the land."

"Tell me about him," she said, kneeling at his side.

"When I was ten my dad tried to make me break a ornery little blue roan named Ribbon Tail. I hated that horse with a passion. Some mornings I would rather have died than climb on that little beast. He about destroyed any love I had for horses. Then Gusto came along. He was grace and mercy wrapped in horseflesh. He taught me to believe in second chances."

"You feel that way about people, don't you?" she said, drawing closer to him. "You know my past but you believe in me. You believe in Diamond even though she is terrified of you."

"Jesus is the Lord of second chances," Ezra said.

"You don't even hate Pratt, do you? You would even like to see him have another chance."

"Who am I to judge anyone? I was once a drug-abusing hippie up to my neck in Eastern religions, the occult, and the martial arts."

"You are a strange blending of toughness and mercy, Ezra. Not to mention the contradiction of hippie and cowboy."

His canvas jacket parted and she noticed the pistol holstered on his hip. She looked away. "I've always wanted to live in the country," she said. "Not a big ranch or anything, just a small ranch or a farm. I like watching things grow. I like animals."

"It is how most of us were meant to live," he said, his eyes drinking in the vastness of the landscape.

"You love the land so much," she said.

"I love it because I see God's handiwork in it. Last winter I was walking down a creek bed after a fresh snow. The banks were lined with red stems of willows, the sky was a warm gray, and the bare cottonwoods stood like big black sentinels. It was just me sliding along on the fresh snow. No tracks, nothing. And I remembered what Jesus said about our sins being as white as snow, and I thought, *I can never be this pure.*"

"We can, though, can't we?" she asked. "I mean, through His salvation?"

"In eternity, I suppose," he said. "But in this world it is the land that talks to me about higher things. That's why I can't hate Pratt. We both listen to the land. He just hears the wrong voices."

"What does your son want?" she asked, gazing at the meadows and hills. "Does he want this life?"

"I think so," Ezra said. "But that is my one great failure. I have not been able to provide him a birthright. There is no guarantee he will ever be able to live here."

Her tone changed to a new seriousness. "Ezra, how can I help you? You seem so distressed, and not on a superficial level, but deep down. Tumultuous. That's how I would describe you."

"You can't help me," he said. "But I appreciate your concern."

"May I get personal?"

"Sure," he shrugged, his eyes on the horizon. "Nothing's stopped you before."

"How are things with you and Anne? She seemed very disjointed yesterday in church."

He granted only the facts. "It is a hard time for Anne," he said. "She is in the middle of finals, ministering to an emotionally scarred young woman, and living in a strange house while her husband is in the hills with a madman."

"I don't mean to pry," she said. "But she must understand that you are trying to protect her by having her stay in town."

"She doesn't like protection by displacement."

"I know. I understand. If I were her I would want to be here with you too."

"Well, you are here right now, and I appreciate your friendship. But this is our last time together until Pratt is caught. I will not put you and your family at risk."

"We can't meet at the church?"

He shook his head. He had things to say that he knew she did not want to hear. "No, we can't meet at the church. In fact, our counseling relationship might be over, Lilith. Pastor Tom will be back in a couple of weeks. Your counseling should resume with him."

The disappointment clouded her face, solidified, and slid into her chest. "I want you for my counselor," she said.

He shook his head again. "We have reached the point where we can be friends or we can be counselor and counselee, but we can't be both. And," his voice softened, "I think the choice is yours."

"Why?" she demanded.

"I let our relationship cross a couple of lines that should not have been crossed," he said.

"Are we too close?" she asked.

"In a way we are, Lilith. I'm serious. You will have to choose between having me as a friend or as a counselor."

Her face was pained. "That is not a choice I want to make. I will have to think about it. I can't imagine Pastor Tom as a very good counselor, not compared to you."

Ezra fiddled with his reins. "He's a little dry and academic, but that distance is healthy sometimes. It provides objectivity."

"But you have such deep insight."

"Maybe, but he has discipline and fundamentals."

"Well, you're a much more interesting preacher," she intoned righteously.

He tried to defuse her. "I've only preached four Sundays," Ezra said. "That's hardly a career."

She looked across his body to his hip. "Why are you carrying a gun?" she asked. The question was pointed as if she was regaining the offensive.

"Because Pratt is dangerous, and I am responsible for your safety. Does the gun bother you?"

"No, but are you afraid?" she asked. "He wants to kill you, doesn't he?"

"I don't think Pratt knows what he wants."

"You seem resigned. Almost fatalistic."

"I'm not resigned to death. I'm resigned to an encounter with death. I want to live, but if I were to die my son is almost raised, and Anne has a new career before her. They'll be okay."

"That sounds selfish," she reproved him.

"No. That's reality. Facing death is stepping naked into the dark night. You can't pack a lot of baggage."

"Sometimes you're scary," she said.

"That is why you find me interesting."

"Oh? Is that it?" she challenged, and punched him lightly on the arm.

"Yes. We both walk close to the edge, Lilith. There's something in us that likes the view."

"And what is this *something?*"

"I don't know," he said, rising to his feet. "But it can be deadly if we're not cautious." He gave her a hand up. "We should be going," he said.

She did not let go of his hand. "Well, thank you for bringing me to Gusto's grave, it's like visiting a holy place."

He shook his head and took his hand away. "No," he corrected her. "It's not a holy place. It is a hill with a nice view where I buried my horse."

CHAPTER TWENTY-NINE

For lunch he burned a hamburger. The surface was black but the inside was raw so he fed it to Beaner. The pup was having the best day of her life. She was getting to chase cows and eat them too.

Ezra weighed himself on the bathroom scale and realized he was down to 154 pounds because he had no interest in food; he ate just enough to keep his strength up.

He was saddling Cajun for the day's second ride when another vehicle drove into the yard. As he led the colt from the tack room stall, he met Dylan coming into the corral.

"Hi," Ezra said. "What are you doing out of school?"

"I had a free period," Dylan said, brushing a strand of hair from his eyes. "I thought I'd come out and see how you're doing."

"How did your matches go in Billings?" Ezra asked.

"They creamed us, as usual," Dylan said.

"But your ankle is better," Ezra noted.

"Yeah, Mom and Diamond prayed for it." He announced his healing with implication in his voice.

Ezra nodded. He could read between the lines. The father was the preacher but the mother and the Indian girl could pray miracle prayers. "That's good," Ezra said. He reset the saddle and pulled the cinch snug. Dylan stood by in quiet anticipation.

"Something on your mind?" Ezra asked. The short silence had been as heavy as an April snow.

The boy nearly burst with concern. "Dad, what's going on between you and Mom?" he asked. His tone was respectful but urgent.

"There's lots going on," Ezra said, leading the chestnut colt to a post. "There's Pratt and Diamond and your mother's schoolwork. And there is some sort of spiritual warfare going on too."

"What kind?" Dylan asked.

Ezra smiled self-consciously. "I don't want to embarrass you, but have you had any really unusual dreams lately?"

The boy blushed. "One," he said. "But I thought it was because I ate too much lasagna."

"Let me guess. It happened in our house, and the dream was sexual. You're not the only one who has experienced this, Dylan."

"So what does it mean?" Dylan asked. "I thought it was just hormones. I've felt terrible about it since it happened."

"I don't know what it means," Ezra said.

Dylan frowned. "That's all you can say? I mean, you and Mom are not even living together, and you think these sexual dreams have something to do with it? I dunno. It just seems like there's more to it than that. There's a division between you and everyone else, and I don't think it's safe." He cleared his throat to summon his courage. "I want to move back out here," Dylan declared.

Ezra leaned an arm across the chestnut's rump. "I appreciate that, Dylan, but you know I can't allow it."

The boy stiffened. "Dad," he said. "I think you're being selfish. You've made it all your battle. What about me and Mom? It's our battle too."

"That's true, Dylan. But you have a different battleground. You and your mother have school and Diamond to take care of. This isn't a good place for Diamond. What would she do out here while the two of you are in school? She's not ready to be alone with me, and the ranch represents something she can't deal with yet. Just like the church does."

"The church?"

"Yeah. The way she ran out of the church two weeks ago. I know she came back with you yesterday, and that's great, but she sat there as nervous as a chicken in a fox den."

"Dad, Diamond's my friend. We talk. And I can tell you, her running out that day had nothing to do with the church. Yeah, she felt something evil. But it wasn't the church, it was . . . somebody."

"Who, Dylan? I am the only person that stands out."

"I don't think it's you," Dylan said. "She likes you, but you intimidate her. I think you remind her of Deemie, I mean, Pratt."

Ezra measured his maturing son with a thoughtful gaze. "You could be right," he said. "But, in any case, she needs you and your mother right now. Your mother needs you too. And I need you, Dylan, but not here. I need you in town."

"I think you're wrong, Dad, and I think you're being selfish. Can you accept that?"

"Yes," Ezra said. "I can accept your sincerity."

"You're an extremist, Dad. You could leave the ranch. What's the worst that could happen? Pratt might burn the house down? Insurance would cover that. You've made it a personal thing, like what you've told me about you and Mikal lifting weights. Everything is a competition with you. Pratt is just another competitor."

"It's more than that, Dylan. I wouldn't risk my life or the lives of others over an ego trip."

"Maybe, except this one involves land. I've spent my life watching you break your back over a few thousand acres of gumbo and grass. I've watched you nurse cattle through tough winters only to have an April storm kill twenty or thirty of their calves. You have a bad back, tendonitis in both elbows, and a torn rotator cuff. Life for you is a fight, Dad. You want it that way."

Ezra nodded slowly. "Some things are worth fighting for, Dylan. Our life on the ranch has been hard—we have never had enough of either money or time—but it's been worthwhile. You're a great kid who is becoming a terrific man. The ranch helped in that development, and that alone was worth the struggle."

"Dad, I love the ranch too. But it's not worth dying for. I don't care if it's Pratt or you breaking your back tossing hay bales all winter. The ranch is killing you."

"We are often undone by that which we love."

"And you're not going to walk away from a confrontation with Pratt," Dylan said. "Not for Mom. Not for me. Not for anyone."

"Was that a question?"

"No, it was an observation."

"It was a correct one," Ezra said. "I can't walk away, Dylan. I can't do it. And I can't allow you to enter the fight."

The boy nodded at his father's hip. "You're wearing a handgun," he said.

"Yes, I'm sure your mother told you that Mikal gave it to me."

"And you're not playing the hero, Dad? This isn't some modern day western that's come to life in your mind?"

"No, Dylan. This is not a fantasy."

"Okay," Dylan said and he sighed deeply. "So, are you going to royally kick butt or what?"

"Yeah." Ezra smiled. "I am."

Dylan stepped forward and gave his dad a hug. Ezra received it clumsily at first, then slowly warmed to his son's embrace. "Take care of yourself," Dylan said.

Ezra nodded. He was too choked for words.

The boy walked to his truck.

Ezra felt humbled as if he had been blessed by a father, not a son, but he burned with a new determination as he watched Dylan drive away. Pratt was doing this. Pratt was stealing his family.

Ezra mounted and started Cajun up the creek. The colt moved gingerly, as if trotting on ice, and turned its head sideways to nicker at the buddies left behind. Ezra lined him out with a slap on the neck. Beaner trotted at the colt's heels. There were more cattle to be moved, and Ezra was eager to give the dog more training. Suddenly a cottontail rabbit burst from the brush and scooted for the sandstones beneath the cliff. Immediately Beaner gave chase.

"Beaner!" Ezra yelled. "Come back." The dog raced on gripped by the thrill of the chase.

"Beaner!"

The rabbit escaped into a small opening in the rocks. Beaner stood poised at the opening, eyes bright, back arched, tail wagging hopefully.

"Beaner. Come here."

She did not even turn her head.

"Beaner! Come!"

Ezra rode closer. His yelling made the colt nervous and the colt's nervousness made Ezra more angry.

"Beaner!" he shouted. "Come here."

The pup turned and began trotting proudly back until she felt the anger radiating from her master. Then she lowered her head and slunk into the brush where she lay looking up fearfully.

Ezra broke a branch from a willow, took her by the collar and spanked her hard three times. She yelped twice and tried to pull away.

"When I say come, I mean *come*," he snarled. The pup cringed and tried to roll onto her belly as a sign of subservience. "You don't chase anything unless I tell you to," Ezra said, knowing the pup could not understand.

He was frustrated. The pup did not know what she had done wrong—she had simply obeyed an instinct—and as angry as he was, Ezra did not want to make her a scapegoat for his tensions. He sighed and rubbed her head. "It's okay," he told her. Her eyes brightened and her tail wagged. She forgave easily. "Just stay close to me, okay?" he asked.

He got to his feet. The pup stood up restored. All was forgotten. She was ready to continue their adventure. As Ezra turned for the saddle he noticed the green wound where he had broken the branch from the willow. There were other wounds, other broken branches. He led Cajun into the stand of willow trees. Something had broken a dozen willow trees.

It was too early for buck deer to be rubbing velvet from their antlers, he told himself. He measured the breaks.

Arrow-length. And no, they were not broken. They had been cut neatly with a sharp knife. Ezra counted the sheared stalks. Twelve smaller willows had been cut. Twelve arrows. One larger stump stood just a few inches tall. It had been the tree that provided the bow.

The weapon is from the land itself, Ezra thought.

He finished his ride with exhausting vigilance. Not a bird flew that he did not see. Not a single deer crept unnoticed from cover. Even the insects on the leaves of grass, the stems of brush, and the trunks of trees caught his eye.

His nerves were fried by the time he returned to the corral. He entered the unsaddling stall with vivid memories, and his right hand gripping the holstered pistol. When he turned Cajun out of the gate, he did not pause to absorb the moment, to listen to the colt's nickering call or feel the hoofbeats upon the beloved sod. He walked to the house weighed down with dread and checked the answering machine. Nothing. And the clock—it was only 7 P.M. Then he collapsed, still wearing his boots and spurs, on the sofa.

Sleep was not a relief. He merely ran headlong into a wall of fatigue and fell backward into himself. He lay there in the stagnancy of his exhaustion, the emblems of his fears sticking to him like wet leaves to a log. A sudden slumber had crawled like a giant cat onto his chest and curled there heavily sucking his breath.

Something more powerful than a dream returned.

He was in a spiritual world, but the attack and its manifestations were physical. He was besieged by passion and lust. The pleasure was excruciatingly painful and its grip unrelenting. In the geography of the dream world, he was deeper into the badlands than where the small foxes denned; he was past ethereal and mystic landscapes and was tumbling to a bottomless abyss, pulled by a giant winged creature, its talons firmly rooted in his back.

He was falling, falling.

The portable phone rested on his chest. Its ringing jolted him awake, the alarm sounding like the electronic cry of a beaten child.

"Hello?" Ezra's voice was weary. And wary.

"Ezra." The other voice was that of a friend calling from the bright side of the tunnel.

"Yes?" Ezra said, still gaining a toehold on reality.

"Ezra, it's me, Jubal."

He quickly came awake. "Jubal. What's going on? What have you found?" His voice was lacquered with desperation.

Jubal paused. "Are you okay, man?" he asked.

"Things are intense," Ezra said. His heart was beating like a trip-hammer.

Jubal knew his ministry was one of information. "I don't know if I have anything for you or not," he said. "But I have certainly been digging around."

"What have you got?" Ezra pleaded.

"Let me tell you what I don't have first. I can't come up with any sacred Indian sites in your area. Nothing."

"No strange rock formations or records of human sacrifices?"

"Not a thing, brother. The only Plains Indian tribe that regularly performed human sacrifice was the Pawnee. And they were not native to eastern Montana."

"So you haven't found anything?"

"Nothing that concerns Indians. I do have a lead on something though about wolves—"

"Wolves!" Ezra interrupted. "What is it?"

"It's just a lead, Ezra. We have a lot of Native American inmates and history buffs here. This evening in the mess hall a guy told me he once read about a strange occurrence near Yellow Rock. It happened about a hundred years ago."

"Give it to me," Ezra said. His hands were clenched and the fingers bent like hooks.

"A cowboy was headed north out of town when he thought he saw a couple of wolves. He got his six-gun out and was going to try and collect the bounties when all of a sudden the prairie came alive around him. What he thought was sagebrush was more wolves. He had ridden into a pack of some 250 buffalo wolves."

"What happened?" Ezra knew the man's fate might be a key to his own.

"Mexican standoff. Nothing happened. The wolves eyed him and his horse but knew he was armed. He passed slowly through them then got the heck out of there."

"This is documented?" Ezra asked.

"Yeah, it's in a book. The guy couldn't remember the title for sure. Something about 'Open Range.' The cowboy who experienced this was the author. His name was Sweetman or something like that."

"And it happened north of Yellow Rock?"

"For some reason that's the one thing this guy did remember. He remembers the creek—Sunday Creek. He thought that was an odd name for a creek. He thinks it happened about nine miles north of town."

The realization hit Ezra like a blow to the head.

"Ezra? That would be close to you, wouldn't it?" Jubal knew he had found a key. He could hear it turning in the lock.

"Yeah," Ezra said and he turned and looked north through the blackened window of the kitchen. "That would be just about in Solomon's yard."

"That could be it," Jubal said. "That could be Pratt's mythical *thin place*."

"It is it," Ezra said. "I can feel it, but I have to have proof. I need to read that book."

"Your town library must have one," Jubal said.

Ezra looked at the clock. The Yellow Rock Library closed in twenty minutes. "Jubal, thanks. Hey, I gotta run." He hung up the phone, locked the house, ran to his truck, and sped toward town. The pistol was still on his hip. He had become so accustomed to it he had forgotten it was there.

The library was closing when he walked in. The librarian knew him and greeted him by name. She may have turned someone else away but Ezra was a local writer. He was a friend of books.

"I need a book," Ezra said, trying to conceal his desperation. "Something about the 'Open Range' by a guy named Shortman, or Sweetman. Something like that."

She gave him her librarian's efficient, competent look. "*Backtrailing on Open Range* by Luke Sweetman," she recited.

"Yes. That's it. Do you have it?"

"No," she said. "We had it until this afternoon. It was a resource book that couldn't be checked out. We kept it in the Montana Room upstairs."

Ezra couldn't conceal his concern. "What do you mean you had it until this afternoon?" he asked.

"Someone stole it. This guy has been coming in a lot lately to browse though the Montana Room books. He's spent hours up there." She raised her eyebrows and lowered her voice. "He's rather odd, and I was suspicious of him from the beginning, so I've kept an eye on him. He came in this afternoon, and when he left two books were missing. He'd just taken them and walked out."

"A tall, raw-boned guy with brown hair and a beard?"

She nodded with disgust. "That's him," she said as if wanting to slap the culprit's fingers with a ruler. "He took *Backtrailing on Open Range.*"

"You said he took two books. What was the other one?"

She gave him a maternal, patronizing look as if he should have known. "Why, he took yours," she said. "He stole our copy of *Leaving the Land.*"

CHAPTER THIRTY

I t was his nightmare. His to end.

Ezra parked his pickup near his uncle's mailbox. He had stopped at his own place only long enough to change clothes—from a black cowboy hat to a dark canvas baseball cap, from cowboy boots to Hi-Tech Magnum hiking boots, and from a nylon jacket to a faded black denim—and to lock the house and bunkhouse and pocket a handful of kitchen matches.

The night was cool with a pale sky, pinpoints of stars, and a full moon that tinseled the clouds and cast thin shadows that lay like carpets woven of air.

The old house, its faded aluminum siding glowing in the moonlight, rose from a dark cluster of formless outbuildings. The cold, blue light of a television projected through the front window, but the rest of the house was dark.

Ezra remembered the cowboy Luke Sweetman as he adjusted the holster on his belt. A hundred years before him Sweetman had descended onto a sagebrush plain only to see the land come alive as ghosts of the past rose from the brush baring toothy grins.

The old white house, the ghetto of musty outbuildings, and the shrouded surrounding hills held a legion of Ezra's ghosts, but they did not worry him. He only wanted Pratt.

The *thin place,* if it existed at all, was Pratt's obsession, not his.

He came down the gravel lane alert, light on his feet, and hugging the woven wire fenceline. His advance was slow, and he stopped often to test for sights, sounds, and smells. The Ruger remained holstered. He crossed the stark lines of an iron-barred cattle guard then jogged quickly to the slouching bulk of the old garage. He tiptoed past the rusting shells of ancient cars to the crumbling concrete steps of the house. He glanced through the door and saw Solomon's balding head reflecting the blue glow of the television. The set was blaring with the western conference finals of the NBA, Houston versus San Antonio. Dark figures raced across a polished stage.

He moved slowly around the house testing the small, dirty windows in the building's foundation. There were four of them. The third one was unlatched. Ezra looked about him. Pratt could be denning in any of the ancient buildings: garage, barn, the numerous chicken houses and granaries, the rubble of the original homestead, or the old schoolhouse with its huge cupboards stacked with outdated, dust-covered books.

He moved to the wooden back steps where the door was fastened with a heavy padlock. Ezra dug a key from his pocket. Solomon had insisted Ezra keep one because the old man often locked himself out. He unfastened the lock and eased slowly into the back porch. Moonlight came through a row of rickety windows to illuminate a maze of cardboard boxes, empty coffee cans, discarded feed sacks, and the door that led downstairs to the cellar. He moved one slow step after another to the door until the cool brass knob was in his bare hand. It opened with a slight creaking. He stepped onto a staircase built from heavy planking. The earthen basement was warm, heated by a large coal furnace that sat in the middle of the room like a glowing giant heart, its vents steaming upward like arteries. He stepped to the basement floor. To his left was a black mountain of coal that was nearly invisible in the darkness. Past the furnace a sagging door opened to two other rooms.

Ezra reached across his body and unfastened the guard strap on his holster. It made a slight popping sound. He pulled the .357 Magnum out. Its cool, stainless body felt awkward in his hand. It was neither friend nor foe. He advanced slowly toward the door, his left hand out, feeling for obstacles, the revolver in his right hand, the arm cocked back with the Ruger gripped near his right ear. The sagging door opened only two feet wide. Ezra squeezed through into the small room where his uncles had cut agates. He smelled the thick, musty odor of the oils that had lubricated the saw and tumblers. His left hand reached out and felt the sharp corner of a saw table. He jostled a coffee can filled with agate slabs. It rattled slightly. Another door was to his right. It opened to a tiny, rectangular storage room lined on three sides by crudely built shelves stacked with canning jars. A window above him let in enough moonlight to trace a soft glow on the lips of the jars. It was the unlatched window.

Ezra closed the door behind him, crouched down, and reached with his left hand into a coat pocket for a kitchen match. It hissed into a blue-orange flame when he scratched it against the door. By holding the match inches above the earthen floor, he could see a vague but recognizable impression, the imprint and depression formed by a sleeping bag. Pratt had slept there, probably on the colder nights, and had left the door cracked open so heat would seep in from the furnace room.

A whisper came out of the air behind him riding on its own chill: "Watchman, what of the night? The morning comes, and also the night."

A tremor spread through Ezra's body and his hand tightened on the revolver. A mist of sweat broke on his forehead. Pratt had been there all along, probably standing behind the furnace. Above him the dull roar of Solomon's television silenced for a second, and Ezra heard the creak of a heavy foot on steps. Pratt was going upstairs.

Panic seized him for an instant, and he imagined he was in the cellar of his youth, locked in by his older sister, fighting claustrophobia and hysteria, letting his eyes adjust to the lack of light until he saw what he was afraid to see: the bull snakes gliding like slow, quiet trains, the scurrying mice, the slimy salamanders in the cellar's moist corners.

No, he told himself. He was not a child. He was a man with a decision to make. Should he rush after Pratt not knowing if he was armed, or trail him quietly? His safety depended on the right call, and so did Solomon's. He stepped through the door into the agate room. The television was blaring again. The door to the furnace room was closed.

Had Pratt locked him in? A wave of claustrophobia returned and he imagined Pratt burning the house with him locked in the cellar, the structure collapsing on him in an avalanche of flame.

He tried the door. It opened and Ezra breathed a short gasp of anxious relief as he stepped next to the furnace. It seemed alive with the low rumble of a large animal dreaming in its sleep. He moved more quickly up the stairs before pausing in the porch. The television silenced again as if it were his partner, and in that instant he heard the clicking sound of someone trying the lock on the front door.

Was it Pratt? If so, where was Solomon?

He went up the stairs on his toes, the pistol extended only inches out from his body, and felt his way to the kitchen. Light from the television bounced off the windows and cast a ghostly blue pallor on the rims of coffee cups hanging from hooks and dishes stacked in piles on the old wooden table. He knew the room by heart and moved past the rickety chairs and avoided the clutter of empty cereal boxes, old egg cartons, and sacks of potatoes. He moved to the entrance of the living room. The front door was only a few feet away. It was still locked from the inside. He peered around the corner. Solomon was not on the couch, but a light was on in the tiny bathroom. The television muted momentarily, and Ezra heard the compression of weight on the ceiling above him. Pratt, unable to decipher the tricky lock on the front door, had taken the only other escape route. He was upstairs.

Another quick decision to make, Ezra realized. Should he go outside to catch Pratt coming off the roof, or follow him and chance a strange encounter with Solomon as he tiptoed across the living room with a revolver in his hand?

He had to follow. Something demanded he follow Pratt step for step. He eased into the room, listened for sound in the bathroom, then skirted to the stairwell door in three lengthy strides. He stepped into the high, narrow staircase, and in the final inches before the door closed he saw Solomon step from the bathroom and shuffle toward the couch.

Ezra closed the door, put his left hand on the railing, and began climbing the steps on his tiptoes as if he were ascending the steep slope of a mountainside.

He stepped onto the landing. The upstairs was a single room his grandfather had designed like a barracks to bed an army of seven sons. Moonlight streamed through a small attic window on the south side illuminating the railings on a host of old beds. Wool blankets, musty and moth-eaten, were crumpled on each as if the bodies of his uncles still slept there; clothes hung on doorless closets; hundreds of cheap paperbacks lined rickety shelves, and boxes of magazines cluttered the floor. This had been his culture. A culture without dance or music. A culture of dusty paperback books and mindless idleness.

Pratt could be behind any of the beds, he thought. Then he noticed the room seemed too cool. A window was wide open with a beam of pale moonlight flowing through. Ezra listened and the silence of the empty night squeezed one telltale creaking for him to hear. Pratt was on the roof.

Ezra moved past Solomon's bed—the one with the covers pulled back—and lifted himself up and through the window. He slowly closed it behind him. The slope of the roof was steep and the old weathered shingles were slick. He took a deep breath and looked around him. The windshields of old cars and the porcelain of junked washing machines glowed in the moonlight. He was surrounded by a ghost town of shaded buildings. He heard a soft thump. Pratt had moved to the porch roof then jumped to the ground. Ezra scrambled to the roof's peak, took a deep breath, and brought the Ruger up in a two-handed grip. He aimed at an opening between old buildings near Solomon's clothesline. He saw a tall dark figure move tentatively into the opening. Then it was obscured by the soft glow of stainless steel. He had Pratt in his gunsights but he could not shoot. He could not chance killing a man because of assumptions. He crawled across the rooftop and dropped first to the porch roof, then to the ground. Ezra knew Pratt had to have another hideout. Somewhere in that maze of rotting, mice-infected buildings he had his supplies, his weapons, and perhaps even a hidden dirt bike. What building was Pratt destined for?

Pratt was a psychotic, Ezra reasoned. A victim of his own delusions. If he imagined the *thin place* to be in Solomon's yard, he probably also imagined it to have a vortex or center, a place to do his incantations or spells. That could be anywhere, Ezra knew. Would Pratt move toward that power spot, toward his weapons, or would he flee? He didn't have time to think about it; he expelled a deep breath and decided to simply reenter the night, the domain of the poacher, and trust that the darkness itself would guide him to its source.

Anne looked up from her books. She could not concentrate on her studies. Everything around her was strange—it was Tom and Darlene's home, not hers—and only the Lord knew what was going on with her husband. Anne's heart was at the ranch, but her mind was supposed to be in her books. She left Pastor Tom's study and went downstairs to the kitchen. Dylan and Diamond were sitting at the table looking at catalogs and laughing. Diamond was years behind in popular culture.

Dylan looked up. "How's it going, Mom?" he asked.

Anne poured herself a glass of water. "Not so great," she said. "Have you reached your father yet?"

"Not yet," Dylan said. "I tried earlier and the line was busy. For the past hour there's no answer."

"Did you leave a message on the machine?" Anne asked.

"No," Dylan said. "I'll just keep trying. Dad doesn't always check the machine."

Anne saw Diamond's eyes glaze. "Diamond," she asked. "What is it? What are you feeling?"

The girl's slender body quivered and tightened like a bowstring. "I was afraid to mention it," she said. "But I felt that evil again in the church yesterday. I made myself sit still this time. I pretended I was only imagining it."

"My dad thinks you're afraid of him," Dylan said. "He thinks you believe he is the source of the evil."

"Oh, no," she said, shaking her head with conviction. "He's not the source. He's the target."

"Diamond, are you sure?" Anne said.

The girl nodded.

"What is the evil?" Anne asked.

Diamond shook her head and her thin eyebrows knotted with fear. She could not force herself to talk.

Anne put the glass of water down and stared resolutely out the kitchen window. "I'm going to the ranch," she said.

Dylan glanced at Diamond then looked at his mother. "Do you want me to come?" he asked.

"No, your dad is probably just in the bunkhouse writing. But I won't sleep or study until I know everything is all right."

Dylan rose from his chair. "I don't think you should go alone," he said.

She patted his chest as she brushed past him to the hallway closet. "I'll be okay," she said. "You two keep an eye on each other."

She went out the door to her car, backed into the street, then pulled up to a stop sign. The quickest way to the ranch was to go right. She turned left, wondering why as she did it.

The church was five blocks away and she felt an urge to simply drive past it on her way to the ranch.

Everything looked okay; the building was dark, and there were no cars parked in front. She went around the block. From the back she thought she saw a soft glow of light coming from the sanctuary. Armon was in charge of the Sunday night services, perhaps he had forgotten to turn a light off. She pulled over, parked, and went to the front door, sorting through the keys on her key ring as she walked.

She didn't need a key. The front door was unlocked. She went up the stairs and into the foyer. Music was coming from the sanctuary. She eased a door open and entered the church's small auditorium. Someone was at the piano, playing and singing softly, the keys lit by a single candle.

A shiver went up her spine. The room was so dark, the music so low and soulful. Anne was in the shadows where she could not be seen so she moved several steps forward and stood partially obscured by a support beam. She could hear better now. The tune was low and mournful, but the delicacy and dexterity of the playing was spellbinding. The voice, though deep and pain-ridden, was beautiful in its haunting, velvet alto. Anne could not make out the words to the song, but she knew the choruses were primarily a series of single-syllable moans that crawled up and down the ladder of notes.

The pianist's hair glowed red in the candlelight, and her perfect features were cut on her face, half in light, half in shadow.

Anne stepped into the aisle and began walking slowly toward the dais.

The singing flowed into a greeting. "Good evening," the singer said as if she had been aware of Anne's presence from the beginning.

"Good evening, Lilith."

The playing continued for a full minute as if the performer was compelled to finish the song. Anne moved closer. The singing finally stopped and Lilith turned and looked down at her. "I suppose you wonder what I'm doing here," she said.

"You're playing the piano."

"Yes," Lilith laughed. "Yes, I am." Then her voice changed to one of rational explanations. "I go for walks at night sometimes," she said. "I just need to be alone. I was walking past the church and thought I'd try the doors. If by chance they were open, I thought I would come in and pray. They were open."

"They are supposed to be locked," Anne said.

"I know. I've tried them before."

"I have a key," Anne said. "I can lock up. That is, if you are done playing."

Lilith stepped away from the piano and walked down to the aisleway. She stopped a couple of feet from Anne and stood there as if measuring the woman.

Anne parted her lips as if to say something but no words formed.

Lilith stepped forward and put her arms around her. Surprised, Anne did not return the hug.

"I just want you to know that you play and sing beautifully," Lilith said. "And I have never seen anyone lead worship as well as you do."

Anne stepped back, breaking the embrace. "Thank you," she said cautiously.

"No, I thank you," Lilith said. "You have given me more than you know." Then Lilith turned and glided up the aisleway toward the foyer. She moved gracefully without a hint of effort, as if her feet treaded a carpet of air.

But Anne felt awkward as she started for the door, as if she was trudging uphill in mud, and a splitting headache erupted at the base of her neck and webbed upward, covering her head like a hairnet. She suddenly became so ill she nearly vomited before reaching the cool outside air where she locked the church's front door, then collapsed against the side of the building, drinking in the night freshness to cleanse her mysterious nausea.

Why do I feel so sick? she asked herself. She looked up and down the dark streets for Lilith but the neighborhood was quiet and empty. Then, as quickly as it had come, her headache and nausea were gone, and her desire to get to the ranch intensified. *I feel like I have entered a bizarre storybook,* she thought as she got in her car, *and someone else is turning the pages.*

Ezra looked up at the stars and moon, seeking help from above. What he saw was a dark formation of clouds approaching the moon from the west. The night was going to grow darker.

He decided to investigate the old buildings one at a time. In front of him was a long row of chicken houses. Unused for decades, they stretched together to form a single long building with intersecting doors. He entered through the west side. The air was musty with old manure and dust, and the dry, gritty ground beneath his feet made him remember being small and checking the henhouse with his grandmother. As the nervous hens squawked, the old woman robbed them of their fruit, putting the eggs in the large front pockets of her soiled white apron, or handing them to Ezra, who packed them gently in an old coffee can. If the hens didn't lay, they became fryers. She wrung their necks, then plucked the feathers by the back porch, where breezes collected and stirred the feathers like silken leaves while stray cats carried the hens' heads into the bushes.

He stepped through a narrow door into the next partition. The scurrying of mice, and the stale and suffocating air made him think of the dangers of hantavirus, a potentially fatal disease associated with rodent manure. He looked outside. One moment the chicken wire over the windows was traced against the pale sky, the next moment it was gone, invisible against the invading clouds. He stepped out of the chicken house and up to a heavy wooden gate, shouldered it open, and moved into the corral. He was exposed for a moment and imagined with a sudden, sickening fear that Pratt was watching him with a night-vision scope. It made sense for a poacher to utilize the latest gadgets, and Pratt might, too, even though he hated technology.

Ezra moved quickly to the shelter of corral planking. If Pratt had night vision they were not on equal ground. He imagined an arrow, cut from the trees of his own land, rushing silently through the night air, its arrowhead—carved out of Sunday Creek agate—whistling toward his heart.

No, he won't do it that way, he said silently. He remembered the *conversation of death* and Pratt's obsession to look into Ezra's soul at the decisive moment and read his nature. *Pratt wants to look into my eyes,* he reminded himself. *He wants to be close when he kills me, or forces me to kill him.*

He moved down the planking to a large, earth-covered barn, pushed the heavy doors open, and stepped inside. He felt the wall for a light switch and turned it on. The large barn filled with dim light. Ezra quickly measured the contents, his handgun following his eyes past the pens—"jugs," Solomon called them—for lambing ewes, the stanchion for pulling calves, the old freezer where grain had been stored. Nothing. He snapped the light off.

Think, Ezra told himself. Pratt had been in Solomon's basement because he was chilled. If he had spent nights anywhere else it was somewhere almost as warm. The only building more secure than the barn was the old garage. It had been built in the fifties out of railroad ties coated with stucco.

Ezra followed the corral planking back toward the yard. Pratt had led him on a detour, perhaps even letting himself be seen for the instant Ezra had raised the revolver. If Ezra could somehow beat Pratt to his nest he could gain an advantage. He quickened his walk, shifting into a half-jog when the moon peeked briefly from the clouds. Because the house was between the corrals and the garage, he decided to check on Solomon. He crept up to a window behind the television set. He could see Solomon still lying on the couch, but Ezra couldn't tell if the old man was awake or not. He moved past two rusting cars, the satellite dish, an old tractor abandoned for so long the wheels had sunk into the ground, and trotted to the large sliding garage doors that joined in the middle. They were locked but could be opened by sliding the two as a whole. He pushed them open a crack and slid into the garage. It was more cluttered than either the basement or the barn, and Pratt could be lying in ambush anywhere. He flicked on a light, then crouched, holding the .357 Magnum in a two-handed grip, and spun in a semicircle. The lightbulb was dim and it barely lit the old building.

He investigated by quadrants. In the northwest corner he found the small dirt bike he and Mikal had always suspected Pratt was using. It was hidden under a pile of old saddle blankets. The little motorcycle could be easily pushed to the highway, started, and ridden to town, and Solomon would never be the wiser. Pratt could return, also at night, or even during the day when Solomon was on one of his long walks. The gravel and grass would not retain many tracks if one was careful. Ezra jerked the plug wires from the distributor and threw them in different directions.

He turned his attention upstairs to the barn's storage attic. It was probably the cleanest place for a man to sleep, but would be cold on nights when the wind blew through the cracks in the seams between the railroad ties.

He moved up the stairs, his finger heavy on the trigger, flicked a light switch, but no light came on. The bulb socket was empty. An assortment of stored furniture and clothing—a mattress and box spring, two dressers, a wicker rocker, several old trunks, old suits hanging on a length of wire—gave the attic the appearance of a bedroom. Ezra could feel Pratt's presence. If he wasn't in the attic, he had been there. This was the place. Not the *thin place,* perhaps, but surely his nest. He moved in a careful crouch, the revolver in both hands, his steps slow and quiet. This time he would fire at the slightest noise and deal with the consquences later.

He moved to the bed. Enough light filtered through a small window for Ezra to see the glint of fur and the dim shine of book pages. He paused, imagining Pratt's cold voice cutting through the air or the fur suddenly springing to life. He breathed deeply to calm himself, then reached into a pocket for a kitchen match, struck it against the headboard, and held it above the bed.

On the covers was a silvery hide. He first thought it was a coyote pelt, but then he realized the size. It was a wolf hide. On the hide were two books lying open and facedown. *Leaving the Land* and *Backtrailing on Open Range*. He held up the latter. It was opened to the pages of the author's encounter with the large pack of buffalo wolves. The match burned down to his fingers, and Ezra blew it out and hurriedly lit another. He picked up Sweetman's story:

> . . . I was heading for the upper reaches of Sunday Creek one
> bright sunshiny day. . . . I came face-to-face with a band of
> gray wolves (often called loafers or buffalo wolves). They were
> coming down the creek straight toward me. . . . I said in-
> wardly, "Here's where I may get a shot or two at easy range,"
> and examined my six-shooter as I rode on toward the wolves. I
> now realized they numbered at least two or three hundred and
> were not changing their course in the least. . . . These shaggy
> monsters were as an army bearing down on me. It was evident
> they realized their strength; not at any time did one of them
> give an inch of ground while I rode half a mile steadily through
> the center of the pack. . . . I thought fast and said to the pack,
> "Hold your fire and I'll hold mine," for if blood had been
> drawn then how easy for a wolf to hamstring my horse, an-
> other to cut his throat—that done and the entire pack could
> have been on us in a moment. . . . I was grateful for a six-gun
> full of lead to finish my ride through the pack and grateful for
> the small voice telling me what to do, otherwise I would not be
> here now to tell the tale.

Ezra had to break himself from the fascination of the tale. Sweetman had ridden a considerable distance through the pack as he traveled up Sunday Creek, so Pratt's self-created *thin place* could be anywhere on the creek, but the vortex had to be powerful enough to produce evidence of its existence.

Pratt thought *Leaving the Land* was that evidence. A cold reasoning settled on Ezra. Pratt was hiding at Solomon's only for the convenience. The center of Pratt's *thin place* was the womb where Ezra's writing had been conceived. Ezra's home was the *thin place*.

And having flushed Pratt from his nest, Ezra had forced him to hasten any rituals his madness had conspired. Perhaps fire, or the blood of domesticated animals, or Ezra's own blood for atonement for his sins. But the site for any violence from Pratt would be in Ezra's own yard.

He dropped the book, holstered the Ruger and hurried for the stairs, banging first into a chest of drawers, then into an old saddle that hung from the rafters by baling twine. He clamored down the stairs, squeezed through the garage door, and ran up the gravel road to the highway. He was out of breath when he reached his truck. He jumped into the cab and dug into his pocket for his keys. They weren't there. He dug frantically through each pocket. He had lost his keys, probably when he had jumped from Solomon's roof.

There was no time to search for keys. It was a mile to his house. He had raced competitively before his ailing back had forced him to quit, so he put pain and stiffness out of his mind and began running at a carefully measured pace—a lone figure in dark clothes jogging the highway at ten o'clock at night.

CHAPTER THIRTY-ONE

As worried as she was for Ezra, Lilith's presence in the church had disturbed Anne, and as the Barber home was on her way out of town, she stopped there to settle the question of the unlocked door.

Betty Lou came to the door in a pink bathrobe that matched her hair and her face muddied with a green facial mask. "Anne," she said, "what brings you out this late?"

"I was driving by the church," Anne said, "and saw a light on. Someone was in there. I was wondering if you and Armon locked up last night."

"Of course we locked up," Betty Lou huffed. "I locked the door myself. Who was in there? What were they doing?"

"It was Lilith Foster. She was playing the piano."

"Playing the piano? Well, I guess that isn't so evil. How did she get in?"

"She said she was out for a walk and decided to test the doors, and the front door was unlocked."

"Well, that just can't be. Like I said, I locked the door myself. No one locks a door like I do. I rattle them and make sure they are locked."

"Maybe someone was in the church today," Anne quizzed. "Maybe Armon or another board member."

"Oh, I doubt it. Armon was with me all day. I had him rototilling the garden. He was wore out by supper and went to bed early. I don't know of anyone else who has keys to the front door, just me and Armon and you and Ezra. That's it."

"Okay," Anne said. "I just thought I'd check." Her thoughts turned back to Ezra, and she nearly ran for her car. She felt as if she were waking late in a bad dream that continued into reality. She sped to the ranch driving faster than she had in years.

The house and outbuildings were dark, and there was no sign of Ezra's truck. *He could be in bed,* she thought, *and the pickup could be in the garage.* She parked her car and rushed up the steps. The front door was locked. She expected that and pounded on it. "Ezra!" she shouted. "Ezra." When no lights came on she took her own key, unlocked the door, and stepped in. She turned on a light and called his name again. On a sudden impulse she locked the door behind her, then turned on lights as she went through the house. The bed was made and dishes were done, but there was no sign of her husband. A tiny red light flashed in the living room. She rushed to the answering machine and pressed the message button.

"Ezra," the voice said. "This is Jubal Lee. I'm curious about what you have found out. I have permission to stay in the office a while longer, so call me back quickly if you can." He left the number.

Anne quickly punched it. It was after hours, and the call bypassed the prison switchboard and rang directly in the chaplain's office.

"Ezra?" the voice answered.

"Jubal. It's Anne. I just got to the ranch and everything is dark and locked up, and there is no sign of Ezra or his pickup. What can you tell me? You must know more about what's going on than I do."

"I called earlier," Jubal said. "I told Ezra that I thought I knew what Pratt was looking for. The key is a book that was written many years ago. Ezra rushed to the library to get a copy. I just wanted to know what he found out."

"Do you know where the *thin place* is?" Anne asked urgently.

"I'm not sure, but I think it's somewhere on Sunday Creek."

"What does the book say, Jubal? What is this all about?"

"All I know is it has to do with the eradication of the buffalo and a gathering of wolves that threatened the life of a cowboy riding near your creek."

"Wolves?" Anne asked, and she felt a chill move through her bones. "You are sure it has to do with wolves?"

"Absolutely. That's the one thing I am sure of."

"Jubal, did Ezra tell you about Betty Lou's dream, the one about coyotes?"

"He mentioned it. Something about three coyotes attacking him and how it was similar to a dream he had years ago."

"Two coyotes and a wolf, Jubal. The coyotes came from the ground and from the air. The wolf sprang out of his own chest and turned on him. I need an interpretation, Jubal. I need to know who or what the coyotes and the wolf represent."

There was silence as Walker processed the information. "I need to know more," he said. "I need to talk to Betty Lou."

"There isn't time, Jubal," Anne insisted. "Just give me something. Anything!" she snapped.

"Well, a coyote out of the ground could represent the world system, and the one from the air could repesent Satan. The wolf coming out of Ezra's chest would be the flesh."

"But who would they be?" Anne said, as much to herself as to Jubal. "The coyotes and the wolf must represent people."

"The coyote of the world could have to do with money or power. Maybe Solomon," he suggested.

"No, no," Anne said impatiently. "That doesn't fit."

"His sisters?" Jubal suggested.

"No, it's got to be Shorty Wilson," she exclaimed. "Ezra broke his nose a few days ago. Now how about the coyote from the air?"

"Has to be Pratt," Jubal said. "He certainly represents the devil."

"You don't think he's the wolf?"

"I don't think so," Jubal said. "Not if the wolf represents the flesh."

"Then who is the wolf?"

"I don't know. Who else is involved in Ezra's life right now?"

Anne thought. "Just Diamond," she said. "And me and Dylan."

"Hmmm, that doesn't fit. If my interpretation is correct, there has to be someone else."

Anne remembered the church and the piano music. "There is a woman," she said. "A woman he's been counseling. Mrs. Foster."

"What's her first name?" Jubal asked.

"Lilith."

"Lilith?" Jubal said, his voice carrying an electric undercurrent of alarm. "Are you sure it's Lilith?"

"Yes," Anne answered apprehensively, sensing Jubal's concern. "Why?"

"In Hebrew mythology, Lilith was known as the mother of all demons and Adam's first wife. She was an incubus spirit that seduced men and killed babies."

"What?" Anne felt as if the room was spinning. "Incubus? Mother of all demons?"

"It's mythology, Anne, not Scripture," Jubal explained. "But many Bible commentaries point out that Psalm 91 and Isaiah 34 both make reference to this Lilith creature."

"But incubus—isn't that some sort of sexual thing?"

"Oh, yes," he said seriously. "And they exist. Believe me, incubus and succubus spirits do exist."

The atmosphere of the house seemed to darken and pulse with energy. Anne again felt sick to her stomach and the dull ache returned in her head. She forced herself to become rational. "We don't know she is the wolf," she said. "Lilith is just a name, that's all. It doesn't mean anything." Anne could not imagine how Lilith could be the main threat compared to Pratt. Lilith was a problem, but a small one. Pratt was the main concern. "If the dream means anything at all, Pratt has to be the wolf," she insisted. "Lilith Foster is only a coyote. Cute and cunning."

"You're probably right," Jubal said. "Pratt probably is the main threat."

"Yes," Anne agreed. "Yes, he is. Jubal, where do you think Ezra is?"

"He probably went to check on his uncle."

"Of course," Anne said and wondered why she hadn't thought of it. "He watches basketball with Uncle Solomon."

"I bet that's where he is," Jubal said. "I have to go now. They tend to have certain rules in this establishment."

Anne thanked Jubal, hung up, then dialed Solomon's number.

After almost a dozen rings his raspy voice answered.

"Uncle Solomon," Anne said. "Is Ezra up there?"

"Nope." He snorted. "Ain't seen 'im. I thought he'd come up to watch the game but there ain't been no one up here 'cept me."

"Thanks," Anne said and put the phone down. If he wasn't up there, where was he?

He had to be in town, she thought. Maybe he was at the Jablonski house waiting for her.

Then a more terrible thought hit her, one that staggered her inner core and shook the foundations of her existence: Maybe he was with her. With Lilith! Perhaps Lilith had even been waiting for Ezra at the church.

When Ezra topped the hill between his house and his uncle's, he saw the lights flash on in his home.

Who was in the house? Pratt?

He quickened his pace, knowing he had more than a thousand yards to go, and in his present condition it would take him at least six minutes to run that far. He could shorten the distance by running cross-country, but the footing would be more difficult. He decided to stay on the highway rather than risk spraining an ankle running through sagebrush at night.

After cresting the hill he increased his stride to utilize the downward momentum. Below him lay a deep gully that dissected the highway berm through a large steel culvert. Suddenly two sixteen-wheel cattle trucks roared over the hill from behind him, one passing the other. They were lit up like carnival rides and the straining of their diesel engines sounded like two freight trains racing down a homestretch to a finish line. The semi in the passing lane swerved toward Ezra. An air horn blew. Ezra jumped from the blacktop into the darkness, and the slope of the hill fell away beneath him. The trucks roared past, and Ezra tumbled over and over, down the steep grade into the grass and mud at the edge of the culvert. He crawled to his feet, shaken and muddy, but not injured. He had to get to the house. He scrambled uphill to the highway and resumed running. The cool night air burned his lungs as if it were hot water.

He saw the lights go off in his house and, moments later, the headlights of a vehicle flashed on. He ran harder, his momentum nearly spinning him out of control. A cloud obscured the moon, and the world became several shades darker.

It was Anne's car coming up the lane. It stopped at the mailbox, and she signaled to take a left turn toward town. He had to reach her. His tired legs flew in front of him, his feet absorbing many times his weight in impact, and pain shot violently from his sore hip to his heel. He sucked air like a thirsty horse drinking water and was only yards from his mailbox when the car turned and started for town.

"Anne!" he shouted. "Anne!" He heard her car shift gears and pick up speed. He had missed her. His body began to collapse as if someone had turned off his ignition; his arms flailed wildly, his rubbery legs began to quiver, and he fell and rolled into the barrow pit, coming to rest on his back, his lungs aflame and his heart beating against his chest.

Above him the cloud passed from the moon. The stars shone again. Everything seemed so pure and bright.

Anne drove to town wondering about her husband. Who was this man who had started packing a handgun and had developed a relationship with a beautiful young woman? And who was Lilith, and what was her problem? Why was she seeking counseling in the first place? Those were questions she knew she should have asked Ezra weeks ago but somehow she, Ezra, Dylan, Diamond, Pratt, and Lilith had all become tangled in twisted threads of fate, and details had slipped through the netting.

Because she didn't know where Lilith lived, she stopped at a Mini-Mart and looked in the phone book. The Fosters weren't listed, but she was certain the Jablonskis would have the address. Pastor Tom kept a membership list at both the house and the church. She went to the house.

Diamond met her as she came in. "I have news," the girl said, her eyes bright with excitement

"What's that?" Anne asked, moving past Diamond to the pastor's study where she began flipping through the Rolodex on his desk. Diamond followed her quietly.

"Melinda called."

"Your cousin?" Anne said, looking up. "She finally got our message?"

"Yes. She is coming next week to get me." The girl seemed overflowing with hope, as if everything was taken care of and people she had learned to love would no longer feel threatened.

"Diamond, that's wonderful," Anne said, and she reached over and gave her a hug. "I am happy for you. I really am, but I have to find something." She returned to the desk, found the Foster address and scribbled it on a notepad. She tucked the note into her pocket. "I have to go back out for a little while," she said. "Where's Dylan? He's here, isn't he?"

"No," Diamond shook her head. "He got worried and went to look for you."

"Dylan's not here?" Anne looked around the room as if hoping an ally would materialize from the walls. "Listen, Diamond, you don't mind being alone a while longer, do you?"

"I'm okay," the girl said. "Melinda is coming for me," she repeated.

"I know, and that's wonderful, and we will miss you very much," Anne said. "Now, listen. I'll be gone just a little while. Keep the doors locked."

Diamond stared at her with questions she was afraid to ask.

"Everything's okay," Anne said as she brushed past her. She hurried out the door to her car and backed from the driveway and onto the street. At the corner she stopped, turned her dome light on, and looked at the address. It was on the other side of town. If Lilith had walked to the church, she had walked a long way. She put the car into gear and sped forward, narrowly missing a vehicle coming into the intersection from a side street. The driver blared his horn angrily.

Anne let out a deep breath. "Calm down," she told herself. "You don't know Ezra is over there. You don't know anything."

The Foster home was a small house in a neglected area of town where the streets were unpaved and unlit. The neighborhood was so dark Anne had trouble reading the house numbers. Finally she found the house she thought was Lilith's. Ezra's pickup was not there. Anne decided to stop anyway. Dogs from surrounding homes barked at her as she pulled to the curb. She knocked at the door not knowing what to expect.

The door opened after several moments and Ben stood there with Hillary in his arms. "Mrs. Riley," he said, surprised.

"Excuse me for intruding so late," Anne said.

"That's fine, that's fine," he said, eager for company. "Come in. I was just trying to put Hillary down. That can be quite a war sometimes."

The small house was cluttered with toys and clothing. "Excuse the mess," he said. "I haven't caught up on the cleaning."

"Yesterday in church someone said you and Hillary were out of town," Anne said.

"Oh, no, I haven't been anywhere since Thursday. That's the day I go to Colstrip and Hardin. Hillary had a small fever yesterday, so I stayed home with her."

"Ah, where's your wife?" She couldn't help but look around suspiciously.

"Oh, she's out walking. She walks a lot. Sometimes she takes the car and parks it somewhere, then walks. I really don't like her walking around here. This neighborhood is so dark, and there are some mean dogs down the street."

"She walks at night because you are home to watch Hillary?" Anne suggested.

"Yes, well, that and her condition. Her condition doesn't allow her to be out in the sun very much, and when she is she has to wear hats and sunscreen and more clothes than are sometimes comfortable."

"She has a skin condition?" Anne asked.

"Skin condition?" Ben laughed. "It's much more serious than that. She has SLE."

"SLE?" Anne said. "I'm a nursing student, but that one doesn't ring a bell."

"Systemic lupus erythematosus," he said.

"Lupus?"

"Yes. She was diagnosed with it about six years ago." He juggled the girl lightly on his shoulder hoping to rock her to sleep.

"Lupus. Isn't that Latin for—"

"Wolf. Lupus means wolf. Erythematosus means red. Red wolf. The red is because of the rash it causes." His smile was both proud and ironic.

"Lupus is one disease we know a lot about," he said. "If you ever have to write a paper on it, just come talk to me or Lillie."

"Lillie?" Anne said. "Do you call her Lillie instead of Lilith?"

His face paled and he gripped Hillary tighter. "Oh, no," he said. "She isn't doing that again, is she?" His neatly trimmed blond mustache drooped at the edges.

The little girl leaned back and looked at her father. "Dad-dee," she said. "Mom-mee name is Lil-Lilth, not Lillie."

Ben Foster quickly pulled his daughter back into his shoulder. His face was lit with a pale terror.

"Doing what?" Anne demanded. "You hope she isn't doing what?"

"Being Lilith," he said sickly, and he squeezed his daughter tighter. "She promised me she wouldn't do that anymore."

"Do what?" Anne insisted. "What are you talking about?"

"I can't say," he whispered, nodding at the little girl. He held her tightly as if absorbing her into himself. "Besides, why do you want to know? Why do you want to see Lillie?"

"She was alone tonight in the church playing the piano."

"That's nothing," Ben snapped defensively. "She loves to play. Music is her life. Look around; we don't have a piano. She has to play somewhere."

"That's fine," Anne said, trying to soothe him. "She wasn't doing any harm."

"Then why do you want to see her?" he whispered. The girl had fallen asleep on his shoulder.

"Ah," Anne paused. "Well, actually, I'm looking for Ezra. He isn't home, and I thought maybe he had a counseling session with Lilith—ah, Lillie."

"But you said Lillie was at the church." He seemed to be grasping for hope.

"Yes, but she left."

"Well, maybe they are there now. Did you think of that?"

"Yes. I drove past the church on my way here. It's dark."

The man's shoulders sagged, and he buried his face in his daughter's neck. "Oh, God," he mumbled. "This is going to be messy again, isn't it?"

"Messy? What do you mean?"

He looked up. Tears were streaming down his face. "Lillie has times when her disease flares up. It's very rare with lupus victims; most people don't even know about it, but she gets seizures, and it affects her mind. She gets blamed for things because people don't understand her. She's not a bad person. She's just sick."

"Gets blamed for what kind of things?" Anne asked.

He shook his head. "I don't want to talk about it," he said, holding his daughter and sobbing quietly. "Maybe you should leave, Mrs. Riley. Maybe everything will be cleared up tomorrow."

Anne backed toward the door. Ben Foster did not see her out. He just stood in the middle of the cluttered living room, clutching his daughter desperately; the tears squeezed from his clenched eyes wetted Hillary's nightgown.

Ezra got to his feet and walked quickly down the lane while taking measured breaths to calm and ready himself. Beaner came running to him joyfully. Ezra did not stop to pat the dog but walked directly to the front door. It was locked.

He had extra keys hanging on a nail in the tack room. Keys to the house, garage, bunkhouse, his pickup, even Solomon's back door and the church. Beaner followed at his heels as far as the corral gate, then stopped and sat down, knowing the corral was off-limits to her unless she was invited.

The dark barn seemed ominous, and Ezra remembered his earlier attack. He felt at his hip for the revolver Mikal had given him. It was gone. He lifted his jacket and stared down at the empty holster. He had lost it in one of his falls.

Great. First the keys, now the pistol. His rifles were in the bunkhouse, but the bunkhouse was locked. He went to the barn door cautiously and reached in and flipped on the light switch. A dull light bathed the unsaddling stall. The other stalls were dark. He took a quick step to the tack room, opened its door, and switched on the interior light. Everything was there—his saddles, ropes, bridles, halters—everything except the keys. The nail above the door where the keys normally hung was bare.

His mind raced. How long had the keys been missing? When was the last time he had noticed them? He couldn't remember. When was the last time he had used them? He had never used them, he realized. He had hung them there a couple years before on Anne's insistence but had never needed them before.

He heard a strange sound from the outside. No, it wasn't strange, it was Beaner barking. But it *was* strange. It was a warning bark. Weak and unsure, but a warning just the same. She barked again. He strained to hear if a vehicle was driving into the yard. Maybe Anne had returned. There was nothing but silence. He glanced around the tack room for a weapon. There were several ropes, a horseshoeing rasp, a stockwhip. Nothing else. What was close? he wondered.

The pitchfork. Upstairs in the hayloft was a pitchfork. But he had to leave the basement portion of the barn, climb out of the corral, and enter the upstairs through one of its two side doors. He had no choice, it was either that, or lock himself in the tack room and shiver through a long night of fear. He turned off the lights and stepped out of the barn. He could not see his dog. "Psst, Beaner," he called quietly. "Beaner, come."

There was no response.

Ezra moved quietly along the side of the barn to the corral planking, then put his toe between the cracks to climb over. His toe didn't fit. Normally he wore his pointy-toed cowboy boots. They fit between the cracks easily, but his round-toed Hi-Techs were too large. He grabbed the top plank and pulled himself up and over. He landed lightly on the other side and crept up the small hill to the steps that led to the hayloft.

He stepped in. It was very dark. He knew he could not chance turning on the light. He tried to remember where he had last used the pitchfork. *On the other end of the loft,* he thought. He moved slowly and quietly across the plywood floor, his left hand reaching and feeling hay bales stacked on each side of the loft with a narrow passageway in the middle.

It was like being in a long dark tunnel with the sides bristling with straw. His claustrophobia rose. He could be cornered in that narrow passage, his way blocked by a crazy man with weapons.

No, he told himself, the wide door is on this end. Besides, the pitchfork is there.

He reached the end. He felt in the bales and the scattered loose hay on the floor. No pitchfork. His heart tripped against his chest. It had to be there. He was sure it was there. He felt again, his hands running down the sides of bales, reaching to the tops, feeling in the rafters and along the wall. He even got to his knees and sorted through the hay on the floor. The pitchfork definitely was not there.

He could not stand staying there. He had to get out. He found the handle on the wide, overhead door and turned. It wouldn't budge. It was locked.

When did I lock this? Ezra cried to himself.

The night Diamond had arrived. The night he had spent alone in the corrals with the Mini-14 in his lap. He had locked both barn doors with the keys on his pickup ring. The next morning, through normal usage, he had only unlocked the one.

He had to get out of there. He was trapped in a tight place. He was poised to rush down the passageway toward the door when he was stopped by something cold and hard that came through the air like a black-winged bat.

A voice.

Diamond LaFontaine stood trembling in the hallway of the Jablonski house. Someone was knocking on the door. Anne and Dylan had keys. She didn't know if Ezra had a key or not. The knocks were hard and sharp but not as heavy as she would expect from a man.

"Anne. Anne, open up," a woman's voice called.

Diamond edged closer to the door. "Anne isn't here right now," she said.

"She's not? Who are you? Where is Anne?"

"I don't know, but she said she would be right back."

"Listen, I'm Betty Lou Barber. I'm a board member's wife, and this is the pastor's house. Would you please open up? I'm catching a chill out here."

Diamond tentatively unlocked the door.

Betty Lou blew in like a pink blizzard. "Gracious," she said, "why aren't things ever normal around Ezra Riley? There's no answer at his house. He's moved a stranger and his family into the pastor's home, and they aren't even here. Gracious."

Diamond began to melt away from her.

"Goodness, girl," Betty Lou said. "Don't be afraid of me. I don't bite. Not much, anyway. Now where did you say Anne was?"

"I don't know—"

"Where are you from anyway? It seems mighty odd the way you just showed up a couple weeks ago. Then you go running out of church like your tail was on fire. Goodness, Lord only knows I've wanted to do that, run out that is, especially when Ezra Riley is preaching—he is so insufferable, isn't he?—but I have to hand it to you, you had the courage to do it."

"I didn't run because of him," Diamond said.

"Oh? Well, why did you run, then?" Betty Lou asked as she inspected the house, appraising everything her eyes could fall upon.

"There was evil in the church," Diamond said.

"Evil? Evil in our church? Gracious, girl, what makes you say that? There's evil everywhere, but in our church? Mercy, I would think our church would be the one safe place. Even Ezra isn't evil. A major pain in the you-know-what, but not evil."

"It wasn't him."

"Then who was it? What was it?"

The girl shrank farther away and seemed poised to run. She eyed the stairs and glanced at the back door leading from the kitchen. Then Anne walked in.

"What's going on?" Anne demanded. She was tired and worried and it angered her to see Diamond scared.

"Oh, there you are," Betty Lou said, marching across the room. "Where have you been at this time of night?"

"Betty Lou, what are you doing here?" Anne moved past the woman to shield Diamond from her.

"Well, since you came by earlier I have been on the phone. I know it's late, but I got some people out of bed. Didn't bother me a bit—enjoyed it a little, actually. Anyway, some things are important enough to disturb people's sleep."

"What are you talking about?" Anne had an arm protectively around the girl and Diamond folded into it as if it were a wing.

"Well, you know," Betty Lou drawled. "The reason you came by earlier."

"Lilith?"

"Yes, *her*. I've gotten to know her pretty well, you know. Some days she was the only one that came to my prayer group—I have to hand it to her, the young woman understands commitment—but that doesn't mean I've trusted her. She's too pretty, too charming, just glides on life like it was ice. But I got her to talk to me, and she told me about all the towns she's lived in, even mentioned names a time or two. Names of pastors and churches. I think she thought of me as a counselor or something. Lord only knows the woman loves to be counseled."

"And?" Anne asked impatiently. "What's the point?"

"The point?" she said indignantly. "The point is I got some answers. The first couple of places I called the pastors claimed they had never heard of her. Course they were new. New for a reason, I might add. The next place the pastor just hung up on me. Can you believe that? The nerve of some people." She took a deep breath to fuel herself. "Well, on the fourth call I got ahold of a pastor's wife, and she talked. And I mean, boy, did she talk."

"What?" Anne urged. "What did she say?"

"She practically had a file on our friend Lilith. Or, Lillian I should say. Lilith isn't her name at all," Betty Lou said proudly. "Lilith is like a stage name for a role she plays. And what a role! She's all but ruined every church she's been in. Oh, she started innocently enough. No one even suspected, but some of those churches are in shambles now. Just shambles. The church in Boise doesn't exist at all. It's defunct. Extinct."

"Ruined them?" Anne said. "How?"

Betty Lou's hair seemed to flare to a brighter shade of pink. "Why, she seduced the pastors," she said. "She had affairs with them—or in one case it was actually a youth leader. And she went after them; make no bones about it, she was the instigator."

Anne's eyes widened as if seeing for the first time, and her jaw slackened. Her face became as blank as a blackboard.

Betty Lou wrote her own thoughts on it. "Makes you wonder what she's been doing here, doesn't it?" she said.

Anne felt Diamond's arm tighten around her. "That was the evil," the girl whispered. "That was what I felt in the church."

"What, Diamond? What exactly did you feel?"

"It was dark and cold," she said. "At first that's all I felt, just darkness and coldness. Then I felt something else, and that's when I got up and ran."

"What?" Anne's grip increased on the girl. "What *exactly* was it?"

"It was sexual," Diamond said. "That's why I didn't want to tell you. I was afraid I would be misinterpreted."

"Sexual? What do you mean?"

Diamond was becoming scared. "I don't know," she said. Her gentle voice was piqued with a desperate desire to be helpful. "It was just *that*. It was not clean."

Anne's eyes widened as if allowing in light. "Lilith was praying next to you, wasn't she?"

"Yes."

Betty Lou had strained to hear Diamond's every word. "Sex," Betty Lou declared. "Sex and sin." *And this revelation about evil coming from a little waif who has seen her share of improper behavior and was spending an inordinate amount of time with that young Riley boy too.* She glanced at a wall clock. "Well, look at the time," she said. "I'm going to bed. All of this sex and sin stuff can be taken care of just as easily in the morning. At least for me, it can." She started for the door, then turned back. "By the way, Anne, where is that husband of yours? Where *is* Ezra?"

CHAPTER THIRTY-TWO

Pratt's voice was frosted with mockery. "Here kitty, kitty, kitty," he called in falsetto. Then he laughed a high-pitched, piercing laugh. "What a cute game of cat and mouse you have played this evening, Ezra Riley. Do you really think I am nothing but a mouse to be hunted in chicken houses and barns?"

Pratt filled the passageway at the east end of the loft. The night was just clear enough for Ezra to see his form silhouetted against the open door, but he could not tell how he was armed.

"So come here, kitty, kitty," Pratt sang. Then his voice dipped to a professorial tone. "Did you know, Ezra Riley, that feral house cats are a bane to the nation's wild fowl? They kill hundreds of thousands of game birds a year. Fortunately, fox, coyotes, even owls, eat house cats. Come here, kitty, kitty."

Ezra had to still his panic. Courage, he told himself. Calmness. Confidence. The three Cs of the martial arts.

Pratt changed tones. "'Watchman, what of the night?'" he sang. "'The morning comes, and also the night.' The night has come, Ezra Riley. I am the night. I am the prophet of a new and chaotic age. An era of darkness. A time for the night. You Christians love the light, but are you prepared for the night? No? Perhaps the night needs some light." He flicked on an overhead bulb. The high stacks of baled hay diffused the radiance. The hay bales were bathed in a golden glow, but the floor was washed in shadows. Pratt took a step forward. Ezra could see something in his hand. He guessed it to be a bow. Pratt stopped. He sighed deeply as if he were made of wind. "You are not dressed right, Riley. This won't do at all. Hi-Tech Magnums. Good boots, I've worn them myself. And a beanie cap. A practical way to dress for creeping around in the dark, but not at all what I hoped for. This is all about symbolism, Riley. Don't you know that? You are supposed to be wearing your cowboy hat and boots. And spurs and chaps. You are not playing your role well at all."

Ezra knew he had to measure Pratt's madness. "I could go to the house and change clothes," he offered.

Pratt laughed. "Yes, I'm sure you could. And I wish I could allow it. I really am disappointed, but then you surprised me. I didn't expect you to come looking for *me*. Especially not at night. Something must have tipped you off. What was it? Who was it? Was it Diamond?"

"No, it was your old friend Jubal Lee," Ezra said, hoping Pratt might act rashly if enraged. Ezra's right hand was out of Pratt's sight and he quietly searched the bales for any type of weapon or shield. If he could not find the pitchfork, perhaps his hand would touch upon a hay hook. He knew there was one somewhere in the loft.

"Jubal Lee." Pratt laughed. "The fool Jubal Lee. What was he able to give you?"

"The location of your *thin place,* Pratt. He learned about the gathering of the wolves."

"Yes, amazing bit of history, isn't it? All of those beautiful wolves searching for their natural prey, the buffalo. The beautiful American bison eradicated by exploitive Christianized butchers. The wolves should have torn that cowboy and his horse to shreds."

"Is that who I am?" Ezra asked. "Do I represent that cowboy? Am I your Luke Sweetman?"

"How poetic," Pratt laughed. "I suppose you are. Of course, I only discovered the reference to the wolves myself a few days ago. I'd heard rumors of the Sweetman story before, but had seen nothing in print until I came across that book in the library. Actually, I thought your book held the clues, Ezra. That's why I was at the libary. You have my copy, you know. Would you autograph it for me?" he mocked.

"Be glad to," Ezra said. "Do you have a pen?"

"No, and I have no more need of your book. It has *bent power.* It is corrupted by your myth of Christianity. Too bad, your love for the land is so intense, so sincere. You almost worship it, don't you? But you see, that's the problem. *Almost* won't quite do." He took another step forward.

"So, is this simply a conflict in philosophy?" Ezra asked, hoping to stall him. His hand had still found nothing.

"*Philosophy?* What a cheap word. My father was a philosophy instructor, did you know that? Of course you did. I am sure Special Agent Mora told you everything. At Tulane. A full professor at Tulane. And my mother was a whore. And a very common whore at that. But, no, I wouldn't say it was a conflict of philosophy. I would say mythology. The cowboy as myth. The symbol of the Old West. That is what you have become, you know. And that myth must die. It is time for a new west, a new myth. And I am it, Ezra. I am Alpha, the beginning."

"So you are here to kill me?" Ezra asked.

"Am I?" Pratt said, stepping forward. "You are the one with the gun, Ezra, that noisy, ugly, messy weapon of fools."

Ezra glanced at his empty holster. It was on his side away from Pratt and hidden in the shadows. "So you want me to kill you?" Ezra asked.

"I would prefer that. I am your dark side, Ezra. You must kill me. I am the worst that you could ever become."

"I could never have been like you," Ezra said.

"Why not? Do you love the land any less? Do you love the thrill of the hunt any less?"

"No, but I don't beat women," he said, the words punctuated with impact.

Pratt stopped, enveloped by a hostile silence. Ezra's searching hand had reached as far as it could but had found nothing. "That was a low blow," Pratt said. "You don't understand cultural differences. You need a lesson in diversity, Ezra."

"I know brutality when I see it," Ezra said. "Or when I feel it. Is this your second attack on me in a barn? Do barns represent something to you, Pratt? Are they uterine?"

"I never did that," Pratt screamed. "You dishonor me by saying I did that. I have come to stare into your eyes face-to-face. I have come to read your soul. I have come for the *conversation of death.*"

The dog barked in the distance and Ezra heard the low rumble of a vehicle approaching the house. Pratt stepped back and shut off the lights. Ezra strained to hear. A car was pulling up to the house. No, a pickup—Dylan's pickup. He recognized the rattles.

"You better pray he didn't see the light," Pratt whispered.

Ezra heard the pickup door slam. A moment later the front door rattled as Dylan tried to open it, then several hard knocks followed. "Dad," Dylan shouted. "Dad, are you in there?" There was a stretch of silence—Ezra's ears hurt from the strain—then the rattling and knocking sounded from another direction. Dylan was trying the bunkhouse.

Don't come this way, Ezra prayed. *Don't come this way.*

He heard a latch on a corral gate open and faint steps approaching the barn. Dylan entered the tack room. He was directly below Ezra. The tack room light came on and filtered through the seams in the plywood floor. Dylan was checking the saddles to make sure his father wasn't on horseback in the hills. Ezra froze, hoping his son would not feel his weight on the floor. The light went off; the tack room door closed. Dylan was inadvertently following his father's exact route. He climbed over the corral planks. Ezra's heart moved into his throat. His son was at the door to the barn. Ezra could barely see Pratt standing at the door. The door rattled but did not open. Pratt was holding it shut, making Dylan believe it was locked. His steps sounded around the barn, passing by the overhead door just inches from Ezra. It seemed forever, but finally the truck's engine started, and Dylan drove slowly away, the pickup's rattles sounding like a faint serenade of good-byes.

"It's your lucky night," Pratt said. "The kid is gone."

The light flashed back on.

"I'm surprised you didn't call out," Pratt said. "What's the matter, Riley? Are you afraid to use the gun in your son's presence? Maybe you don't think you can shoot straight. Maybe you can't. I watched you practice the other day. Oh, and did you take Mikal Mora's suggestion? Is your

SP101 loaded with .357 Magnums? Surely you don't expect a mere .38 slug to drop Alpha?"

"You are serious about me killing you?" Ezra asked.

"I want to see if you are capable. Besides, maybe I have a death wish. Your wife thinks you have one. What gave her that idea? Your little pity party of a few years back when you got yourself caught in a coyote trap? Or was it a wolf trap? I don't recall. For you, it should have been a mouse trap."

"So you want to be a martyr," Ezra said. He was determined to stay calm and not allow Pratt to provoke him. "It would advance your cause to die, wouldn't it?"

"I'm sure it would," Pratt said. "And in today's legal system who knows what might happen? You might spend your life in prison for shooting a man who only carried a crude bow and arrows fashioned from the willows of your own creek."

"I would gladly shoot you, Pratt—"

"Then do it!" Pratt screamed.

"I would," Ezra said calmly. "But I seem to have a problem."

"What's that?" Pratt snapped.

"I lost my gun."

"You what?"

"I lost it. I fell twice running here from my uncle's. You should have let me shoot you earlier."

"You fool. You lost your gun? I can't believe it. You must kill me within the center of *your* energy, not your crazy old uncle's energy. He is not a lover of the land. That is why I would not allow myself to be killed there. It had to be here. Oh, Riley." He sighed. "You are more incompetent than I imagined. You are not worthy of my kingdom." Pratt stepped closer, and Ezra could distinguish the outline of his beard and hair and the glint in his eyes. "You are not worthy to kill me, Ezra Riley," Pratt continued. "You are not even worthy to live." Ezra's right hand continued to stretch out as if offering a prayer as it searched the dry bales, looking and waiting for a miracle.

Pratt reached over his shoulder and pulled an arrow from a buckskin quiver. He notched it in his little bow. "Let me see your eyes, Ezra Riley," he said, stepping within six feet. "Let us have our talk, one soul to another." He pulled back on the bowstring. "Here kitty, kitty," he sang. "Come to Alpha."

Ezra considered rushing Pratt, but the madman had stayed just far enough away to loose an arrow before Ezra could reach him. "Come closer," Ezra challenged, "if you want to see my eyes."

"Nice try, Riley, but I can see your soul quite well from here. And do you know what I see? I see the soul of prey. I see you giving permission to the predator to kill you because you are weak and I am strong and that is our destiny. You are not a kitty, Ezra Riley. You really are nothing but a mouse." The bowstring was taut with the arrow pointed at Ezra's chest.

"My Lord is a lamb," Ezra said.

Pratt laughed. "A fitting pun to die by," he said. "Are you speaking in tongues yet, Riley?" Ezra didn't answer. Pratt took a deep breath, tensing himself for the kill. Something touched Ezra's hand. It was slightly wet and raspy. His hand was being licked. In the darkness something was licking the salty sweat from his fingers and palm. He moved his hand a few inches toward himself. The licking continued.

"Good-bye, Ezra Riley," Pratt said. "Any last words?"

"*Don't hurt me, Deemie,*" Ezra said.

Pratt paused. Those were Diamond's words.

Ezra grasped Hemingway by the neck, hoisted the cat above the bales, and threw her at Pratt. She landed across his face, her front claws sinking into the corners of his eyes for traction, the back claws raking at his jaw. Pratt dropped the bow, the loosened arrow shot past Ezra's head and embedded in the rafters. Pratt reached to pull the cat off, and Hemingway bit deeply into the bridge of his nose. Pratt screamed and whirled into the side of the bales, slipped on the loose hay, and fell heavily. Ezra leaped over him, sprinted across the loft, through the door, and jumped from the steps. He fell when he hit the ground, but he rolled and came up running. Behind him he heard the soft thump of the cat being thrown against the side of the barn and the clomping of Pratt's big feet as he struggled to get up. Ezra ran past the boxcar where the feed was stored, vaulted over the top plank of the corrals, raced through the pens, and into the creek. The night was a tapestry of moonlight and shadow as he ran quietly on the creek bed gravel avoiding the tree branches that reached out to stab him. He heard something behind him and felt a brushing against his leg. "Beaner," he whispered. He did not have time to command the dog home, so he ran on, moving south, toward town, away from his house and Solomon's, hoping he had the speed and endurance to race Pratt to town if he had to. He cut across his horse pasture toward the highway, squeezed through a four-wire fence, snagging and losing his cap. He left it dangling on the wire and settled into a relaxed, measured run, his dog at his heels. He was going to flag down the first car that came by, but the two-lane blacktop was bare of traffic. After a mile his lungs and legs began to betray him, and the burst of adrenaline wore off. He knew if Pratt had followed he would be gaining. Ahead of him he saw the dim image of a small car parked by the side of the road. *Probably a couple of teenagers drinking beer,* he thought. He knew he would give them the scare of their lives.

As he came closer the car's dome light came on and the front door opened. A person got out. "Ezra," a voice called out. "Is that you?"

"Lilith?" Ezra said, collapsing against the side of the car.

"What in the world—"

"Get back in," he ordered as he opened the passenger door. Beaner looked at him in confusion. Ezra grabbed the dog by the collar and lifted her into the car. "Drive," he told Lilith. "To town, quickly!"

Lilith spun out of the approach and onto the highway. The car's little engine roared as she shifted gears. "What's going on?" she demanded.

"Pratt. He attacked me in the barn again."

"Oh, God. Are you okay?"

"Yeah, but it's a long story."

"Where are we going?"

"To the sheriff's office," he gasped, trying to get his breath.

"Will there be anyone there this time of night?" she asked, her face reflecting the faint glow of the dashboard lights.

"No, you're right. To the police station."

"But this took place out of the city limits," she argued.

"So? I have to report it. They can call the sheriff." Ezra could not understand her recalcitrance.

"Ezra, listen to me," she explained. "You don't have a scratch on you. You'll be rushing into the police station with a strange woman saying a madman has attacked you—for the second time—in your barn, and you know Pratt will be nowhere around by the time anyone gets to your place to investigate."

"What are you telling me?" he asked, but he remembered the attitude of the young deputy a few days before. A city policeman could be worse.

"I'm saying you could look like a chump, like some crazy cowboy preacher having delusions. Let's get you cleaned up, then you can call the sheriff at home and discuss this with him."

"No, no. I won't rush into the police station and I won't act like a crazy person—"

"Ezra, you never saw the first attacker. Did you see Pratt this time?"

"Lilith, he was just a few feet from me with a bow and arrow pointed at my chest."

"A bow and arrow?" she asked pointedly.

"Yeah. A homemade bow and arrow. Made from the willows of my own creek."

"Ezra, listen to yourself. Who in the world is going to believe that?"

Beaner snuggled comfortably against Ezra's chest. "Sheriff Butler will," he said, and he realized Butler might be the only one who would.

"Right," Lilith agreed. "And he's home in bed. But it's the graveyard shift at the cop station. You're probably going to get some rookie city cop who just moved here from Chicago or somewhere. He's likely to put you through a sobriety test. And what's that on your belt?"

"An empty pistol holster."

"Great, that will look real good."

"I can take it off."

"And you're muddy, sweaty, and flushed too."

They were nearing the lights of the town. Ezra sighed. "Okay, okay. I'll call Butler. Take me to Jablonskis'."

"Do you want to wake everyone up and scare that Indian girl half to death? I just drove by there, Ezra. The place is pitch dark. Everyone's asleep."

"But Dylan was at the ranch half an hour ago."

"Well, his truck is parked there now and the house is dark," Lilith insisted.

"Okay. Just stop at any pay phone."

"No," she said adamantly. "The church. You can clean up there."

"Lilith, I don't have any keys. I've lost them all. The way things are going I couldn't open my mailbox."

"I have a key," she said.

"Where did you get a key?"

"Pastor Jablonski gave me one. I needed a place to go to play the piano. We had to sell our piano when we moved here."

"Okay." Ezra shrugged. "To the church." It was tiring to argue with Lilith, and he was making no headway. "By the way," he said. "What were you doing parked out there by the ranch?"

"I just knew you were in some sort of trouble," she said. "Sometimes I drive around and listen to praise music and pray. Tonight I kept praying Psalm 94, and I knew it was for you."

"Well, you were my guardian angel tonight," Ezra said, and he stroked Beaner's head. He did owe her, Ezra thought. So he would do as she wished and let her take him to the church to clean up.

"Your guardian angel?" she said to herself. "Yes, yes I am."

CHAPTER THIRTY-THREE

Lilith parked her car in the back of the church behind an elm tree.

"Why are you parking back here?" Ezra asked.

"Maybe he's following us," she said.

"Pratt? I doubt it. All he has is a little dirt bike, and I pulled all the plug wires out of it."

"Let's not underestimate him," she said, and she started around the side of the building to the front door. "Don't underestimate your enemy, Ezra. That's what you told me." She reached into a coat pocket for a key ring.

"You stay here, Beaner," Ezra told the pup. "You stay." The dog gave him an obedient look and lay down on the welcome mat outside the door.

They went downstairs to the church kitchen. Lilith turned on a light.

"Man, I'm a mess," Ezra said, seeing the mud on his pants and coat. "I rolled all the way down a hill and into a mud puddle."

"And you wanted to run into the police station looking like that." She smiled reprovingly. "I'm going to put some water on for some tea. You need to be calm and collected when you talk to the sheriff."

Ezra washed his face and hands in the kitchen sink and dried himself with a dishtowel. "I should call Butler right away," he said. "Pratt's crazy, he could be running up and down the highway looking for me."

Lilith gave him a patronizing look. "Do you really think he's *that* crazy? He's avoided capture for a long time, Ezra. I don't think he's going to be running down the highway waiting for a policeman to stop and give him a ride."

"He could be," he argued, but he knew she was right.

"Ezra, Pratt's gone by now and you know it. He probably saw my lights as we sped away. He knows you will be coming back with help. He either has a vehicle stashed somewhere or he's going to hide in the hills. Really, I don't think it makes any sense for you and the sheriff to go back out there tonight. You need to rest. You need a good night's sleep."

"You're being a little bossy, aren't you, Lilith? It was my life that was on the line tonight," he said. "I need to report this."

"Ezra," she cooed. "I am not being bossy. I am being rational and practical. Report this in the morning. Even if Pratt is still somewhere close to the ranch, how are you going to find him in the dark? He's likely to attack you again. If you go back out there at night, he has the advantage."

"Well, I don't know how in the world I can get to sleep," he said. "Or *where* I would get to sleep. I'd hate to disturb Anne and Diamond . . ." He realized he had thought of his wife only once since fleeing the barn and that Lilith had quickly detoured him from the idea of going to her.

"We can stay here," Lilith said.

"We?" he asked. He was still wiping at mud on his neck and picking it from his hair.

"Yes, here," she said. "There's a sofa in the pastor's office. I can sleep there. There's another down here where the ladies' prayer group meets. You can sleep here."

"You wouldn't need to stay," he said.

"I don't mind." She reached to a high cupboard where the ladies kept the tea. "Ben and Hillary are out of town anyway, remember? If I went home I'd worry about you and wouldn't get any sleep at all."

"Well, I don't think I can sleep. I need to do something, Lilith. I need to get the sheriff on Pratt's trail."

"What trail?" she said. She pulled two cups from another cupboard. "Ezra, before you call the sheriff why don't you tell me what happened? Rehearse your story."

"I don't need to rehearse it," he snapped.

"Ezra, don't be mad at me. I didn't mean it as if you were making it up or something." She moved beside him and took his hand. "Come on," she said, "it will be a few minutes before the water is hot." She led him to a shadowed corner where a couch and half a dozen chairs formed a square. She sat on the couch. Reluctantly, he sat beside her. "Just tell me what happened," she said. "It may help you remember something important."

"Lilith—"

"No," she said, raising a finger as to a child. "Tell me the story."

"Okay, okay," he sighed. He knew he was tense and needed to relax. Maybe Lilith was right. Maybe he should get his story straight. He told her about the call from Jubal and the information concerning the cowboy and the wolves. He told her about going to the libary and finding two books had been stolen, including a copy of his. Then he went to his uncle's house.

"Why did you go there?" Lilith interjected.

"Jubal had some information wrong. He thought the book said the wolf pack had been at a certain place so many miles from Yellow Rock. That sounded like Solomon's place. The book doesn't say that, but as it turns out, that's where Pratt was." He continued, telling how he had found Pratt in his uncle's basement, followed him upstairs, onto the roof, then through chicken houses, a barn, and into the garage where he discovered the books and a wolf pelt.

He heard the teakettle begin to whistle and looked at Lilith. She urged him to go on.

"I was afraid Pratt was going to burn down my house or something," he said. "So I ran to my truck, but I had lost my keys. So I ran down the highway. I fell once when a cattle truck nearly ran me down. Then I fell again when I tried to catch Anne's car."

"Anne's car?" Lilith asked.

"Yeah, she had come to the ranch. Looking for me, probably." He continued the story, saying he had gone to the tack room but the extra keys were gone, then he heard Beaner bark and went searching for a weapon, and that was how Pratt had cornered him in the barn.

"So how did you get away?" she asked.

"I threw a cat in his face," he said.

"You did *what?*" She gasped.

"I threw Hemingway into Pratt's face. Then I raced by Pratt and down the creek to the highway. Then I found you."

She reached over and held his hand. "Ezra, let's think about this. Have you been listening to your own story? Do you realize how crazy it sounds?"

"Yeah, I admit it sounds pretty far-fetched." It was reality to him, he knew, but he wondered what it would sound like to a sheriff being roused from his night's sleep.

"Do you think you should tell the sheriff everything?" Lilith asked.

"Of course." It was Ezra's nature to believe in the truth.

"Are you sure?" she challenged. "Sometimes we have to be as innocent as a dove but as cunning as a serpent."

"But I have proof. The books are in my uncle's garage. So is the dirt bike."

"Do you think they are still there?"

Ezra's eyes squinted, then they darted left and right as if he were cornered again. "The bike won't start," he said. "It will be there."

"By the time you found me he could have jogged to your uncle's. It would have taken him no time at all to grab his stuff, push the bike to the highway, and roll it into the ditch, or even hide it down the creek somewhere." She glanced at her watch. "It's ten to eleven. He has seven hours of darkness to slip into the badlands to hide or to get another vehicle."

"What are you suggesting?" Ezra asked.

"I'm telling you to wait and call the sheriff in the morning. But check your uncle's garage first and see if the bike is there or not. If it isn't, you're going to look pretty foolish dragging the sheriff up there. And what about your uncle? Are you going to try and tell him that you spent the night pursuing a crazy man through his house and he didn't even know it? The sheriff will ask him about it, you know."

Ezra sighed and slumped into the couch. He didn't want to get Solomon involved. "You're right," he said. "I don't have any proof except the arrow in the barn and he might have taken it too."

The whistling sounded louder from the kitchen. She put a hand on his shoulder. "The water's ready," she said. "I'm going to bring you some hot tea, then we can come up with a plan that makes sense."

She went to the kitchen, poured the tea, turned the basement lights off, and returned with two cups in her hands. "I made it a little strong," she said. "But I put a lot of honey in it."

He took a sip. "Why did you turn the lights off?" he asked. The room was now only lit by the small light built into the kitchen stove.

"I was afraid the neighbors might see the lights and get worried. So, how's the tea?"

"Anything warm tastes good right now." He noticed that the top button on her blouse was unfastened. He wanted to mention it but did not want to embarrass her. "Something's been bothering me," he said.

"Oh? What's that?"

"The way the sheriff explained that Pratt got into the barn without leaving any tracks. He figured he put his feet in the crack between the lower corral planks, held the top plank with his hands and sidestepped his way to the barn."

"That makes sense," she said.

"Yes, except Pratt has big feet and wears big boots. His feet wouldn't have fit. That crack is less than two inches wide."

"He probably wore moccasins. You said he was an Indian freak."

"Could be, but I got kicked in the stomach, and that sure didn't feel like moccasins."

"Are you done with your tea? I'll bring you another cup."

He shook his head. "No. My tea's fine. I really think I should be calling the sheriff," he said. "Maybe Solomon's at risk."

"You don't really think so, do you?" she asked.

"Well, at least let's drive past Jablonskis'. I'd feel better if I knew everything was okay over there. Pratt could still decide to come after Diamond."

"Ezra, Pratt is going to hide in the hills. You know that."

"Do I? You said he might have another vehicle. He might come looking for me at Jablonskis'. He knows Anne and Diamond are there." He took another long sip of tea, then glanced at his watch. It was too dark to read it.

"He would expect the police to be there too. Waiting for him. You need to calm down, let me get you more tea, and relax." She took the empty cup from his hand, rose, and began walking toward the kitchen. "In a little while we will drive past the Jablonski house, and you will see that it is dark and everyone is asleep," she said over her shoulder.

"I hate just waiting. I hate not doing something." He stared at the wall as if it was a movie screen and imagined Pratt commiting a variety of foul acts: attacking Solomon, kidnapping Diamond, even murdering Anne and Dylan. "That's it," he said. "Let's call the police."

She placed his refilled cup on the floor beside the sofa then reached over and took both of his hands. "Wait," she said. "Haven't we forgotten something? Maybe we should pray."

He wanted to tell her to save the prayers for later, but he was a preacher and a lay counselor—he had to consider his roles.

She closed her eyes and took the lead. She prayed for wisdom to know what to do about Pratt and for protection for Anne, Dylan, and Diamond. She prayed for the police and the sheriff, for Solomon, for the church, and for Pastor Tom and Darlene.

Ezra opened his eyes nervously twice, wondering when she was going to quit.

But she continued and continued. She went into detail praying for herself and Ezra, asking that the truths revealed in the counseling sessions would come to full fruition. Her voice became soft, musical, and hypnotic as she asked that she become a better mother and wife, and a better friend to Ezra. She capped the prayer with several minutes of thanking God for the many things He had already done as well as the things He was about to do.

Then she stopped and asked Ezra if there was anything he wanted to pray about. "I don't think so," he said.

She closed her eyes and continued. She prayed for Pratt and for the horses and the livestock. Ezra leaned deeper into the couch. Her voice was so reassuring that she was not hard to listen to. *Long-winded,* he thought, *but pleasant.*

He was even more relaxed when she finally finished. "I'm glad you prayed about truth," he told her. "Because things are not always as they seem."

"What do you mean?" she said.

"You know how worried I was about Shorty Wilson? I've been worried about him for years. And worried about my sisters. Right now I couldn't give a rip about any of that." His eyelids were becoming heavy, and his head slumped against the back of the sofa. "What time is it?" he asked.

"A quarter to midnight," she said. "Here, you should drink your tea before it gets cold." She put the cup in his hands.

Ezra raised his head and gulped it down to be finished with it. He had never cared for tea. "We've been here almost an hour? Doesn't seem that long," he said and slumped back into the couch. "For some reason," he mumbled, "I think it's all over. The three coyotes, I mean. Or two coyotes and a wolf. Whatever." His speech was becoming slurred.

"You mean Betty Lou's dream?" she asked pointedly.

"Yeah. For some reason it feels like it's over. Maybe Pratt won't be coming back at all." He spoke as if exhausted by the forming and expelling of thought.

"Pratt would be crazy to come back," Lilith said. "And I don't think he's that crazy. By morning he will know that every lawman in the state is searching for him."

"I'm still . . . worried . . . about Anne . . . and Diamond . . . and Dylan." His head began to tip toward the armrest.

"Ezra," Lilith said, leaning over him. "Are you okay?"

"Exhausted," he said. "Sleepy. Whole body's numb."

"I'll get some blankets from the nursery. You need to sleep."

"No," he said, struggling to get up. "Gotta go."

She pressed him back against the couch. "You're tired. You need to rest."

"Something's . . . not . . . right."

She quietly watched him for several moments. His drooping eyes stared toward the ceiling from a blank face. Finally she reached over and pulled him down into her lap. His head dropped heavily and lay there, his face up and expressionless. "You're right, Ezra," she said. "Something is not right." She ran her fingers across his eyebrows, nose, and lips. "But I will make things better," she cooed. "I will make things right."

CHAPTER THIRTY-FOUR

ylan had returned to the Jablonski house as Betty Lou was leaving. They nearly collided on the sidewalk. "My," Betty Lou said. "Another Riley keeping late hours. Doesn't anyone in your family have the good sense to sleep at night?" she asked. Dylan didn't answer. He just politely stepped aside and let her go her way.

"What was Mrs. Barber doing here?" he asked as his mother met him at the door.

"She's been doing her own detective work," Anne said. "Where have you been, Dylan? Why did you leave Diamond alone?"

"I went looking for Dad. Something doesn't feel right tonight."

"I know," she said. "I'm going to look again now but I want you to stay here with Diamond."

"Where are you going?" Dylan asked. "I've already been to the ranch. He's not there."

Anne led him down the steps away from Diamond's hearing. "I don't know where I'm going," she said. "But I want you to promise to stay with Diamond. And keep the doors locked. Your father got some information tonight that probably led him to Pratt. I don't know what's happened," she stressed, "but Pratt could be coming here. If you don't hear from me in an hour I want you to call Sheriff Butler."

She left her son and got in her car. Anne didn't know where to drive so she returned to the ranch. Everything was dark. The house was still locked, and there was no sign of Ezra's pickup. Then she noticed that Beaner had not come to greet her. Had Beaner been there when she was out before? She couldn't remember. Anne did not pay much attention to dogs. If the dog and the pickup were gone, it could mean Ezra was broken down out in the hills. She drove north toward the county road.

Once she topped the hill, she saw Ezra's pickup parked by Solomon's mailbox. The truck was unlocked but the keys were missing. She looked down at the house. It was dark except for the sterile light of the television. She was confused. She had already called Solomon once, and he hadn't seen Ezra. She got in her car, drove down to the house, and was about to knock on the door when she looked in the window and saw Solomon asleep on the couch. Something senseless was on television. It looked like a home shopping program in Spanish. She got back in her car and drove away. Nothing was making sense. She decided her suspicions had been wrong. The threat had to be Pratt—not Lilith—if Ezra's truck was near Solomon's but he and his dog were missing. She tried to put a scenario together: Ezra had been coming home from checking cows when someone stopped him. No. Why was his truck pointed north? He had to be going north when something caused him to park the pickup. And if he had parked it there in the daylight, Solomon would have seen it and mentioned it to her.

Now she was sure Beaner had been at the ranch when she was there earlier. She remembered how hurt the dog seemed when she didn't take time to pet it. She pulled back into the ranch yard, got out, and called for the dog. After several minutes she heard Hemingway yowl from the barn. She heard nothing else.

She tried again to make sense of it all. Ezra's truck was parked near Solomon's mailbox, but his uncle had not seen him. The dog had been home an hour and a half ago but now was gone.

She got back into the car, determined to drive straight to the police.

Lilith traced a finger around Ezra's lips. "My darling Ezra," she said. "Can you hear me? I have a confession or two to make. Be a good counselor now, and hear my confession." His eyes closed and his head dropped to the side. She cradled his head under one arm and pulled him into her. "What's wrong, Ezra, do you have a slumbering spirit?" His eyes slowly opened but seemed unfocused. "It wasn't true when I told you I just bought your book recently. I got it a year ago. You can imagine how surprised I was when we moved here and I discovered you in the congregation of our new church." She stroked his hair. "I love writers. And dancers and artists and musicians. We creative people are so free and so tormented at the same time. We live a life of ambiguity and contradiction. By the way, Ezra, about the key to the church, I did ask Pastor Jablonski for one, and he promised to give me a copy. Then he left on his trip. I just happened to find yours." She was speaking in fragments, a disjointed stream of consciousness passing across the light of her own memory. "My first trip to the ranch, the day you confronted Shorty Wilson for me, I went into your tack room to find a bridle for Shiloh, and there was this ring of keys on a nail. I thought: *I wonder how many doors do these keys open?* Quite a few as it turns out." She began rocking slowly, holding Ezra's head as if it were a baby. "You gave Pratt too much credit, Ezra. I was the one who came to your house at night. I touched your foot while you were sleeping. You and Anne lying there. It made me so jealous. I left the eagle feather on the table and the magpie feathers downstairs. I wanted to drive Diamond away because I didn't like you having another woman in your house, especially a pretty one who is younger than me. I knew you would blame Pratt. Men are so predictable."

She reached down and took a sip from her cup. "I prayed for you daily, did you know that? Sometimes I went to the ranch in the mornings while you were out feeding and Anne and Dylan were in school, and I just walked the creek bottoms and prayed for you. That's how I found the eagle and magpie feathers. But I visited mostly at night. I am a creature of the night, you know. Because of my condition." She laughed sweetly to herself. "My darling little Ben thinks my condition is my problem. That I am a victim of a disease. I am not a victim of anything, Ezra, and least of all a disease. Lupus is simply a very convenient cover, an excuse to seek the night."

His eyes closed again, and she looked at him angrily. "Ezra," she said, slapping his cheek. "Pay attention while I am talking to you. My confession isn't over. I am getting to the good part." She kissed the tips of two of her fingers then dabbed Ezra's nose. "I was the one who attacked you in the barn," she whispered. "I didn't know if I could do it or not. I was still getting to know you then, but you see, from our very first meeting I knew I would never have you. I wanted you so bad, Ezra, but you are so stubborn, so principled. Oh, you were attracted to me. That was obvious. But was there any chance you would betray your precious wife? No, I didn't think so. Your other lover is the land, Ezra, and I could tell there simply would not be room for me. So I had to do something."

There was a noise at the upstairs door and she stopped, her eyes whitening with intensity. "Your dog." She smiled. "I keep forgetting about your silly dog. Now, where was I? Oh, yes, the attack. When I was a small child, I remember my father telling a story of when he was in the Navy. A couple of sailors rolled drunks down by the piers. They took rolls of coins, knotted them in the end of a long sock, then swung the sock and hit the drunks over the head. For some reason it fascinated me and I thought, *My, now there is something I would like to try sometime.* I used a pair of my nylons, Ezra. I thought you would appreciate the intimacy." She paused to drink from her cup.

"You got everything else right. Or I should say the sheriff did. I came down the planks just like he thought, and I waited in that horse stall forever and ever. It got quite chilly."

She heard a noise again. "Your dog is uncomfortable, but I am not going to let it in. I hope it doesn't start barking. I hate barking dogs." His eyes had closed, and she opened them with her fingers. "So that's how it happened, love. I had to make myself swing the first blow, but after that it was easy. It was fun. I added the kick as a special touch, but not to really hurt you. I didn't really want to hurt you, Ezra. I wanted to *have* you. I wanted to possess you."

The door rattled. "Oh, that dog. What do you call her? Beaner? That's a stupid name, Ezra. A really stupid name. I don't like dogs," she repeated. "Now, I like your cat, Hemingway. There is a name with class. Hemingway." She put both hands into his hair and dug her nails into his scalp. "Speaking of animals, my dear, you were quite wrong about Betty Lou and her stupid dream. Of course, Shorty Wilson is a coyote. Everyone knows that. But Pratt? Oh, you overestimated him if you thought he was a wolf.

He was just another coyote, a trickster. Do you know now who I am, Ezra?" She pulled his face close to hers, stared into his dim eyes, then kissed him passionately on the mouth.

She pulled back with a smug satisfaction. "I am Lilith," she said, "I am lupus erythematosus. The Red Wolf." She laughed and the sound of her voice chilled the room. "Of course, lupus did not cause me to be the way I am. Thousands of women have the disease, but they are not like me. Lupus merely gave me an identity, Ezra, my dear one. Lupus is not a disease for me, it is an honor, a naming of my nature. It has taught me to love the night. So why am I the way I am, Ezra? That was for you to find out. You were the counselor, remember?"

The door rattled harder. "Errr," she growled. "That dog is making me so mad." She lifted Ezra's head and got to her feet. "Don't go anywhere, my sweet," she said. "Your pretty baby will be back for you."

She looked in the kitchen for an implement and noticed the phone on the wall. She had to get a couple of calls out of the way. "I better do this first," she said softly, then sighed deeply as if casting a spell of deceit upon herself, and punched the numbers.

The phone rang a dozen times before it was answered.

"Hello, Betty Lou?" Lilith said, a false urgency in her voice. "This is Lilith. I am so sorry for getting you out of bed, but this is important, and I didn't know who else to call." She made herself sound as if she were on the verge of tears. "Can you meet me at the church first thing in the morning? Please? About seven-thirty. Oh, thank you, Betty Lou." Lilith laughed to herself. *You are such a dope, Betty Lou. You think you are so clever and insightful, but you're just an old buffalo wallowing in the mud of life.*

She hung the phone up, shook her head as if wringing water, then dialed again.

"Ben? Hi. Listen, something has come up and I won't be home tonight. Ben, don't beg. You know how I hate it when you beg. I will be home in the morning. It's important, Ben. It's my ministry work. I will be home before you have to leave for work."

She hung up and resumed her search for a weapon. There was a wide assortment of knives in the utensil drawer, but she didn't like knives. They were so messy. She settled for a heavy wooden mixing spoon. She slapped the rounded end in her palm to test for weight and impact and nodded approvingly. She moved past the stove where the tea water simmered in a glass kettle, then stopped at the base of the steps.

She turned and looked back at the shadowed form of Ezra Riley lying unconscious on the sofa. "Your puppy needs a spanking," she said, and she bounced lightly up the steps.

It was a sudden and clear thought, like sheet lightning flaring across the sky, that made Anne turn from her route to the police station and drive past the church. She pulled up to the front. The building was dark except for a soft glow in the basement that she knew was the small light above the stove. People were always forgetting to turn it off.

Well, I don't have time to do it now, she thought. She was putting the car in gear to leave when a dog on the steps sat up and stared at her. Its ears perked and its tail began wagging slowly. At first she thought it an odd place for a neighborhood dog to sleep, then she realized the dog was Beaner.

Anne shut the car off and got out. "Beaner?" she said.

The pup trotted to her friskily, her tail spinning like a propeller.

Anne crouched down and the pup licked her hands. "What are you doing here?" Anne whispered. The pup whined as if trying to reply. Anne looked around for any sign of another vehicle. There was nothing nearby. She stood up, sorted through her ring of keys, and approached the door. "You stay here," she told Beaner, then she unlocked the door and stepped in. Her instinct was to turn on a light, but she stopped herself. If Ezra was betraying her, or if he was in trouble, it was better to be cautious. Everything upstairs was dark. She decided to move toward the only light and began slowly descending the stairs, her right hand resting lightly on the railing. She stopped once to listen and look. All she could see below her was the soft reflection of the stove light on the smooth concrete floor. It reminded her of moonlight on water. She continued carefully to the basement landing. To her right was an entrance to the kitchen. She could see the smooth chrome and porcelain contours of the stove. The large, bare basement in front of her looked dark and empty. To her left was an open door leading to a storage room.

That door should be closed, she thought. She turned and stared into the room's dark void. When she heard a sound, Anne instantly raised her arms and screamed. The spoon handle caught her on the left forearm and spun her backward into the kitchen. She ducked a second blow, and the spoon splintered against the basement wall. Anne reached out for something to use for a shield, and her hand grasped the handle of the glass teakettle. She whirled it up, striking Lilith full in the face. The glass cracked, and hot water sprayed in all directions. Lilith dropped to the floor. The kettle separated from its handle and crashed to the cement floor, spraying shards of glass in all directions. Anne took two steps back, her chest heaving, the handle to the kettle still in her hand. She brought her free hand to her mouth as she looked down at the form on the floor. There was broken glass and blood everywhere, but Anne could not see the person's face.

Lilith stirred slowly. Anne took a step back, holding the kettle handle as if it were still a weapon. Suddenly Lilith leaped to her feet, as quick and graceful as a cat, and fled up the stairs. Anne heard the front door open and slam shut. She dropped the kettle handle and staggered against the wall, her heart beating against her chest. She groped for the row of light switches and hit them all at once. The basement came alive with light. Across the room, lying as lifeless as a rug, was her husband.

"Ezra?" she called out.

He did not respond.

Anne ran to him. "Ezra, what's wrong?" He lay face up, his eyes closed, one arm dangling to the floor. She shook him. "Oh, God," she cried. "Oh, Jesus." She reached for his wrist and searched for a pulse. It was so faint she could barely feel it. She ran to the wall phone and dialed 911. "This is Anne Riley," she said. "My husband is unconscious in the basement of the Community Believers' Church. I don't know what the problem is."

The dispatcher asked for an address and told her to stay on the line.

"I want to go to my husband," Anne argued.

"Please stay on the line, Mrs. Riley. An ambulance is on the way. Now why is your husband unconscious? Has he fallen?"

"No, no, he's just lying on the couch. I think he's been drugged."

"You think he's been drugged. Did he take the drugs himself?"

"No, no. There was a woman here. She attacked me. I think she did it."

"She attacked you? And you think she drugged your husband?" There was a pause as if the dispatcher was taking notes, checking a clock, or talking to someone in Central Dispatch. She came back on the line. "That must be quite a church you have there, Mrs. Riley. Do you have any idea what the substance was that rendered your husband unconscious?"

"No, you would have to ask the woman."

"And what is her name?"

"Foster. Lilit—no, Lillie Foster. Mrs. Ben Foster."

"And what is her relationship to your husband?"

"She's, uh . . . my husband is a church counselor, and he was counseling her."

"In the middle of the night?" the dispatcher asked suspiciously.

"I don't know, I don't know," Anne said angrily. In the distance she heard the wail of sirens. She dropped the phone and ran back to Ezra. On the floor by the sofa were two cups. One contained a residue of murky tea. The other was half-filled with water.

Three paramedics and a police officer were soon in the room. They took Ezra's vital signs, strapped him onto a gurney and started a glucose IV. "The breathing is shallow but the pulse is okay," a paramedic said. "What's in this guy, lady?" he asked Anne.

"I don't know," she said. She handed the police officer the dirty cup. "Whatever it is, it was in this cup." The officer sniffed the cup. He looked at a paramedic and shook his head.

"Okay, let's roll him," the paramedic said. "We'll do a nasal-gastril and blood and urine screen in ER. Is there an easier way out?"

Anne pointed to a basement door and they began wheeling Ezra toward it. "I want to ride with him," she said.

"Sorry, ma'am," one of them shouted back. "We're short on room."

The policeman reached out and restrained her by an arm. "You are his wife?" he asked.

"Yes." The officer was young and handsome and didn't look much older than Dylan. Suddenly Anne felt very old and tired, as if life was speeding away on fast wheels and she was cornered in a basement with no escape. Ezra was her life and where he went she had to go.

"And you were attacked on these premises?" the officer asked.

Anne's eyes were on the basement steps and her heart was in the ambulance. She had forgotten her own pain. She absently rolled up the sleeve of her blouse to show a red and swollen forearm.

"We better have that X-rayed," the officer said. "Who attacked you?" She did not hear him.

"Mrs. Riley," the officer said. "The name of your attacker again?"

"Mrs. Ben Foster. Lillian Foster," she stated calmly, then reiterated, "I have to go to the hospital."

"You can ride with me," the officer suggested. "You shouldn't drive in your condition."

"If we go to Lilith's house we can find out what was in the drink," Anne said.

"Lilith?" The policeman frowned. "I thought you said her name was Lillian?"

"It is. She uses both."

"I can't permit you to go to this woman's house," the officer said. "Come with me, please, and I will take you to the hospital. You can be with your husband, and you can have your arm X-rayed." He took her lightly by the arm that was not injured.

As she seated herself in the front seat of the patrol car, she heard the ambulance siren fading into the distance. The young policeman radioed a report to Central Dispatch as he pulled away from the church. He requested another officer to go to the Foster residence. "Can you give me this woman's address?" he asked Anne.

"No," she said. "I know where the house is, but I don't remember the address. The address would be in the church somewhere," she added. "In the pastor's office."

"Do you know the make or color of her vehicle?"

"No," she said, realizing she had never paid any attention to the Fosters' cars.

"I am taking you to the hospital to have your arm checked," the patrolman said. "Then we will locate this Mrs. Foster."

"Can you call Sheriff Butler?" Anne asked.

"The sheriff? Why?"

"He's been working with my husband," was all she could think of saying.

"About this Mrs. Foster?" the officer asked.

"No," she said. "About something else. But I think he should know." She saw the brick structure of the hospital ahead of them. The empty ambulance was parked in the Emergency entrance. Inside she knew people were moving frantically to save her husband's life. She prayed they would succeed.

CHAPTER THIRTY-FIVE

Uncle Joe threaded his nineteenth bluegill onto his stringer. "I notice you been spendin' a lotta time out in the hills by yourself," he said. "That's okay if you're out there huntin' arrowheads, agates, or rabbits. But if you're just out there to be alone, to get away from people, let me tell ya, that ain't ever gonna be the answer. That's what your uncle Solomon does. Just gets alone in the hills. But you're never alone, even in the hills. No matter where you go, you're always with yourself, and besides, who knows? Maybe ya can't trust the hills, either." He took a deep breath and stared straight ahead. He had said a mouthful and it had him all tuckered out.

Leaving the Land

Ezra was in an electric world where the grasses glowed green, the sky was a vibrant blue, and the badlands pulsed with their own energy. The land seemed alive with an overwhelming beauty.

Shiloh stood beside him. Ezra could read his horse's thoughts. Shiloh was at peace and glad to be a friend at service.

Two other friends had just left him. He could not see them anymore. Was it Jim Mendenhall that had ridden north or had it been his father? Or Austin Arbuckle? Was it Rick Benjamin that had ridden east, or was it Jubal Lee Walker or Mikal Mora? He wasn't sure. The missing riders seemed to be an amalgamation of the mounted men of his memories.

But they were gone. There were no other people, but he was hardly alone. The land was there. His horse was there.

He wondered how old he was. It was an amusing thought. It seemed to make no difference. He had no age.

He knew he had people in his life somewhere. Vague memories of Anne and Dylan and other faces passed like clouds changing in the wind. They were not formless, but not formed either. Below him a herd of red cattle trailed toward water. They sparkled like little jewels. A hawk soared in the breeze.

He pinched the earth and let a trickle of dirt run between his fingers. He plucked a stem of grass and sucked on the shoot.

The breeze against his face was warm. The world around him was beautiful and peaceful.

But something was wrong.

The more he thought about it the more wrong it seemed.

Everything was too good. It did not seem real.

The breeze cooled, even became chilling.

In the maze of badlands he saw a tawny motion.

It was a coyote trotting his direction.

Ezra told himself that the coyote would soon catch his scent and run away.

But the coyote kept coming.

Shiloh lifted his head from munching grass and pricked his ears.

What do you make of this, fellow? Ezra thought.

Unusual, Shiloh answered.

It did not seem strange to Ezra that he and his horse were communicating.

The coyote moved closer. It was on a direct line toward them following a faint deer trail that led out of the badlands.

Ezra thought, *It knows we are here but it doesn't care.*

The horse took a step backward.

The coyote was close enough now that Ezra could see the bright, beady eyes and its pink tongue.

My horse is gone, Ezra realized. Shiloh had not run away; he was simply gone. Ezra was afoot, dismounted. Alone.

The coyote trotted as if Ezra was in its sights. Its course was direct and purposeful, and the animal seemed self-contained with energy.

Ezra began to feel fear.

The coyote was now but a few feet away. The energy radiating from it was bombarding Ezra with thoughts. It was trying to talk to him.

Ezra considered running or grabbing a stone to throw, but he was paralyzed. A coldness gripped him, and though his heart beat rapidly, his breathing became shallow.

The coyote was upon him. It stood inches away, its eyes sparkling, saliva dripping from a smooth, tapered tongue.

Ezra's mouth did not move but he heard himself say, *You are not real.*

The coyote seemed to smile. *I am as real as you make me,* it said.

I thought you were a wolf this time.

I am whatever you want me to be, it said.

Ezra could feel the weight of the animal upon him. He felt its hot breath against his face.

He had brief flashes of memory—the other times the coyote had crossed his path: Himself on a cold bus returning home to his father's funeral. Himself in a cold trailer house after having moved to the ranch. And snatches of scenes from the same chilling dream.

The face of the coyote came back into view.

Tell me your name, Ezra said.

I am the land.

No, Ezra thought. *You are the curse upon the land.*

The coyote's breath was hot and stale. *I am death,* it said. *And I have come for you.* The coyote lay upon his chest, put its mouth against his, and began to suck his breath.

So this is death, Ezra thought. Not a ripping or tearing, but a quiet wearing down. A slow absorption.

Then he remembered he was not ready to die. It was an unexpected thought that descended like a plunging hawk. He heard a shriek that he knew was his own will to live.

I won't have you, Ezra said, though no words came from his mouth.

The coyote took one step back, and hate radiated from its small black eyes.

It is set before me this day life and death, Ezra thought.

The coyote sat on its haunches and stared curiously.

I choose life.

Wakefulness flowed through him like liquid light. His eyes opened, and life and light hurt his eyes. His nose, throat, and stomach were very sore and irritated. But that wasn't the worst of it. His groin was burning.

"Romazicon," he heard someone say. "It works wonders. It knocks the heck out of Valium every time."

Where was he? Everything seemed too bright, too white, too sterile. The light of remembrance slowly began filling his mind. He wondered if someone had turned on all the lights in the church basement. And who were these people? Where was Lilith? Was Beaner still sitting outside the door?

"Where am I?" he asked. His voice was so raspy he did not recognize it as his. "Where's Beaner?" The last thing he remembered was his dog making noises at the door.

"You are in the emergency room of the hospital," a nurse told him. "Who's Beaner? Your wife? She was here minutes ago."

He didn't bother to explain. He had tubes running down his nose that he wanted very badly to pull out and other tubes running into his arm. "What happened?" he asked.

A doctor came forward. "Someone gave you an almost lethal dose of Valium," he said.

The truth swirled in his head like a formless presence, a fog. "Lilith," he said.

The doctor placed a gentle hand on his shoulder. "We want you to stay awake for a little while but to rest. No more questions until later," he said. "If you find your groin area to be a bit sensitive, it's because we had to do a urine screen. We just removed the catheter."

"Anne?" he asked. "My wife."

The doctor nodded. "She's here somewhere," he said.

"Pratt," Ezra said. Images were coming back in black patches of shadow. A man in a barn. Himself running down the creek. A car sitting by the highway.

"Who?" the nurse asked.

"Pratt," he rasped.

The nurse frowned.

"Sheriff . . . sheriff . . ."

"No more questions," the doctor said. They wheeled him to a room. When he became alert enough to fully remember, his body also realized its exhaustion. He slept.

Anne's X ray revealed her arm to be badly bruised but not broken. She wanted to be with Ezra but was told he was out of danger but asleep. "Valium," a nurse told her. "It might have killed someone less . . ."

"Stubborn?"

"I was going to say *strong*." The nurse smiled.

"A policeman wanted to talk to me," Anne said. "Do you know where he went?"

The nurse shrugged. "He was here a minute ago."

While she was being X-rayed, she had heard the policeman tell someone he could not locate an address for a Foster family. Anne could and she knew that is what they wanted from her. But where did he go? She stopped another nurse. "You haven't seen a policeman or Sheriff Butler, have you?"

The nurse hadn't. Anne looked in the emergency room. The doctor and nurses were busy with a drunk who had fallen off his bar stool and cut open the back of his head. She got Ezra's room number from the desk and went to his room. He was asleep. While she was peeking in on him a nurse came by and told her she really shouldn't be there. "I'm his wife," Anne said.

"But you can't be," the nurse said. "I just hung up the phone from talking to a woman who said she was his wife. She wanted to know how he was."

Lilith!

Anne was not going to wait any longer. She had questions that needed answers. She slipped out a side entrance without being noticed. It was only six blocks to her car. She walked at a quick pace, assisted by a mental kicking of herself. How could she have been so blind? If Ezra had not seen the danger in Lillian Foster, why hadn't she? She hadn't been around, she realized. She had been consumed by schoolwork and ministering to Diamond. And Ezra had not seen because he had been preoccupied with Pratt, preaching, and running the ranch.

She had planned on getting the address and going to the police, but after Lilith had called the hospital pretending to be Ezra's wife, Anne no longer wanted a policeman with her. She wanted Lilith all to herself. She had lived her life being nice, trying to get along with everyone, turning the other cheek, even capitulating at her own expense when necessary, and had preached the same gospel of mercy to her husband, but suddenly she wanted to fight, not on her knees in some mystical combat, but with her hands. She knew where the Fosters lived and would go there herself. She drove to the dark neighborhood on the edge of town. It was quieter and sleepier than when she had been there several hours earlier. Only one dog barked in the distance when she got out of her car. There was a vehicle parked in the Fosters' driveway, the same one that had been there before, she realized. She knew Lillian and Ben had separate cars. She did not see a second one.

She knocked on the door loudly. There was no answer. Another neighborhood dog began barking. She knocked harder until a light came on in a back room.

Ben answered in a bathrobe, his hair tousled and eyes half-open.

"I'm sorry to awaken you," Anne said. "Is your wife home?"

"Lillian? No. She's not here," he said.

"Where is she, Ben?" Anne demanded.

"Mrs. Riley, it's one in the morning. Why do you want to see Lillian?"

Anne rolled up her sleeve and held up her arm. "She did this," she said, showing him the bruise. "And she almost killed my husband."

He trembled slightly and his head shook spastically. "That's crazy," he said. "Lillian would never do anything like that."

"Where is she, Ben?" Anne's voice was almost fierce, and she was tempted to grab him by the lapels of his bathrobe and shake him. She could do it, she knew. She was three inches taller than the man and outweighed him by twenty pounds.

"I don't know," Ben said. "She called earlier and said she had something important to do but would be home in the morning. I think it had something to do with Mrs. Barber."

"Betty Lou?"

"That's just a guess. Lillian sometimes has trouble sleeping, so she walks and prays. Mrs. Barber has been her prayer partner lately."

"Does she take anything to help herself sleep?"

"She has a prescription for Valium, but she hates to use it. She needs to keep her blood clean because of the lupus."

"Ben," Anne insisted, "none of this is a surprise to you, is it? You know she's done this before."

"I don't know what you're talking about," he said forcefully, but his eyes dropped to the floor. "She has a disease, that's all. She's sick."

"Wake up, Ben. None of this has anything to do with lupus. She does what she does because she enjoys it, but she's crossed the line this time. The police are waiting to talk to her."

"Lillian is always being blamed for things that aren't her fault," he whined. "She can't help it if men are always after her."

"Ben, it's the other way around."

"No, it's not," he said, and he slammed the door in Anne's face.

As she stood there, all the lights in the small house extinguished. Where would Lilith be? Anne wondered. Where would she go next?

Anne drove to the Barber home and rang the doorbell until Betty Lou finally answered. She wore fluffy pink slippers and a pink bathrobe that opened to show knee-warmers beneath her nightgown. Flakes of a green facial mask had dried around her eyes. "Anne Riley again?" Betty Lou said. "What's going on? Is it everyone's mission in life to keep me awake tonight?"

"Have you heard from Lilith?" Anne asked.

"Not for a couple of hours. Why?" She felt around her eyes and began flaking off the facial mask.

"She drugged Ezra," Anne said. "He's in the hospital having his stomach pumped. What did she tell you? What did she want?"

"Drugged Ezra? Oh, my. Lilith called about eleven. She was coherent but very disturbed. She said it was very important that I meet her at the church at 7:30 this morning. Is Ezra okay?"

"He'll live, but don't expect Lilith to make your meeting," Anne said. "She was setting Ezra up. She wanted you to find her there with him, probably on the couch together, asleep under blankets."

"Oh, my," Betty Lou said again, picturing the scene. "I would have crucified him."

"Betty Lou, remember your dream? The third attack was by an animal you thought was a wolf."

"Yes?"

"Lillian Foster has lupus."

"So?"

"It's not the disease, Betty Lou. It's the name. Lupus is Latin for *wolf*."

Betty Lou Barber seemed to cave in on herself as she stepped backward into her house. She brought a hand to her lips. "Oh, my. And we prayed so many prayers together. And always about your husband."

"Hers were directed *at* my husband," Anne said. "Not to God *about* my husband."

"What do you mean?" she asked weakly, hesitant to hear the answer.

"Betty Lou, you have been under her influence like the rest of us. For the past month you have been praying with a witch."

Betty Lou took another step backward and bumped into a hall table cluttered with angel figurines. Several fell to the floor and shattered. "A witch?" she said. "What do you mean? Spells and potions?"

"No, I mean manipulation and domination." Anne could tell the woman did not understand. Or did not want to understand. "Keep all of this just between us," Anne told her. "Because no one is going to believe it anyway."

"But what about Lilith?" Betty Lou said. "What are we going to do?"

"That's up to the police now," Anne said.

"The police?" Betty Lou gasped. "But the scandal—"

Anne nodded. "It is a scandalous thing," she said.

When Ezra awakened about eight Anne was at his bedside. "Good morning," she said. "How are you feeling?"

He squinted and brought his hand to his face. "Terrible. Where am I? Why am I here? My nose and throat hurt and my stomach . . ."

"They pumped your stomach," Anne said.

Ezra tried to rise up in bed. "Ow," he moaned. "Catheter. I remember that part. How did I get here?"

"I found you unconscious in the basement of the church."

"Where's Lilith?"

"I don't know," Anne said. "But there are a number of people looking for her."

"And Beaner?"

"I took her home."

A deeper concern covered him as his memory returned. He saw the image of a dark barn and a silhouetted figure and became suddenly alarmed. "Where's Pratt?" he said, pulling the sheet aside to rise.

"Pratt? I don't know," Anne said. "What about him?"

Ezra's head spun again with night scenes of him creeping though Solomon's cellar, a revolver in his hand; him falling down the highway embankment; him alone in the barn with Pratt, then running down the highway toward Lilith's car. He looked around the room. "Why am I here?" he said. "Didn't Pratt put me here?"

"No," Anne said, putting a hand on his chest to keep him from rising. "Lilith put you here. She nearly killed you with Valium."

"Lilith?" he said, and his face contorted in confusion.

"Ezra, she's not at all who she pretends to be."

"But where's Pratt?" he said, struggling to get up. "I have to get to the ranch." He fell back onto the bed. He was about to vomit, and he had to go to the bathroom. "I'm sick . . . ," he said.

"You're going to have diarrhea all morning, Ezra. They won't release you until noon."

"But Pratt—" he said, his mind still trying to sort the images. "You better call Sheriff Butler."

"I have talked to him," Anne said. "He and the police want to talk to you later. About Lilith," she added.

He stared at the ceiling. Hospital rooms were so ugly, he thought, then he turned and looked at Anne. "Is Dylan okay?"

"Yes, why?"

"He was a few inches from Pratt last night. And Diamond?"

"She's fine. Her cousin called and is on her way."

"But Pratt is still out there somewhere," he said.

Anne nodded. "So is Lilith," she said.

CHAPTER THIRTY-SIX

The sun was setting, killdeer were screeching, and night-hawks were soaring. I reeled in my flyline and embedded the hook of the black gnat in the corked end of the fly rod. "You think I could end up like Solomon?" I asked Uncle Joe. He rose heavily from his five-gallon bucket and began laboring toward the truck, the string of fish dangling from his left hand. "We all gotta end up like somebody," he said. "If you got a temper problem, you'll be like your dad. If it's drinking, you'll be like Sam or Willis. If it's eating, you'll be like me.

"Maybe that's why people go to church," he continued. "To break the mold and try to be someone they're not." His breathing was labored and his steps short and shaky as he climbed the reservoir's dike. "Maybe they wanna be like Jesus," he gasped. He stood on the dike, huffing and puffing. "Not that I know what that would be like," he added.

Leaving the Land

Ezra was released from the hospital Tuesday afternoon. He spent the remainder of the day giving statements to the police about Lillian Foster, to Sheriff Butler about Pratt, and he did his best to explain everything to Anne, and to himself.

Anne did not attend classes all day. She and Ezra both knew what that meant. Ezra had urged her to go, but she insisted on spending the day moving herself, Dylan, and Diamond back to the ranch. "I'm not leaving you alone anymore," she said. "They say nature abhors a vacuum, and so does the supernatural. Lilith tried to fill a void, Ezra. We can't let that ever happen again."

"But you are throwing away two years of school," he argued.

"No, I'm losing one semester," she said. "If a nursing degree is something I really want, I'll get it, Ezra. But I don't have any regrets about the past few weeks. My family comes first, and Diamond has become part of our family."

Butler arrived at the ranch early Wednesday morning and searched the hayloft for clues. All he found was a trace of blood on the floor and an indentation in a rafter where the arrow had struck.

"We need to search your uncle's garage," he told Ezra.

"I really want to keep Solomon out of this," Ezra said.

"Can you get him off the place for an hour?" Butler asked.

Ezra could. He had Anne call Solomon and ask if he wanted to go to town for groceries. Solomon always wanted to go to town for groceries. Especially with Anne. When she drove up to get him he was already standing on the concrete steps with his checkbook in his hand. "Thought you were supposed to be in school," he said. His tone was loud but not threatening, like a dog's friendly bark.

"I've dropped out," she said.

He shuffled to the car shaking his head. Women didn't make any sense to him at all. He got in and slammed the door. Being the consummate reader of the Yellow Rock paper, he had noticed that Ezra had been admitted and released from the hospital. "What's wrong with Ezra?" he said. "Slackin' off, again? I saw his name in the paper."

"Food poisoning," Anne said, stretching the truth to the point of breakage. "He was pretty sick."

Solomon grunted. For eighty-three years he had eaten anything that dared crawl within reach of his fork. He'd never been food-poisoned. It proved to him what he had always suspected, the younger generation just didn't have any constitution at all.

Once Ezra and Butler saw Anne drive past with Solomon, they searched the garage. Neither of them was surprised to not find anything except the plug wires Ezra had pulled from Pratt's bike. Ezra was relieved to even find those. It helped him believe his own story. But the bike, books, wolf pelt—anything that Ezra had recalled seeing—were gone. They even checked Solomon's basement and barn.

"There's one more thing I have to do," Ezra told Butler. "I need to find the revolver Mikal Mora gave me. I need to search the two places where I fell."

The closest of the two was the culvert under the hill. Ezra rolled up his sleeves and poked about in the puddle where the culvert drained. His fingers settled on something smooth and hard. He pulled the revolver out. "I found it," he called out. "A good cleaning and it will be like new."

"I've found something too," he heard Butler call back. His voice was shadowed by an echo. The sheriff had entered the five-foot-high culvert. Ezra ducked his head and walked in onto the corrugated steel floor. He met the sheriff pushing a small dirt bike his way. "Bingo," Butler said. "At least we have something substantial."

"So what do we do now?" Ezra asked.

"I'm going back to town and arrange to get a deputy in the air," he said. "I'm going to call in a couple reserve deputies and have them drive the back roads of the ranch. And if you can loan me a horse, I think you and I should get horseback."

"Then you think Pratt is still nearby?"

"I don't know if he is or not," Butler said. "But we're going to operate under that assumption. When I come back in an hour or two, I'll let you know if there is anything new on Lillian Foster."

Ezra went home and cleaned the revolver thoroughly, scouring the mud and grass stems from the bore, cylinder, and action, then coating the parts with a light oil. He decided he was going to stay armed until Pratt was caught and was holstering the revolver when Diamond came up from her downstairs bedroom. She watched him quietly. Anne had told her the full story of Ezra's experience with Pratt and Lilith. Her eyes were deep and sad.

"I don't want to hurt him," Ezra said.

Her face did not move except for the slight parting of her lips to speak. "He is already dead," she said. "He died many years ago."

He had no answer. Their eyes locked for an instant, and for the first time she was looking at him with affection instead of apprehension. If there was fear in her eyes, it was for him.

But even that brief sharing made her uncomfortable. "My cousin comes tomorrow," she said. "I must get ready." She rose and drifted away like a feather on a breeze.

Ezra went to the corral and saddled Shiloh and Cheyenne. He scabbarded his father's old .30-30 carbine and hung it from the right side of his saddle. Beaner danced excitedly by the gate. "Yeah, yeah," Ezra told her. "You've earned it. You can come."

Butler drove in a few minutes later. "I have some news," he said as he walked to the corral carrying his chaps and binoculars. "The police went to the Foster residence this morning and the place was empty. The husband took the little girl and slipped away sometime during the night."

"He's joining his wife somewhere," Ezra said.

"Speaking of her," Butler said as he zippered his chaps, "the county attorney has filed attempted murder charges against her."

"She wasn't trying to kill me," Ezra said.

"But she almost did. If and when she is caught, she can do her convincing in front of a jury."

"Well, she's good at that," Ezra said dryly.

"One more thing," Butler said as he hung the binocular case from his saddle horn. "The police checked the plates on a Wyoming pickup that's been sitting in the parking lot at County Market for the past week. It's been reported missing from a ranch near Buffalo. The ranch is owned by Antonio de la Rosa."

Ezra mounted Shiloh. "If we have his bike and his truck, then Pratt is still around."

"You forget one other thing," the sheriff said, nodding at the house. "You still have the girl. She might mean more to him than you think." He pulled himself up onto the dun.

Ezra still didn't know what Diamond meant to Pratt. Did he love her or had she been merely a servant, a slave for fulfilling his physical needs and an audience for his eccentric beliefs? "The girl leaves tomorrow afternoon," he said.

"Then I would guess we have an interesting twenty-four hours ahead of us," Butler said, and he pulled his hat brim down, snugging the Stetson to his head.

Ezra looked up the lane and saw Anne returning from taking Solomon to town. "Then maybe I shouldn't be leaving them here alone."

When the car stopped in front of the house, Ezra noticed there was someone else in the front seat. It didn't look like Solomon. Anne stepped out of the car, and so did another woman. She wore a uniform and a gun belt. "My jailer," the sheriff said. "Anne and the girl won't be alone."

They rode until dark combing the coulees and creek bottoms for some sign of Pratt. They found nothing, but the search provided Ezra a good opportunity to ride around the cattle. Butler was not discouraged after they unsaddled and walked to the house. "Every law enforcement agency in the county will be keeping an eye on this place for the next few days," Butler told Ezra as he got in his truck. "The Highway Patrol will drive by every hour or so. Brand inspectors, game wardens—anyone with a badge is going to find a reason to be on the north side. The town cops will even be driving out this far to burn a little carbon out of their cars, and the ADC pilot will have one of us in the air at first light." He handed Ezra a radio. "Your pastor carries this when he serves as police chaplain. Listen to it, and you will know most of what we're doing."

"I appreciate all of this," Ezra said.

"Well, it's time we all took this Pratt guy a little more seriously. I even got the governor to raise cain with the USFWS. I expect their man in Billings to be down here by tomorrow. We'll get this guy, Ezra. I guarantee it."

Ezra felt better after hearing the sheriff's report, but as soon as Butler and the jailer had driven away, he still felt exposed and vulnerable. Pratt had become the myth he wanted to be. He seemed as prevailing as the night, as untouchable as the wind. Ezra considered moving everyone, himself included, back to town. But what would he do with Solomon? The old man would refuse to leave his house, and Anne was likely to be just as stubborn.

For Diamond's sake he tried not to appear threatened, but the moment the sun went down Ezra flooded the ranch with light. He turned on the yard lights, the porch lights, and the lights in the bunkhouse, garage, and barn. He parked his pickup directly in front of the house and moved all of his guns inside to the basement. When he came upstairs Anne, Dylan, and Diamond were sitting around the kitchen table. "What are you doing?" he asked.

"We're going to pray," Anne said. "Will you join us?"

"You're doing the right thing," he said. "But I have something else I have to do." He got in his pickup to drive to Solomon's. Though Ezra didn't think Pratt would threaten the old man, he simply could not leave his uncle unprotected.

"How's the game going?" Ezra asked as he walked in and took his customary seat near the roaring television.

"Ol' Shag ain't doin' so great tonight," Solomon said. He always pronounced Shaquille O'Neal's name incorrectly, calling him Shag instead of Shaq as if he were a sheepdog and not a seven-foot, 300-pound center. "How's the grass comin'?"

"It's looking pretty good," Ezra said.

"Cheat grass takin' the country?"

"It's trying," Ezra said, knowing the usual routine of questions was coming his way like expressway traffic at rush hour.

"Seen your buddy lately?" Solomon asked.

"Who's that?"

"The arrowhead man, the beardie."

"Pratt?" Ezra asked curiously. "No, I haven't seen him. Have you?"

"Nope." Solomon seemed disappointed. "He ain't been by here for a few days now." He lay quietly for a few minutes, a horizontal diver poised on the springboard of his next question, and stared at the television with a fierce intensity. "What was that plane doin' today?" he finally shouted. "The one that kept flyin' up and down the creek."

"ADC," Ezra said, "hunting coyotes."

"Hunting coyotes? It flew all day long, up and down the creek," he repeated, "then into the hills and back. Never did hear no shootin'. We losin' calves?"

"Could be," Ezra said. "There's one bad coyote in the country."

"Well, you can't hunt just one coyote like that," Solomon said. "You're just going to wise 'em up." He settled back into a long stare. Sometimes it amazed him how stupid the world had become. "They ain't huntin' coyotes," he said.

"No," Ezra admitted. "The guys in the plane are looking for Pratt."

Solomon scowled. "For the beardie? They're flyin' just to nab a poacher?"

"Solomon, I told you, this is one bad dude."

"Humpf. Waste of money flyin' that plane. I could catch him anytime. You quit feedin' yet?"

"I quit a few days ago," Ezra said. Five months of hard labor had come to an end, but he didn't expect any appreciation from his uncle.

"Saw you were in the hospital," Solomon teased. "Goldbrickin' again, huh?"

"Yeah, I needed a day off so I went to the emergency room." Ezra saw Solomon's mind coil again for a springboard dive into a new wave of questions. He began to lose his concern for the old man. If Pratt was around, Solomon would talk him to death.

"Hmmff," his uncle grunted. "That ole Shag is so big he should be fed from a sack."

That's next, Ezra thought. Solomon wasn't content with Ezra shoveling feed for cows half the year. He would have him feeding basketball players next. He stood up. "Well, I have to get back," he said.

Solomon looked concerned. "It ain't even halftime," he said.

"Orlando is going to win."

"Houston and San Antonio is on next," Solomon said, baiting his nephew to stay late.

Ezra went to the door. "You keeping this door locked at night?" he asked.

"Always do," Solomon said. "Ain't no one gettin' in here."

Ezra heard the false security in Solomon's voice as if he believed nothing was going on that he didn't know about and couldn't handle and Ezra should watch his own self; he was the one having trouble with coyotes and food poisoning. "If you see Pratt, call me immediately," Ezra warned.

"Haw." The old man snorted. "Why would I wanna do that? I just end up talkin' to that 'idiot in the box.'"

Ezra shook his head. He knew the old man would die a slow death before speaking to an answering machine.

When Ezra got home Anne met him at the door. Dylan and Diamond had gone to bed. "Is Solomon okay?" she asked. She was always more concerned about Solomon than Ezra was. Her gift of mercy.

Ezra was a realist. "Ornerier than usual," he said.

"Did you tell him about Pratt?"

"Yeah, but he didn't believe me. How's everything here?"

"Fine, I was just getting ready for bed. We had a good prayer time. Oh, and Jim Mendenhall called. He's going to be out in the morning to pick up his two horses."

"That's it? Nothing from the police or the sheriff?"

"Nothing."

"I think I better sleep in the TV room," he said. He wanted to sleep in the big chair by the stove so he could stay dressed, armed, and near the front door.

She came up to him and unzipped his jacket. She unbuckled his belt and pulled it from his pants, taking the holstered pistol and laying it on the clothes dryer. "No, you're not," she said. She pulled his jacket off and laid it over the revolver, then took his hand and started leading him down the hall. "You're sleeping with me," she said.

CHAPTER THIRTY-SEVEN

As a child my father gave me two horses. The first one, a blue roan, was a curse, and I was ridiculed constantly for not being able to master him. Night after tormented night I prayed to die rather than face the blue roan. My mother would slip into the room as I feigned sleep and take a chair beside the bed. "Your father is a good man," she would tell me. "And the only man I could ever love. But he isn't a good father. He doesn't know how." Her words did not help me understand my father or work miracles in breaking the blue roan, but they taught me about commitment. Her Johnny Riley was a good man. And most important, he was her man. She would have no other. She had housebroken my dad. She probably could have broken the blue roan.

Leaving the Land

Ezra Riley awakened with his wife in his arms. She was sleeping with her head on his chest and one leg across his. He felt possessed in the right and honorable sense of the word. He lay still feeling her breath against his skin and remembering how he was when she first met him: withdrawn and moody, a poet of dark imaginings desperately striving to find God and destiny in the spiritual freak show of drugs, martial arts, and Eastern religions. When his father died she had moved with him and their baby to a harsh, hostile environment and an alien culture where stoicism was praised, emotions were repressed until they festered, and men did not worry about thoughts deeper than discussing the weather. It had been her quiet, persevering faith that had led him to a belief in Christ. Through all of their many trials—spiritual, economic, relational—she had stood beside him, not passive, but peaceful; not subjected, but submitted.

Where would he be, *what* would he be without her? An alcoholic? Drug addict? A successful but tormented writer who had traded his soul to fulfill the burning desire for accomplishment and notice? How many deals with the devil had Anne's caution and wisdom prevented him from consummating?

He felt settled, rooted to peacefulness, nourished by deep waters. He slept again.

When he awakened a second time his eyes opened to hers. "Any dreams?" she asked.

"None," he said with gratitude and relief. Someday he would tell her about the dark visitations of the night, the trespassing of the incubus spirit that Lilith had somehow willed from the dark, roily waters of the unconscious. Someday. But not yet. He needed more daylight in his life before he again talked of the night.

Anne rolled onto her back and stared at the ceiling. "Diamond leaves today," she sighed. "I'm going to miss her."

"You will always have her," he said.

She rolled back to him, snuggled closer, and put her lips next to his ear. "Are you disappointed with me for blowing this semester of school?"

"Not at all."

"Maybe I'm not meant to be a nurse," she whispered. "Maybe I'm meant to be here with you."

"You still can't rope," he teased.

She punched him playfully on the arm.

"You do what you want to do," he said. "And I'll support you." Then his eyes drifted away, and he felt the pangs of self-doubt and the shame of not rewarding this woman and his son with more material things.

"Don't say it," she said, seeing the dark clouds hover above the horizon of his mind. "Don't apologize for what you think you haven't given us." She pulled him close, and her lips descended on his. There was a clean, fresh hunger in her body.

The four of them had breakfast together. Diamond was silent. In her downcast eyes and trembling hands Ezra read both excitement and sadness. He could not detect any remorse in her for leaving Demetrius Pratt. It was Anne and Dylan—maybe even himself—she was saddened to leave.

"Can I stay home from school today?" Dylan asked. "I was through with all my tests yesterday." Ezra knew his son needed closure with Diamond. Dylan wanted to meet Diamond's cousin, say good-bye, and watch the girl drive away to a new life.

"Yeah," Ezra said. "No problem. Why don't you go out and feed the horses? Put Jim's horses in a separate pen and throw them some hay from the loft."

Ezra had already patrolled the yard armed with his revolver. He had turned off the lights in the bunkhouse and garage and was going into the hayloft when the mail truck stopped. He got the morning mail instead. "Make sure you turn the lights off in the barn," he called after Dylan.

Diamond was picking at her scrambled eggs. She didn't seem very hungry. Anne came over, stood behind her, and began massaging her shoulders.

"Diamond," Ezra said softly. "Are you going to be okay?"

She nodded.

"Be patient," he told her. "You have lived a very strange life for the past five years. It will take you a while to adjust."

"I know," she said softly. She reached up and held Anne's hand.

All of their heads turned when the front door crashed open and Dylan burst breathlessly into the house. "Dad," he shouted. "There's someone in the barn."

Ezra tipped his chair over as he jumped up and rushed down the hallway. "What?" he said. "Did you hear something?"

"No," Dylan said, his face flushed with excitement and exertion. "I saw him. He's lying on the floor."

Ezra unholstered the Ruger. Anne came running down the hallway. Fear was carved into her face like initials in sandstone. "Don't go up there," she pleaded.

He ignored her request. "Lock the door after I go out," he told Dylan. "And call 911. Tell the sheriff to get somebody out here." He glanced down the hallway. Diamond still sat at the table. She looked hard and frozen and stared out the window, away from them, toward something no one else could see.

He stepped outside. *It has come to this.* The revolver no longer seemed awkward in his hand; instead the barrel was an extension of his fingers, the grip was part of his palm, and the bullets were missiles of his heart. He was so calm he almost felt Mikal Mora standing, armed, beside him. His walk to the corrals was nearly casual except he held the Ruger in a two-handed grip with the barrel pointed to the ground to his right. Beaner poked her head out of the doghouse. She did not offer to follow him.

He went around the corrals to the west then behind the back side of the barn to the eastern door. He stepped lightly up the wooden steps and eased the door open.

Hemingway bounded out and Ezra's heart jumped to his mouth. The cat leaped to the corral rails, turned, sat, and began preening herself. Ezra took a deep breath to steady his nerves, then pushed the door open wider.

"Pratt," he announced. "I am coming in, and I am coming in armed."

He pushed the door wide open. Morning sunlight flooded in, bathing the wooden floor in a warm, golden glow, illuminating dust motes in the air, and causing shadows to form on the stacks of hay. The shadows ran down the narrow corridor to where two big feet were pointed toward the ceiling. The rest of the body faded into blackness.

Ezra cocked the hammer of the Ruger and kept a finger resting lightly on the trigger. He came forward slowly. "Pratt," he said.

There was no answer.

Ezra stepped up and looked down at the man. The glazed eyes stared up from a red and swollen face with a yellowish pus oozing from a crimson web of bites and scratches. The body seemed stiff and empty, frozen in a dreadful terror as if molded from a nightmare and coated with wax.

Ezra backed away slowly, fighting to keep his breakfast down, feeling his way toward the door. He uncocked the revolver and let it dangle idly from his fingers. When he stepped from the barn he gulped deep soul-washing breaths of fresh air as Hemingway stared at him from her perch. The cat yowled once, then treaded lightly away on the top corral plank, pulled by her feline self-importance. Ezra saw Anne and Dylan staring from a window by the front door and wanted to wave to let them know he was okay, but he could not move his arms.

Shake it off, he told himself. *It's over.* He was still standing there minutes later when the sheriff's car sped up to the corrals. Gravel sprayed against the planks like little bullets as the car slid to a stop. "Whadya got?" Butler called up to him.

"Pratt," Ezra said. "He's dead."

The sheriff said something to the deputy. The deputy used the radio, then both men pulled on long plastic gloves that reached all the way to their shoulders. They walked to where Ezra was standing. "You're sure he's dead?" Pratt said.

Ezra nodded.

"Cover me," Butler told the deputy. The young man pulled his 9mm Glock from its holster. They entered the barn.

Several minutes later they stepped back out. The deputy looked bewildered and ill. He rushed away from them. Ezra didn't know if he was going to the car or pardoning himself to vomit.

"Not a pretty sight," Butler said. "But not one that I can say I am sorry to see."

Ezra finally felt the Ruger dangling in his hand and holstered it. "What killed him?" he asked.

Butler pointed across the corral to where Hemingway sat on a tall railroad tie watching the barn swallows dip and dive. "Your cat," he said.

"My cat?"

"Cat scratch fever," Butler explained. "Or staph. One or the other. Either one could kill a man if he didn't get treatment. Especially a man in Pratt's condition. He doesn't look like he had eaten for days. He's all gaunted up."

"Fasting," Ezra said. "It must have been part of his ritual."

"I opened his shirt," Butler said. "I've never seen anything like it. His body is riddled with scars, some of them are recent."

"Self-mutilation," Ezra explained. "Sitting Bull did it before the Battle of the Little Big Horn."

"Well, I don't think it helped Pratt's condition any. Neither did the exertion of eluding us in the hills the last few days. But I wonder why he came back here to die? Do you suppose he was wanting help, wanting to turn himself in?"

"No," Ezra said. He said it because he knew it was true, and because he would give Pratt the dignity of dying with his principles no matter how wrong those principles had been. Pratt had been honest. He had not attacked Ezra in the barn or prowled his house. "He would never have turned himself in," Ezra said.

"An ambush then, I suppose," Butler said. "One last attempt on you." His cool blue eyes fell on Ezra with a probe of questions.

Ezra didn't say anything but he shook his head. Pratt wasn't coming back to ambush anyone. He had come back only to die where his troubled mind believed a gateway existed. But to discuss the *thin place* only seemed to give it more power, and to Ezra's way of thinking, the *thin place* no longer existed. The gates were closed.

"Well, the ambulance is on the way," Butler said. "We will get him out of here. I don't suppose there's anyone to claim the body."

"Yes, I think there is," Ezra said. "Tell the U.S. Fish and Wildlife Service to notify Antonio de la Rosa." He turned and walked away. The sun was warming as it tipped above the cottonwoods that lined the banks of Sunday Creek. Beaner finally left the doghouse and came to greet him. She followed at his heels as Ezra went to the house to tell Diamond what the girl already knew.

CHAPTER THIRTY-EIGHT

I learned to write for all the wrong reasons. I was driven to it by the stone-cold silence of the world around me. I had to express myself or explode like a volcano. Sometimes I stood outside my parents' bedroom door and read my poems softly to my mother. "That's good, Ezra," she would say quietly as if not to awaken my father. But I imagined him awake. Awake and lying there like a big slab of muscle, his hazel eyes staring into the darkness and realizing that his boy could write. By golly, if nothing else, his boy could write.

Leaving the Land

Saturday morning Ezra awakened before dawn with a fresh desire to write. He had not felt this hungry for self-expression since Pastor Tom's lengthy sermonizing had inspired him to transcribe *Leaving the Land* on the backs of church bulletins. He didn't even bother to make coffee. He just went to the bunkhouse, turned his Macintosh on, and sat down.

The words began to flow. They started as a trickle but soon gathered their own momentum. It wasn't classic work. He knew everything he wrote would be rewritten several more times, and some of it would be trashed, but the spirit and the desire were present. Beginning a book was like the first two hundred yards of a marathon—everyone ran it too fast before settling in for a long, torturous ordeal that some would never finish.

He began a novel. He safely decided not to use any of his family members as characters nor to set it in Yellow Rock. His characters would include Jubal Lee Walker and Mikal Mora. He decided not to use Pratt. Pratt was just too unbelievable.

He didn't stop when he heard the horses come in for their feeding. Let them wait, he decided. Nor did he stop to get the mail or have breakfast.

When he finally stepped away from his computer, he had been writing for almost three hours, but it only felt like minutes. He was exhilarated when he stepped outside. He knew it was a false high—there would be hundreds of hours of drudgery before the book was completed—but at least he was back at his craft.

Anne was smiling when he came to the house. "You're writing?" she asked.

"Yes." The smile that filled her eyes was one he had not seen in a long time. Maybe that was his fault, he thought. "Good," she said. "By the way. Someone called but I didn't want to bother you. The voice seemed familiar but I didn't recognize the name."

"Who was it?"

"Someone named Mark Anderson."

Ezra smiled. Mikal had learned that the conflict with Pratt was over. He would call him later and amuse him with the details. Pratt killed by a cat; Ezra losing the Ruger in a mud puddle. He could cause Mikal no end of consternations.

That afternoon Ezra stopped at his uncle's to watch television. He actually wanted to be near Solomon, to let the old man know that the loose ends were knitted together. Loose ends that Solomon did not even know about. Ezra wanted his presence to establish closure and peace.

"Whatcha been doin'?" Solomon shouted.

"Been on Dead Man," Ezra said. "The grass is comin' good except the cheat grass is taking the country. The Red Hills reservoir has water. The cows are looking good. Wilson's cows are all gone. Guess he sold them to begin payment on his legal bills."

Solomon was stumped. He had his first string of questions answered before he could ask them.

"Jim was out this morning," Ezra continued. "And got his horses. He's doing fine. Says he's going to quit drinking for good and lose forty pounds."

"Haw!" Solomon's grunt was a loud acclamation of cynicism.

Ezra rolled on. "Dylan is finished with school, but he is going to need some college money. I think you should hire him for the summer. I need the help and you need the tax deductions. Today I have him fixing fence over by the old windmill."

Solomon's face looked like it had struck a wall. The discussion had turned to money. His money.

"By the way," Ezra tossed in. "I'm preaching again tomorrow. Want to come to church?"

The old man stared straight ahead—he would not hear that question and could not respond to what he hadn't heard—and began rolling rocks from his mind in an effort to uncover a question of his own. He unearthed an unusual one. "Where's that pretty gal you had helpin' ya?" he blurted.

"She disappeared," Ezra said. "Anne hit her in the face with a kettle of hot water."

Solomon never blinked. He had the stare of an animal blinded by headlights. After a moment, he tried again. "Where's that beardie? You seen the arrowhead man?"

"Pratt?" Ezra asked. "Pratt's dead."

Solomon's bushy brows came together like two pads of steel wool.

"My cat killed him," Ezra added.

Solomon was still processing everything when the phone rang. Ezra got up to get it. If Anne knew he was at Solomon's the calls were usually for him. "Hello?" he said.

"Ezra, I think you better come home," Anne said. "A Mr. De la Rosa is out in the yard. I didn't invite him in." He hung up the phone and turned to his uncle.

"Bet that's your wife," Solomon grunted, regaining his sarcastic energy. "She wants ya to come home and do some work."

"Yeah, that was Anne," Ezra said, crossing the room to the door. "But she called to tell me there's a rich Brazilian at the house waiting to see me."

Solomon grimaced as if his thoughts were wild horses and he was trying to gather them for one last stampede. His canine eyes read the truth in his nephew, but his mind was overloaded; he had too much information to process at once. The arrowhead man was dead, killed by a cat; Anne had hit the pretty gal with a kettle of hot water; Jim Mendenhall was on a diet; and who in Hades was the rich Brazilian?

"Gotta go," Ezra said, and he smiled to himself as he got in the truck. It seemed almost cruel to bait his uncle like that, but Ezra knew he had given Solomon what the old man wanted most, a reprieve from monotony. A full day's ponderings, large and firm like a block of granite, were left in the old white house, and Solomon would chip away at them with a bedeviled diligence. Pounding, pounding, pounding, until he had chiseled his own conclusions and opinions.

CHAPTER THIRTY-NINE

Uncle Joe opened an orange soda, tipped his head back,
poured half the can down his throat, then stared
through the dirty windshield as Sam drove us home.
"So, ya still thinkin' about bein' a writer?" he asked me.
I said yes. "Well, if you ever write about your family, re-
member that most of us drank too much and scrapped
too often, but we never failed to help a neighbor if he
asked, and no amount of tough winters or dry summers
ever broke us. We all coulda left. Your father could have
left years ago and then you wouldn'ta been here en-
joyin' the sunset and watchin' a fat man catch bluegills.
That woulda been a shame, wouldn't it? A darn shame
if your pa had ever left the land."

Leaving the Land

Antonio de la Rosa was leaning against a silver Land Rover when
Ezra pulled into the lane. Ezra noticed Beaner was glaring from
her doghouse. The usually friendly dog wanted nothing to do
with de la Rosa. Ezra parked his old Ford next to the corral and
walked across his yard. The Brazilian was alone. There was no bodyguard
in sight.

"Ezra, my friend," de la Rosa said, extending a warm handshake. "It
is so good to see you again."

"What can I do for you, de la Rosa?" Ezra asked.

"I came for Demetrius's body. He has no family, you know."

"So I understand."

There was a pause as the two measured each other's intentions.

"I have a rather unusual request to ask of you," the South American
said. Ezra waited. De la Rosa had tried to dress western. He wore a shirt
with pearl snaps, Wranglers, and cowboy boots made of ostrich skin. "I
was wondering if Demetrius could be buried on your ranch?"

"You gotta be kidding?"

"I can arrange everything, including the paperwork. It would have to be done quickly, say, by this evening. And I will pay you well."

Ezra shook his head in amusement. "De la Rosa," he said. "You are a piece of work. Have you ever not gotten what you wanted?" he asked rhetorically. "No disrespect for the recently departed, but no way is Pratt being buried on this ranch."

De la Rosa smiled. "I understand," he said. "I know you and Demetrius had your misunderstandings."

"Misunderstandings? He tried to kill me."

"Whatever." He put an arm around Ezra's shoulder and began steering him toward the creek. "There are other things we need to talk about, my friend. I would like to see some more of your ranch if you would be so kind."

Ezra leveled an appraising look, then shrugged. "Sure," he said. "Get in my truck."

"Oh, we can take the Land Rover."

"No," Ezra declined. "I wouldn't want to see you put any scratches in it." They got in the old Ford. De la Rosa sat on the torn seat covers next to a can of rusty staples, a faded denim jacket, and half a dozen mismatched leather gloves.

Ezra drove through sagebrush bottoms beneath the shade of towering cottonwoods. Shiloh, Cheyenne, and Cajun lifted grazing heads as the old truck bounced by. He stopped at the base of a large, cedar-fringed hill. Its steep sides were coated with dry gumbo and dotted with outcroppings of yellow rock. "Let's climb to the top," Ezra said.

Before de la Rosa could protest Ezra was out the door and beginning the steep ascent. The toes of his Vibram-soled cowboy packers dug into the brittle gumbo, and he propelled himself forward, leaning like a sprinter, his arms pumping in a timed coordination with his legs. De la Rosa struggled to follow. The slick leather soles of his new cowboy boots provided no traction, and he slipped several times and had to grasp the rough stems of greasewood with his bare hands to keep from falling. He was out of breath and dirty when he finally arrived at the top.

Ezra had been waiting for several minutes. He squatted silently on his haunches sucking a grass stem he had plucked from where Gusto was buried. He looked straight ahead with a thousand-yard stare.

De la Rosa took a deep breath and pretended he wasn't strained. "Beautiful," he said, drinking in the view. "Another prima vista."

"Yeah, it's not bad," Ezra said.

The South American paused until his breathing was normal, then came forward, stood slightly behind Ezra, and put a hand on his shoulder. "You have a deep love for this ranch, don't you?"

"Yup," Ezra said.

"I have reconsidered my earlier offer. I want to help you own all of this, not merely manage it. What would be your greatest dream for this land?" he asked.

"Oh," Ezra said. He sucked on the grass stem thoughtfully as if drawing life from grass nourished by Gusto's bones. "I guess I would like to see it stocked with buffalo and wild longhorn cattle. And I would do most of my work in a saddle on a good horse. In the winters the buffalo and longhorns would mostly fend for themselves, and I wouldn't be breaking my back day after day feeding cows from a sack, throwing hay bales off a truck, and breaking ice in old silted-in reservoirs. Instead, I would put a gas furnace in my bunkhouse and write novels."

"An admirable vision," de la Rosa said. "And all of it is possible and more. Just increase your vision by tenfold. I will have the Wilson holdings by summer's end. The interior fences will be ripped out, and the wheat and CRP will be seeded back to native prairie. I can combine the Wilson land with the Riley ranch and put you in control of over 400,000 acres. For your wages, I will see that all of the Riley land is put in your name. Your uncle and two sisters will be more than compensated for their shares."

"Pretty tempting," Ezra said.

"You could build a future for you, your son, and his children after him."

"A legacy would be nice," Ezra said.

"So, what do you say? Do we have a deal?"

Ezra rose and let de la Rosa's hand drop from his shoulder. He turned and looked the South American in the eye. "Didn't I see you the other night?" he asked.

"I beg your pardon. I don't understand."

"Monday night," Ezra said. "I was lying on a hospital bed at the point of death when I found myself on a hill somewhat like this one. You came trotting up out of the badlands, came right up to me, and began sucking the breath from my body."

"Ezra," de la Rosa pleaded. "Is this some sort of joke? I do not understand what you are talking about. Is this a riddle?"

"No, it's not a riddle," Ezra said. "It's about choices. Life or death. Blessing or curse."

De la Rosa was perplexed. "I still do not understand."

"No, you certainly don't," Ezra said, and he stepped to the edge of the hill and began skidding downward, sliding as he had learned to do as a child, a skiier on a slope of gray gumbo.

"Ezra," de la Rosa shouted after him. "Where are you going?"

"Home," Ezra said. He left the truck for the Brazilian and began walking, pulled toward the badlands not by the hills themselves but by a power deep within himself that surged through his bloodstream with a thermal intensity. His steps were long and strong, each foot coming down, making contact with the earth, then pushing away, leaving that small piece of soil behind, claimed, stamped by his footprint as a signet of his possessing it. He walked as a priest performing a silent exorcism, not delivering the land of original sin, but delivering himself of memories—an unhealthy attachment to the past—that swirled about him like dust devils. He dispelled them with deep breaths of fresh air—his own little winds of forgiveness.

He walked the deep coulee of silent cedars where he had been entrapped before being found and released by his son. He had left the trap—a Newhouse No. 4—embedded in the sandstone, its rusting chain trailing into the soil like a dried umbilical cord. The steel jaws were clenched shut, like a demon whose mouth had been bound by prayer.

The tall needle grasses whipped across his denim legs as he crossed the high flat where he and Jubal Lee had raced the Thoroughbreds, and where later he had said his final good-bye to Gusto. A repentant Jubal Lee had provided restitution for his debts. Gusto was buried but never gone. His memory was one of redemption, an intervention of mercy.

Ezra felt like Joshua claiming the promised land: driving out Amalekites, taking no prisoners, claiming no bounty. The echoes of screaming men dimmed as the angry voices of his father, uncles, and Charley Arbuckle retreated into cavernous washouts and fell away to a dark silence. The generational line was broken. His own son had been raised with nurture, not spite, and cultivated with attention, not neglected to fend for himself and survive like the seed of a thistle blown to the badlands.

The shadows lengthened and the day cooled, but his pace remained constant. He did not have time to walk all the way to Krumm Spring, but he walked far enough to see it from a distance. He stopped on top of the Grassy Crown, the highest point on the Riley ranch, and was poised there, as immobile as a sheepherder's monument, as the sun dipped beneath the western horizon. The prairie grasses glowed golden as the sky painted itself with colors no number of Crayolas could describe. When the highest clouds began to fade, he left the hill and walked the serpentine twists of Crooked Creek, following the shallow pathway to its confluence with Sunday Creek. It was dark when he turned southward. Unknowingly he traced the path of Luke Sweetman's wolves as they had searched for their legacy, their heritage of buffalo. But he wasn't thinking about wolves or Demetrius Pratt.

He thought once about Wilson and how his own fears for the ranch had been imagined. The threat was still there, but it was unformed. But there would always be threats. If it wasn't a person it would be drought, blizzards, poor markets, or taxes. Life was hard. That was a fact his mother and father had always tried to tell him, but it was a realization shaped like an old leather glove. It had to be soaked in sweat then dried in the sun while fitted to one's own hand.

He thought of Lillian Foster. No one knew where she was, but he knew she was out there, tangled in her deception and denial, while spinning yet another web to ensnare a well-intentioned man motivated by mercy. A daughter of duplicity. He wondered if she was scarred or burned, if her loveliness had been branded by the smashing of the kettle of hot water against her face. He didn't think about her for long. The night was too fresh and clean to allow his mind to harbor passing defilements.

He began to feel tired. Whatever energy had driven him was slowly waning. Owls hooted in the dark trees. Somewhere in the distance a coyote yapped. He passed the specter of Solomon's house, the constant television light radiating out of a single window like the eye of a cyclops.

It was cool in the humid pockets of the creek valley, but the night warmed as he neared his house. He met the grazing horses. They let him approach, and he ran a hand down Shiloh's broad back. He ached to be on horseback. Just being near a horse excited his soul. He gave Shiloh an affectionate rub behind an ear and walked away.

Beaner did not bark as he neared the yard. She simply materialized at his heels as he passed the corrals. Somewhere Hemingway yowled. Her complaint was muted as if coming from inside the barn.

He knew it was late because the house was dark, but he had no idea of the time. He had walked past its dictates and had only now reemerged into a world of temporal measurements. He eased through the front door, pulled his boots off, hung his hat on a nail, undressed in the bathroom, and went to bed.

Anne was lying there silently.

He slipped under the covers and put an arm across her bare skin. He laid his head on her breast. She was the earth to him. She was the nurturer. His refuge. All good things were born from her.

"Were you worried about me?" he asked quietly.

She drank in the odor of his skin and hair. He smelled of cedar, sage, horses, and fresh air. "No," she said softly. "I knew you were coming home."

About the Author

John L. Moore's works have been published in *Reader's Digest* and *The New York Times Magazine,* as well as other daily papers and national magazines. Moore, who lives near Miles City, Montana, is a rancher, lay minister, husband, and father to two teenagers. He has received many awards, such as being a Western Writers of America Golden Spur Award runnerup, *Christianity Today*'s Critics Choice Award winner for fiction, and a Western Heritage Award nominee—sponsored by the National Cowboy Hall of Fame. His previous books include *Bitter Roots, The Breaking of Ezra Riley, Loosening the Reins,* and *Leaving the Land.*

Other Books from
John L. Moore

Bitter Roots
A Novel

This compelling novel of the McColley family in the Big Sky country of eastern Montana unfolds the powerful tale of how one father's sins are visited upon his wayward sons. In the tradition of Larry McMurtry's *Lonesome Dove*, this tale combines intense storytelling drama with a forceful theme of a family healing against incredible odds.

0-8407-6759-5 • Paperback • 240 pages

The Breaking of Ezra Riley
A Novel

As Ezra Riley battles the elements of the rugged and unforgiving Montana land, he struggles to find the love and forgiveness he craves in this extraordinary novel of a man's coming of age. 1991 *Christianity Today* Critics' Choice Award Winner for Fiction.

0-8407-6760-9 • Paperback • 276 pages

Leaving the Land
Sequel to *The Breaking of Ezra Riley*

Ezra Riley faces a new crisis of faith. When an old friend that he hasn't seen since his youth appears, Ezra must discern the difference between image and reality. This stunning sequel explores Ezra's rebellious past, and his uncertain future as a Montana rancher.

0-7852-8288-2 • Paperback • 252 pages